The Fairy Doll

& Other Tales from the Dolls' House

RUMER GODDEN was one of the UK's most distinguished authors. She wrote many well-known and much-loved books for both adults and children, including *The Dolls' House*, *The Story of Holly & Ivy* and *The Diddakoi*, which won the Whitbread Children's Book Award in 1972.

She was awarded the OBE in 1993 and died in 1998, aged ninety.

The Fairy Doll

& Other Tales from the Dolls' House

Rumer Godden

With a foreword by

Jacqueline Wilson

MACMILLAN CHILDREN'S BOOKS

The Dolls' House first published 1947 by Michael Joseph, London
Impunity Jane (1955), *The Fairy Doll* (1956), *Candy Floss* (1957),
The Story of Holly & Ivy (1958), *Miss Happiness and Miss Flower* (1961), and
Little Plum (1963) all first published by Macmillan London Limited
This collection published 2012 by Macmillan Children's Books

This edition published 2013 by Macmillan Children's Books
a division of Macmillan Publishers Limited
20 New Wharf Road, London N1 9RR
Basingstoke and Oxford
Associated companies throughout the world
www.panmacmillan.com

ISBN 978-0-330-53574-8

Text copyright © Rumer Godden 1947, 1955, 1956, 1957, 1958, 1961, 1962
Foreword copyright © Jacqueline Wilson 2012
Illustrations copyright © Jane Ray 2012

The right of Rumer Godden and Jane Ray to be identified as the
author and illustrator of this work has been asserted by them in accordance
with the Copyright, Designs and Patents Act 1988.

1 3 5 7 9 8 6 4 2

A CIP catalogue record for this book is available from
the British Library.

Printed and bound by CPI Group (UK) Ltd, Croydon CR0 4YY

Contents

Foreword

When anyone asked me what I wanted for a birthday or Christmas present when I was young I always begged for a book or a doll. We were quite poor and I borrowed most of my books from the library, but I was desperate to add to my own small shelf of paperbacks and cheaply printed two-and-sixpenny (twelve and a half pence!) children's classics. You couldn't borrow dolls so I craved them even more. Way back in the 1950s when I was a child, girls played with dolls right up until secondary school without any embarrassment whatsoever.

We had wonderful dolls too, not just the vacant-looking baby dolls and Barbies you get nowadays. I had soft little girl dolls with intelligent faces and plaits and many sets of outfits: school uniform complete with little ties and badges, lace-trimmed party dresses, duffel coats with miniature toggles, striped pyjamas and tartan dressing gowns, and small slippers trimmed with fur and tiny pom-poms. I had a very showy Italian teenage doll with a real figure and an ultra-fashionable wardrobe. I pretended she led a very outrageous celebrity life when my back was turned. I had a great big toddler doll who was knee-height when I stood her up and helped her walk in her pink plastic shoes. I also had a whole boxful of tiny pink penny dolls no bigger than my thumb, brilliant for when I wanted to play orphanages.

Imagine my delight one Christmas when I was given *The Dolls' House* by Rumer Godden. It's a satisfyingly long story about a family of very different dolls with distinct personalities. I'd read cosy stories about dolls before – it was an Enid Blyton speciality! *The Dolls' House* was exhilaratingly different. The beautiful malevolent doll Marchpane brought a whole new dimension to the story. I'd never encountered a truly evil doll before. My heart turned over reading Chapter 20!

The Dolls' House is full of suspense and quiet horror, but thank goodness there's a bittersweet resolution.

The heroine Tottie reassures anxious Mr Plantaganet that good things will happen now, and they will be happy. I loved Tottie, the little wooden Dutch doll with glossy black hair and painted pink cheeks and blue determined eyes. I ached to own a tiny Dutch doll just like Tottie but I couldn't find one anywhere. I had to wait until I was grown up. Now my own little Tottie sits on a bookshelf near my desk and smiles at me reassuringly whenever I look up.

Rumer Godden doesn't just write about dolls'-house dolls. *The Fairy Doll* is about Elizabeth, the youngest child in the family, who is teased for being a clumsy crybaby – and the little fairy doll on top of the Christmas tree helps her develop confidence. Modern children might raise their eyebrows in astonishment that six-year-old Elizabeth is considered a baby because she forgets matches or flour or marmalade when she's sent to the shops alone for Mother or loses the money for her bus fare. Children were expected to be pretty independent when Elizabeth (and I) were little girls.

Candy Floss is about a little fairground doll who lives in a coconut shy. She sits on Nuts, a little wooden horse, and works for a boy called Jack who owns a cute dog called Cocoa. Candy Floss isn't a toy. She has a job to do, attracting customers to the coconut shy – but she unwittingly also attracts the attention of a very rich, whiny little girl called Clementina. She snatches Candy Floss. We read on anxiously, wondering if she'll ever get back to her home with Jack and Cocoa and Nuts.

Perhaps my favourite out of all Rumer Godden's doll books is *The Story of Holly & Ivy*. Holly is a beautiful doll with real golden hair, dressed for Christmas in a red dress. She's longing to be bought for Christmas and live in a real home instead of a toyshop. Ivy is a spirited little girl who doesn't have a proper home at all. She lives in an institution and has nowhere to go for Christmas. But this is a story about wishing – and in the most magical, intricate way Holly and Ivy find their heartfelt wishes eventually come true.

Of course it isn't just girls who are proud doll owners. Gideon is an imaginative little boy of seven in the story *Impunity Jane* – and Jane herself is his little pocket doll. They have the most splendid adventures together, and Gideon proves to Joe McCallaghan's gang that he definitely isn't a sissy.

There's a delicacy and charm in all these stories. The dolls are all carefully housed and fed and clothed in style. No one tries harder to please her dolls than Nona in *Miss Happiness and Miss Flower*. Nona is a sad little girl sent to England from India to live with her cousins. She is shy and withdrawn and homesick, and finds seven-year-old Belinda particularly trying. But when Nona is sent two little Japanese dolls, she's determined to learn about Japanese customs and make them their very own Japanese house.

There's a touching sequel called *Little Plum*, which tells how rough tough Belinda eventually manages to make friends with Gem Tiffany-Jones next door, who has a Japanese doll called Little Plum. There's a common theme in all these books – lonely children and dolls somehow forming friendships against the odds and learning to be kind to each other. Each story will give a nimble-fingered imaginative child many fantastic ideas for things to make and do for dolls.

Towards the end of *Little Plum* the children hold a special Doll Festival on the third day of the third month, making painstaking efforts to make everything perfect and authentic. Perhaps we should all hold a special Doll Festival in honour of Rumer Godden herself.

I went to a public lecture she once gave when she was already an elderly lady. I listened, entranced, as she spoke in a voice as precise and poetic as her prose. She looked very elegant, with silver hair and a beautiful big aquamarine ring the same colour as her eyes. She lived until she was ninety, as dignified and delightful an elderly lady as the great-grandmother in *The Fairy Doll*.

All the dolls' stories are about wishing in one way or another. *I* wish that thousands of modern girls (and boys) discover these sensitive, superb stories and love them as much as I do.

Jacqueline Wilson

The Dolls' House

For Janaki Paula Mary Foster with love

Fain am I to work these nosegays
Gathered from my tranquil days
In gentle rain, mild storm and sunny weather . . .

From Great-Grandmother's sampler

Chapter 1

This is a novel written about dolls in a dolls' house. The chief person in it is Tottie Plantaganet, a small Dutch doll.

Dutch dolls are scarce now, but Tottie was made a long time ago when they were plentiful and sold in every shop that had toys for sale; and large ones cost a penny, the middle size a halfpenny, and very small ones, like Tottie, were sold for a farthing each.

At present she lived in the nursery of two little girls called Emily and Charlotte Dane. I say 'at present' because Tottie had lived a long while; once she had lived with two other little girls who were Emily and Charlotte's great-grandmother and their Great-Great-Aunt Laura.

How strange that a little farthing doll should last so long. Tottie was made of wood and it was good wood. She liked to think sometimes of the tree of whose wood she was made, of its strength and of the sap that ran through it and made it bud and put out leaves every spring and summer, that kept it standing through the winter storms and wind. 'A little, a very little of that tree is in me,' said Tottie. 'I am a little of that tree.' She liked to think of it.

She was made of that wood, neatly jointed at the hips

and shoulders and sockets (she had sockets for elbows and knees), with a sturdy inch-wide yoke for shoulders and a round little head with glossy painted hair. She had glossy pink cheeks and her eyes were painted with bright firm paint, blue and very determined.

Emily and Charlotte had chosen two other dolls to be Tottie's father and mother; their names were Mr Plantaganet and Mrs Plantaganet, but Mrs Plantaganet had another name and that was Birdie. Of course Tottie knew, just as you and I know, that Mr and Mrs Plantaganet were not her real father and mother, that she had no real father and mother, unless it were that felled tree of whose wood she was made. She knew that, just as she knew that her little brother Apple, the doll they had given her for a little brother, was made from plush (which is a kind of velvet), and Darner, the dolls' house dog, had a backbone made from a darning needle; if you have ever played at Fathers and Mothers, and of course you have played at Fathers and Mothers, you will remember what a very good feeling it is; that was exactly the feeling between Tottie and Mr and Mrs Plantaganet – Birdie – and little brother Apple and Darner the dog.

It is an anxious, sometimes a dangerous thing to be a doll. Dolls cannot choose; they can only be chosen; they cannot 'do'; they can only be done by; children who do not understand this often do wrong things, and then the dolls are hurt and abused and lost; and

# The Dolls' House

when this happens dolls cannot speak, nor do anything except be hurt and abused and lost. If you have any dolls, you should remember that.

Listen to the story of Mr Plantaganet (before he was Mr Plantaganet); for a long while he was hurt and abused and lost. He was a delicate little doll, rather larger than Tottie, with a china face and brown glass eyes and real brown hair. He was a boy doll and he always said he remembered once being dressed in a kilt as a Highlander, with toy bagpipes stuck to his hand with hard painful glue, painful when you tried to get it off. He was bought for some children – not, I am glad to say, Emily and Charlotte, quite other children – who took no care of him at all. It was they who dragged the bagpipes off and took some of the painted skin off the palm of his hand as well, and tore his clothes off too, and let their puppy bite his foot until it looked half nibbled. One of the boys drew a moustache on his little top lip with indelible pencil ('indelible' means it can never come off); then they threw him into the cold dark toy cupboard, where he lay for weeks and months and might have lain for years if they had not been ordered to tidy the toy cupboard because children were coming to tea. As it was, they left him lying on the floor under the table and Emily, who was one of the visitors, nearly trod on him.

'Oh! I am sorry,' cried Emily, but nobody seemed to think it mattered. 'What a dear little doll,' said Emily,

7

picking him up. 'Who is he? Whom does he belong to?' He did not seem to belong to anyone. She noticed that his eyes were filled with dust. The children said Emily could have him, and she wrapped him up in her handkerchief and took him home.

She and Charlotte saw at once that he was made to be a little man doll. They sponged the dust and glue off him with hot water and dried him carefully, and, though the moustache would not come off, they knitted him a sock for his spoilt foot and put plaster on the palm of his hurt hand; and their mother made him a check flannel suit and a blue shirt and a tie of red silk ribbon. Emily cut him tiny newspapers out of the real ones to read.

'I like him with a moustache,' said Emily.

'It makes him look more like Mr Plantaganet,' said Charlotte.

He could still not quite believe he was Mr Plantaganet. He was still easily made afraid, afraid of being hurt or abused again. Really you might have thought that Tottie was the father and he was the child; but there are real fathers like that.

Mrs Plantaganet was not quite right in the head. There was something in her head that rattled; Charlotte thought it might be beads, and it was true that the something made a gay sound like bright beads touching together. She was altogether gay and light, being made of cheap celluloid, but, all the same, nicely moulded and jointed and painted.

She came to Charlotte on a cracker at a party. Yes, Mrs Plantaganet started life as part of a cracker, to which she was fastened by silver tinsel. She had been dressed in blue and green feathers. At first they had not thought she was anything more than part of the cracker. First Charlotte kept her on the cracker; then off the cracker; then one day she decided to dress her and pulled the feathers off.

The feathers were glued on Mrs Plantaganet and here was her difference from Mr Plantaganet: the glue coming off did not hurt her at all; it came off easily with hot water, leaving not a trace, and her body only gave out a warm celluloid smell and turned even more pink.

'There is something brave about this little doll,' said Emily. 'I don't usually like celluloid dolls.'

'Nor do I,' said Charlotte. 'But I like her.'

Emily made Mrs Plantaganet a red skirt with blue rickrack braid on the hem, a blue blouse with red spots; the spots were pin spots, but they looked large as buttons to Mrs Plantaganet. 'I think she likes them large and bright,' said Emily. They sewed her hair, which was fluffy yellow cotton, into a bun; but Emily thought again and let the hair out of the bun, loosed and flyaway. 'I think she was wishing we could let it fly away like that,' said Charlotte. 'I think she likes her hair.'

They put her next to Mr Plantaganet and they seemed to suit one another at once. They seemed to suit Tottie too. Tottie had on a little apron that was embroidered with red daisies; both Mr and Mrs Plantaganet thought she looked the very pattern of a nice small wooden girl; they were to think even more of her later.

'We must get Mr Plantaganet a walking stick,' said Emily. 'And Mrs Plantaganet must have a hat with a tiny feather.'

There was still something of the cracker and feather look about Mrs Plantaganet as there was still something of the dark toy cupboard about Mr Plantaganet.

'But Tottie has been ours always,' said Emily.

'Even before always,' said Charlotte.

As for Apple, there were no fears for him. Come fog, come fine, no one could be unkind to Apple. He was as big as Emily's thumb, plump and made of warm plush, coloured pink-brown. He felt nice and he was nice, with chunky little arms and legs and sewn-in dimples and a wig of brown darning-wool hair. Perhaps it was the darning wool that made Darner so fond of him. Apple wore a buster suit, scarlet felt trousers and a white cambric blouse, white socks, and red felt shoes that were fastened with the smallest of small pearl buttons you can imagine. No one ever saw Apple without exclaiming, 'What a little love of a doll!' Tottie and Mr Plantaganet felt that too, though they knew how naughty he was; Birdie, Mrs Plantaganet, felt it, but she did not know that he was ever naughty; she only loved him.

You had to be very careful how you touched Darner because he had a prick at his head end; it was his darning-needle backbone and it made him difficult to handle. The rest of him was clipped wool, gone a little grey with London grime, over pipe-cleaner legs. Emily and Charlotte used to take him, in his turn, as they took the rest of the family, to the Park, where he liked to be stood in the shelter of a fallen leaf (if it were autumn and there were fallen leaves), so that he could bristle at other real-size dogs. He also liked staying at home.

That was the trouble. There was no home.

Chapter 2

The shortage of dolls' houses was acute.

There were a few in the toyshops but they were very expensive and made of cheap papier-mâché or plywood. 'Not worth the money,' said the children's father. 'They wouldn't last any time.'

'I want one to last,' said Mr Plantaganet with a catch in his breath. 'I want one to last for always.' More than anything in the world Mr Plantaganet wanted a home. 'One that will shut. One that will last. Do you think they will ever buy a house for us?' he asked. Being a doll, he could not say, 'Do you think we shall ever buy a house?' He had to wait until Emily or Charlotte, or Emily and Charlotte's father, had the idea of buying one for him. Even if they had the idea, these days it was too expensive and he knew that the money Emily and Charlotte put into his pockets was only gold and silver paper. 'I don't think we shall ever have a house,' said Mr Plantaganet.

'One will come. One will come,' sang Birdie.

'How do you know?' asked Mr Plantaganet.

Birdie could not say how she knew. The thought of it rattled in her head with the thought of that tiny raffia hat that Emily had now found for her; it was no bigger than a half-crown and Emily had fixed in it a feather

12

The Dolls' House

from her aunt's canary. Remembering that, Birdie suddenly remembered what she had thought about the house. 'Emily fixed the hat,' she said. 'Someone will fix the house.'

Of course there were dolls' houses advertised in the newspaper, even sometimes in the part of the newspaper Emily cut up for Mr Plantaganet. *Dolls' house for sale. Four rooms, fully furnished, electric light, loggia. Garage with miniature cars. £25.*

'That's an enormous heap of money,' said Charlotte.

'But I don't want electric light,' said Mr Plantaganet. 'A little pretending candlestick would do for me, and I wouldn't know how to drive any kind of car.'

But even the plain dolls' houses, *Four rooms . . . Two rooms . . . Some furniture . . .* were seven or eight or three even four guineas each, and neither Emily and Charlotte nor their father had that much money to spare. 'We shall never get one,' said Mr Plantaganet.

At the moment the Plantaganets were as uncomfortable as anyone in London; they had to live crowded together in two shoe-boxes that were cramped and cold and that could not shut; when they hung their washing out to dry, even the smallest pattern duster, it made the cardboard sodden and damp. 'You can't play with them properly,' wailed Charlotte.

'It doesn't feel like home,' said Mr Plantaganet. 'Though of course it is ever so much nicer than the toy cupboard,' he added hastily. 'But I am too heavy for it, and so is Apple. It doesn't feel safe.'

'I don't mind it,' said Birdie, but then Birdie, aggravating creature, never minded anything. She was happy anywhere.

'It slips about. Everybody knocks it over. It doesn't feel safe,' said Mr Plantaganet.

'Long long ago,' began Tottie in her comforting voice (and it is the best wood that gives out the most comforting voice – ask the men who make pianos and violins and flutes), 'long long ago, I knew a dolls' house. I lived in it. It belonged to Laura. She was Emily and Charlotte's great-great-aunt. That was a hundred years ago,' said Tottie.

Tottie had stayed the same all that time, for all that hundred years. Does that surprise you? It is easier for dolls than children. From the moment they are made, finished, they never have to alter, they never have to grow. 'I wouldn't be a child for anything,' Tottie often said. 'First you have to be a baby, then a little child, then a bigger child, then a schoolboy or girl, then a big boy or girl, then grown up.' Of course Tottie knew she could not, even if she would; there is no power of growing in dolls, and she knew that was why, for instance, any live little girl, however stupid, had power over her. 'I am as I am,' said wise little Tottie. 'I couldn't be all those things. In all these years, these hundred years, I can still only be me.' It is very important for dolls that children guess their right ages; some thoughtless children make their dolls vary between six and six months. Mr Plantaganet for instance was born twenty-eight years old. Tottie was about seven. Apple would always be three. Darner was so cross that it was easy to guess he was old. Birdie was more difficult, it was her flightiness, but even Birdie was easily seen to be between twenty and thirty.

'I was telling you about the dolls' house,' said Tottie. 'It was not too big. It could stand comfortably on the table and outside it was a glossy cream colour painted with ivy. It looked as good as real ivy,' said Tottie.

'It would be better than real ivy,' said Mr Plantaganet. 'Real ivy chokes things and can even pull down a house. Painted ivy is safer. I like painted ivy. Go on.'

'Go on. Go on,' cried Apple. Emily had put him on a chair, but he had deliberately fallen off upside down because he wanted to practise standing on his head.

'Don't do that, Apple dear,' said Tottie. 'The dolls' house? Oh, yes. In the front there was a front door with steps leading up to it.'

'How many steps?'

'Six,' said Tottie, 'and the door was painted green with a knocker; it didn't really open but that didn't matter, because the whole of the front swung open, leaving the inside ready to be played with.'

'Leaving the steps?' asked Mr Plantaganet anxiously.

'Leaving the steps,' nodded Tottie, and she added,

remembering, 'On the steps was fixed a little tiny scraper.'

'Would my foot go on it?' asked Apple, 'my foot, in its red shoe?'

'Perfectly,' said Tottie. 'And yours,' she said to Mr Plantaganet before he need ask. 'There was a kennel,' she said, 'just outside.'

'For Darner?' asked Apple.

'But would he go in it?' asked Mr Plantaganet doubtfully.

'In this kennel I think he would,' said Tottie.

Darner did not growl as he would have if he had thought the kennel was dangerous. He always growled 'Prrick' at danger.

'There was a hall with a staircase and a polished wooden floor. I remember the floor particularly,' said Tottie, 'because it looked like a draughtboard. Draughts is a game you play on a board checked in squares of light and dark wood,' she explained to Apple. 'The walls of the hall were red. Red paper,' she said, 'that looked like satin.'

'Are you sure it did?' asked Mr Plantaganet doubtfully. 'I haven't seen any paper like that.'

'You would have once,' said Tottie. 'I am quite certain. I remember it looked cosy and rich. There was a hall window with lace curtains; the white looked pretty on the red; there were Christmas scraps for pictures and a clock glued on the wall, and two dolls' house dark wood chairs and a tiny rug.'

'Everything!' said Mr Plantaganet.

'Everything. And in the hall,' said Tottie, 'was the figure of a butler.'

No one asked her why she said 'the figure of a butler' instead of 'a butler'. They knew that whoever had made, or tried to make, that butler had not been successful. There are some dolls like that. There was no need to pity him because he never had been a butler.

'We could put him outside,' said Mr Plantaganet. 'Go on.'

'To the left was the kitchen,' Tottie went on. 'You know which the left is, Apple, your left hand, the one you don't shake hands with. On the left, then, was the kitchen.'

'What was it like?'

'What was it like?'

'What was it like?'

'There was a blue tin stove with saucepans and a kettle. There was a heavy iron on a stand, no bigger than Emily's fingernail. There was a rolling pin and a wooden pudding basin smaller than a thimble. There was a dresser with flowered china cups and plates on it, a table and another rug and kitchen chairs and a mangle and a pot of pretending geraniums on the window sill.'

'Oh, dear!' said Mr Plantaganet longingly.

Up to now the thought of the house and the thought

of her hat had been knocking together in Birdie's head; now she asked, 'Was there a little feather broom?'

'I think there was,' said Tottie.

'Dear!' said Birdie, and the feather broom and the feather in her hat seemed to float before her eyes.

'Could you make buns for tea in that kitchen?' asked Apple. 'What is a bun?'

'To the right of the hall,' said Tottie, 'you know your right hand, Apple dear, the one you do shake hands with, to the right was a sitting room. It had a green carpet,' said Tottie, 'the colour of holly leaves, and it had real wallpaper, like the hall, only this one was white with cream stripes. On the wallpaper were two little pictures; their frames were made of glued-on shells that Laura had picked up at the seaside. There was another window —'

'Did it open?'

'No, it didn't open, but it had lace curtains too, and there was a fireplace and a fire of shining red gelatine paper. There was a sofa covered in red velvet and two chairs to match, and a table and a piano; its notes were paper notes glued on. On the table,' said Tottie slowly, 'was a lamp with a white china shade; it would really light if you used a birthday cake candle.'

'We should have to be careful of Apple with that candle,' said Birdie suddenly, and they all stared at her because that was such an unusually clear thing for Birdie to say.

'You are right to be afraid of fire,' said Tottie. 'You are celluloid, Birdie, and that would flare up in an instant if you went anywhere near fire.'

'You would, you know,' said Mr Plantaganet. 'Better not go near the candle, Birdie.'

'I?' asked Birdie, surprised. 'I was thinking of Apple.'

'Also on the table,' said Tottie, 'there was a vase of wax roses; they were modelled in wax and they were no bigger than a thimble.'

'Like the pudding basin,' murmured Mr Plantaganet.

'Yes,' said Tottie, 'and in the sitting room there was a golden cage and inside the cage was a bird.'

'A bird?' asked Birdie. 'A-ah! Did it sing?'

'No, it couldn't sing,' said Tottie, 'but it was there.'

'It could sing,' said Birdie, and her eyes seemed to shine. 'I know how it sang.' Scraps and pieces of all the songs she had ever heard knocked together gently in her head with bird songs, chiefly sparrow because she had heard little else, being a London doll; she could not sing any one of them but they all ran together and seemed to make a chain of song in her head such as might be sung by a bright toy bird. 'A-ah!' sighed Birdie. Music, delicate clockwork musical-box music, was what Birdie liked to hear.

'Upstairs,' said Tottie, 'there were two bedrooms. One had a pink flannel carpet and one had a blue. There were beds with nicked-round blankets, and there was a white tin bath with taps, and there was a cot with bars.'

'Would it do for me?' asked Apple.

'It would be a good fit,' said Tottie gravely. 'There was a jug and basin and a pail to match them, for carrying the water downstairs.'

'Very thoughtful,' said Mr Plantaganet. 'Did the taps on the bath really run?'

'Yes, if you put the water in the tank behind the bath,' said Tottie.

Mr Plantaganet nodded. Apple was thinking about the cot. Birdie was thinking about the bird in the birdcage.

'Occupied, of course?' said Mr Plantaganet suddenly.

'Occupied?' asked Tottie.

'I mean there are other dolls living in it, of course?'

'It was a long time ago,' said Tottie. 'Maybe it has gone, been sold or broken up. I don't know where it is now,' said Tottie sadly. 'That Laura, Great-Great-Aunt Laura, had a little girl, but the little girl is a great-aunt herself now. Why, she is Emily and Charlotte's great-aunt. Maybe she has given it away or given it up. I don't know.'

'But dolls lived in it then,' said Mr Plantaganet. 'You lived in it once. Did other dolls live there with you? Don't you remember them?'

'I remember one,' said Tottie slowly. 'Yes, I remember her,' said Tottie, very, very slowly.

'Why do you say it like that? What was her name?'

'Her name was Marchpane.'

'What a funny name. What does it mean?'

'Marchpane is a heavy, sweet, sticky stuff like almond icing, very old-fashioned,' said Tottie. 'You very quickly have enough of it. It was a good name for her,' said Tottie slowly.

'But what was she like?' asked Mr Plantaganet.

'What was she like?' asked Birdie.

'What was she like?' asked Apple.

'She was valuable,' said Tottie. 'She was little and heavy.'

'What was she made of? I am made of celluloid,' said Birdie, and 'celluloid' knocked in her head against other words like it – 'cellophane', 'cellular', 'celanese'. Now she did not know which she was made of, but any of them seemed to describe her well.

'I like you to be made of celluloid,' said Mr Plantaganet quickly, as if he were afraid that what Tottie said might hurt Birdie, but Birdie did not mind.

'Marchpane was made of kid and china,' said Tottie.

'Kid? What is kid?'

'It is a kind of leather, white leather,' said Tottie. 'Her body was made of it and stuffed with sawdust and jointed; her joints worked more smoothly than mine. Her head was china, and her eyes were china too. Her hair was real, in a plait that they pinned round her head. You could plait it and unplait it.'

'Was it yellow?' asked Birdie.

'Yes,' said Tottie mournfully.

'Is there – much – difference between real and unreal? I wouldn't know,' said Birdie.

'Well – ye-es,' said Tottie as gently as she could.

'Did her clothes take on and off?' asked Apple, who hated to have his clothes taken off.

'She was in wedding clothes,' said Tottie. 'They took off and they were all white.'

'White? I shouldn't like that,' said Birdie more cheerfully. 'I like pink and red and yellow and blue.'

'But they were beautiful. They were stitched with tiny featherstitching.'

'Is there a stitch called featherstitching? Oh, I should like that!' said Birdie, forgetting Marchpane.

'And they were edged with narrowest real lace.'

'Prr-ickkk!' said Darner suddenly. They looked at him in surprise. They all looked round for the danger and could not see any.

'Were those curtains real lace curtains?' asked Mr Plantaganet. 'Those curtains in the house?'

'I shouldn't suppose so,' said Tottie. 'Real lace is very expensive.'

'If it were my house,' said Mr Plantaganet, 'I should have real lace curtains. Nothing less,' said Mr Plantaganet firmly. 'Think! To live in a house like that.' His eyes, that Emily now kept quite free from dust, shone (being glass, they shone quite easily). 'Not to live in a shoe-box any more.' His voice changed as he said that; he sounded as if he were shut in the dark toy cupboard again.

'I could get out of my cot,' said Apple suddenly. 'I would. I could climb through the bars and Emily and Charlotte would think I had rolled out.'

Birdie was thinking about the bird, her songs, her hat, its feather, featherstitching, the feather broom.

'And when they had finished playing with us,' said Mr Plantaganet, 'they would shut up the front and we should be alone, quite private in our own house.'

'Yes,' said Tottie. 'I had forgotten how good that can be.'

She had forgotten Marchpane as well.

Chapter 3

It was late autumn.

How do dolls know when it is autumn? The same way that you do. They smell the London autumn smells of bonfires, of newly lit chimneys, of fog and leaves soaking in the wet. When they go out they see that Michaelmas daisies are out in the Park and chrysanthemums are in the flower shops and violets have come back on to the street flower-sellers' trays. The grownups talk of the first winter colds, and winter coats, and the difficulties of central heating, and the children begin to think of parties and dancing class and even Christmas.

It was also, of course, much colder. It was cold in the shoe-boxes in the colder weather; their cardboard sides were thin and too low to keep out draughts, and Mr Plantaganet began to suffer. He was a delicate little doll and he looked quite drawn with cold. Emily was knitting Tottie a cloak in red wool. 'I do wish she were knitting a muffler or a little waistcoat for Mr Plantaganet instead,' said Tottie. She could go no further than wishing. Dolls cannot tell anything, but often their wishing is as strong as telling. Have you never felt a doll's wish? I am afraid Emily did not feel Tottie's; she finished the cloak and tried it on and

Tottie looked very well in it. Mr Plantaganet remained cold, a little miserable, a little neglected, and draughty in the shoe-box.

Then it happened, in that very autumn, that Emily and Charlotte's great-aunt died, the very great-aunt who had been the little girl of that Great-Great-Aunt Laura who had owned the dolls' house and gathered the shells at the seaside. Her relations and friends found a dolls' house in the attic, an old dolls' house on which the cream paint was dirtied and hung with cobwebs, but on which painted ivy could be seen. It had a green front door with a knocker and six steps going up to it, exactly as Tottie had described.

'Fancy this being here,' said the friends and relations.

'What shall we do with it?'

'It could be sold,' they said. 'It is really as good as new.'

This was not quite true, for it was dusty and thick with dirt; the butler had gone quite to dust, the velvet of the sofa and chairs was rotten and ripped, the shells had come off the pictures in places, and the lace curtains were torn.

'Still, it would fetch a good price,' they said.

'I don't think it ought to be sold,' said one relation who perhaps had more heart than the others. 'It was played with by Great-Aunt, perhaps by her mother. Are there no little girls in the family who might like to play with it now?'

There were two little girls. There were Emily and Charlotte.

The letter came at breakfast when the Plan-taganet family were on the hearthrug where Charlotte had arranged them, pretending it was a park. When Mother read the letter they listened with all their ears, except Apple, whom Charlotte had incautiously put to play up on the fire irons. He was sliding dangerously near the dirty coals. Tottie was watching him from the corner of her eye.

'Can we have it, Mother?' begged Emily and Charlotte.

'Oh, can we?'

'Can we?' begged the Plantaganet family, except Apple.

'You had better ask Father.'

'Can we, Father?'

'Can we?'

'Can we?'

'Can we?' begged the Plantaganets.

Apple was getting nearer and nearer to the coal.

'We had better take it,' said Father. 'And then we can advertise it in the newspapers and get twenty-five pounds.'

'Do we need twenty-five pounds?' asked Mr Plantaganet, but Tottie told him Father was only teasing.

The Dolls' House

'I wish he wouldn't only tease,' said Mr Plantaganet. Mr Plantaganet could never tell when Father was teasing. 'Ought fathers to tease?' he asked wistfully. 'Perhaps I am not a proper sort of father.' He very much wanted to be a proper sort of everything. 'A house!' said Mr Plantaganet, forgetting Father. 'I suppose it is that house, Tottie?'

'I should think it must be,' said Tottie in her calming, calm wood voice. 'An old dolls' house that belonged to Great-Great-Aunt Laura. What else could it be?'

'That – that dream house?' said Mr Plantaganet.

'You didn't dream it, I told you of it,' said Tottie, who was strictly truthful; she could see Mr Plantaganet was getting into a state.

'I can't believe it,' said Mr Plantaganet. 'I can't.'

'Yes, you can,' said Tottie, 'easily. Now Father has said "Yes", it is going to happen.'

'No more shoe-boxes!' said Mr Plantaganet, with a catch in his voice. 'And it has been awfully cold in those shoe-boxes sometimes, hasn't it, Tottie?'

'Yes, but that's all over now,' said Tottie. 'At least, soon it will be over. Apple! Apple! Take care!'

'That little doll is nearly in the coal,' said Father, and he touched Apple with his foot.

Charlotte picked him out of the fender just in time.

'And Birdie will have her birdcage, and Apple will have his cot, and Darner his kennel.'

27

'And you will be able to wish Emily and Charlotte to shut the front when they have done playing with us, and I am sure they will,' said Tottie. 'And we shall live there happy ever after.'

'Yes. Oh yes! Oh YES!' said Mr Plantaganet, and he said to himself, 'No more shoe-boxes. No more dark toy cupboards. No more dark at all; we shall have the little lamp and even if they forget the candle, with a lamp it is easy to pretend that it is light. Red walls,' whispered Mr Plantaganet, 'taps that really run (if you fill the tank first), wax roses in the vase, nicked blankets on the beds.'

His eyes looked as if they might break their glass. No doll can cry tears, they have to keep their tears in, but Mr Plantaganet's eyes looked as if they held tears of joy. Did you know people could cry for joy as well as for sorrow? They can, and dolls would too sometimes if they could.

'Happy ever after,' said Mr Plantaganet. 'Happy ever after, Tottie.'

As I told you, they had forgotten Marchpane.

Chapter 4

When the dolls' house arrived, Marchpane was not in it.

She had been sent to the cleaners.

That was very bad for Marchpane. The cleaners took such care of her that it went to her head which, being china, was empty, which is a very dangerous kind of head to have. Mr Plantaganet had one too, and it had been filled with his gloomy thoughts of dark toy cupboards and boys who drew moustaches, but now it was more happily filled with thoughts of the dolls' house. Marchpane's was filled with thoughts of Marchpane; and at the cleaners she thought how wonderful Marchpane was: how valuable Marchpane was: how beautifully Marchpane was made: what elegant clothes Marchpane had, with what small exquisite stitching. 'I am a beautiful little creature, really I am,' thought Marchpane. 'I must be worth a fabulous amount of money. No wonder they are so careful of me. They can hardly be careful enough. I am so very important,' said Marchpane. There was no one to contradict her and her thoughts of Marchpane grew larger and larger till you would have thought her little head was hardly big enough to contain them.

The cleaners took off her fine-sewn wedding

clothes and washed and cleaned them exquisitely so that they were whiter than snowdrops or snow. Then they cleaned Marchpane herself all over and she was whiter too, but they cleaned her with petrol, and after it, I must confess, she smelled strongly and nastily of petrol: in fact, ever afterwards, she had a faintly nasty smell (which was quite right, because she was nasty).

The cleaners redressed her, and replaited her hair, which they had cleaned until it looked like golden floss; then, having politely asked permission first, they put her on the counter of their shop, with a card:

Mid-nineteenth-century doll, as cleaned by us.

Marchpane stood on the counter and everyone who came into the shop looked at her and admired her. Marchpane liked being looked at and admired more and more, though she thought of course it was only her due, and that the people were very lucky to have a chance to see such an elegant and beauteous doll as Marchpane.

Chapter 5

Charlotte and Emily, the Plantaganet family, had been busy.

The dolls' house was exactly as Tottie had described it, but . . .

'Oh dear!' said Mr Plantaganet, and if the corners of his mouth had been made to turn down, they would have turned down.

'Oh dear! Oh dear! O-oh dear!'

On the dolls' house, and in it, were years and years of dust and grime and cobwebs and mould and rust. The children and the Plantaganets looked at the tattered chair and sofa covers, at the torn old curtains, at the sea-shells fallen off the picture frames, at the remains of the butler. The blue tin stove was rusty and so was the bath, the mangle was stuck, some of the kitchen chairs were broken and the nicked-round blankets were grey with mildew. 'Oh dear! Oh dear!' said Mr Plantaganet.

'Stop staying "Oh dear!"' said Tottie sharply.

'But what shall we do? What can we do?'

'We can wish,' said Tottie still sharply because, truth to tell, she was feeling worried and anxious herself. Could the children, would the children, be able to put it in order? That was the question in Tottie's mind.

'It's dusty. It's dirty. It's horrible!' cried little Apple.

'Is it?' asked Birdie anxiously. She could not herself see anything more than the birdcage and the bird. They were so wonderful to Birdie that she could not see anything else, and, being two things of the same kind, she did not feel the thoughts of them knocking together in her head.

'Is it dusty and dirty, Tottie?' asked Birdie.

'Wish! Wish! Wish!' said Tottie, and every knot and grain of her seemed to harden. She came from a tree.

'What shall we do? What can we?' said Mr Plantaganet.

'Don't bleat. Wish,' said Tottie hardly, and her hard voice made the word sound so hard and firm that even Mr Plantaganet took heart and they all began to wish. 'Wish that Emily and Charlotte can put our house in order and make it good again. Go on, all of you. Wish. Wish. Wish,' said Tottie.

At that moment, among the Plantaganets appeared hands, Emily and Charlotte's hands, lifting them on to the mantelpiece out of the way where they could see. Then those same hands began to strip the dolls' house.

'What did I tell you?' said Tottie.

'But – they are not making it, they are taking it all away.'

'Taking it all to pieces.'

'Taking it all away.'

'Wait and see,' said Tottie. 'Wait and see.'

32

The Dolls' House

Emily and Charlotte and their mother took everything out of the dolls' house; they took the carpets up from their tintacks and with the carpets came layers of dust. They did not look like carpets but pieces of crinkled old grey flannel. Birdie hid her face in her hands. 'I wanted the pink one and there isn't a pink one,' she said.

'Wait and see. Wait and see,' said Tottie.

'The carpets are filthy,' said Mother. 'I will take them to wash and iron.'

'What did I say?' said Tottie.

Meanwhile Charlotte was brushing down the walls and roof, Emily was brushing out the rooms and stairs. Then Charlotte fetched a pail of water and a cake of soap and her nail brush.

'Charlotte, do you think you ought to use that?'

'Hush!' said Charlotte, beginning to use it. She washed the walls and roof and Emily, after watching a moment, joined in and, fetching her nail brush, began to wash the floor and walls and ceilings. She was a little astonished because she was the one who usually thought of things; it was unusual for Charlotte to be the first. 'H'm,' said Emily, scrubbing hard. 'Charlotte must like the dolls' house very very much.' The grime was so deep, the dust so thick, that they had to change the water in the pail three times.

'London grime,' said Tottie, watching. 'A hundred years of London grime.'

33

'I hope she doesn't miss the front steps,' said Mr Plantaganet, but Charlotte did not miss the front steps. She missed nothing at all. By the time she had finished she herself was filthy, with a filthy overall and dirt marks on her cheeks. Then she took a dry cloth and dried the walls and roof and steps all over; then took a duster and polished them. Emily watched again and followed her.

'Good work, Charlotte,' she said.

'Yes, good work,' said Tottie.

'Good work,' cried all the Plantaganets.

'Why, it begins to look new,' said Emily, stepping back from the dolls' house.

Indeed it looked much better. The good paint, and paint was good in those days, had come up well, and the wallpapers, from their brushing, had lost their look of grime. Charlotte had knocked down a few more shells from the pictures, but Emily had fetched the glue and glued them on again, which was unusual for Emily because she did not usually do things for Charlotte. She also brushed and dusted the furniture and rubbed the rust off the stove with sandpaper; she pulled the curtains down from the windows to which they had been fastened with drawing-pins and ripped the covers off the sofa and the chairs. Soon beds, chairs, and windows were left quite bare.

'Are you still wishing, Tottie?' asked Mr Plantaganet anxiously.

'Yes,' said Tottie firmly.

'You – see what I mean, don't you?' said Mr Plantaganet.

'You must wish about the curtains,' said Tottie. 'You must wish about the couch and chairs. You must wish about the beds.'

'Curtains, chairs, beds,' said Mr Plantaganet. He wished he could shut his eyes in order to wish harder but, of course, he could not because they were not made to shut.

'Over and over again,' said Tottie. 'You must never leave off wishing.'

'Beds, chairs, couch, curtains; beds, chairs, couch, curtains; beds, chairs . . . '

'My cot. My own little cot,' wished Apple.

'My bird-broom-feather.' Birdie still did not know which to think of first.

'Beds, couch, curtains, chairs . . . '

The door opened and the children's mother came in.

'Could she have washed those carpets already?' asked Mr Plantaganet suspiciously.

She answered him herself. 'I have washed the carpets,' said Mother. 'They have come up beautifully. Now I have brought the scrap bag; we shall need new mattresses and pillows and sheets and blankets for the beds.'

'And pillow cases,' said Charlotte, 'for mouse-size pillows.'

Emily stared at Charlotte, and so did the Plantaganets. It was not usually Charlotte who said things.

'Could I have a mouse-size pillow?' asked Apple, excited. 'A pillow for a very small mouse?'

'I shall fetch the cotton wool,' said Emily, 'and then I can stuff them as you make them.'

'But – but – I don't want cotton for mine,' cried Birdie, 'I want – want – want –' Her head rattled so that she could not say what it was she wanted. Tottie began to wish.

'I think Birdie ought to have a feather bed,' said Charlotte suddenly.

'A-aah!' said Birdie rapturously.

'Here are some bits of flannel for blankets. We can nick them round the edges,' said Mother. 'And what do you think? Shall we make Apple a patchwork quilt for his cot?'

'Could you make the patches small enough?' asked Emily. Mother thought she could.

'It is getting better and better and better,' said Mr Plantaganet.

'Yes!' said Birdie.

'Yes, but you must go on wishing,' said Tottie. 'You mustn't leave off wishing.'

'While I am in this cleaning mood,' said Charlotte, 'I am going to wash the windows. What shall we do about curtains?' asked Charlotte.

The Dolls' House

'They should be lace,' said Mother.

Then Emily spoke. 'They must be real lace,' said Emily.

Mr Plantaganet smiled.

'Real lace is very expensive,' said Mother.

'I shall get my money box,' answered Emily.

'Get mine too,' said Charlotte.

'What is the difference between real lace and not-real lace?' whispered Birdie.

'It is made by hand and not by machine,' said Tottie slowly, 'and it shows the care that was taken to make it, and besides being fine, it is strong, every least bit of it, and it looks different and it feels different. You would know the difference if you saw the two together.'

'Do you think I would?' asked Birdie humbly. 'Real things and not-real things, they seem the same to me. My bird and its songs –' She knew one was real and one was not, but she could not say now which was which.

Emily came back with the money boxes. They were rather empty; hers had a threepenny bit, a half-crown and a florin and a sixpenny bit in it. 'Five shillings and threepence,' said Emily. Charlotte's had a florin, sixpence, four three-penny bits, and a penny. 'Three shillings and sevenpence,' said Emily, 'eight and tenpence altogether. That might be enough but – there are other things we want as well,' said Emily. There was a gleam in her eyes as she looked at the old couch and chairs.

'I shall measure the windows,' said Charlotte and she measured them with Mother's tape measure. They were six inches long. 'Six inches, and there are four windows. Four times six is twenty-four, twenty-four inches, and twenty-seven inches is three-quarters of a yard. We should have to buy three-quarters of a yard of that real lace,' said Charlotte. 'And we should have three inches over. We could make a lace apron for Tottie.'

'Yes, but we need a new couch and chairs.'

The couch and chairs, now they were stripped, certainly looked in very bad repair; their wooden arms and legs were scratched and stained and they had no stuffing left on their seats and backs at all.

'Not a little patch of that red velvet,' said Mr Plantaganet.

'There are others in the shops,' said Charlotte uncertainly.

'Yes, ordinary ones,' said Emily scornfully.

'Wouldn't – wouldn't ordinary ones do?' Charlotte was a little like Birdie. She was happy with ordinary things, but Emily was not.

'This dolls' house is special,' said Emily. 'You know it is, Charlotte. It is an antique,' said Emily.

'What is an an— what she said then?' asked Mr Plantaganet.

'Yes, what is it?'

'What is it, Tottie?'

38

The Dolls' House

'Old things are antiques,' said Tottie. 'Things that have lasted for many years, usually because they were beautifully made of good materials in the beginning.'

'Like real lace,' said Mr Plantaganet.

'Yes, and usually they have been given great care or they would not have lasted all that time,' said Tottie.

'Like the dolls' house?' asked Birdie. 'It is an antique. Emily said so.'

'Are you an antique, Tottie?' asked Apple suddenly.

'I suppose I am,' said Tottie.

'I know what would look very beautiful on that holly-green carpet,' Emily was saying slowly. 'Do you know, Charlotte?'

'What?' asked Charlotte.

'Do you remember looking at that shop in Wigmore Street?' said Emily, 'where they had that little set of dolls' house chairs and couch? They were very old and they were made of real oak – it said so – and they were red velvet too.'

'And there was a table,' said Charlotte dreamily, 'and it had a red runner and a fringe.'

'Yes,' said Emily.

'Yes,' said Charlotte.

'Yes,' said the Plantaganets.

'I shall have sixpence for my tooth when it comes out,' said Charlotte.

'Oh, Charlotte! Don't be silly,' said Emily. 'Those were terribly expensive.'

'Then – we shall have to have ordinary lace and chairs.'

'Oh no!' cried Mr Plantaganet. 'Oh no! Please no!'

'I don't mind ordinary chairs,' said Birdie. 'I can make do with anything.'

'We can't,' said Emily. 'We shan't.'

'But – what shall we do?'

'We shall do what other people do when they want things,' said Emily. 'We must make money.'

'But how?' asked Charlotte.

'How?' asked all the Plantaganets.

'Somehow,' said Emily.

Chapter 6

Tottie and the dolls' house were not the only things in the house that had belonged to Emily and Charlotte's great-grandmother and Great-Great-Aunt Laura. There was, as well, a sampler.

'What is a sampler?' asked Apple.

'It is a needlework picture to hang on a wall,' Tottie explained to him. 'It is all worked in cross-stitch on fine canvas, and sometimes, most times, the stitches are very fine indeed. Do you remember, in *The Tailor of Gloucester*,' asked Tottie, 'when it says, "the stitches were so small – so small, that they could only have been made by mice"? Well, the stitches in samplers look like that, but they were not made by mice,' said Tottie. 'They were made by little girls; and hours and hours of stitching went into them. They had letters and alphabets and a great deal of writing. I remember them well,' said Tottie. 'I feel glad that little girls do not have to make them now,' said Tottie.

Great-Grandmother's sampler hung in the children's room. It was long in shape and framed in a narrow wooden frame. It was worked in baskets of flowers on a cream background, and it had a verse that said in tiny pale-blue stitches:

Tales from the Dolls' House

Fain am I to work these nosegays
Gathered from my tranquil days
In gentle rain, mild storm and sunny weather,
A friend to flower, flesh and fur and feather,
Content, please God, my time on earth to dwell
Till death shall claim me and I say farewell.

'I remember those *f*'s,' said Tottie. 'They gave her a great deal of trouble.'

Charlotte did not like to look at the sampler, she said it gave her a headache and she did not understand the poem in the least, but Emily liked it. Sometimes she begged Mother to give her a certain little set of clothes, Tottie's first clothes, as old as the sampler. These clothes were not beautiful ones like Marchpane's; they were the ordinary clothes that might have been made for any little doll in those times: a bodice with infinitesimal tucks where stay-bones should have been, a pair of long-legged drawers scalloped to match, and a dress of India muslin embroidered in blue flowers, and a very little blue bonnet to match that had white embroidery that looked like quilling on the edge. Emily liked to dress Tottie in these and stand her underneath the sampler.

'Let's put her there today, Charlotte,' said Emily next afternoon. 'Mrs Innisfree is coming to tea.'

Both the children loved Mrs Innisfree, who was gay and serious as need arose and who was always interested in their dolls. Emily dressed Tottie and stood her under the sampler and even wrote a ticket that said, not unlike the cleaners' notice for Marchpane: *Example of a real old sampler worked by a little girl in 1846.*

'Poor little girl,' said Charlotte indignantly.

Emily took no notice. She wrote: *Example of a farthing doll, dressed by that same little girl in 1846.*

'Her mother must have helped her,' said Charlotte. 'No little girl could make that quilling. You ought to put in about the mother, Emily.'

'Well, I shan't,' said Emily. 'It spoils the notice.'

There was a sound of footsteps outside the door and Mrs Innisfree came in. She admired Tottie and the sampler and she admired the dolls' house, and she sat down by the fire and listened to the whole story of it.

'It's a pity about the chairs and couch,' said Mrs Innisfree.

Emily told her about the set in Wigmore Street, and then she and Charlotte fell silent.

'They sound the very thing,' said Mrs Innisfree. 'Will you buy them?'

'No-o,' said Emily.

'No-o,' said Charlotte.

'At least, not yet,' said Emily with a faraway brightness in her eyes.

'I see,' said Mrs Innisfree, and her eyes went to Tottie. 'It is strange,' she said, 'that you should have arranged Tottie like that for me to see. I am having an exhibition,' said Mrs Innisfree, 'at least a part of it is mine. It is called "Dolls Through the Ages", and it is to help the Blind Children's Fund. I wonder if your little doll and sampler could be in it.'

'You mean, just as they are now?' asked Charlotte. '"*Example of a real old sampler worked by a little girl in 1846*" (poor little girl), and "*Example of a farthing doll dressed by that same little girl in 1846*" (only you ought to have put in about the mother doing the quilling),' said Charlotte.

'Yes, I mean that,' said Mrs Innisfree. 'I think your mother would let you, and,' said Mrs Innisfree, looking at Emily and Charlotte and at the shabby little chairs and empty windows of the dolls' house, 'we pay for some of the dolls, and I should like to pay you for Tottie.'

When Tottie heard these words she gave a little gasp, but no one heard her.

'How much would you pay?' Charlotte was saying. 'Would you pay a whole pound?'

'Charlotte!' said Emily and tried to kick her gently on the ankle.

'But we need a whole pound,' said Charlotte.

'We should pay a guinea,' said Mrs Innisfree.

Tottie gave another sound and this time it was a groan, but Apple was tugging at her skirt.

'How much is a guinea?' whispered Apple.

'A pound and a shilling,' said Tottie faintly. 'Mrs

Innisfree is giving that for me. O-oh! Oh!'

'That would be enough,' said Charlotte, nodding her head.

'After a hundred years!' cried Tottie.

'Then will you let me take Tottie and the sampler away?' asked Mrs Innisfree.

'Take Tottie away –' cried Mr Plantaganet, and stopped.

'Tottie? Going away?' asked Birdie.

'Tottie go away?' asked little Apple, and he said firmly, 'No.'

'Now, Apple –'

'No! No! No!' cried Apple.

'It is to get the chairs,' said Mr Plantaganet.

'Don't want any chairs.'

'Now, Apple!'

'I don't want any either. Bother the chairs,' said Birdie. 'Can't we sit on cotton reels? They would do.'

'We have to have elegant chairs,' said Mr Plantaganet slowly. 'Here is a good way of Tottie earning them. Isn't it like Tottie,' asked Mr Plantaganet, 'to be the one to earn us a couch and chairs, and the table with the runner, and the real lace curtains perhaps as well?'

Tottie said nothing at all. She stood as if, instead of being wood, she had turned to stone, and when Emily picked her up and wrapped her in white paper to give to Mrs Innisfree, Tottie lay cold and heavy in her hand.

Emily felt misery and reproach from Tottie, but she did not understand why. Can you guess why?

Tottie was wrapped up and packed in a box, the box laid on top of the sampler with the two notices, and they were all handed to Mrs Innisfree.

Chapter 7

In the night Apple would not sleep without Tottie,
Birdie had no wish to sleep, and even Mr Plantaganet
did not feel quite comfortable.

'Go to sleep, Apple, do,' he said.

'You go to sleep,' said Apple.

But Mr Plantaganet could not. Emily and Charlotte
were strangely restless too.

'Emily,' said Charlotte at last from her bed.

'Yes, Charlotte.'

'You will be cross,' said Charlotte.

'I don't think I will,' said Emily. 'I-I think I know
what you are thinking, Charlotte.'

'Well,' said Charlotte, and she lay on her back
looking thoughtfully up at the ceiling. 'Well, people
usually do, don't they?'

'Do what?'

'Lend, not be paid,' said Charlotte.

'Ye-es,' said Emily miserably.

'I mean, for an exhibition like that, which is to help
people, people usually lend their things, don't they, to
help the other people?'

'That's what I was thinking – remembering,'
said Emily. 'Do you remember the animal carving
exhibition we went to see? It had labels: *Head of a deer,*

47

lent by Mr So-and-So. Rabbit, lent by Mrs Somebody Else.'

'Ye-es,' said Charlotte.

'It didn't say, *Hired from Mr So-and-So,*' said Emily, 'and that is what being paid means. We have hired out Tottie.'

'That is what she didn't like,' said Charlotte, and she was near the truth though that was not the whole truth.

'I felt her being miserable, but I didn't take any notice – then,' said Emily.

'Nor I,' said Charlotte. 'But I wish I had.'

'I believe Mrs Innisfree offered to pay us because she was sorry we couldn't get the chairs,' said Emily.

'We shall go to Mrs Innisfree in the morning and tell her,' said Emily. 'I believe she knew we really ought not to have been paid.'

'I believe we really knew that too,' said Charlotte. 'It was my fault,' she added. 'I said we needed a pound.'

'No, it was mine,' said Emily. 'I wanted the chairs more than you did. How funny. I want things so hard, Charlotte, that I don't think what I am doing. I don't want them so much now,' said Emily.

'Then we shall have ordinary ones?' asked Charlotte.

'No,' said Emily firmly and shortly.

'Then what will you do?'

'I don't know what I shall do,' said Emily, 'but not this,' she said.

Mrs Innisfree was surprised to see them when they

called at her house next morning. She seemed more surprised and pleased when Emily laid the pound note and the shilling on the table.

'After all,' said Charlotte, 'we are not blind and if we don't get paid for Tottie, the children who are blind will get more money.'

'Certainly they will,' said Mrs Innisfree, and she looked at Emily, who had put down the pound note and the shilling and who could not trust herself to speak.

'Emily,' said Mrs Innisfree, 'you wanted those chairs badly, didn't you?'

'Yes,' said Emily, 'but Charlotte likes the dolls' house just as much as I do.'

'It was your idea to get those chairs?'

'And the couch and the table and the runner,' put in Charlotte.

'Well – I saw them first,' said Emily.

'Emilys usually see things first,' said Mrs Innisfree gently. 'And it is usually they who have the ideas. I am like Emily; it was my idea to pay you for Tottie, but of course it is far nicer that you yourselves have decided to lend her to me. Now I have another idea,' said Mrs Innisfree.

(You must remember that while this was happening Tottie was packed away in her box under her paper and had no idea of it at all. You must keep remembering that.)

'I want,' said Mrs Innisfree, 'to see those old chairs and that old couch. The ones that were in the dolls' house when it came.'

'But – they are all torn and unstuffed.'

'But the wooden part, the legs and arms and frames?'

'That is still there,' said Charlotte.

'They should be as good as new, if they were as good in the first place as I think they were. As good as the Wigmore Street ones,' said Mrs Innisfree. 'Go and get them now,' she said.

'What now? Straight away?' asked Charlotte, but Emily's eyes gleamed.

'Straight away,' said Mrs Innisfree. 'I might be able to do something with them if they are as I hope.'

'Are they?' asked Charlotte an hour later when she and Emily had come back.

'Are they what?'

'As you hoped?'

'Yes, they are,' said Mrs Innisfree.

The sofa and chairs stood on the table in her drawing room. 'Look,' she said, and with her scissors she ripped off what Emily had left of the stuffing, the torn bits, and dirty old cotton; soon the chairs and sofa were bare down to their seats. 'Look,' said Mrs Innisfree, 'the wood is good, quite solid. Do you see, Emily, the little legs are turned. They are scratched and discoloured, but the good work is there. Do you see that when things are beautifully made, how beautifully they last?'

'These don't look as if they had lasted,' objected Charlotte. 'They look fit to throw away.'

'That is because you haven't looked into them. Wait and see,' said Mrs Innisfree. She opened a drawer and took out two pieces of sandpaper and rubbed them against each other. 'That's to smooth them a little because they are too rough – they must not scratch the wood too deeply.' She picked up a little chair and began to rub its leg.

'But – you are taking all its polish off.'

'And the dirt and scratches. Now you and Charlotte rub them, and when they are quite clean and smooth we shall take them to a man I know who is a French polisher, and we shall ask him if he will help us. I think he will,' said Mrs Innisfree.

'But – would a real French polisher polish them?'

'He might, if we can make him interested,' said Mrs Innisfree. 'People will do anything if they are interested.'

'But what about the seats and arms and backs? They were all cushioned before.'

'They can be cushioned again.'

'But with what? Mother says that nowhere, any more, anywhere, can you buy stuff like that they were cushioned with,' said Emily.

'Have you seen this?' asked Mrs Innisfree, and she

picked up a footstool that was standing by the table and showed it to them. Its top was of embroidery, flowers, worked very finely, in the same mice stitches that Tottie had talked about, stitches like the sampler, only finer.

'This is called *petit-point*. Have you ever seen a chair like it?' asked Mrs Innisfree. 'A tapestry chair?'

'Oh!' said Emily. 'Oh! You mean—'

'Yes. What could be better than tiny tapestry chairs and couch?' asked Mrs Innisfree.

'Dolls' tapestry would have to be very, very fine,' said Emily slowly. 'Could anybody work it?' she asked doubtfully.

'I have worked it so that it was very fine indeed.'

'It would be beautiful,' breathed Charlotte. 'But we couldn't do it, not Emily, nor I. It would take us years and years to learn. Our great-grandmother could have done it. Perhaps there was some use in working samplers,' said Charlotte mournfully. 'Now who – who – who –'

Mrs Innisfree had not answered. She had opened a drawer and was taking out a roll of fine canvas and a box of silks.

'You!' said Emily and Charlotte together. 'You! You mean you would work it for us?'

'It would not take me very long,' said Mrs Innisfree. 'I think I could do it. Anyway, I could try. Suppose you stay to lunch with me and then we could choose patterns and colours. Of course we shall need an upholsterer as well as a French polisher,' said Mrs Innisfree, 'but I have another friend who would do that for us. I think it will be far nicer and of course far cheaper,' she said with a sideways look at the children, 'than the little set in Wigmore Street that you wanted to buy.'

'What a great deal we are learning about things,' said Emily, 'all these beautiful old things.'

'But you mustn't think it is only the old things that are beautiful,' said Mrs Innisfree. 'We can do as good work nowadays if we have the same patience.'

'Yes – patience!' said Charlotte. Truth to tell, her hand was aching very much from the sandpapering, but she went on rubbing.

They had lunch with Mrs Innisfree. What did they have? They had plaice, which is fish, and green peas and mashed potatoes, and a cherry tart from Mrs Innisfree's bottled cherries.

After lunch they looked through the patterns and silk and chose a small pattern that was part of a larger pattern; it was moss rosebuds in crimson and pink, with green leaves, on a cream background. 'And we must have this copper colour for the stems,' said Mrs Innisfree, 'and I shall use this peacock blue for the shading.'

'Can you shade so tiny?' asked Emily.

'I think I can,' said Mrs Innisfree.

'I think you can do anything,' said Charlotte, and that evening she said to Emily, 'Do you know, Emily, Mrs Innisfree reminds me of Tottie.'

'Of Tottie?'

'Yes.'

'Can a real person remind you of a doll?'

'I don't know,' said Charlotte, 'but Mrs Innisfree does.' She thought for a moment. 'Perhaps it's because Tottie never breaks or gets spoilt. I miss Tottie,' said Charlotte.

They had asked to peep at Tottie before they left Mrs Innisfree, and how surprised Tottie was to see their faces bending over her.

'Is this all a bad dream?' asked Tottie of herself. 'Am I at home again?' But as soon as Charlotte lifted her up she saw that she was in a strange room and that the box still lay on the table. 'It isn't a dream,' cried Tottie in Charlotte's hand. 'Oh! Oh! Oh!'

'Why does she look so unhappy?' asked Charlotte.

'A pound and a shilling! A guinea. After a hundred years,' said Tottie.

'She looks – angry,' said Emily. Both of them could feel Tottie wishing, but they could not understand why she should wish, and they put her back into the box and covered her up with tissue paper.

'When does she go to the Exhibition?' she heard Emily ask, just before they put on the lid.

'To the Exhibition! To the Exhibition!' said Tottie in a cry so loud that every knot and grain of her felt twisted, but, of course, not a sound came out of the box.

Chapter 8

Marchpane had been seen by someone at the cleaners who had taken her address and written to the great-aunt's relations to ask if Marchpane too might not come to the Exhibition.

The great-aunt's relations said yes.

Marchpane was delighted.

Chapter 9

When Tottie was next taken out of her box she found herself in a large cold room that had long tables, covered with blue cloth, against each wall, and a number of ladies all busy unpacking dolls.

Tottie had never seen so many ladies and so many dolls, particularly so many dolls. There was every kind of doll: baby dolls, little girl dolls, boy dolls, lady and gentleman dolls, soldier dolls, sailor dolls, acting dolls, dancing dolls, clockwork dolls, fairy dolls, Chinese dolls, Polish, Japanese, French, German, Russian. There was a white wax doll with exquisite white china hands, and a Dutch fisherman with a basket on his back, and a Flemish doll in market clothes, and her cook sitting down with her basket. There were Japanese dolls with blank white faces, and Chinese dolls whose faces were as alive as snakes, with painted snaky eyebrows and long noses; they were dancers and ceremonial dolls with satin trousers and red-painted shoes. There were two little German dolls with yellow fringes and gentle brown eyes and peasant clothes, and a Polichinelle, very old, with his legs drawn up and a carved, frightening, evil face. There was every kind and sort of doll and they filled the room, each standing in its place and showing what kind of doll it was. Some of them were very handsome and imposing; all of them, without exception, were far, far larger than Tottie.

She felt small and shy and longed to go home. 'But I can't go home,' said Tottie. 'I shall never go home again,' and her secret trouble filled her so strongly that, if wood could have drooped, Tottie would have drooped. 'Oh! Oh! Oh!' cried poor little Tottie, and she thought of them all at home: Mr Plantaganet, Birdie, Darner, Apple; when she thought of Apple she felt as if she must break into splinters, but of course, being made of such good wood, she gave no outward sign.

A lady took her up in her hand. 'Where shall we put this darling little thing?' she asked. 'Look. She goes with this sampler.'

'What a charming idea,' said another, but Tottie did not think it was in the least bit charming.

'A farthing doll!' said another lady. 'Why, I should think she must be unique.'

Tottie did not know what 'unique' meant (if you don't, go and look it up in the dictionary), for all she could tell it might be something rude, and she wished she could hang her head, but of course a wooden neck will never, never bend and so she stayed, staring as woodenly as possible, straight in front of her. The ladies took her and set her up on the centre of one of the long tables, with the sampler behind her and two square cards and one longer one in front of her. From

Tottie's point of view, these cards were upside down, so that she could not read them. They looked like this:

LITTLE GIRL OF 1846
DRESSED BY SAME
FARTHING DOLL

SAMPLER WORKED
BY A LITTLE GIRL
IN 1846

LENT BY HER GREAT-GRANDDAUGHTERS,
EMILY AND CHARLOTTE DANE
IN 1946

On the table opposite Tottie were four dolls under a glass-domed cover. Next to her, on her right side, was a wax doll with a satin dress, and on the other side a walking doll dressed in blue satin with a bustle behind and white flounces. She held, tiptilted, a blue parasol, and in the other tiny hand, a fan.

'Who – who are those in the case?' asked Tottie.

'They were Queen Victoria's dolls when she was a child,' said the wax doll.

'O-ooh!' said Tottie. She remembered Queen Victoria of course.

'La! We 'ave been put in one of ze best positions, is it you say? in ze room,' said the walking doll.

'Why does she talk like that?' asked Tottie in a whisper of the wax doll.

'She is French,' said the wax doll. 'She is very proud.'

The walking doll held her tiptilted parasol and her

58

fan and glanced at Tottie. 'What ees it you are made of?' she asked. '*Pardonnez-moi*, but la! I do not recognize ze substance.'

'I am made of wood,' answered Tottie with dignity.

'Wood? La! La! La! Tee-hee-hee.' Her laughing sounded as if it were wound up. 'Tee-hee. La! La! I thought doorknobs and broom 'andles and bedposts and clothes-pegs were made of wood, not dolls.'

'So they are,' said Tottie. 'And so are the masts of ships and flagpoles and violins – and trees,' said Tottie.

She and the walking doll looked at one another and, though the walking doll was quite ten inches taller than Tottie, Tottie did not flinch.

'I am made of keed and porcelain,' said the walking doll. 'Inside I 'ave a leetle set of works. Wind me up and I walk.'

'Walk, walk, walk,' cried the other dolls.

'*Merci! Je ne marcherai pas que si ça me chante,*' which means she would not walk unless she wanted, but of course she could not walk unless someone wound her up.

'I once knew a kid doll,' said Tottie. 'I did not like her.'

'Who is talking about kid dolls?' came a voice from the opposite table. 'Who did not like kid dolls?'

'I don't,' said Tottie firmly though, at the sound of that voice, she felt as if instead of being wood all through, she might have been made hollow inside.

'And who are you?' said the voice.

'It is a leetle object,' said the walking doll, 'that 'as found its way in 'ere. La! It is made of wood.'

'Of wood?' said the voice. 'Once I knew a little doll made of wood and I did not like her at all!'

'I 'ave nevaire see one,' said the walking doll.

'They were sold in the cheaper shops. A shilling a dozen or four for a penny. The children, silly little things, would waste their money on them.'

'La! Children! *Merci. Je ne mange pas de ce pain là.* 'Orrible leetle creatures. *Je les déteste.*'

'Silly little things! Little creatures! Those are children they are talking of!' said the wax doll, shocked. Her voice, after the others, was meltingly soft. 'How dare they!' said the wax doll. 'They don't deserve the name of "doll". But tell me about those things you were talking of – the ships and flagpoles. It must be good to be made of something hard,' said the wax doll.

'It is,' said Tottie. At the moment all the good wood in her was standing firmly against the things the voice and the haughty doll had said. Tottie knew that voice. She looked across at the other table and she saw whom she had expected to see. She saw Marchpane. Marchpane saw her.

'Oh, it's you,' said Marchpane.

'Yes,' said Tottie.

'Strange!' said Marchpane. 'I thought you would have been broken or thrown away long, long ago.'

'No,' said Tottie.

'What is it they used to call you?' asked Marchpane. 'Spotty, Dotty. Surely it was Dotty.'

'Tee! Tee-hee! Tee-hee!' giggled the walking doll. 'Tee-hee-hee! Tee-hee!'

'My name is Tottie,' said Tottie. 'It always has been.'

'I couldn't be expected to remember,' said Marchpane. 'There were so many of you.'

'Not in our family,' said Tottie. 'I was the only one.'

'She is the only one now,' said the wax doll. 'The only one of her kind in the Exhibition. I heard them say so.'

For some time there had been whispers going on among the dolls and now the walking doll was listening. 'La! Is it possible?' she asked. '*Non. Non. Je m'en doute.*'

'What is it?' asked Marchpane.

'Dey say that some of the dolls 'ere are to be sold, sold out of their families.'

'What? Sold by your own family?'

'Sold!'

'Sold!'

'Sold!' ran the whisper among the dolls.

'*La! Quel malheur!*' said the walking doll. 'My museum would nevaire part with me.'

'Nor mine,' said Marchpane quickly.

'Nor mine,' said the wax doll, but she said it with a fluttering sigh.

You notice that Tottie had said nothing all this time.

This was Tottie's secret trouble. Yes, Tottie thought that Emily and Charlotte had sold her to Mrs Innisfree. If you look back to page 44 of this book you will see why. 'We pay for some of the dolls,' Mrs Innisfree had said. 'I should like to pay you for Tottie.'

'How much would you pay?' Charlotte had asked. Oh, Charlotte! 'Would you pay a whole pound?'

Tottie shuddered when she remembered that.

'We should pay a guinea,' said Mrs Innisfree.

Of course Tottie did not know that Emily and Charlotte had given the guinea back to Mrs Innisfree. She thought she was sold and would presently be sold again. She was filled with shame.

'It must be there on those cards,' thought Tottie. 'Only they can't read them because they are upside down and Marchpane is too far away on the other table. But soon they must know!' thought Tottie.

'La! I am glad I am not standing next to such a one,' said the walking doll.

'But you are. You are,' thought Tottie. She wished she could sink through the table.

The other dolls were longing for the Exhibition to open. Marchpane, of course, was eager for the people to come and admire her, and so was the haughty doll. The wax doll was excited. She had been packed away in a box so long. 'Do you think there will be any children?' she asked with longing in her voice.

'Children? I hope not!' said Marchpane.

The Dolls' House

'I 'ope zey will not touch,' said the haughty doll.

'They had better not touch me,' said Marchpane. 'That must certainly not be allowed.'

'But – were you not meant to be played with?' asked the wax doll. 'I was. I was.'

'La! You are un'appy?'

'I am shut away in a box. Away from children, and it is children who give us life,' said the wax doll.

'And tumble one about and spoil one,' said Marchpane, and the walking doll shuddered to the tip of her parasol.

'Isn't that life?' asked Tottie.

'I want children,' cried the wax doll. 'I-I –' She stopped. It had been on the tip of her tongue to say, 'I wish I could be sold.' She wished she dared to say this aloud, but wax is not very brave stuff and so she remained quiet.

Tottie wished the Exhibition would never open. 'But it will,' thought Tottie, 'and then – then – someone will buy me. I shall be sold and when the Exhibition closes I shall go away to a new home. Oh!' cried Tottie. 'Oh Apple! Darner! Birdie! Mr Plantaganet! My little home! Oh! Oh! Oh!' But no sign of grief showed on her wooden face. She stood as firm as ever.

'Is it true,' said one of the dolls, 'that this Exhibition is to be opened by a queen?'

'Queen Victoria?' asked the wax doll, looking at the dolls in the glass case. Tottie whispered to her that

Queen Victoria had been dead long, long ago.

'Forgive me,' said the wax doll. 'I have been shut away so long.'

'A queen?' said Marchpane with great satisfaction. 'How right and proper. She will be sure to notice me. They always do,' she said, though Tottie was sure she had never seen a queen before. 'I am so glad I have been cleaned.'

'I always stay clean,' said Tottie. 'Wood can be washed and be none the worse.'

'So can scrubbing brushes,' said Marchpane tartly. 'I am afraid Her Majesty will have rather a disagreeable surprise,' said Marchpane. 'She can't have been told that there are farthing dolls in this Exhibition. Why, I don't suppose,' said Marchpane, opening her china-blue eyes wide, 'that she knows that such things exist.'

'Even queens can learn,' said Tottie quietly.

Every evening, when the Exhibition room was shut, a child came to look at the dolls.

'A child! A child! A child!' The whisper would go through the room because so many of the dolls through being rare and precious had been for a long while put away in boxes or kept on shelves or in museums. They had not been near children for so long. They yearned toward this little girl who crept in to look at them. None of them yearned more than the wax doll.

The child was thin, with poor clothes, and she kept her hands behind her as if she had been told not to

64

touch. She went from one doll to the other and stared with eyes that looked large in her thin face.

'La! You would think she 'ad nevaire see a doll before!' said the walking doll.

'Perhaps she hasn't, as close as this,' said Tottie. 'Dolls are scarce now and very expensive.'

'Quite right. They should never be given to children to be played with,' said Marchpane.

The wax doll looked at the child as if her heart would melt. 'Little darling!' she said. 'How good she is! How gentle! See, she doesn't even touch.'

At that moment the child took one hand from behind her back and stretched it out to the wax doll and, with a finger, very gently touched her satin dress. The wax doll trembled with pleasure from head to toe. After that the child came most often to look at the wax doll.

'I believe she is the caretaker's child,' said Marchpane.

'She is my child,' breathed the wax doll.

Now the day came for the Exhibition to be open. By eleven o'clock everything was dusted and ready; the ladies were waiting, the dolls were waiting, and a great number of other ladies and gentlemen and a few children, invited guests, were waiting. Marchpane and the haughty doll were preening their necks to hold them to the greatest advantage and setting off their dresses; the wax doll was looking at the children and thinking they were not as good as the caretaker's child; Tottie stood dreading and fearing the moment when someone would buy her and her secret must be told.

The Exhibition ladies kept coming along the tables and shifting and tidying what was arranged and neat already, and putting straight what was straight before.

'I do wish they wouldn't,' sighed Tottie.

'They are showing us every attention, naturally,' said Marchpane. 'We are very important – at least,' she corrected herself, 'some of us are.'

'I don't like attention,' said Tottie who had been dusted and flicked with a feather broom and stood up and down until she felt giddy.

There was a stir, a pause, the Queen had come. Presently they heard her voice. The Queen's voice was as clear, her words as distinct, as separate drops of water. '*Clear and cool, clear and cool.*' Tottie had heard that about water once, and the Queen's voice sounded to her like that.

'I have great pleasure in declaring this Exhibition open,' said the Queen's voice, and there was an immediate clapping of hands.

'Why are they clapping?' asked the wax doll.

'They are clapping us, of course,' said Marchpane.

'They are clapping the Queen,' said Tottie.

Now the ladies and gentlemen, following the Queen, who was attended by the ladies of the Exhibition and her own lady-in-waiting, began to come down the tables, looking at the dolls. The lady-in-waiting carried a bouquet of chrysanthemums. 'That is for us, I expect,' said Marchpane.

'How could it be for us? It's too big,' said Tottie, but by now Marchpane was so far gone in conceit that nothing looked big to her.

'But – she isn't wearing a crown!' said the wax doll, disappointed.

'She only wears a crown when she goes to Parliament and places like that,' said Tottie, who had learned about kings and queens when her little girls, from Great-Grandmother down to Charlotte, learned their history.

'She has the most elegant hat with grey feathers,' said Marchpane. 'I shall have one copied for myself. Shh. She is coming this way.'

'La! I am nairvous,' said the walking doll. *'Je ne me sens pas bien du tout,'* which means she did not feel well. The wax doll trembled, but the people thought it was their footsteps shaking the room. Tottie remained woodenly staring in front of her.

On the Queen came, stopping, looking, touching, this doll or that, asking questions. Then she stopped directly in front of Marchpane, as Marchpane had known she would.

'What a beautiful doll,' said the Queen. 'Surely she is the smallest in the Exhibition?'

Now in Marchpane's ears, the Queen could not

have asked a more unfortunate question. Marchpane was not the smallest doll in the Exhibition. Tottie was, and Marchpane hated her for that. She almost cracked her china as she heard Mrs Innisfree say, 'There is one even smaller, Ma'am. This little farthing doll,' and saw the Queen turn away to Tottie.

'Oh!' said the Queen. 'Oh! I used to play with wooden dolls like this when I was a little girl.'

'A queen! With wooden dolls! How very surprising!' said the other dolls.

'*La! Comme c'est drôle!*' said the walking doll. As for Marchpane she said nothing. She was afraid she really would crack if she did.

'I haven't seen one for years and years,' said the Queen. 'My nurse used to buy them for me.' And then she asked the very question Tottie was dreading to hear. 'Is she for sale?' asked the Queen.

Every knot and grain in Tottie hardened as she waited for the answer to come. Whispers ran up and down the dolls.

'I should like to buy her if she is,' said the Queen.

'Birdie, Emily, Charlotte, Mr Plantaganet, Apple, Darner, Apple, goodbye,' whispered Tottie. She wished she could close her eyes to shut out the faces but, naturally, she had to keep them woodenly open. But – what was this that Mrs Innisfree was saying?

'I'm afraid not, Ma'am,' said Mrs Innisfree. 'She isn't for sale. She is the very dear possession of two little girls,' and she pointed to the card.

The Queen picked up the cards and read them out:

'"*Sampler, worked by a little girl in 1846.*" "*Farthing doll dressed by the same little girl in 1846.*" "*Lent by her great-granddaughters, Emily and Charlotte Dane, in 1946.*"'

'Of course,' said the Queen, 'she must be a great treasure. May I look at her?'

And Tottie was picked up in the pale grey glove of the Queen, who examined her and examined her clothes.

'Dear little thing,' said the Queen, and gave Tottie back to Mrs Innisfree and passed on down the tables.

'My dear, you 'ave 'ad a *succès fou!*' said the haughty doll. Tottie did not ask what a *succès fou* was. For the first time her wood felt weak, bending, and then one of the ladies ran forward with a cry. 'Oh dear!' she said, 'the little farthing doll has fallen over and rolled down right off the table.'

Chapter 10

Tottie was not hurt.

Such happiness flowed through her that she felt as though the sap of her tree had risen in her wood, as it once had every spring, and was running through her.

'Tottie is happy because the Queen wanted to buy her,' said the other dolls.

'She is happy because the Queen couldn't buy her,' Tottie could have corrected them. 'But what was it all about?' asked Tottie. 'Emily and Charlotte must have had a change of heart.' That was as near as Tottie ever came to understanding the truth, and it was very near the truth.

'God bless the Queen,' said Tottie. 'God bless the Queen.'

But Marchpane was bitterly jealous.

Chapter 11

Meanwhile the Plantaganet family had moved into the dolls' house.

They had made it completely their own. Though the chairs were not ready yet and the lace curtains had not come, Mr Plantaganet, Birdie, Apple, and Darner had settled down. The house was clean from top to bottom. There were new sheets and pillows, those mouse-size pillows, and nicked-round blankets on the beds. Apple had his patchwork quilt. The carpets were nailed down and their washing had made their colours fresh. 'Mine is pink, as pink as roses and apple blossom and nail polish,' sang Birdie. The rust had been scoured and scraped from the stove and pots and pans, and the sea-shells had been glued back again on the picture frames.

No family could have been happier than the Plantaganets were now. Darner had his kennel to himself, and it was filled with real chopped-up straw that Emily had begged from a stable in the mews and cut up with her scissors. Apple had the whole house to play in and he had learned the dangerous practice of somersaulting down the stairs. He wished that Charlotte would sit him at the top and then, quite soon, he would manage to overbalance and somersault down to the bottom. Birdie had her room with the pink carpet, and every morning she dusted it with her feather broom while she sang all the songs that she felt her bird in the birdcage would sing, though what of her was dusting and what singing, Birdie sometimes did not know.

'Do I sing with my hands and dust with my voice?' asked Birdie. 'I might, I do not know, but I am happy, happy, happy,' and she flicked with the feather broom and sang a trill. 'So happy,' sang Birdie. Emily had made her a flyaway apron with embroidery cotton strings that were pink like the carpet. 'My carpet,' sang Birdie. 'How I like pink! Trr-la! Trr-la! Trr-la-la!' How different was the sound of Birdie's 'la' from the walking doll's.

And Mr Plantaganet? Mr Plantaganet was different. He looked heavier, the porcelain of his face and hands seemed brighter, cleaner, the checks on his suit seemed more clearly marked, his red-ribbon tie more crisp. When he held his walking stick it looked as if he would swing it at any moment.

The house was a house to be proud of, well built, solid down to the last window sill and up to the wooden chimney. It was warm, gay, comfortable, and there was the lamp and its birthday cake candle for when it was dark. Emily and Charlotte often lit it, and when they had finished playing they shut the front and left the Plantaganets safe inside.

The Dolls' House

While Birdie dusted and Apple somersaulted on the stairs and Darner lay in his kennel, Mr Plantaganet sat in the sitting room reading the little papers Emily made for him and thinking what it would be like when the new chairs and curtains came. For the moment he had to sit on one of the bedroom chairs. He was quite happy, sitting in the sitting room, but he began to feel that, if he were a real master of the house he should, like Father, go to the office. 'I wish they would think of getting me an office,' said Mr Plantaganet. 'I should like to go to the office very much.'

They had kept a place for Tottie. There was a bed waiting for her in the same room as Apple, the room with the blue carpet. Mr Plantaganet slept with Birdie. Tottie's clothes were in the cupboard, her red knitted cloak hung in the hall with Birdie's straw hat with the feather. 'Of course we are all waiting for Tottie,' said Mr Plantaganet.

'Trr-la, trr-la, I wish Tottie were here,' sang Birdie. 'Then we could cook, little pretending flour pies and hundred-and-thousand sweets.' (Do you know hundreds-and-thousands? They make good dolls' house sweets.)

'If Tottie were here she wouldn't let me somersault downstairs, but I wish Tottie were here,' said Apple.

'It doesn't feel like our home without Tottie,' said Mr Plantaganet, then his face looked stiff and he dropped his walking stick. 'Birdie,' he said, 'suppose it isn't our home after all? Suppose we have made a mistake? They couldn't take it away from us, could they, Birdie?'

'I don't understand,' said Birdie, and she lowered her broom and the embroidery cotton strings of her apron sank and were still. 'What do you mean? I don't understand,' she said with a sound like a whimper.

'No. No. Don't think about it. I was only joking,' said Mr Plantaganet quickly.

'W-were you? It didn't sound like a joke.'

'Don't think about it. You go on with your dusting, my dear.'

'M-may I? Are you sure?'

'Of course, Birdie dear. Of course. Forget about it.'

Mr Plantaganet soon forgot about it himself. He had discovered that, when the birthday cake candle in the lamp was lit, the roses in the vase threw a tiny real shadow of themselves on the table.

Chapter 12

The Exhibition was almost over. Many people had visited it; it was a great success.

Most of the people had taken notice of Tottie. 'What a love of a doll,' they had said. 'But that is what they say about Apple,' said Tottie. 'Oh, Apple. I long to see you again.'

Emily and Charlotte had been several times to visit her. 'Dear possession,' thought Tottie, 'a great treasure.' That was what Mrs Innisfree and the Queen had said. Tottie could look them in the face now, happily. 'She doesn't look hurt any more,' said Emily.

'And we never found out why she did,' said Charlotte. 'That is the worst of dolls. They are such secret people.'

They showed Tottie a cutting from a newspaper. It gave an account of the Exhibition: '. . . and the smallest doll is a hundred-year-old farthing doll, lent by Emily and Charlotte Dane.' If anyone had listened, they might have heard a tiny gritting sound. It was Marchpane grinding her china teeth.

Emily and Charlotte had looked at Marchpane and admired her very much, especially Emily; they knew she had belonged to Great-Great-Aunt Laura, but they did not know she had lived with Tottie in the dolls' house.

Tottie was longing to go home, but the other dolls were, for the most part, sorry the Exhibition was over. They would be packed away again or sent back to their museums.

'What is a museum like?' asked Tottie.

'It is cold dere,' said the walking doll suddenly. She sounded quite unlike herself.

'Nonsense. It is grand and fine,' said Marchpane. 'It is filled with precious and valuable things kept in glass cases.'

'I shouldn't enjoy that,' said Tottie, looking at Queen Victoria's dolls. 'How can you be played with if you are in a glass case?'

'One wouldn't want to be played with,' said Marchpane. 'When I was at the cleaners, people said I ought to be in a museum.'

'It is cold dere,' said the walking doll again.

'It is grand and fine,' said Marchpane.

'C'est vrai mais –' said the walking doll, 'Mais –' Her voice sounded as if her works had quite run down.

'I don't want to go back in my box,' said the wax doll. 'It is too dark and quiet. I wish . . .' She was thinking of the caretaker's child who still crept out to look at her in the evenings when the people had gone. 'I wish . . .'

76

The Dolls' House

The last day came. Tottie, with every minute, grew more happy and excited.

'You are lucky,' sighed the wax doll.

'Tell us about dis 'ouse you are in,' said the walking doll.

'Yes, tell us. Then I can think about it when I lie with my eyes shut in my box. I can think and pretend. Tell, Tottie. Tell us.'

All the dolls took up the cry. 'Tell us, Tottie. Tell.'

Tottie had always thought it better not to talk about the house in front of Marchpane, but now she was so excited and happy herself and so sorry for the other dolls that she forgot to take care. She began to tell about the dolls' house.

She told them about its cream walls and the ivy and Darner's kennel. She told about the red hall and the sitting room with the holly-green carpet and the struggle to get the chairs (though she did not tell that she had thought that she herself had been sold to get them). She told about the rooms upstairs and the pink and blue carpets and the bath with the taps, and she told about Birdie and Mr Plantaganet and Darner and Apple. She told them from the beginning to the end, from the bottom to the top. When she had done, there was a long soft silence, and then a-aahs and sighs from the dolls.

'If only . . .'

'I wish . . .'

'It might have been . . .'

'I wish . . .'

'If only . . .'

'If only . . .'

'Oh, lucky, lucky Tottie!'

'Oh, Tottie, you are lucky!'

'Don't you believe her,' cried Marchpane in a loud voice. 'That isn't her house. It's mine.'

All the dolls looked at Marchpane. Then they all looked at Tottie.

'It is in our nursery now,' said Tottie.

'You stole it while I was at the cleaners.'

'It was sent to us, as you were sent to the cleaners. It needed cleaning and taking care of,' said Tottie. 'We cleaned it and took care of it.'

'How dare you!' cried Marchpane. 'You think because the Queen noticed you, you can do anything. Wait and see. Wait and see,' cried Marchpane. 'I shall have that house back.'

'How can you?' asked Tottie. 'It's in our nursery.'

'Wait and see,' said Marchpane. 'Wait and see.'

The Exhibition was closed. The dolls had been taken away, the room was empty, and when the caretaker's child came in the evening there were only long blank tables where Tottie and Marchpane and Queen Victoria's dolls and the walking doll and the wax doll and the other dolls had been.

Did the caretaker's child think of the wax doll? And

The Dolls' House

the wax doll, in her lonely box, think of the caretaker's child and of the finger that had touched her satin dress? Did the dolls think of Tottie's welcome home by Emily, Charlotte, Birdie, Mr Plantaganet, Apple, and Darner?

I think they did.

Chapter 13

It was winter when Tottie came back to the dolls' house. If you would like to know how winter looks to a doll imagine yourself as looking into a crystal ball, a ball of glass, in which a Christmas-frost snowstorm is being shaken down on little splinter trees and cardboard houses. Children were given those snowstorm balls when Great-Great-Aunt Laura and Emily and Charlotte's great-grandmother were young. Winter looks like that to dolls because they are not often taken out in the winter, and they see the snow and snowflakes through the windowpanes of glass.

Tottie came back and it was winter, but so far there was no snow.

Emily and Charlotte took her with them when they went to Mrs Innisfree's house to fetch the couch and chairs.

'Tottie ought to go, because it was Tottie who really got the chairs for us,' said Emily.

'Are the couch and chairs really coming, Tottie?' asked Mr Plantaganet. 'We have been wishing and wishing. I have never really stopped wishing,' said Mr Plantaganet. 'But it was you who got them for us, Tottie,' he said.

'Dear Tottie, but I should have been quite

content with cotton reels,' said Birdie.

'Oh, Birdie dear!' said Mr Plantaganet impatiently. Sometimes he found it hard to be patient with Birdie.

Apple was not there. He had a plan, unknown to Tottie, that he might climb up to the dolls' house chimney. He thought he might climb up the ivy, it looked so real, but of course it was painted too flat and the paint was far too slippery.

Emily made Tottie a cotton-wool cap and a cotton-wool muff to go out in, as it was beginning to be bitterly cold. 'But we are cosy in the dolls' house,' said Mr Plantaganet. The whiteness of the cotton wool looked pretty with Tottie's glossy black hair and painted cheeks; she shone with happiness. Birdie did not want a cap or a muff. She wanted a feather boa.

'What's a boa?' asked Apple, forgetting the ivy.

'It's a long scarf, but made out of feathers, and it is round all the way down,' explained Tottie.

'Like a caterpillar?' asked Apple, who had seen a caterpillar in the park.

'Yes, a caterpillar would make a very good boa for Birdie,' said Tottie.

'If it were made out of feathers,' said Birdie. 'But it's not.'

Tottie was carried along to Mrs Innisfree's on the palm of Charlotte's hand. Charlotte had on a red woollen glove, Tottie had on her red woollen cloak, her cap and muff. They went well together.

*

It was a clear, pale, cold sunny day; the bare branches of the trees in the Park stood out against a clear pale sky. The cold touched Tottie's cheeks and the sunlight made them glisten.

Emily and Charlotte were talking of Christmas, and Tottie was suddenly reminded of a little sunshade, a parasol, not made, like the walking doll's parasol, from satin, but of paper from a cracker. 'I saw one long ago,' said Tottie. 'It was gay as a little paper wheel. How Birdie would love that,' thought Tottie. 'How I should like to give her one for Christmas. She would like it better than the feather boa, but you don't see them nowadays. I wish . . . ' said Tottie, sitting on Charlotte's hand; 'and for Apple a marble. A marble would make him a good ball, and for Darner a tiddlywinks plate, a nice big purple one. And for Mr Plantaganet? I wish they would think of getting him a toy post office,' thought Tottie. 'Then he could go to business; if he went to business every day he would be very happy. I wish and wish they would get him a toy post office.'

When they arrived in Mrs Innisfree's house, Tottie forgot even about Christmas and Christmas presents. There, on the table in Mrs Innisfree's drawing room, were the couch and chairs.

Emily did not recognize them.

Charlotte did not recognize them.

Tottie did not recognize them.

82

Their wood, having been carefully sand-papered, had been polished by Mrs Innisfree's French polisher until it shone with a real furniture dark wood shine of its own. Then the *petit-point* seats and arms and backs had been fastened over new cushions. Mrs Innisfree had worked the cream background and the tiny roses and leaves; she had even worked their shadings, though the flowers were scarcely bigger than knots or dots.

'Oh!' cried Emily.

'Oh!' cried Charlotte.

'Oh!' cried Tottie. 'Oh! It was worth going to the Exhibition.'

'Even the Queen's dolls' house,' said Emily, 'hasn't a better set than that.'

'Yes, that is perfectly right,' said Tottie. She felt now she knew something about queens.

Mrs Innisfree put down on the table two pairs of fine white lace curtains, each curtain six inches long. 'I saw the piece of lace,' she said. 'It was the right width and just the right length, and there is a piece, three inches, over, so I made an apron for Tottie. Do you see, Emily, the lace is worked with ferns? Your great-grandmother's drawing room might easily have had lace curtains worked with ferns. They were very fashionable then.'

'We shall keep them always, we shall never change them,' said Emily solemnly. 'Nor will our children's children.'

'Do you suppose Tottie will see them?' asked
Charlotte. 'I mean our children's children, not the
chairs.'

'She may,' said Emily.

'That makes me think,' said Charlotte, and she
added, 'I seem to have been thinking a great deal of
thinking lately.'

It was a solemn morning. Mrs Innisfree and Emily
did an account and it seemed that the cost of the
lace curtains, of Mrs Innisfree's French polisher and
upholsterer, and of the silks and canvas for the chairs,
came to eight and tenpence, which was just the money
they had had in their money boxes, though Charlotte
now had the sixpence for her tooth and Emily had
saved another half-crown.

'I believe you are saying eight and tenpence,' said
Emily, looking hard at Mrs Innisfree, 'because you knew
it was eight and tenpence that we had,' said Emily.

'And if I am?' said Mrs Innisfree. 'If I enjoy it?'

'And we can't pay you for the time,' said Charlotte,
'nor for the thinking. I wonder what makes thinking,'
said Charlotte. 'It is funny how one thing begins another.'

'And how it all leads on,' said Emily.

'Yes, it joins,' said Charlotte, wrinkling her forehead.
'I have been thinking of thinking. And there is no
knowing where it leads to, or when it will end, or where.'

Chapter 14

On Christmas morning the Plantaganets woke to hear real carol singers in the street outside.

'*Peace and goodwill among men,*' sang the carol singers.

'And among dolls,' said Mr Plantaganet. 'I hope among dolls.'

'*Peace and goodwill.*' The voices brought Christmas into the dolls' house. 'Can such a large thing as Christmas be in a dolls' house?' asked Mr Plantaganet. 'It is so large. See, it has spread over the whole world, and for so many years, nearly two thousand years,' said Mr Plantaganet, the dark brown of his eyes looking large too. 'How large it is,' said Mr Plantaganet.

'It is beautifully small too,' said Tottie. 'Perfectly small.'

You might think that, to a doll, many things would seem too large, but no. A doll is not as small as a beetle, for instance, and a beetle's world is just right for a beetle. When, too, you have lived as long as Tottie, you will learn that small things are not as small as they seem, nor large things as large; nothing is small and nothing is large when you have become accustomed to the world. Now the carols brought the spirit of Christmas into the dolls' house.

'I like "Peace and Goodwill",' said Tottie.

Tales from the Dolls' House

'I like "The Holly and the Ivy",' said Mr Plantaganet. 'They are like the colours in this house. I like "Prince of Peace"; that suits it too. I know about peace now,' said Mr Plantaganet. 'In the days of the toy cupboard –' he began and his eyes looked darker and he did not go on. 'Yes, I like "The Prince of Peace", but the one that I like best of all is "God Bless the Master of This House", because I am the Master,' said Mr Plantaganet.

Birdie liked the rocking carol, only she mixed it with 'Rock-a-Bye Baby', but after all it was nearly the same thing.

'*Peace and goodwill*,' sang the carol singers.

The dolls' house, that Christmas, looked very pleasant. Emily and Charlotte had decorated it; they made wreaths of moss on curtain rings, that looked like holly wreaths, and they had strung holly berries for garlands. Emily had even made a paper chain with very small links. Birdie liked the paper chain best of anything. The new chairs and couch looked handsome in the drawing room, and there was a Christmas tree, six inches high, standing in a wooden pot. It was the kind of Christmas tree you have on Christmas cakes; it was just right for the Plantaganets.

'Would you like to give one of the Plantaganets this for Christmas?' asked the children's mother, coming into the room. 'I must have had it at a party long ago.' She showed them a parasol made of white paper printed with a pattern of purple and scarlet feathers. It could be put up and down, and had once fitted into a cracker.

'Oh! For Birdie,' cried Emily at once.

'How odd,' thought Tottie. 'How lovely and how odd.'

'And for Apple, a marble. Wouldn't a marble make a ball for Apple?'

'More and more odd,' thought Tottie, 'and still more lovely.'

'Darner might have a new plate,' said Charlotte, looking in the toy cupboard. 'This big tiddlywinks would do. The rest are all lost. It's a purple one. That would suit him nicely.'

'More and more odd,' thought Tottie again, 'and more and more lovely.'

For Mr Plantaganet they hung a buttonhole on the tree. It was made of woollen flowers. 'I don't much like that,' thought Tottie.

Mr Plantaganet did not much like it either. 'Is my Christmas spoilt?' he whispered to Tottie.

'No. *No*,' said Tottie. 'But I wish I could make it better.'

'I wish that too,' said Mr Plantaganet. He suspected it was spoilt.

At that moment the postman's knock sounded from the front door. Emily and Charlotte ran to open it. He had brought two parcels, a light thin one, the shape of a flat cardboard box, and a small one, the shape of a child's shoe-box. It was very heavy.

Emily opened the flat light one first.

'What is it?' asked Charlotte. 'What is it? Oh!' she cried as Emily set up a cardboard counter painted with netting. 'Oh! It's a post office. A toy post office.'

'Oh!' cried Tottie, and she caught Mr Plantaganet's eye.

'Look at the stamps,' said Emily, 'and the stamper.'

'Let me look at the stamps,' cried Mr Plantaganet.

'Let me look at the stamper,' cried Apple.

The toy post office was complete. It even had two letter boxes labelled PACKETS AND NEWSPAPERS and LETTERS. It had stamps and certificates and postal orders and telegraph forms and letter paper and postcards and stamped envelopes. It had a red tin telephone and a purple inkpad for the stamper.

'But what shall we do with it exactly?' asked Charlotte.

'We can tell you,' wished Tottie and Mr Plantaganet together, and Emily, as if she had felt them wishing, looked at them. Then she looked only at Mr Plantaganet. 'I know,' said Emily slowly. 'I know, Charlotte. It shall be Mr Plantaganet's office. He shall go there to business every day.'

'As a postman?' asked Charlotte.

'As a postmaster,' said Emily.

'A postmaster!' said Mr Plantaganet, and his

waistcoat seemed to swell and grow bigger. 'Did you hear, Tottie? I am a post*master*. Did you hear, Birdie dear? Now I have nothing left to wish for. Did you hear, Apple? Oh, how happy I am. Did you hear –' He was about to say, 'Did you hear, Darner?' when he remembered that Darner was a dog and could not be expected to recognize the difference between Mr Plantaganet, Postmaster, and plain Mr Plantaganet. He stopped. His attention was caught by Darner.

Darner was looking at the other parcel. All his wool stood on end. 'Prrickckckck,' said Darner at the parcel. 'Prrick. Prrick. Prrick! Prrick! Prrrrrrickckckck!'

Chapter 15

At the moment Darner barked at the parcel the Plantaganet family were all in the post office that Emily had set up on the table. Apple was playing with the scales, Birdie was tinkling the telephone; it had a bell and Birdie liked the sound of it. She wondered if a musical box sounded like that. Tottie had told her about musical boxes and she often longed to hear one. Tottie was looking at the postcards. Mr Plantaganet was trying not to wish that they would all go away and leave him alone with it.

As Darner barked, Tottie remembered the other parcel, and for no reason that she could put a name to, she found herself wishing and wishing and wishing that Emily would put them all back in the house. She must have wished very purposively, as Emily raised her head and said, 'I think they must all go back into the dolls' house now.'

'In the house, and behind the door. Shut the door,' wished Tottie.

'After all, Mr Plantaganet wouldn't go to the office on Christmas Day,' said Emily.

'Wouldn't he?' asked Mr Plantaganet.

'Wouldn't a postmaster? The postman does,' said Charlotte.

The Dolls' House

'A postman doesn't go the office,' said Emily, 'he goes on his rounds. You can't send parcels on Christmas Day, you only get them.'

'I wish you didn't,' said Tottie. She felt worried, a little frightened and a little angry; she felt as if her wood had gone stiff.

Charlotte put the Plantaganets tidily back in the house: Apple on the stairs, ready to somersault; Birdie in her bedroom, with the pink carpet, taking off her hat with the feather; Mr Plantaganet on one of the new chairs in the sitting room; and Tottie in the kitchen. 'Now you are all in your happy little house,' said Charlotte. She did not close the front.

'Our happy little house,' sang Apple as he began his somersaults. He reached the bottom and to his great joy Charlotte looked up and said, 'Oh, he has fallen downstairs, poor little Apple,' and put him up again.

'Our happy little house,' sang Birdie, twirling her feather.

'Our happy little house,' hummed Mr Plantaganet, 'and office,' he hummed as he read his paper. He went on humming: sometimes 'The Holly and the Ivy', sometimes 'Peace and Goodwill among Men'.

Charlotte had given Tottie the pudding basin tied in a scrap of white muslin and said she was turning out the Christmas pudding, but Tottie felt too nervous to think about puddings. She could hear Darner in his kennel still saying 'Prrick,' and Darner never said 'Prrickck' except for danger.

Through the open front of the dolls' house Tottie watched Emily undo that parcel.

Emily undid the string and then carefully she unwrapped the paper. It was a small shoe-box. Tottie shivered all through her wood. 'Shoe-boxes are unlucky for this family,' she said. 'The last shoe-box made Mr Plantaganet awfully unhappy.'

The shoe-box was padded with cotton wool and paper. Emily and Charlotte lifted it out, piece by piece, and then Emily gave a cry of admiration and pleasure. 'Look, Charlotte. Look. It's a doll. That doll. That lovely doll.' And she lifted Marchpane from the box.

There was a sudden light clatter in the dolls' house kitchen, but nobody heard.

'Oh! I loved her at the Exhibition,' cried Emily. 'You remember her, Charlotte. She has been sent to us because she was Great-Great-Aunt Laura's doll. Look, the letter says she would have come before only she was sent to the cleaners and the Exhibition. She goes with the dolls' house, you see.'

'Does she?' asked Charlotte doubtfully. She looked at Marchpane and then at the Plantaganets so happily settled in the dolls' house. Emily had no eyes for anyone but Marchpane. 'Look at her clothes,' said Emily.

'My clothes,' said Marchpane in a complacent voice.

'They take off and on. Look at the tiny buttons and the lace edgings.'

'The lace edgings,' said Marchpane still more complacently.

'And her hair! We can really brush it and comb it.'

'It's real hair,' said Marchpane.

'And her eyes. Look. They open and shut. None of the others' can open and shut.'

'Mine open and shut. They are the best blue glass,' said Marchpane.

'She doesn't smell very nice,' said Charlotte.

'Oh, Charlotte. I loved her at the Exhibition,' said Emily, 'and now she is ours.'

'I don't remember her very well at the Exhibition,' said Charlotte slowly. 'She wasn't ours then and we went there to see Tottie.'

'Yes, but we looked at her.'

'I didn't. I looked at Tottie.'

'Don't be such a little silly, Charlotte,' said Emily. 'What is the matter with you?'

'I don't know,' said Charlotte. 'I have a funny feeling.'

'Well, you are very silly. She is perfectly beautiful. She must be our best doll.'

'But –' began Charlotte, and then she said in a low voice, 'Do you think we ought to have a best doll, Emily? Do you think it is kind to the others? They were here first.'

'No, they were not,' said Emily. 'Marchpane was Great-Great-Aunt Laura's doll.'

'Well, Tottie was our great-grandmother's doll,' said Charlotte, and then she gave a cry. 'Oh, Emily, look! Tottie has dropped the Christmas pudding bowl down on the floor and it has rolled right under the kitchen table.'

Chapter 16

They brought Marchpane into the dolls' house.

Tottie stood by the kitchen table, stiff and hard. 'It was nearly I, and not the pudding, that fell,' thought Tottie. 'I fell once, for joy, but I shall not fall for fear of Marchpane. Trees, good trees, don't fall down in storms,' said Tottie.

Charlotte picked up the pudding basin and, as it was lunch time, she untied the muslin and turned out a morsel of real plum pudding onto a plate. 'I wish I could give you a sprig of holly small enough to stick in it,' said Charlotte kindly.

Emily brought Marchpane into the kitchen first. 'You should remember each other,' she said to Tottie.

'We remember each other,' said Marchpane and Tottie. Tottie had never looked more wooden. Marchpane's eyeballs gave a sudden click.

'You jerked her,' said Emily to Charlotte.

'No I didn't,' said Charlotte.

'Of course, they first knew each other years and years ago,' said Emily. 'They must know secrets about each other that we don't know.'

'We do,' said Tottie. Marchpane said nothing at all.

Presently Emily took her into the sitting room and sat her on the couch by Mr Plantaganet, and then she shut the front of the dolls' house and went away to lunch.

When Mr Plantaganet saw Marchpane sitting opposite him with her golden hair and blue eyes and white clothes, he was quite dazzled. He dropped his newspaper and stared with both his dark glass eyes.

'Don't do that,' said Marchpane sharply.

'Don't do what?'

'Stare and stare and stare,' said Marchpane. 'It's very rude.'

'I am sorry,' said Mr Plantaganet politely, 'but I can't help staring.'

'I suppose they are fixed,' said Marchpane, looking at him.

'Fixed?'

'They don't open and shut?'

'Open and shut?'

'Your eyes,' said Marchpane. 'Take them off me at once.'

'Excuse me,' said Mr Plantaganet still more politely, 'my eyes are not on you. They are in me.'

'Faugh!' said Marchpane. 'You should be in the hall, not sitting in a chair. If you sit at all, it should be in the kitchen.'

'Excuse me,' said Mr Plantaganet again as he grew more and more bewildered. 'Why should I be in the hall and kitchen? Why shouldn't I sit? I'm jointed.'

'Are you not the butler?' asked Marchpane. 'There

The Dolls' House

used to be a butler, I'm sure.'

'The figure of a butler,' Mr Plantaganet corrected her. 'He is gone to dust. I don't know what a butler is,' said Mr Plantaganet, 'but I know I am not one. I am a postmaster, and, besides, I am the master of this house. Do you know that carol?' he asked, '"*God bless the Master of this House, God bless the Mistress too*"? Well, I am the master and Birdie is the mistress.'

'That she certainly is not,' said Marchpane.

'Oh yes, she is,' said Mr Plantaganet positively.

'She isn't. I am,' said Marchpane.

'You?' asked Mr Plantaganet. 'Oh no! How could you be? I have never seen you before and I have seen Birdie. Do you know who I thought you were? I thought you might be the fairy off the Christmas tree. Birdie is always talking about her. Are you the fairy off a Christmas tree?'

'A fairy?' said Marchpane scornfully. 'I am real. Far more real than Birdie.'

'Does Birdie know that?' asked Mr Plantaganet anxiously.

There was a sudden bump, bump, bump, on the other side of the wall.

'What is that?' asked Marchpane.

'That is Apple.'

'Apple?'

'The little boy doll. Our little boy. He belongs to us.'

'Does he?' asked Marchpane thoughtfully.

There was a light sound of rustling from upstairs.

'What is that?' asked Marchpane.

'That is Birdie.'

'It is too light,' objected Marchpane, 'to be an anyone.'

'Birdie is light,' answered Mr Plantaganet.

'I am heavy,' said Marchpane.

Mr Plantaganet did not answer. The rustling sound came again.

'What is she doing?' asked Marchpane.

'I expect she is dusting the paper chains with her feather broom,' said Mr Plantaganet.

'Paper chains? With a feather broom? What a very odd thing to do! What did you say her name was?'

'Birdie.'

'It does sound like a bird rustling,' said Marchpane.

Mr Plantaganet thought of that and it seemed to him that Marchpane was right and Birdie was, truthfully, very like a bird, a small light bird with thin legs and bright eyes. 'One that goes for short flights,' thought Mr Plantaganet. 'One that collects bits of things to make its nest.' Yes, Birdie in her bedroom, busy with her private affairs, twig after twig, was very like a bird building its nest.

'It's an aggravating noise,' said Marchpane.

'I like to hear her,' answered Mr Plantaganet, and his voice sounded as if he were smiling.

 98

'I wish you would stop her.'

'Oh no,' said Mr Plantaganet. 'I shouldn't like to disturb her.'

'I shall disturb her!' said Marchpane.

'But – you wouldn't. You couldn't,' cried Mr Plantaganet in alarm.

'Why not?' asked Marchpane.

'It – it is cruel to disturb a bird in its nest,' said Mr Plantaganet. That was not what he had meant to say but it seemed to say what he wanted even better than the words he had meant to use.

'Faugh!' said Marchpane and the blue glass balls of her eyes seemed to glare. Mr Plantaganet felt quite frightened. 'Oh!' yawned Marchpane. 'I do wish Emily and Charlotte, or whatever their names are, would come and put me in my own room.'

At that, a thought came into Mr Plantaganet's mind. A horrible thought. To make quite sure he went, in his mind, through the whole dolls' house, through the kitchen and hall, sitting room, and the upstairs pink room and blue room. Then he looked at Marchpane. 'Excuse me,' said Mr Plantaganet timidly, 'but – er – which is your room?'

'The one with the pink carpet of course,' said Marchpane.

'But that is Birdie's. She chose it. That is Birdie's nest.' He meant to say 'room' but he was so upset that he was confused and again 'nest' seemed to suit

Birdie even better than 'room'. That is Birdie's nest – bedroom.'

'If you really want to know,' said Marchpane in her flat, heavy voice, 'the whole house is mine.'

'Wh-a-t?' cried poor Mr Plantaganet. He could not believe his little porcelain ears. 'But it's our house. Ours. That we dreamed of – that we wanted – that we wished for,' said Mr Plantaganet.

'I can't help what you did for it,' said Marchpane, yawning. 'It is mine. Mine, and really,' said Marchpane, yawning again, 'I can't live in it with all these people, bumping and rustling and having silly ideas that it is theirs. I must tell Emily and Charlotte,' said Marchpane, and she yawned still once again.

'Oh, don't say that. Don't say that,' cried poor little Mr Plantaganet.

'But I do say it,' said Marchpane.

'But – you don't understand. This is our house. It is full of us. It was for us. We were on the hearthrug when the letter came. We saw Emily and Charlotte clean it and make it new again and we helped them by wishing. We wished so hard – you don't know. We waited for the curtains and the blankets on the beds and the couch and chairs. You don't know. Now I shall go every day to the office and come back again . . . And this Christmas was so beautiful. You don't know,' panted Mr Plantaganet, 'oh, truly, truly you don't know.'

'What you don't know, and had better know,' said Marchpane, 'is that I was here, here in this dolls' house, long, long years ago. Long, long before any of you.'

'Not before Tottie you weren't,' said Mr Plantaganet, and as he said it his eyes grew steady and his voice grew suddenly firm. 'Tottie has been here as long as you have. Why, she remembers your coming. She has been here longer.'

'Tottie! A farthing doll!'

'A farthing, or a penny, or sixpence, or a pound, she has been here longer. Tottie is Tottie. She always is and she always had been. Tottie! Tottie! Tottie!' called Mr Plantaganet.

At that moment Charlotte opened the front of the dolls' house and picked up Tottie.

'I don't see,' said Charlotte, 'why you should be left all alone in the kitchen while she sits on one of your chairs. You shall come into the sitting room, Tottie,' and she sat Tottie down on the couch next to Marchpane. 'There,' said Charlotte to Marchpane, and shut the dolls' house front again.

'Did you hear what she said?' whispered Mr Plantaganet to Tottie as soon as Charlotte had gone. In his agitation he had lost his manners, but Tottie had not lost hers.

'How strange it must seem to you to be back,' she said to Marchpane. ('Yes, I heard,' she said quietly to Mr Plantaganet.)

'Did you hear what she said about Birdie, and our house, our dear, dear house? Oh, Tottie! Oh, Tottie! I feel as if we were in danger,' said Mr Plantaganet.

'We are in danger,' thought Tottie, but she did not say it aloud because she knew Marchpane must not know they were in the least frightened. Instead she thought of all the bravest things that were made of wood: the bowsprits and figureheads of ships, for instance, that have to drive into the sea and meet the waves: or their masts; of the stocks of rifles and of guns; of flagstaffs that fly flags high up in the air, and of her tree. 'I am made of the same stuff as they,' thought Tottie. 'Wood. Good strong wood. After all, nothing very strong is made of kid.' She smiled at Mr Plantaganet and he felt as though she had reached out and patted his hand and said 'Courage'. She smiled at Marchpane and said again, 'How strange for you to be back.'

'Not nearly as strange as for you,' said Marchpane.

'Why?' asked Tottie.

'One hardly expected you to last for so long.'

'Why?' asked Tottie.

'Cheap material, shoddy stuff.'

'Wood is neither cheap nor shoddy,' said Tottie, and again she thought of the bowsprits, the gun stocks, flagstaffs, trees, and she smiled.

'Don't you mind what she says?' asked Mr Plantaganet.

'No, I don't mind because it isn't true,' said Tottie. 'I can remember the day they brought you here,' she said, turning to Marchpane. 'When Laura brought you here. Those two little girls!' she said. 'Sometimes I think Emily and Charlotte are they all over again.'

'Funny how people don't last,' said Marchpane, yawning. 'But I am tired. Don't talk to me about them. I am not interested in little girls.'

'Not – interested – in – little – girls!' said Mr Plantaganet, shocked.

'No. Not in Laura, nor her sister, nor Emily, nor Charlotte, nor any of them,' said Marchpane distinctly.

'But they are alive! It is only they who make us live.'

'Faugh!' said Marchpane rudely.

'Marchpane doesn't like to be played with,' said Tottie quietly.

'Not like to be played with? Then what is she for? Why was she made? I should sooner be broken,' said Mr Plantaganet, 'or thrown in the toy cupboard, than never be played with at all.'

'Well, I shouldn't,' said Marchpane.

'You are not a doll,' cried Mr Plantaganet; he had forgotten to be frightened. 'You are a *thing*.' And then he remembered and cried, 'Oh, what are we going to do, Tottie?'

'We must wish,' said Tottie openly; she was no longer trying to be polite to Marchpane. 'We must wish and we must never stop wishing for a moment.'

'I can wish too,' said Marchpane. 'I am heavier than you!'

'To be heavy doesn't mean to be strong,' said Tottie.

'I am very strong.'

'Nothing, nothing,' said Tottie, 'nothing can be stronger than good plain wood.'

Chapter 17

'Charlotte,' said Emily, 'we must take Birdie and Mr Plantaganet out of the pink bedroom. We need it for Marchpane.

'But,' began Charlotte, 'you gave it to them.'

'Well, where is she to go? Would you put her in the attic?'

'N-no, but where are *they* to go?'

'Marchpane will need that big bed all to herself,' said Emily. 'They must go in with Tottie and Apple.'

'There isn't room.'

'Then they must go in the attic.'

'There isn't even a bed, Emily.'

'There is a cotton-reel box,' said Emily. 'They must sleep in that. We can make it quite pretty for them.'

So, instead of their room and their brass, painted bed Birdie and Mr Plantaganet were put to sleep in the attic in a cardboard box with *J. Coats Ltd., Manchester*, on its side. Emily did not take much interest in it, but Charlotte made a mattress of cotton wool and tried to nick round the edges of blankets, but her hands were small and clumsy. 'Oh dear! It doesn't look nice,' said Charlotte.

There was not even time to warn Birdie. Emily turned all her clothes and her apron out of the cupboard and cut down the paper chains. 'Marchpane doesn't go with paper chains,' said Emily, and she swept them all into the attic before anyone could say a word of warning to Birdie.

'What will she do? What will she say? My poor Birdie,' cried Mr Plantaganet. 'She will never understand.' But, oddly enough, Birdie understood only too well.

'Of course,' said Birdie, 'she couldn't sleep in a cotton-reel box, could she? Her eyes open and shut and her hair is yellow like mine, only it's real –'

'Yes,' said Mr Plantaganet. 'When I first saw her I thought she was a Christmas tree fairy.'

'Did you?' asked Birdie and, for the first time, her voice sounded wistful. 'I suppose – I am never – anything like a Christmas fairy?' There was silence, and then Birdie said in her own brisk light voice, 'After all, I came from a cracker box, why shouldn't I sleep in a cotton-reel box?' The words 'cracker box' and 'cotton-reel box' began to knock one another gently in her head. 'I came from a cotton-reel box. Why shouldn't I sleep in a cracker box? Cotton box, cracker box, cracker-reel box?'

'You are getting muddled,' said Mr Plantaganet, 'and remember, Birdie, don't go into her room.'

Birdie could not remember. She was always being found in Marchpane's room, still thinking it was hers.

The Dolls' House

'Don't you like my pink carpet?' she would ask Marchpane.

'My pink carpet,' said Marchpane.

'No, mine,' said Birdie. 'Certainly. Emily and Charlotte gave it to me.'

'It wasn't theirs to give.'

'Isn't everything theirs?' asked Birdie in astonishment.

'Faugh! Get out of my room.'

'My room,' cried poor Birdie.

'My room, my carpet, my bed. Get back to your cotton-reel box.'

'She is cruel,' said Mr Plantaganet, trembling. 'She is cruel. I hate her.'

'Don't waste time hating,' said Tottie. 'You must wish. I wish. We must wish.' But the wishing showed no sign of changing anything, or perhaps Marchpane was wishing harder. Emily was now doing everything for Marchpane, nothing for the Plantaganets, though Charlotte tried to prevent this.

'Charlotte is on our side,' said Tottie.

'Yes, but Emily isn't, and Emily is the one who does things, far more than Charlotte.'

'Emily has the ideas, she thinks of things and does them while Charlotte is far behind. If you go ahead like that, sometimes you must go wrong. Think if you were ahead, walking, on a road by yourself, and there were not any signposts,' said Tottie. 'Sometimes you must make a mistake. It is easy for the one to come behind and say, "This was wrong, that was wrong." They only know it was wrong because Emily went there first. They know the right way. They don't have to choose. Emily often chooses wrong things,' said Tottie, 'but I know Emily. She has plenty of sense. We must be patient, and go on wishing. One day Emily will find out she is wrong.'

'She will find out that Marchpane isn't the beautiful doll she seems? That she is a thing?' asked Mr Plantaganet.

'Yes, she will.'

'You are – certain, Tottie?'

'Certain,' said Tottie in her most wooden voice.

Chapter 18

Perhaps Marchpane was very powerful or Emily had less sense than Tottie thought; at all events, she showed no sign of changing and things grew worse and worse for the Plantaganets.

'I know,' said Emily one day. 'Let us pretend they are the servants. They can sleep in the attic and stay in the kitchen. Let them be Marchpane's servants.'

'Oh no! Emily, oh no!' said Charlotte, shocked. 'How can they be? They are themselves. Marchpane is more like their aunt or their step-sister.'

'She isn't like a sister,' said Emily, and that was certainly true. 'She is a lady. A great lady. I don't want them in the sitting room with her.'

'Why shouldn't they be in the sitting room?'

'They are so ordinary. So like ordinary people.'

'Then I like ordinary people.'

'Yes, but they don't go with Marchpane.' Emily had her way, and the Plantaganets were told to keep in the kitchen.

Mr Plantaganet couldn't understand it. 'The master of the house to stay in the kitchen, not to go into the sitting room, not to go where he likes in his own house? Father goes where he likes. I am the father, the master of the house, Tottie?'

109

'Of course you are,' said Tottie firmly.

'I am not – what she called me, Tottie? I am not the butler, am I?'

'You shan't be the butler,' said Tottie, but Emily put in her hand and took up Mr Plantaganet. 'You are the butler,' said Emily. 'Go and open the door.'

'I am a postmaster, the master of the house, postmaster, house master,' cried poor Mr Plantaganet, struggling.

'A pretty postmaster!' said Marchpane. 'Emily hasn't opened your post office for days.'

'Shouldn't we put up the post office for Mr Plantaganet?' suggested Charlotte.

'He can't have it now,' said Emily. 'He is being the butler. And Birdie can be cook.'

'But – would Birdie make a very good cook?' asked Charlotte miserably. 'You know how muddled she gets. Suppose she were muddled between sugar and salt.'

'Or coffee and curry power, or beans and sultanas.' Emily laughed, but the Plantaganets did not laugh. 'Very well, she can be the maid and Tottie can be the cook.'

'Tottie – can – be – the – cook?' said Charlotte, reeling.

'Yes, we can make her a dear little cap and apron.'

'But Tottie – Tottie, Emily!'

'I don't care,' said Emily in a hard voice. 'I want a cook for Marchpane and Tottie must be cook. I don't

The Dolls' House

see anything in it,' said Emily loudly. 'We often make her cook.' Charlotte was silent. 'Don't we?' said Emily more loudly. 'She likes cooking.'

Charlotte was silent. 'I don't care,' said Emily again. 'She is the cook, so there!'

'You have to do as you think with dolls,' she said to Charlotte's silent face. 'You have to play with them.'

'Yes, poor dolls,' said Charlotte.

'I'm only playing with them,' said Emily defiantly.

'Yes, poor dolls,' said Charlotte.

Chapter 19

Now the Plantaganets, of the dolls' house, were only allowed to use the attic and kitchen. Marchpane lay in their big bed, bathed in their bath, sat on their chairs, ate and drank out of their flowered china, looked out of their windows. She sat by the lamp and saw the shadow of the roses; she had Birdie's birdcage, and her feather broom. If Birdie's hat had fitted on her head, you can be sure Emily would have given it to her.

And Apple? Apple was still Apple in the house. He would not stay in the kitchen, not because, like Birdie, he could not remember, but because he did not want to stay in the kitchen.

'You are naughty, Apple,' said Tottie.

'I want to be naughty,' said Apple.

He was not afraid of Marchpane. He did not dislike her. He was not afraid of anybody, and he liked everybody as everybody liked him. 'Sing me a song,' he said to Marchpane, as he would have said to Birdie and Tottie.

'I don't know any songs,' said Marchpane, and Apple laughed in high delight because he thought Marchpane was teasing. 'Go on, sing it,' said Apple.

But Marchpane really did not know any songs. She had lived for all those years in nurseries and she did

112

not know any songs. This was because her head was so filled up with thoughts of herself that there was no room for the smallest song to enter; but she was very clever. She knew that the Plantaganets did not like Apple to be with her and so she said, 'You sing to me.' This was clever because most people, however small, like to sing their own songs best, and Apple began to sing to Marchpane. Every day he sang her a song and she pretended to love it. Soon he had a habit of going in to Marchpane.

'Apple, don't do that,' said Tottie.

'Will,' said Apple.

'Don't,' said Tottie.

'Don't,' said Mr Plantaganet.

'Don't, don't, don't,' said Birdie.

'Do,' said Marchpane, 'do.'

Apple liked people who said 'do' better than people who said 'don't' and he continued to go in to Marchpane.

'She will get him into mischief,' said Tottie.

'I am very uneasy about him,' said Mr Plantaganet, but they were far too proud to go in after Apple and show Marchpane they cared. Birdie was not too proud. She went straight in and brought Apple back. That surprised them.

'There were no two thoughts about it,' said Birdie, and she looked surprised herself. 'Sometimes there are not,' she said. 'Sometimes there is only one thought and then I know what to do. Sometimes, but not very often.'

'And why don't you let him play with me?' asked Marchpane.

Birdie could not answer. As soon as Marchpane spoke to her, she became confused, and thought of heaviness and lightness, and yellow hair that was not real and was real, and eyes that were painted and eyes that opened and shut, and wedding clothes and cracker feathers and the fairy off the Christmas tree. She could not speak to Marchpane, but Tottie answered her.

'Because we do not choose,' said Tottie.

'*You* do not choose?'

'You let him do dangerous things,' said Birdie suddenly.

'Do I?' asked Marchpane and smiled. 'Yes, I do,' she said, 'if I want.'

'You had better not,' said Tottie. 'He is our little boy.'

'Is he? Fancy that!' said Marchpane. She glared at Tottie. 'Wait and see,' said Marchpane. 'Wait and see, you little splinter!'

Suddenly, just after that, Emily said to Charlotte, 'I know, Apple shall be her little boy.'

'Whose little boy?'

'Marchpane's.'

'Marchpane's?'

'Yes. Marchpane's.'

'But he isn't Marchpane's little boy. He is a Plantaganet. You can't change him now.'

'Why can't I?'

'You can't. I won't have it,' said Charlotte.

'Charlotte, who is the Eldest?'

'You can't be the Eldest all the time,' cried poor Charlotte.

In the dolls' house there was silence. Marchpane, Birdie, Mr Plantaganet, Tottie, and Darner had all heard. Apple was not listening; he had made a white gumboot out of the little bedroom jug and was trying it on his foot over his red shoe and now he could not get it off.

Darner was the first to break the silence. 'Prrick!' said Darner. 'Prrick! Prrick! Prrick!'

'Did you hear?' asked Mr Plantaganet then, in a long, long whisper. 'Tottie, did you hear?'

'Did I hear? Or did you? Did I? Did you? Did I?' said Birdie, rattling terribly.

Tottie did not answer. She was wishing desperately, her wood as hard as if it were full of knots and grains. 'Oh, Emily! Emily! Emily! Emily! I wish. I wish. I wish,' wished Tottie. 'Oh, Emily. Emily!'

But Marchpane only smiled her heavy china smile.

Chapter 20

If it were impossible for Birdie to remember that her room was Marchpane's, how could she remember that Apple was now Marchpane's little boy? She forgot all the time and this, of course, gave Marchpane many opportunities to pounce on her, and Marchpane loved pouncing on Birdie. 'She is like a cat with a poor little bird,' said Mr Plantaganet indignantly. 'Oh, I hate to see her,' and he begged Birdie, 'Birdie, do try and remember. Remember that your room is her room. Remember that Apple is her little boy.'

'You say that?' said Birdie.

'I have to say it,' said Mr Plantaganet sadly.

'I shall never say it,' said Birdie.

Tottie looked at her. 'Birdie, do you try and not remember?' she asked.

Birdie did not answer.

'But she is so cruel to you,' said Mr Plantaganet.

'Yes,' said Birdie, 'but I don't mind. I don't remember it.'

Tottie and Mr Plantaganet looked at her. 'How strange Birdie is,' they were both thinking. 'She looks as if she had grown lighter,' thought Mr Plantaganet. 'And how untidy she is. No wonder Marchpane teases her. She looks as if she had forgotten about her hair and her apron strings, and the feather on her hat and her parasol. She looks as if she might fly away. And how bright she looks,' thought Mr Plantaganet, 'like someone standing near a candle.'

'Like a doll in a lit shop window,' thought Tottie. 'Like a doll on a Christmas tree,' thought Mr Plantaganet.

'Birdie, do try and remember,' urged Tottie. 'Try and remember not to go in after Apple. We must give him up for the present. Just for the present,' said Tottie firmly. 'We shall get him back,' said Tottie.

Mr Plantaganet was too sad to speak. Darner did not even growl, but turned over in his kennel with a sharp little flop; Birdie said nothing, nor did that bright look on her face alter at all.

It happened that Mrs Innisfree gave Emily and Charlotte a musical box. It was a small wooden one, painted with kittens and fans, and it was made in Switzerland. When it was wound up, it played music that was the smallest tinkle, delicate and thin. Emily had put it in the dolls' house sitting room for Marchpane and Apple to hear, and the sound of it filled the house. 'Tinkle, tinkle,' played the musical box. It drew Birdie from the kitchen.

'What is it? What is it?' asked Birdie. 'Oh, how beautiful! How beautiful it is!' It seemed to her more beautiful than anything she had ever heard or ever imagined. 'It is like the songs I meant my bird to sing, only I didn't know them then. How could I know? I am only a cracker doll, but I know now,' said Birdie. 'I know now.'

It drew her from the kitchen across the hall to the closed sitting-room door.

Birdie had tried to remember what Tottie and Mr Plantaganet had asked. For two whole days she had not followed Apple, not gone into her bedroom, not gone near Marchpane. Now, as she stood at the sitting-room door, the tinkling of the musical box delighted her so much that it tinkled in her head and she could no longer remember what anyone had said.

She had no idea of going in, nor of anything else but the music, when suddenly she heard a sound that upset the running of the tinkling and spoilt it.

'Oh, hush!' said Birdie. 'Don't, don't.'

She tried to listen to the music again, but again came that ugly sound.

'No!' said Birdie. 'Hush. Hush.'

But it came again. Again. Suddenly Birdie, as if she had woken up, knew clearly what it was. It was Darner barking. 'Prrick,' came the sound. 'Prrick! Prrick! Prrick!'

Clearly, in that instant, Birdie had one thought, and only one. 'That was Darner,' thought Birdie clearly, 'Darner barking. Something is happening to Apple. Apple. Apple is in danger,' thought Birdie, and she opened the sitting-room door.

The Dolls' House

'Tinkle. Tinkle. Tinkle. Tinkle. Tinkle.' The sound of the music met her so much more full and clear near the musical box that the sound of it knocked against the sound of Darner's barking in her head and confused her. She did not know she had come in; she could not see what was happening to Apple.

For Apple was standing on one of the tapestry chairs, which was dragged up near the table, and he was leaning over the lamp with his darning-wool wig near the candle flame; there was a strong smell of singeing, and it was just going to send the whole of Apple up in flames.

Marchpane was sitting on the couch, watching him and smiling her china smile.

'Tinkle. Tinkle,' went the musical box.

'Prrick!' barked Darner. 'Prrick! Prrick! Prrick! Prrrrrickkkckckckck!' he barked frantically.

'Isn't that Darner?' asked Tottie in the kitchen.

Marchpane went on watching, watching with her smile.

'It is Darner,' said Mr Plantaganet, and he dropped his newspaper.

'Emily!' said Charlotte suddenly. 'Something is happening in the dolls' house.'

'Tcha!' said Emily. She was not liking the dolls' house at present. They could hear the musical box, 'Tinkle. Tinkle. Tinkle. Tinkle.' 'Nonsense. What could happen?' asked Emily.

'I smell singeing,' said Charlotte, sniffing. 'Emily, did you light the birthday candle?'

'Prrick! Prrick! Prrrrrickkckckckck!' barked Darner so loudly that Birdie heard him clearly over the music.

'Darner. Tinkle. Darner. Tinkle,' fluttered Birdie, while Marchpane smiled. 'What am I to do?' cried Birdie. 'Which is it? Is it which?'

'P-R-I-C-K!' barked Darner.

As the candle caught the edge of Apple's fringe and he screamed, as Tottie and Mr Plantaganet tumbled in at the door, and Emily and Charlotte swung open the dolls' house front, the sound of Apple's scream tore the sound of Darner's barking and the tinkling music out of Birdie's head. She had one thought, and she threw herself at the lamp.

'Birdie! Back! Back! Back!' cried Mr Plantaganet.

'Birdie! Let me!' screamed Tottie. 'Birdie, you are made of celluloid, remember!'

'Celluloid!' said Birdie in her light calm voice, and the lightness of the real candle was in her face. Light as she was, she threw herself between Apple and the lamp, and Apple fell off the chair face downward on the carpet and put out the spark of fire in his wig.

There was a flash, a bright light, a white flame, and where Birdie had been there was no more Birdie, no sign of Birdie at all, only, sinking gradually down on the carpet beside Apple, floated Birdie's clothes, burning, slowly turning brown, and going into holes;

last of all, the fire ran up the pink embroidery cotton of her apron strings and they waved up in the air, as they used to wave on Birdie, and then were burnt right up.

'Tinkle. Tinkle. Tinkle,' said the musical box.

Marchpane smiled.

Chapter 21

'But where did Birdie go?' asked Charlotte.

'She was celluloid. That is highly inflammable,' said Father.

'What is "highly inflammable"?'

'It burns up in a flash, leaving nothing behind it.'

'Birdie left nothing behind,' said Charlotte sadly.

'But what happened? What happened? I still don't understand what happened,' said Mr Plantaganet.

'Apple was standing on the chair far too near the lamp. You must have put him there, Charlotte,' said Emily.

'I didn't,' said Charlotte.

'Don't be silly, Charlotte,' said Emily. 'And his wig must have caught fire. That was what we smelled singeing; and we opened the front so quickly that we tumbled Tottie and Mr Plantaganet over, and Birdie was standing too near, though I have warned you, Charlotte, and they tumbled her over so that she fell against the lamp and knocked Apple over, and was burned herself.'

'She gave her life for Apple,' said Charlotte.

'What a good thing it was only Birdie,' said Emily, but she did not say it very certainly.

'She gave her life for Apple.'

'I suppose she did in a way. I suppose – if you like to call it that.'

'She gave her life for Apple.'

'Don't go on and on, Charlotte.'

'Tottie tumbled in at the door,' said Charlotte, 'and Mr Plantaganet did too. I put them in the kitchen. I didn't put them in the doorway, although you say I did. I didn't put them there nor Apple on the chair, nor, nor – Birdie near him. The only one who never moved,' said Charlotte loudly, 'was Marchpane.'

'Yes, Marchpane,' said Emily slowly.

'I should like to take her up by a pair of tongs,' said Charlotte, 'and drop her in the fire.'

'Oh, Charlotte. She is far too beautiful.'

'She isn't beautiful at all,' said Charlotte. 'She is nasty and she smells nasty too. She isn't beautiful.' A thought struck her. 'Emily,' she said, 'wasn't Birdie beautiful when she went up in that flame? Like a fairy, like a beautiful kind of silver firework.'

'Birdie would have liked that,' said Emily, and she sounded like the old Emily who knew so well what all the Plantaganets liked. 'Oh, Charlotte!'

'Yes, Emily?'

'I – wish . . . '

'Yes, Emily?'

'I wish the dolls' house was like it was – before Marchpane.'

'Yes, Emily.'

'Suddenly,' said Emily, 'I don't like Marchpane very much.'

'Nor do I,' said Charlotte decidedly.

'I didn't like the way – she sat there – when Apple – when Birdie –'

'Nor did I,' said Charlotte.

'I'm sorry now,' said Emily. 'I wish – but what are we to do with her, Charlotte? She is too valuable and beautiful. We should never be allowed to throw her away. We must do something with her.'

'She must go out of the dolls' house,' said Charlotte. 'She must go out at once.'

Marchpane sat all this time on the couch, staring in front of her with her smile on her face, as if she had not heard a word, as if she were something stuffed in a glass case.

Perhaps it was that that put it into Charlotte's head. Charlotte who so seldom had ideas. This was Charlotte's idea, not Emily's, or perhaps it was Tottie's, for it came to Charlotte like a voice, and it might have been Tottie's voice. It was Tottie who knew how Marchpane had liked being at the cleaners, and at the Exhibition. Cleaners. Exhibition. The thought came clearly into Charlotte's head.

'I know,' said Charlotte. 'We must give her to a museum.'

Chapter 22

Marchpane enjoyed being in the museum. She was in a glass case, between a lace collar and a china model of a King Charles spaniel. She was dusted very carefully twice a week and a number of people came to look at her. Sometimes young men and girls came to the museum to make drawings, and Marchpane was always quite sure, no matter what they drew, that they were making drawings of her. Every day she increased a little more in conceit, and the glass case made her safe from ever being played with.

Chapter 23

Towards six o'clock, just after tea, Charlotte brought Mr Plantaganet back from the post office and put him in his chair in the sitting room and gave him his paper. Emily brought Tottie in from shopping; she had found Tottie a raffia shopping basket the size of a nut, and she made Tottie hang it up with her cloak in the hall. Then she went in to sit with Mr Plantaganet. Apple was upstairs. He had been sent to bed early by Tottie so that he could not play with the lamp. Charlotte still said she had not put him on the chair, and Emily had lately given up saying that she had. Apple was safely in bed, tucked up in his patchwork quilt so that only his round head showed. Emily had clipped his burnt fringe straight with nail scissors and his plush had not been hurt at all. Darner lay quietly, snugly, in his kennel.

'Shall we let them have a little music?' asked Emily, and she wound up the musical box. It went 'tinkle, tinkle' and Darner stirred in his dreams.

Mr Plantaganet could not tell one of its tunes from the other. 'I have to have words,' said Mr Plantaganet. 'Words help me to know what it is. Like those carols, Tottie. Do you remember them?' And he began to hum 'God Bless the Master of This House'. 'Do you remember them, Tottie?'

The Dolls' House

'I remember everything,' said Tottie, listening to the music.

'Yes, I suppose you must, and for so long,' said Mr Plantaganet. 'Such a long time, Tottie.'

'Yes,' said Tottie.

'Things come and things pass,' said little Mr Plantaganet.

'Everything, from trees to dolls,' said Tottie.

'Even for small things like us, even for dolls. Good things and bad things, but the good things have come back, haven't they, Tottie?' asked Mr Plantaganet anxiously.

'Of course they have,' said Tottie in her kind wooden voice.

'Good things and bad. They were very bad,' said Mr Plantaganet.

'But they come and pass, so let us be happy now,' said Tottie.

'Without Birdie?' asked Mr Plantaganet, his voice trembling.

'Birdie would be happy. She couldn't help it,' said Tottie.

And Birdie's bright tinkling music went on in the dolls' house and, on her hat that still hung in the hall, and on her feather broom, and on her bird and on her parasol, the colours and patterns were still bright.

Miss Happiness
and
Miss Flower

My thanks are due to Edmund Waller, who designed the Japanese dolls' house described in this book, and who with his brother Geoffrey, aged twelve, made it; to Fiona Fife-Clark, aged eleven, who furnished it, painted the scrolls and lampshade and sewed the dolls'-house quilts and cushions; to Miss Anne Ashberry and Miss Creina Glegg, of Miniature Gardens Ltd, Chignal-Smealey, Essex, who made its garden and grew the tiny trees; to Miss Stella Coe (Sogetsu Ryu) for her advice over the meaning of flowers in Japanese lore and for reading the book; and finally and especially to Mr Seo of the Japanese Embassy, for his valuable help and advice and for the loan of books.

Chapter 1

They were two little Japanese dolls, only about five inches high. Their faces and hands were made of white plaster, their bodies of rag, which meant they could bow most beautifully – and Japanese people bow a great deal. Their eyes were slits of black glass and they had delicate plaster noses and red-painted mouths. Their hair was real, black and straight and cut in a fringe. They were exactly alike except that Miss Flower was a little taller and thinner, while Miss Happiness's cheeks were fatter and her red mouth was painted in a smile.

They wore thin cotton kimonos – a kimono is like a dressing-gown with wide-cut sleeves – and they each had a wide sash high up under their arms which was folded over into a heavy pad at the back.

Miss Happiness had a red kimono patterned with chrysanthemums, Miss Flower's was blue with a pattern of cherry blossom; both their sashes were pink and on their feet they had painted white socks and painted sandals with a V-shaped strap across the toes.

They were not new: Miss Flower had a chip out of one ear, her pretty kimono was torn and the paint had come off one of Miss Happiness's shoes. I do not know where they had been all their lives, but when this story begins they had been wrapped in cotton wool and tissue

133

paper, packed in a wooden box and tied with red and white string, wrapped again in brown paper, labelled and stamped and sent all the way from San Francisco in America to England. I do not think they had been asked if they wanted to come – dolls are not asked.

'Where are we now?' asked Miss Flower. 'Is it *another* country?'

'I think it is,' said Miss Happiness.

'It's strange and cold. I can feel it through the box,' said Miss Flower, and she cried, 'No one will understand us or know what we want. Oh, no one will ever understand us again!'

But Miss Happiness was more hopeful and more brave. 'I think they will,' she said.

'How will they?'

'Because there will be some little girl who is clever and kind.'

'Will there be?' asked Miss Flower longingly.

'Yes.'

'Why will there be?'

'Because there always has been,' said Miss Happiness.

All the same, Miss Flower gave a doll shiver, which means she felt as if she shivered though it could not be seen. Miss Flower was always frightened; perhaps the child who made the chip in her ear had been rough. 'I wish we had not come,' said Miss Flower.

Miss Happiness sighed and said, 'We were not asked.'

Miss Happiness and Miss Flower

*

Children are not asked either. No one had asked Nona Fell if she wanted to be sent from India to live with her uncle and aunt in England. Everyone had told her she would like it, but 'I don't like it at all,' said Nona.

'Nona is a good name for her,' said her youngest cousin, Belinda. 'All she does is to say No, no, no, all the time.'

With her dark hair and eyes, her thinness, and her skin that was pale and yellow from living so long in the heat, Nona looked a stranger among her pink-cheeked, fair-haired cousins. There were three of them: Anne, who was fourteen, slim and tall; Tom, who was eleven, with freckles; and Belinda, who was a rough tough little girl of seven.

Nona was eight. Her mother had died when she was a baby and she had been brought up by an old Ayah – an Ayah is an Indian nurse – on her father's tea garden, Coimbatore in Southern India. It had been hot in Coimbatore, the sun had shone almost every day; there had been bright flowers and fruit, kind brown people and lots of animals. Here it was winter and Nona was always cold. Her cousins laughed at her clothes; it was no wonder, for they had been chosen by old Ayah who had no idea what English children wore in England, and Nona had a stiff red velvet dress, white socks, black strap shoes and silver bangles. They laughed at the way she spoke English, which was no wonder either, for she talked in a sing-song voice like Ayah.

She did not like the food; living in a hot country does not make one hungry and she had not seen porridge, or puddings, or sausages, or buns before, and 'No thank you,' said Nona. She said 'No thank you' too when anyone asked her to go out for she had never seen so many buses and cars, vans and bicycles; they went so fast it made her dizzy. She said 'No thank you' when her cousins asked her to play; there had been no other English boys and girls in Coimbatore and she had never ridden a bicycle, or roller-skated, or played ping-pong, or rounders, or hide and seek, or even card games like Snap or Beggar-my-neighbour. All she did was to sit and read in a corner or stand by the window and shiver. 'And cry,' said Belinda. 'Cry, baby, cry.'

'Belinda, be kind,' said Nona's aunt, who was Belinda's mother. Nona called her Mother too. 'Be kind. We must all help her to settle down.'

'I don't want her to settle down,' said Belinda.

All through Christmas Nona was unhappy and when Christmas was over it was no better. She stood by the window and ran her bangles up and down her wrist, up and down and round and round. They were thin and of Indian silver; she had had them since she was almost a baby and to feel them made her seem closer to Coimbatore.

Miss Happiness and Miss Flower

'Come to the park, Nona. We're going to skate.'

'No thank you.'

'I'm going to the shops, Nona. Come along.'

'No thank you.'

'Have some of this nice hot toast.'

'No thank you.'

At last Mother spoke to her seriously. 'You really must try to be happier, Nona. You're not the only small person to come from far away.'

'I'm the only one here,' said Nona.

At that moment the bell pinged and the postman's rat-tat sounded at the door, and 'You go,' said Mother.

When Nona opened the front door the postman gave her a brown paper parcel. It had American stamps, it felt like a box and was very light. I wonder if you can guess what it was.

Nona took the parcel from the postman and brought it to Mother. Written on it was 'The Misses Fell'. 'It's for Anne and Belinda,' said Nona.

'It might be for you as well,' said Mother. 'You are a Miss Fell.'

'Am I?' asked Nona in surprise.

'Don't you know your own name, stupid?' asked Belinda.

Nona shook her head. Ayah used to call her Little Missy, but no one in Coimbatore had called her Miss Fell.

'It's from your Great-Aunt Lucy Dickinson,' said Mother, looking at the writing. 'It must be a late Christmas present.'

'A late Christmas present! A late Christmas present!' shouted Belinda, and she shouted for Anne to come.

'Undo it, Nona,' said Tom.

'Why should Nona . . . ?' began Belinda.

'Because I said so,' said Tom in such a terrible voice that Belinda was quiet.

Nona took off the brown paper and found the wooden box with the red and white strings. 'Cut them,' said Belinda impatiently, but Nona's small fingers untied the bow and the knot and carefully smoothed out the strings. 'Oh, you are *slow!*' said Belinda.

'She's not, she's careful,' said Tom.

Nona lifted the lid and carefully, perhaps even more carefully than usual because Tom had praised her, she unrolled the cotton wool and tissue paper, and there on the table, looking very small and cold and white, lay Miss Happiness and Miss Flower.

'What queer little dolls,' said Belinda, disappointed, and Nona answered, 'They're not queer. They're Japanese.'

You can imagine how frightened and lost Miss Happiness and Miss Flower felt when they found themselves on the big slippery table. They had to lie there looking up into the faces of Nona and Belinda.

138

Miss Happiness and Miss Flower

If Nona and Belinda had been Japanese children, one of them, Miss Flower was sure, would have made her and Miss Happiness bow. 'We can't even be polite,' said Miss Flower in despair, and she cried, 'Can one of *these* be the kind and clever girl?'

'Wish that she may be,' said Miss Happiness. 'Wish.' As I have often told you before, wishes are very powerful things, even dolls' wishes, and as Miss Happiness wished, Nona put out a finger and very gently stroked Miss Flower's hair. Her finger felt the chip, and 'You poor little doll,' said Nona.

'They're not even new,' said Belinda in disgust. 'Stupid old Great-Aunt Lucy Dickinson,' and in a temper she began to crumple up the wrappings. Then she stopped. She had found a piece of paper written on in spidery old-fashioned writing. Mother read it out. It was from Great-Aunt Lucy Dickinson. 'I send you with my love,' wrote Great- Aunt Lucy Dickinson, 'Miss Happiness, Miss Flower and Little Peach.' 'Happiness and Flower,' said Mother. 'What pretty names.' (See note: *Names*, p. 216.)

'Peach is the one I like best,' said Belinda. 'But where *is* Little Peach?'

'Was there no other doll in the parcel?' asked Anne.

'No. There were only two, not three.'

'Nothing in the wrappings?'

'No.'

'In the cotton wool or tissue paper?'

'Nothing.'

It was very odd. There was no sign of Little Peach. 'And he is the one I would have liked best,' mourned Belinda.

'Never mind,' said Mother. 'Anne is too big for dolls so there is one each for you and Nona.'

'They have been a long time getting here,' said Anne, looking at the postmark on the brown paper. 'Poor little things, spending Christmas in a parcel.'

'They don't mind about Christmas,' said Nona quickly.

It was strange how Nona seemed to know about these little dolls. '*You* have never been to Japan,' said Belinda rudely.

That was true, but, like Miss Happiness and Miss Flower, Nona had come from far away, and could feel for them. 'Perhaps,' said Miss Flower, 'she might be the kind and clever girl.'

'Why shouldn't they mind about Christmas?' argued Belinda.

'They don't have Christmas in Japan.'

'Don't be silly.'

'I'm not silly. They don't.'

'What do they have then?'

Nona was not sure but, as you know, she was always reading, and it seemed to her that in some story about Japanese children or in a geography book she had

140

read . . . What did I read? thought Nona, wrinkling up her forehead to try and remember. Then, 'They have a Star Festival,' she said.

'A *Star* Festival?'

'Yes,' said Nona. They were all looking at her and she blushed and stammered, though she remembered more clearly now. 'S-something to do with the stars, t-two stars,' she said. 'I think they are the spirits of two people who loved each other long, long ago, a thousand years ago, and were separated. Now they are up in two stars each side of the M-milky Way, and one night each year they can cross and meet.'

'Across the Milky Way?' said Anne. 'How pretty.'

'Yes,' said Nona again, and now her eyes shone so that she, too, looked almost pretty. 'And on earth that night children – grown-up people as well, but mostly children – write wishes on pieces of coloured paper and tie them outside on the bamboos, all over Japan,' she said, her eyes shining.

They looked at her in surprise. 'Why, Nona', said Mother, 'you seem a different child when you tell a story like that.'

'I didn't know you could,' said Anne. 'It's a beautiful story.'

'Jolly clever to remember it like that,' said Tom.

'It comes of reading,' said Father. 'That's what I'm always telling you children. Good girl, Nona.'

He gave Nona a pat on the head and Nona felt so

pleased that she smiled at him quite like a happy little girl, but Belinda was not pleased at all.

Belinda was the youngest and she had always been Father's pet, and Tom's and Anne's; she did not like it when they praised Nona. 'You needn't think you're so clever,' she said to Nona when everyone else had gone. 'You can't do anything *but* read . . . and cry, cry-baby. They only say you're clever because you were so stupid before.'

Nona did not answer but the happy look faded from her face.

'Why did you come here?' asked Belinda. The more she talked the angrier she grew. 'Why did you have to come? We don't want you. Why don't you go home? Why don't you have a house and a family of your own?'

Nona still did not answer.

'Star Festival! Rubbish!' shouted Belinda.

'It isn't rubbish,' said Nona in a hard little voice; now she was pale again and her eyes blazed, but Belinda did not see; she had flung out of the room.

When Nona was alone she went and stood by the window and presently a tear splashed down on the window-sill, then another and another. A home and a family of your own . . . 'Coimbatore, old Ayah,' whispered Nona, and the tears came thick and fast.

I do not know how long Nona stood there by the window, but the room, and then the garden, grew dark.

Miss Happiness and Miss Flower

She could hear the others talking in the playroom and Mother singing in the kitchen, but she stood there in the dark room staring out of the window.

I wish I could go home, thought Nona. I wish I could see my *own* father. I wish I could see Ayah. I wish . . . Now the wish was so big that it seemed to run out of her right up into the sky, and . . . 'Why, the stars are out!' said Nona.

Across the garden she could see the shapes of trees, bare against the sky, and above them and behind them were stars, bright because of the frosty winter dark. There was a glass door into the garden and Nona opened it and stepped outside. It was so cold that it made her catch her breath, but now she could see the whole night sky. There's the Milky Way, thought Nona – her own father had often showed it to her – and she wondered which of the stars were the two that held the people in love.

By the glass door there was a little tree. It was not a bamboo, of course, but as she looked at it Nona's face suddenly grew determined and she came in and shut the door.

She switched on the light, and taking a piece of paper and a pencil from Mother's desk – 'Without even asking,' said Belinda afterwards – she tore the paper into narrow strips and began to write. 'I wish I could go home,' wrote Nona through more tears. 'I wish I had never come.' 'I wish I was back in Coimbatore.' 'I wish I

143

had a house of my own.' 'I wish there wasn't a Belinda.' She took a piece of cotton from Mother's work-basket, cut it into short bits and threaded one through each of her papers, and rolled them up tightly so that no one could read them. There was a blazer belonging to Tom in the basket, waiting to be mended; Nona slipped it on and went out and tied her wishes on the tree.

It seemed to help her unhappiness to put the wishes on the tree and she went back to write some more, but she had said all there was to say. The Japanese dolls were lying close by her elbow and now she looked down at them. The light caught their eyes so that they shone up at her. I believe *they* like tying wishes on the tree, thought Nona. Of course, it's their Star Festival.

'Our Star Festival!' said Miss Happiness and Miss Flower.

It was not, of course, the right night, but that did not seem to matter. Nona took another piece of paper and cut that up, then ran into the playroom and quietly fetched her paint-box and a cup of water; then she painted the new strips in colours, red and green and blue and yellow. When they were dry she began to write again.

'What is she doing?' whispered Miss Flower.

'Writing wishes.'

'I wish she would write some for us.'

Nona began to cut the strips into smaller, narrower ones.

'What is she doing now?'

'Writing wishes.'

'But such tiny ones. Do you suppose . . . ?' asked Miss Flower – she hardly dared say it – 'suppose they are for us?'

'They are for us,' said Miss Happiness, and Miss Flower cried, 'Wishes for the River of Heaven!' which is what Japanese people call the Milky Way. (See note: *Star Festival*, p. 216.)

Next morning Anne was the first to look out of the window and see the little tree covered with wishes. How pretty they looked with their colours! Nona had found some tinsel left over from Christmas and put that on too, and had cut out some paper flowers. 'Why, Nona!' said Anne, 'how lovely!' Then she looked again and asked, 'Isn't it . . . ? Yes, it is. Look,' she called to the others. 'Oh, do come and see. Nona has made a Star Festival all by herself.'

'But not on bamboos,' said Nona. 'You haven't any.'

'But lots of wishes,' said Anne.

'Lots of wishes,' whispered Miss Happiness and Miss Flower. They knew what the wishes were.

'Rolled up like secrets,' said Tom.

'They are secrets,' said Nona quickly. She was beginning to feel ashamed of some of them. 'Secrets,' she said again.

'Secrets!' sighed Miss Happiness and Miss Flower. They would have liked everyone to read them. 'Because we *do* want to go home,' they said. 'We *do* want a house of our own. We *do* wish Miss Nona could look after us. It's a pity they have to be secrets.' But the wishes were secret no longer; Belinda had slipped out into the garden and was pulling them off the tree. When she had read some she came in and slammed the door.

'How dare you!' shouted Belinda at Nona. 'They're my dolls as much as yours,' and she snatched them up. 'Mother said so,' shouted the furious Belinda.

Two days ago Nona would have let Belinda take the dolls; she would have gone away by herself and read or stood looking out of the window, but she could not bear to see the way Miss Flower hung limply in Belinda's rough little hand. 'Don't! You're hurting them,' she cried.

'They're only dolls,' said Belinda, more angry than ever, and she cried, 'All right. They want a house. They can go in my dolls' house.'

'House? Did she say house?' asked poor squeezed Miss Flower.

'She said house,' said Miss Happiness.

'Like in our wish?' But Miss Happiness was not at all sure this was like their wish.

'How wonderful,' whispered Miss Flower. She would have liked to close her eyes and dream but, of course, dolls with fixed eyes cannot do this.

Belinda knelt down in front of her dolls' house and swung open the door. 'It's a funny kind of house,' said

Miss Happiness. For the first time she had a frightened quiver in her voice.

To us it would not have been a funny kind of house, but when a Japanese doll says 'a house' she means something quite different. Belinda's dolls' house was white with gables and a red roof. The front opened, and inside were two rooms downstairs and two rooms upstairs; it had flannel carpets, bits of lace for curtains and was filled full of dolls'-house furniture and dolls'-house dolls all belonging to Belinda.

I am afraid she was a careless child and everything was dusty, dirty and higgledy-piggledy. It looked very higgledy-piggledy to Miss Happiness and Miss Flower. 'I don't want to stay here,' said Miss Flower as Belinda sat her on a dusty chair, on which already there was a large pin. 'Ow!' cried poor Miss Flower.

'I don't want to either,' said Miss Happiness.

Perhaps it was because Nona too had known quite other kinds of houses, and felt so unhappy and strange in England, that she could guess what Miss Happiness and Miss Flower were feeling behind their stiff plaster faces. 'I don't think the dolls' house will do,' said Nona.

'Why not?' said Belinda. She did not see anything wrong. 'I'll make room for them,' she said and she swept the other dolls out of the dolls' house, helter-skelter, bumpetty-bump; the other poor dolls were

147

bumped and bruised, their legs twisted round. 'No! No!' cried the Japanese dolls. 'O Honourable Miss, please no! Oh no, not for us! Oh, the poor dolls! No! No!' Miss Flower remembered how her chip had ached when it was done. She saw a little boy doll with his wig half torn off, a girl doll with a twisted leg, and 'Oh, I can't bear it!' cried Miss Flower and she fell off the chair on to the floor.

'Stupid thing,' said Belinda.

When Belinda said that, Nona grew so angry and hot that she had to speak. '*She's* not stupid,' she said. '*You* are. Japanese dolls don't sit on chairs.'

'How do you know?'

'I once saw a picture of a Japanese girl serving tea, and she was kneeling on the floor, like this,' said Nona; she took Miss Happiness and made her kneel. (See note: *Kneeling*, p. 216.)

Miss Happiness had rather more stuffing in her body than Miss Flower; she stayed exactly where Nona had put her and very pretty she looked with her little black head and the big loop of her sash, far more comfortable than Miss Flower had looked on the chair. Then, very gently, Nona took up Miss Flower and straightened her kimono and put her to kneel beside Miss Happiness.

'That's better. That's better,' sighed Miss Flower, and 'Wish. Wish,' Miss Happiness told her. 'Wish that Miss Nona could look after us.'

'Bet they won't like kneeling there for long,' said Belinda. 'The floor's too hard.'

'Cushions,' said Nona. 'Flat sort of cushions.' She said it quite certainly for she seemed to see a heap of bright dolls' house cushions, and she pleaded, 'Let me try to make them cushions, Belinda.'

Belinda looked at the untidy, dirty dolls' house, then at the two little dolls kneeling on the floor as if they were . . . asking? thought Belinda. Indeed they were. Dolls cannot speak aloud, you know that, but now Miss Happiness and Miss Flower wished: 'Please, Honourable Miss. We are your little nuisances but please let us have the cushions.' It was certainly the first time in her noisy busy life that Belinda had felt a doll's wish, and she was suddenly ashamed, but she was not going to let Nona know that. 'You had better make them a whole Japanese house,' she said mockingly.

'A Japanese dolls' house,' said Anne.

'A Japanese dolls' house?' Nona looked startled. Until that moment she had never thought of such a thing. 'I couldn't. How could I?' asked Nona.

At that moment Miss Flower slipped – you remember she had not as much stuffing as Miss Happiness. She slipped and the slip sounded like a sharp breath and her head sank even lower on the floor. She must have knocked Miss Happiness, for Miss Happiness bent over too, and they looked as if they were very much asking.

'But . . .' said Nona, 'I don't know how.'

'You didn't know how to make a Star Festival, but you made it,' said Tom.

'Not properly,' said Nona, but she was pleased, for Tom was the one in the family who really made things. Anne was clever; she could embroider and paint and sew and weave on her loom but Tom had a proper work-bench in the playroom and was making a model galleon – which is a sailing-ship man-of-war. He was making it most beautifully with endless delicate pieces for masts and spars, decks and rails. Tom really knew, and 'You could make a dolls' house,' said Tom.

Chapter 2

It was a week later. Every day Nona took Miss Happiness and Miss Flower out of their wooden box and dusted them and looked at them. 'But where is our house?' asked Miss Flower every day, and every day they both wished, 'Little Honourable Miss. Oh! please, little Honourable Miss, where is our house?' But Nona could not think how to make a Japanese dolls' house.

She got a big cardboard box and cut out doors and windows, but that did not seem right and the cutting hurt her fingers. She tried to arrange an empty drawer with the wooden box for a bed and some rolled-up handkerchiefs for cushions, but it did not look like anything at all. At last she came to Tom's work-table and stood at his elbow.

He had finished cutting the pieces for the hull of his galleon – the hull is the bottom part of a boat – and now was very busy gluing them together. He knew Nona would not talk as Belinda did and so he did not tell her to go away. She stood quite silently watching his clever careful fingers, and a feeling stirred in her own as if they could be clever and careful too. At last the hull sat up firm and neat between its blocks on the work-table, though the glue was still sticky. Then Nona did speak.

'How did you know how to make it?' she asked very respectfully.

'Learnt,' said Tom, rubbing the glue off his thumbs with a wet rag.

'How did you learn?'

'How did you learn about the Star Festival?'

'Oh!' said Nona. 'You mean . . .' and, as she said that, Tom flipped over the book that had the plan of the galleon in it; it was a paper book filled with patterns and designs, and called *100 Ways to Make a Fretsaw Model*. 'Don't lose my place,' said Tom.

'I didn't know you could learn to *carpenter* out of books.'

'You can learn anything out of books,' said Tom.

'A book like this?'

Tom nodded.

'Oh!' said Nona. She stood by him a moment longer and then said, 'Thank you, Tom.'

Mother was very surprised when Nona appeared in front of her wearing her out-door things, her coat, red cap, boots and gloves. 'Do you want to go *out*?' said Mother.

'Oh, please,' said Nona. She was in such a hurry that the words tumbled out. 'I've got my Christmas money. I want to go to the bookshop.'

'Run along then, dear,' said Mother.

Run along! The excitement faded out of Nona's

face. 'By – by myself?' she asked.

'The bookshop is this side of the street. You won't have to cross the road.'

'But . . .' The street with its lorries and cars and bicycles, and all the people, thought Nona; the big boys and the dogs. She shivered.

'If you wait till this afternoon I'll come with you.'

'I can't wait,' said Nona.

As Nona opened the front door all the noise of the street came in: a lorry rumbled past, and a car; a gang of children on roller-skates made a noise like thunder; a big boy whistled. Nona shut the front door and ran upstairs.

She had meant to take off her coat and cap and throw herself on the bed in tears again, but then she caught sight of Miss Happiness and Miss Flower.

They were standing one each side of her clock and . . . Did *I* take them out of the box, thought Nona staring. She must have done, but she had been so excited when she put on her things to go out that she did not remember. Did I take them out of their box? She did not think she had, but there they were, standing by the clock, their feet together, their arms hanging down. It seemed to Nona that they were waiting.

I suppose Japanese people are very brave people, thought Nona, and after a minute she went downstairs and opened the front door again.

*

Just as she was going out, Mother called her back. 'Oh, Nona, if you are going to the bookshop be careful to be very polite to old Mr Twilfit. He's inclined to be cross.'

'Cross! He's an absolute old dragon,' said Anne.

'He once nearly bit my head off,' said Tom cheerfully.

Nona began to shake. 'Oh, Anne, come with me.'

'Can't. I'm busy.'

'Tom?'

'I'm busy too.'

Nona turned back to the door.

'He once chased me out of the shop,' said Belinda.

'If I know you, you were touching the books with your dirty hands,' said Tom.

Nona thought, and then went back upstairs and washed her hands. Even paler than usual, but with her head held high, she went out and shut the door behind her.

'She has gone,' whispered Miss Flower.

'And for us,' said Miss Happiness.

'Is it to do with the house, do you think?'

'I think so. We will wait for her to come back.'

Tick, tick, tick went the clock as the minutes passed. It might have been two little dolls' hearts beating.

Nona's heart was beating too, but . . . once you start being brave you have to go on, thought Nona. She was shaking when she got to the bookshop. Perhaps she expected to meet a real dragon but all she could see in the shop were books, stacks and racks of them, books on shelves and laid on tables, books piled up on the counter. The shop had W. Twilfit, Bookseller, over the window, but though she peeped and peered she could see no sign of anyone at all.

The bell rang as she went in, which made her jump. Very carefully she walked between the tables, and jumped again when she saw a big old man looking at her. In the dark shop he seemed very big, very alarming to Nona; his grey hair stood up in a shock, making him seem even taller than he was, but the most frightening thing about him were his eyebrows that were thick and shaggy as two furred grey caterpillars. When she saw him looking at her, Nona stayed as still as a mouse caught in a trap.

'What do you want? Hey?' His voice was so big that it seemed to rumble round the shop.

'Please' – Nona could hardly make any sound at all – 'Please, have you got a book called *100 Ways to Make a Japanese House?*'

'No such book.' Besides being a rumble it was cross. Nona held on to the edge of a table.

'But Tom said . . .'

'Tom's wrong.'

The shameful tears were near again. Nona bent her head over a book and turned over a page.

'DON'T TOUCH!' shouted Mr Twilfit.

This time Nona jumped so high that she bit her

155

tongue, and the pain and the fright made her speak before she could think. 'I *can* touch,' she said. 'I washed my hands before I came!'

She did not know then that when Mr Twilfit's eyebrows worked up and down, in the way that looked so frightening, it meant that he was pleased. They worked up and down now. '*Washed* them?' said Mr Twilfit, as if he did not believe her.

For answer Nona showed them to him palms upwards. Mr Twilfit bent and looked at them; then he took one, and he could feel how Nona was trembling. 'I didn't know there was a boy or girl in this town,' he said, 'who would wash their hands before they touched books. I beg your pardon, little Missy.'

The rumble was almost soft now. Ayah had called Nona Little Missy. It was too much for Nona; she burst into tears.

'Must it be a Japanese house?' asked Mr Twilfit.

'They are – sniff – Japanese dolls – sniff,' said Nona.

'And you want to make them feel at home,' said Mr Twilfit, and he looked out of the window. Then he said, 'When I was a little boy I knew what it was like to be a long way from home.'

Mr Twilfit had not chased Nona out of his shop, indeed he had taken her into his room behind it and sat her down at his desk while she told him all about Miss Happiness and Miss Flower. His eyebrows worked up and down as she told from the beginning of the postman bringing the parcel, right down to *100 Ways to Make a Japanese House*.

'But I'm afraid I was right,' he said. 'There is no such book. There are others. Can you read?' he rapped out.

'Of course,' said Nona.

'Really read?'

That was one thing Nona was quite sure she could do, and she nodded.

Mr Twilfit got up and went back into the shop; Nona could hear him rummaging and taking down books from the shelves. 'This one is called *Japanese Homes and Gardens*,' he said, bringing in a book. It was nearly half as big as Nona. She took a deep breath.

'I don't think I could pay for one as big as that,' she said.

'It's nearly all pictures. Might be useful,' said Mr Twilfit as if she had not spoken. He went back to the shop. He found another book called *Customs of Old Japan*; then one on how the Japanese arrange flowers, and a book of Japanese fairy tales with more pictures. 'Useful,' said Mr Twilfit.

'I don't understand about the money here,' said Nona. 'Indian money is different.' And she put all her Christmas money, a ten-shilling note, some half-crowns, shillings, sixpences and pennies, on the desk. 'But would this be enough?'

'Can't buy those books,' said Mr Twilfit. 'Out of the question. Cost a lot of money. Will you be careful if I lend them to you?'

'Very careful,' said Nona, and her brown eyes glowed.

'Then give me your name and address.'

'Nona Fell,' said Nona dreamily – she was thinking about reading those books – 'Nona Fell. Coimbatore Tea Estate, near Travancore, South India . . .'

'You are in England,' said Mr Twilfit very gently. 'Your address here?'

Nona looked at him and the glow went out of her eyes. She could have fallen through the floor with shame; even small children, almost babies, know their address, but she had been taken into the house almost as if she had been a piece of luggage, and had never bothered to notice or find out its address. 'I don't know,' she had to whisper.

'I see. You weren't interested,' said Mr Twilfit, and Nona nodded with another rush of tears.

'Is it far?' asked Mr Twilfit.

'Just down the road.'

'Come along then,' said Mr Twilfit.

'Good gracious heavens!' said Belinda, who was looking out of one of the front windows. '*Look* at Nona and Mr Twilfit.'

Everyone crowded to the window to see.

'He has a great bundle of books,' said Anne.

'She's bringing him in,' said Belinda.

'Well, I'll be darned!' said Tom.

It was Mother who really brought him in, for it was she who opened the door. 'Nona, I was getting anxious . . .' then she broke off. 'I see you have found a friend.'

'Have I?' asked Nona. She had not thought of having a friend in England, but it seemed like that when Mr Twilfit came in and sat down and had a cup of coffee.

'And we were fetched down to the room to meet the old and honourable gentleman,' said Miss Happiness.

'She made us bow,' said Miss Flower and she sounded just as pleased as Miss Happiness. 'She is beginning to understand.'

Now every day on the playroom window seat three heads could be seen: Nona's dark one, bent, as she sat cross-legged with one of Mr Twilfit's books, and beside her two very small black ones: Miss Happiness and Miss Flower. She had made them two cushions from pieces of old hair ribbon; Miss Happiness had a red cushion, Miss Flower's was pale blue. 'I like mine best,' said Miss Flower; then she was worried in case Miss Happiness did not like her own, but 'I like mine,' said Miss Happiness.

Nona had no time to stand and look out of the window; she spent all day over Mr Twilfit's books or trotting up the road to see Mr Twilfit. She was learning all she could about Japan; about Japanese houses and gardens and Japanese furniture – though it mostly isn't furniture, thought Nona; about quilts and cushions, bowls and scrolls; about the niche to hold a scroll and flowers; about the way the Japanese arrange flowers. She was learning about Japanese feasts – 'And they do have a Star Festival,' said Nona, 'a New Year Festival and a Feast of Dolls.'

'But not with dolls like us,' said Miss Flower, and she and Miss Happiness said together, '*Honourable* dolls.' Nona learned Japanese names, and about Japanese food and Japanese fairy tales. She was not the only one to learn. 'Everyone else has to learn too,' said Anne, 'willy-nilly,' for Nona sometimes read the books aloud in her sing-song voice. 'Like a reading machine,' said Tom.

'For goodness' sake!' said Belinda, and stuffed her fingers in her ears.

Though Belinda stuffed her fingers in her ears there was one story she always managed to hear. It was in the fairy tale book and was about a boy called Peach. '*We* had a Little Peach who should have been in the parcel but was lost . . . and Mother *still* hasn't written to Great-Aunt Lucy Dickinson,' said Belinda.

The Peach Boy story began with a man and a woman who longed for a child. No child came, until on one hot summer day the woman found a big peach floating in the stream. She took it home for her husband to eat, but no sooner had he touched it with his knife than the top flew off. It opened in two halves and there, in the peach, was a tiny baby boy.

'A *Japanese* baby boy,' said Miss Happiness and Miss Flower.

Belinda loved that story. 'He grew up to be naughty, just like me,' she said, 'and when he was big he went out into the world. I wonder *why* our Little Peach didn't come,' said Belinda.

Chapter 3

Miss Flower could not help being anxious about the house. 'Will Miss Nona know that a Japanese house should have walls that slide open like windows?'

'Paper windows,' said Miss Happiness.

'That it should have a little garden to look at?' said Miss Flower. 'Does she know about quilts, not beds? Chopsticks, not spoons and forks? Cushions, not chairs?'

'You know she knows about cushions,' said Miss Happiness.

'But bowls, not cups?'

'Hush, she is studying.'

Miss Flower tried to hush but she could not help a small whisper. 'It takes so long to study. If we could tell her . . .'

'We can't.'

'What can we do for Honourable Miss?'

'We can wish,' said Miss Happiness, and they wished. Perhaps Belinda felt the wishing more than Nona, for, 'Is she going on reading for *ever*?' asked Belinda.

It really seemed as if Nona would go on reading for ever, but one snowy afternoon Mr Twilfit knocked at the door. He had brought a book. 'Not *another* book!' said Belinda.

'Hush, Belinda,' and Mother asked Mr Twilfit to come into the drawing-room where they all were; but Belinda would not hush.

'She has read and read,' said Belinda, 'and she *still* doesn't know how to make a Japanese house.'

'I do know,' said Nona, and they all looked at her.

'Well, how?'

'I don't exactly know how but I know what it should be like.'

'Well?'

Miss Happiness and Miss Flower, who had been brought down on their cushions, held their breaths.

'Japanese houses are up off the ground,' began Nona, 'so the house should stand on stilts – or up on a box, I thought, with little wooden steps. Some of the walls should be plain, but the other walls should slide like windows; they should be rather like picture frames but with plain paper criss-crossed with wood. Some of the inside walls should slide too, but they are plain.'

'Yes,' breathed Miss Happiness and Miss Flower.

'The roof should be tiles, dark blue or grey . . .'

'Yes. Yes.'

'Inside, there should be a little hall for taking off shoes. Japanese people don't wear shoes in the house. The rooms should be almost empty, with matting on the floor, if we could get it fine enough,' said Nona.

'Lots of homes nowadays do have chairs and sofas and beds but most still have cushions to sit on, and they would have cupboards with sliding doors, or else chests, where they keep rolled-up quilts or mats for beds.'

'Yes,' said Miss Happiness and Miss Flower.

'They would have a firebox – I don't know exactly yet what that is – and in the room there should always be a niche, an alcove for a scroll – that's a Japanese picture – and, by it, a vase of flowers, very few flowers,' said Nona.

'Yes. Yes,' cried Miss Happiness and Miss Flower, and 'Bravo!' said Mr Twilfit.

'Nothing else?' asked Belinda. 'No tables or chairs?'

'A very little table just off the floor.'

'It will look very bare.'

'Japanese houses *are* bare.'

'That is their beauty,' said Mr Twilfit, and his eyebrows worked up and down as he looked at Nona. 'You'll see,' said Mr Twilfit. 'It will be all right once you have got the bones.'

'Do houses have bones?' Nona and Belinda asked him together.

'The foundations, the floors, walls and roofs are the bones. How will you get those, hey?' asked Mr Twilfit.

'They could be carpentered,' said Nona.

'You can't carpenter,' said Belinda.

'No, but . . .'

'But?' Once again they all looked at Nona.

'Tom can,' said Nona with a rush.

'I don't make girls' things,' said Tom.

'Of course they *are* more difficult and delicate,' said Mr Twilfit, and he asked Mother, 'Was it Sir Winston Churchill or the President of the United States who made that beautiful dolls' house for his sister?'

'I don't believe they did,' growled Tom under his breath.

'And of course,' said Mr Twilfit – his eyebrows were busy – 'you would need to be a really good carpenter.'

'I'm making a model galleon,' said Tom.

'And that's horribly difficult,' said loyal Belinda, but Mr Twilfit shook his head.

'That's a model from a plan,' he said. 'Quite, quite simple, you only have to follow it. A Japanese dolls' house wouldn't have a plan. I don't suppose anyone has made one – not in this country. The plan would have to come out of your own head. A boy could hardly be expected to do that.'

'I don't see why not,' said Tom, but Mr Twilfit still shook his head.

'How would you raise it?'

'Make a plinth,' said Tom. 'Like a box upside down,' he explained quickly to Belinda before she could ask him what a plinth was.

'Then the grooves for the sliding walls, they would have to be so very small . . .'

'I could make them,' growled Tom.

'And the frames to hold the paper screens. For a dolls' house they would have to be so very thin. How could you join them?'

'I could,' growled Tom.

But Mr Twilfit still shook his head. 'It would be very difficult,' and, as he stood up to go, he said to Nona, 'You had better save up and we'll see if we can find a proper carpenter.'

Tom scowled at Mr Twilfit – a scowl is a face you make when you dislike someone – and spoke across him to Nona. 'I'll make it for you,' said Tom and under his breath he said to Mr Twilfit, 'You'll see.'

'Nona, would this box be big enough?'

'Nona, if I make this two feet long . . .'

'Would this paper be thick enough for the screens?'

'Nona, I found this shell . . .'

A strange thing had happened. Suddenly it was as if everyone in the house were helping to make the Japanese dolls' house. 'Everyone except me,' said Belinda. 'I won't help.'

Perhaps it was Nona's reading aloud, or Mr Twilfit's interest, or the plan that Tom had drawn from the pictures in the books, 'or because of our wishing,' said Miss Happiness and Miss Flower, but all the family seemed to be running backwards and forwards to Nona, asking Nona questions, bringing things to

Nona. 'Except me,' said Belinda and kicked the table.

'Belinda, you're not jealous of Nona?'

'Of course I'm not jealous,' said Belinda scornfully. 'I'm not even interested in Japanese dolls.' That was not quite true; she very often thought about Little Peach. He would have been like Peach Boy in the story, thought Belinda. To think about him took away the feeling Belinda was beginning to have, a feeling of being left out. 'I *wish* Little Peach had come,' said Belinda.

Chapter 4

'Have you chosen the site?' asked Father. ('You see, even Father is joining in,' said Belinda.)

'What is a site?'

'The plot or place where you build.'

'I'll build it on my work-table,' said Tom.

'But it can't stay there,' said Nona.

'No jolly fear,' said Tom.

'Besides, it has to have a garden.'

'If it has a garden, it should be near a window. Plants need light and air,' said Mother.

'Plants?' Until that moment Nona had not thought of a garden with real plants. 'Where should we find them?' she asked.

'In the fields and woods.'

'Could we take them?'

'Of course. They're wild.'

In Coimbatore flowers grew on trees or creepers or else in the gardens. 'You mean little flowers growing around *loose*?' said Nona amazed. She seemed to see a dolls'-house-size garden full of flowers of dolls'-house size. 'Could we make it on my window-sill?' she asked. 'Could that be the site?'

'Well, I had thought of an old table . . .' said Mother.

'*Please*.'

168

'Oh, let her, Mother.'

'Very well.'

It seemed to Belinda that everyone was spoiling Nona. Belinda kicked the door as she went out.

At the cabinet-makers' Tom found a piece of rosewood. It was dirty and chipped, 'but it's real rosewood,' said Tom, and when he had sandpapered it smooth it was a deep, soft rose-brown colour. 'It will do for the top of the plinth,' said Tom. 'I shall make it a base.'

'But what next?' asked Miss Flower; she still could not help feeling anxious.

Next was a visit to the wood shop. 'A wood shop?' asked Nona. She had never heard of one.

'You can buy pieces of wood, all lengths and sizes, narrow bits and wide ones. I hope you have some money,' said Tom.

Nona had the ten-shilling note, the half-crowns, shillings, sixpences and pennies she had shown to Mr Twilfit. She had her ninepence a week pocket money saved up as well. 'Will that be enough?' she asked Tom.

'Come and see.'

'Come? How?' Tom was getting his bicycle out. 'You mean on the back? With my legs hanging down?' said Nona in horror.

'Of course not. That isn't allowed,' said Tom. 'I'll ride very slowly and you can run beside me.'

'*Run?* In the street? I couldn't,' said Nona.

169

'O.K. No wood,' said Tom. 'I'll get on with my galleon.'

The rosewood floor stood on Nona's windowsill; Miss Happiness and Miss Flower stood near it.

'Bicycles go so fast,' said Nona.

Miss Happiness and Miss Flower appeared not to hear.

'Tom whizzes in and out, between buses and cars.'

They still seemed not to hear.

'Japanese people are *horribly* brave,' said Nona.

They did not contradict her, and Nona came and stood by Tom's table. 'O.K., I'll come,' she said.

The wood shop was a most wonderful place. There were big blocks and planks of wood, tiny delicate mouldings, thin strips, narrow bits and wide ones; there were chair legs and stool tops, every kind of corner and grooving, and handles from great front door ones down to the smallest dolls'-house size. There were sheets of wood of every kind, stains and paints, screws and hinges.

What did Tom buy? 'A terrific great lot of wood,' Nona told the others when she got home. She thought it wonderful that Tom knew what to ask for and that the shopman knew what he meant. 'Because *I* didn't,' said Nona.

It was all packed up and Tom tied the long bits of wood to the cross-bar of his bicycle; the screws and nails and pots of stain and glue and paint he put in his pockets. 'But you'll have to carry the rest,' he told Nona.

'*And* run?' asked Nona faintly.

Tom looked at her. 'Belinda would,' he said.

'O.K.,' said Nona and picked up the parcel.

When you build a real house there is the sound of bricks being piled, of the concrete mixer, of wood being sawn and hammered, of lorries and shouts. The sound of a dolls' house being made is different; there is a tap, tap, tap from a little hammer, the shirring of sandpaper, the whirring noise of the fine drill as Tom made his drill holes; but the building noises made by Tom meant as much to Miss Happiness and Miss Flower as the sound of your real house being built could mean to you. Nona had taken them and their cushions into the playroom so that they could see.

'What is he doing now?' whispered Miss Flower.

'He is making the corners.'

'And now?'

'He is making the hall.'

'And now?' asked Miss Flower.

'He is making the two side walls.' And then one day Miss Happiness cried, 'Oh, Flower . . .'

'Yes?'

'He is making . . . a niche.'

'A niche? For our scroll and flowers? Oh, Happiness!'

Tom and Nona had argued about that niche. 'But

171

I *told* you,' said Nona. 'It's a most important part of a Japanese room.'

'Be darned if you did,' said Tom.

'But I *did*. A niche like a little alcove. I did.' It took Tom four days to think out how to make that niche, but at last he found a way. It was fitted into one of the side walls, making a small alcove in it. 'We'll make it a separate little roof,' said Tom, 'and a low floor inside.'

'Oh, Tom, you are clever,' said Nona.

'Honourable, clever Mr Tom,' said Miss Happiness and Miss Flower.

Tom planned to make an entrance hall. He divided the front of the house into one big window and a small hall. 'A shoes-off place,' said Miss Happiness.

'It should have sliding screens inside *and* out,' said Nona.

'Christopher Columbus!' said Tom. He might well have said it, for they were small and finicking to make, but he made them.

The windows were made of frames, latticed like the sliding screens, on hinges that Tom took off two old cigar boxes of Father's. They swung back so that Nona could open the front of the dolls' house when she wanted to play.

Now the front of the house was finished, and the side walls and the niche were painted, and fixed against the end pillars. Soon, from pillar to pillar, Tom would fix the heavier beams that would hold the roof.

'But what about the screens?' asked Nona. 'The sliding screen doors in the back wall and for the hall?'

'I'll make them,' said Tom. He sounded tired.

'But when? When?'

'Christopher Columbus!' said Tom. 'Can't I ever have a day off?'

To make the sliding screens was most difficult of all. 'I need six hands,' he said. At last he had put in the two back screens with their paper lattice and the plain and latticed screens for the hall; and it was a wonderful moment when Tom and Nona could slide them all backwards and forwards, backwards and forwards. 'Let Mr Twilfit see *that*!' said Tom.

Now the walls were up, and the house only needed the roof 'to have all its bones,' said Nona, remembering what Mr Twilfit had said; but before the roof could be made, something happened that Nona had forgotten about. The something was school.

'I can't go,' said Nona.

'Anne goes, Tom goes, Belinda goes. Of course you must go.'

'No thank you,' said Nona, but it was no use saying 'No thank you', as this was one of the times children were not asked; and one morning Nona had to take off her red velvet dress, her white socks and silver bangles, and dress herself in a tunic and blouse like Anne's and Belinda's, a dark blue coat and a cap with a badge.

173

Then, carrying a case that held a new pencil box, a ruler and her money for lunch, she walked with Anne and Belinda to school.

She came home in tears. 'I knew she would,' said Belinda. 'She cried all day.'

'You mustn't cry here,' the teacher, Miss Lane, had told Nona.

'It's here I want to cry,' said Nona, and she did. Belinda was ashamed, but Belinda did not know how terrifying the big strange new building seemed to Nona. There seemed to be hundreds of girls and so much noise and bustle that it made her head swim. They, too, laughed at the way she spoke, and the little girl she sat next to, a pretty little girl with long golden curls, would not speak to her. By the time they reached home Nona was sick with crying and Belinda was so angry her cheeks were bright red.

Mother led Nona to the fire and took off her coat and cap and gloves. She gave her some hot tea and brown bread and butter; Belinda had some too, and by and by they both felt better.

When they had finished, Mother took out her sewing. The fire was warm, the sound of the needle going in and out was quiet and calm. Nona felt tired but she did not cry any more. She sat on the rug and leant against Mother's knee.

'You'll have to go again tomorrow,' said Belinda.

Then Mother said, 'Why not take Miss Happiness

and Miss Flower to school?'

'They wouldn't be allowed,' said Belinda at once.

'How could I take them?' asked Nona. 'In my pocket?'

'No, in your head,' said Mother, and before they could argue she said, 'If you took them in your pocket that would be breaking the rules, and you mustn't do that, but you could take them in your head.'

'How?' but a watery smile came on Nona's face.

'You say Japanese pictures are scrolls, with painting and writing?'

Nona nodded.

'In school you can learn how to write beautifully and to paint.'

'Can I?'

'You read to us that in Japanese houses they have matting on the floors. You could learn to weave mats on a loom.'

'Like Anne?'

'Certainly. Anne learned to weave at school. Then you can learn to sew. There are all those quilts and cushions to make and the dolls need new kimonos. Miss Lane teaches you to sew nicely. Even Belinda is learning to make tiny careful stitches.'

'I'm not,' said Belinda.

'Do you hear the honourable lady?' whispered Miss Flower.

'Kimonos, quilts, cushions,' said Miss Happiness, her eyes shining.

'Tiny careful stitches!' and together they both sent a fresh wish to Nona: 'O Honourable little Miss Nona, please go to school. Oh, go to school!' And Nona began to think that perhaps school might not be so very dreadful, particularly as Tom said, 'I'll work for you every Saturday until the house is finished.'

It took a long time. 'Saturday after Saturday,' grumbled Tom. Half-term came and went and still the house was not done. 'Children are so slow!' groaned Miss Flower.

That was the first and only time Miss Happiness got cross. 'Slow? They are wonderfully quick,' she cried. 'Quick and kind and clever. Don't you ever let me hear you say things like that again,' cried Miss Happiness, and her little glass eyes flashed.

'We must do the roof,' said Tom one Saturday, and he said, 'In a real house when that is done a bough is put in the chimney and the builders are given beer.'

'Do you like beer?' asked Nona.

'Ginger beer,' said Tom.

'When the roof is made,' said Nona, 'I'll buy you a bottle of ginger beer.' But how was the roof to be made?

'It should be tiles,' said Tom. He had drawn tiles in the plan, tiles like little scallops in rows; now he had to think how he could make them.

176

Miss Happiness and Miss Flower

There was an old tea chest in the garage. It was stamped in big black letters. Tom looked at it. 'It's the right thickness,' he said. He took it to pieces and from two of the sides he cut panels and glued them into place against a ridgepole.

Nona looked at the great black letters. 'But . . .' she began in dismay.

'But what?' asked Tom, as if he could not see anything wrong.

'It looks *horrid!*' said Nona. 'Not a bit like tiles. And why have you put the lettering outside?'

'Why not?' asked Tom.

'It shows.'

'It won't show,' said Tom.

'But it does,' said Nona, almost tearfully.

'Wait and see,' said Tom.

He sounded as if he knew exactly what he was doing, but Miss Flower could not help being anxious too. 'Will it be all right?' she whispered to Miss Happiness. 'Will it?'

'I think it will,' said Miss Happiness.

'Are you sure?'

'Mr Tom has made the house beautifully. He will make a beautiful roof as well. We should trust Mr Tom,' said Miss Happiness.

Miss Flower wanted to trust Tom but she thought it wise to do some wishing as well. 'I wish the house could have a pretty roof. I don't see how it can but I wish it could,' she wished.

'How much money have you got?' Tom asked Nona.

She had four shillings, and Tom went with her to the bookshop, where they bought a large sheet of stiff drawing-paper. Then they bought a pot of dark blue poster paint. Mr Twilfit did up the paper in a roll. 'It's for the dolls' house,' Nona told him.

'It's getting on, hey?' asked Mr Twilfit.

'Very well, thank you,' said Tom coldly, and Mr Twilfit's eyebrows went up and down as he watched Tom walk away out of the shop.

When they got home Tom stretched the paper on his work-table and he and Nona painted it evenly, a deep blue. In the afternoon when it was dry he sat Nona down at the playroom table and told her to cut the paper into long strips, two inches wide. 'Measure carefully,' and he said cheerfully, 'You can manage it.'

Nona looked at the beautiful paper and was not at all sure she could manage it. 'W-won't you do it, Tom?' she asked.

'You must do *some* of the work,' said Tom severely. 'I have to bike down to the wood shop. I need a piece of wood.' He took some more money from Nona and went off.

Nona sat and looked at the paper – she was very afraid she would spoil it. Very carefully she measured off two inches at each side, making dots to mark the width . . . But how can I keep the cutting straight?

thought Nona. Still very carefully, with the big scissors, she started to cut across from dot to dot and, sure enough, the strip was uneven and wandered up and down.

'Silly billy! You'll never do it like that.' Anne had come quietly into the playroom to practise.

'Then *how*?' asked Nona desperately, looking at the dreadful jagged strip she had made. 'Oh, Tom will be so cross,' and she looked as if she were going to cry.

'Look. Fold it,' said Anne, putting down her music.

'Oh, Anne, please help me.'

'You must measure,' said Anne.

'But I *did*. Two inches.'

'Right,' said Anne. 'But you need a knife, not scissors.' She took a knife from Tom's work-table and cut off the uneven piece Nona had left, then measured two inches again, marking with dots as Nona had done, folded the paper, and then slit along the fold; a smooth two-inch strip came off. 'Now try,' said Anne.

'Oh, Anne. You do it.'

'I haven't time.'

'P-please, Anne. I don't want to make Tom cross.'

'Well, I'll fold it. Then you try,' said Anne. 'Come on. It's easy.'

It was easy – 'when you know how,' said Nona. With Anne folding the paper and holding it steady, Nona was able to cut off an even strip.

'And strip after strip,' said Miss Happiness in pride.

'Anne, you have such very clever, neat hands,' Nona was saying.

'So have you, Miss Nona,' said Miss Flower.

When Tom came back the strips were laid out on his table, even and smoothly cut, and he was pleased. 'But now we have to scallop them,' he said. 'Anne, you're the neatest one. You do them.' He did not beg Anne, he ordered her. 'I wish I were a boy,' thought Nona.

'What about my piano practice?' Anne said it as if she would far rather make the scallops.

'Practise afterwards,' said Tom. 'Get the scissors, Nona.'

'They're here,' said Nona, hoping Tom would not look in the wastepaper basket and see the strip she had spoiled.

Anne folded each strip four times and with the scissors cut one edge into even scallops. As soon as they were cut, Nona unfolded the strip and, with a deeper blue pencil, Tom marked a line between each scallop: scallop after scallop, strip after strip. It took longer to mark the lines than to cut the scallops, and when Anne went to the piano to practise, Tom, with Nona to wait on him, was still at work.

After tea Anne helped again. Nona brushed the back of the strips with glue, making them really sticky, and Anne and Tom stuck them one at a time on to the roof panels; they began at the bottom and glued them each a little above the first so that the scallops overlapped. As one row of scallops rose above the other, they began to look very like tiles, and when the roof was covered bottom to top, back and front, Nona and Anne clapped.

'I told you we could trust Mr Tom,' said Miss Happiness.

As Anne and Tom started to make a tiny tiled roof for the niche, Nona slipped out and all by herself went to the grocer. She had to cross the road but, holding her purse very tightly, she crossed it. She was not nearly as afraid now as she had been that first day when she set out for Mr Twilfit's shop. At the grocer's she spent two of her last three ninepences on two bottles of ginger beer; the grocer gave her coloured straws for nothing. On her way home, as she was not sure Anne liked ginger beer, she stopped at a flower barrow and bought a spray of white blossom; she had no money to buy any more.

Miss Happiness and Miss Flower were puzzled when they saw Nona arranging the ginger beer on a tray. 'We should have served tea,' said Miss Flower, and she said longingly, 'In the tea ceremony.' 'Ceremony' is a word Japanese dolls use a lot; it means doing something in a very respectful and special way.

'In England it is the ginger beer ceremony,' said Miss Happiness, and she comforted Miss Flower. 'See, our Miss Nona knows how to arrange flowers almost as we do; she does not put too many in the vase.' Miss Happiness did not know that there had been only one ninepence left.

'And plum blossom means hope,' said Miss Flower.

'It *is* hope,' said Miss Happiness. 'Look, Flower, look!'

Nona had put the dolls on the pretty tray she was carrying to the playroom. She had stopped just inside the door, looking. Now Miss Flower looked too, and 'Aaah!' whispered Miss Flower.

On Tom's work-bench stood the little house with its tiled roof, its tiny hall and the screen walls that slid, its two side walls and the niche. There was, of course, no chimney, but where the chimney might have been Tom had put a twig of green leaves for a bough.

'How happy and gay they all are!' said Miss Happiness.

'One person isn't happy,' said Miss Flower, and suddenly she had a doll shiver. 'Listen,' said Miss Flower.

'Belinda, have some ginger beer.'

'I'm busy.'

'Belinda, come and see the Japanese house with its new roof.'

'I'm very busy.'

Belinda was still feeling left out. The next time she went into the playroom she gave Tom's worktable a good shake, but Tom had made the house so well that nothing moved or broke. 'I wish Japan were at the bottom of the sea!' said Belinda; but it was not Japan that made her miserable, for as soon as she heard the story of Peach Boy again or thought about Little Peach she felt warm and comfortable; it was when she thought about the Japanese dolls' house – 'and Nona!' said Belinda, gritting her teeth – she felt so jealous and cold and hard that she might have been a small iron Belinda.

Chapter 5

Nona was still not very happy about going to school. 'Why, Nona?' asked Mother. 'Belinda doesn't mind and she is younger than you.'

'It's all right for Belinda,' said Nona. 'She has lots of friends.'

'You can have friends.'

'No I can't,' said Nona tearfully.

'Why not?'

The tears overflowed. 'There's only one girl I like and she sits next to me,' sobbed Nona.

'If you like her why should you mind?' asked Mother, mystified, which means she could not understand at all; it certainly was difficult to understand. 'Why should you mind?' asked Mother.

'She's too pretty and stuck-up to speak to me.'

'She means Melly,' said Belinda. 'Melanie Ashton. You know, her mother keeps the hat shop.'

'But Melly's a nice little girl.'

'She won't speak to me.'

'Perhaps she's shy.'

'No, I'm the one who's shy,' wept Nona.

Except for Melly, school was not really so dreadful now. Nona was learning to write and paint and sew, as Mother had said. When she read aloud now it was

184

not in a sing-song, and nobody laughed at her English. Then one day, on the new page of her reading book, she came across a tiny poem. It was so small it might have been made for a dolls' house:

My two plum trees are
So gracious . . .
See, they flower
One now, one later.

Underneath was written: 'Haiku. Japanese poem.' (See note: *Haiku*, p. 216.)

'Are all Japanese poems as little as that?' Nona asked Miss Lane. 'Are they all as little?'

'Not all, but a great many,' said Miss Lane.

'Could I copy it?' asked Nona, and began to tell Miss Lane about Miss Happiness and Miss Flower.

'Is the house finished?' asked Miss Happiness.

'Oh no!' cried Miss Flower, and 'Now I have to make the steps,' said Tom.

The steps were four pieces of wood, the same length but different widths. Glued one on top of the other, they made a set of steps leading up to the front door. 'You can put dolls'-house tubs of flowers each side,' said Tom.

'Is the house finished now?' asked Miss Happiness.

No, it was not finished yet.

Tom stained the frames and the angle pieces a beautiful dark brown. He had painted the walls and the underside of the roof an ivory colour, but the niche he painted pale jade green. Last of all the house was dusted and cleaned, carried into Nona's room from the playroom, and put on the windowsill. 'Now show that to Mr Twilfit!' said Tom.

'First it must be furnished,' said Nona. 'I need scraps of cotton and silk.'

'You haven't got any,' said Belinda.

That was only too true. The pieces in Mother's scrap-bag were bits of flannel and oddments from old cotton dresses. There was some velveteen, but velveteen is thick and heavy for a small doll. 'I need thin bright silk in different colours,' said Nona.

'Well, you can't have it.'

'I know I can't,' said Nona mournfully. She had spent that week's ninepence on extra things for Tom. 'And I need a lamp and a low table, and the book says Japanese people keep their quilts in cupboards with sliding doors. How can I . . .' Nona broke off and sat quite still. 'A cupboard with sliding doors,' she whispered.

'Nona, I'm talking to you,' said Mother. 'I'm asking you if you want any more pudding?' These days Nona often had more pudding, but now she did not answer.

'Nona. Are you dreaming?' Yes, Nona was dreaming – of Melly's pencil-box.

Miss Happiness and Miss Flower

It was a new pencil-box of plain light wood. It had a compartment down the middle and, most fascinating of all, it had a roll top of slatted wood that rolled back as soon as you touched it. 'It would make a perfect little cupboard,' dreamed Nona, 'empty and standing on its side. Perfect!' And then a daring thought came to her: I wonder if Melly would swap it? – Nona had not been in school very long but already she knew all about swapping. Swap, but for what? It would have to be something very beautiful. After lunch Nona went slowly upstairs and pulled out her drawer; next morning when she went to school she wore her silver bangles.

'Oh, how pretty!' said Melly.

Nona had seen Melly looking at the bangles and had pulled the cuff of her blouse back so that they would show more as she let her hand lie on the desk. They clinked gently against one another and their silver shone above the wood of the desk. 'You like them?' whispered Nona.

Melly nodded, and her curls bobbed. Nona slid off the bangles and when Miss Lane was busy she passed them to Melly. '*Very* pretty,' whispered Melly, looking at them.

'You can put them on if you like.'

Now that they had spoken Nona could not think why she and Melly had not spoken before.

Perhaps Mother had been right and Melly was shy; she blushed as she slid the bangles on. They looked beautiful on her pink and white wrist, and 'Very, *very* pretty,' whispered Melly.

Nona felt an ache in her heart; she had had her bangles almost since she was a baby and they reminded her of Coimbatore, but she had the dolls to think of now. 'I'll swap them if you like,' said Nona.

Melly's grey eyes widened. 'But . . . they're silver!' she said.

'Yes, but I'll swap them.'

'For what?'

'For your pencil-box,' said Nona lightly, but her heart was beating.

'Melly Ashton, Nona Fell, are you talking?' asked Miss Lane, but the two heads, Nona's dark one and Melly's with its golden curls, were bent over their desks, and their pens scratched away. Yet, if Miss Lane had noticed, she would have seen that Melly's pencil-box was on Nona's desk and Nona's bangles were on Melly.

Standing on its side in the Japanese dolls' house the pencil box did look like a real cupboard. 'The quilts shall go in the bottom – when I have the quilts,' said Nona. 'The bowls in the top – when I have the bowls.' The rolltop slid backwards and forwards like a real cupboard.

188

Miss Happiness and Miss Flower

'It might have come from Japan,' said Miss Flower, and Miss Happiness said, 'It has "Made in Japan" stamped on it. I saw it.'

'Nona, you are to go into the drawing-room. Mother wants you,' said Anne.

'You have done something,' said Belinda. 'Mrs Ashton is there.'

'Who is Mrs Ashton?' asked Nona.

'Melly's mother,' said Anne.

'What have you done?' asked Belinda.

Mrs Ashton was sitting on a chair by the fire when Nona came in. In her hand she held the bangles.

'They're quite valuable,' she was saying to Mother. 'Real silver. I'm sure you wouldn't want Nona to give them away and I couldn't possibly let Melly accept them.'

'But I didn't give them,' said Nona. 'I swapped them.'

'Swapped them?'

'For Melly's pencil box.'

'A *pencil box*?' Both the mothers stared at Nona as if she were ill.

'But you could buy a pencil box for a shilling or two, you silly child.'

'Not that one,' cried poor Nona. 'There isn't another one like that. Oh, don't you see? That's

189

the only one that will do.'

Mrs Ashton was very like Melly, with the same golden hair and grey eyes, the same smile. Nona had spoken to Melly, and now she found courage again. 'If you would come upstairs,' she said, 'I could show you,' and she slipped her hand into Mrs Ashton's. It was the first time Nona had put her hand into anyone's since she had left Coimbatore.

Mrs Ashton looked at Mother, who nodded. 'Show me,' said Mrs Ashton.

'But Mother will make you give it back,' said Belinda. 'You needn't think she won't.' And sure enough, 'You must give it back,' said Mother.

'But Mrs Ashton wasn't cross,' said Nona.

'All the more reason,' said Mother.

'And Melly didn't mind.'

'But you are not allowed to swap things at school, not expensive things,' said Mother. 'I'm sorry, Nona, but you must keep the rules.'

Very slowly Nona took the pencil box out of the house.

'It is right and proper,' said Miss Happiness with a sigh. 'She must keep the rules.'

Miss Flower did not answer. She was too sad.

Indeed it seemed that the dolls' house was not getting on at all. On the way to school Nona and Belinda passed a shop where, in the window, four dolls'-house tea sets in delicate flowered china were set out. 'What about those?' asked Belinda.

'It's bowls, not cups, I need,' said Nona.

'There's a sugar bowl.'

'Only one.' Each set had two cups, a teapot, a milk jug and a sugar bowl.

'You could knock the handles off the cups,' said Belinda cheerfully.

'And give them something chipped!' said Nona. She knew without being told that Miss Flower would not like that. 'Anyway, they are four shillings and sixpence each,' she said.

Another shop had table mats in fine, fine bamboo. 'Like dolls'-house matting,' said Nona, 'and Japanese houses always have matting on the floor.' But the mats were a shilling each, 'and I should need two,' said Nona. In the same shop as the tea sets was a round dolls'-house table in dark wood. 'If Tom cut the legs shorter it would look Japanese. Oh, I don't know where to begin!' said Nona, and pressed her face against the glass of one shop, then another. In the end she bought the table, and Tom, with his smallest saw, cut the legs down for her so that the table was only an inch from the floor. It was just right for a Japanese table, but it looked bleak and plain in the empty room. 'It will *never* be furnished,' said Nona.

*

Miss Flower was terribly alarmed. 'You heard what she said,' cried Miss Flower, and if she could have wrung her little plaster hands she would. 'Never be furnished! Oh, we're only dolls. What can we do?'

'Wish,' said Miss Happiness. She was still smiling. Perhaps that was because her smile was painted on her face, but it made Miss Flower angry.

'What's the good of wishing?'

'You never know,' said Miss Happiness.

You never know. Sometimes when things seem farthest off they are quite near. Next morning Melly came to school with a small bundle. She put it on Nona's desk. 'Mother sent you this,' she said.

The bundle was wrapped in a piece of soft paper. Inside were scraps and pieces and snippets of silk, satin and taffeta, in pink and scarlet, blue and lemon colour, white, green, purple and mauve.

'But . . . but . . . how did she *get* them?' asked Nona.

'Well, she does make hats,' said Melly, and laughed at Nona's face. 'These are bits left over. And she says if your mother will let you come to tea she, my mother, will help you with the cushions and quilts. She's a very good sewer,' said Melly.

Nona hardly knew if she were standing on her head or her heels. To go to tea with Melly; to make the quilts and cushions; to have this heap of soft and beautiful stuffs! 'What is the matter with Nona?' asked Father, who happened to be looking out of the window as

Nona and Belinda came back from school. 'She looks as if she were dancing on the pavement.'

Then, at the beginning of the holidays, it was Easter.

Nona had not kept Easter before. She had never seen Easter eggs or Easter rabbits or chickens. 'Your own father has sent me some money from Coimbatore,' said Mother, 'to buy you all Easter eggs. Ten shillings for each of the others,' she told Nona, 'a pound for you.'

'A *pound!*' said Belinda, her eyes round.

'Is that twenty shillings?' asked Nona. She was trying to do a sum in her head.

'You could buy an enormous huge great Easter egg for that,' said Belinda. 'One of those huge chocolate ones with chocolate and chickens inside.'

'Oh no!' cried Nona.

'No?'

'Please, please no,' – in her agitation Nona could hardly speak – 'I don't want an Easter egg.'

'Not want an egg for *Easter?*'

'No. At least, only a tiny one, about sixpence.'

'Well, what is it you want?'

'Four tea sets,' said Nona, 'and two table mats.'

'What extraordinary things to want.'

'I want them,' said Nona certainly.

On Easter Sunday, as they were coming back from church, Melly came up the road to the gate. She was carrying a package tied with yellow ribbon. 'Why, Nona! She has brought you another Easter egg!' but it was a queer shape for an Easter egg, for the package was long and thin. Before Nona opened it she knew what it was, and her fingers began to tremble. 'It's your pencil box.'

'Not mine,' said Melly. 'It's the same as mine. Mother bought it in London in the same shop. Happy Easter,' said Melly, and ran off.

Happy Easter!

'In Japan we have the New Year Festival,' said Miss Flower, 'when fathers and mothers dress the children in their best clothes and take them to visit the shrines and give them money.'

'Lots of money,' said Miss Happiness.

'That is something like this,' said Miss Flower.

'But I like Easter,' said Miss Happiness, and she said, 'We have the Star Festival, of course, and the Boys' Festival, when the boys have paper carp fish and play games.'

'But I like Easter,' said Miss Flower, and she said, 'We have the Doll Festival, when the festival dolls are brought out and the little girls put them up on steps covered with red cloth.'

'I think this is a doll festival day,' said Miss Happiness, smiling.

Indeed, it seemed to be, for the Japanese dolls'

house was almost finished at last. The pencil box stood against the wall; the quilts were rolled up on its bottom shelf. Nona had been to tea with Melly on two or three Wednesday afternoons when the hat shop was shut, and after tea they had sewed quilts and pillows, pale pink for Miss Flower, while Miss Happiness had blue.

On the Tuesday after Easter, Nona had hurried over breakfast and run all the way to the shops in case the tea sets were sold, but they were still in the window and she had been able to buy all four.

'*Four* tea sets?' Belinda had asked.

'So that I can get four bowls.'

'And waste all the cups?'

'I have to,' said Nona sadly.

'Christopher Columbus!' said Belinda, just like Tom.

Nona put the cups, the jugs and all but one teapot on one side, but the four sugar bowls and all the plates and saucers and the one teapot she arranged on the top shelf of the pencil box; with its green leaves and pink flowers the china looked Japanese.

Japanese people eat their food with polished sticks called chopsticks: Nona cut pine needles into inch lengths to make some, and they were put beside the china. From the table mat shop she chose two mats in fine cream-coloured bamboo; they almost covered the floor when they were put down. On the matting were cushions made from Mrs Ashton's bright silks;

Nona set them round the low table.

'It must be ready now,' said Belinda, but Nona shook her head.

Tom helped to make a lamp from an empty cotton reel. (See note: *The Lamp*, p. 218.) He ran a flex up through it with a tiny electric bulb and Nona made a paper shade to fit it. She cut a strip of stiff paper, painted it deep pink and joined it into a circle with sticky-tape. 'And I'm going to model a lantern in clay, like the Japanese stone lanterns, for the garden,' she said.

'What garden?' asked Belinda.

'The garden I am going to make.'

Every Japanese house has a firebox. (See note: *Firebox*, p. 218.) Nona made hers from a matchbox, painted dark brown and filled with shining red paper from a Christmas cracker. Tom put another of his tiny bulbs in it and joined the flex to the lamp. When it was lit the firebox seemed to glow.

'Now we need a scroll,' said Nona, 'and I must put flowers in the niche.'

'Well, put some,' said Belinda, but Nona said, 'I have to learn about them first.'

'Learn about flowers? Pooh! What is there to learn? Oh Nona, you are so slow.'

'*Please* leave Honourable Miss Nona *alone*,' wished Miss Happiness and Miss Flower. 'Leave her. She is doing things in the Japanese way.' (See note: *Flower Arranging*, p. 218.)

196

Miss Happiness and Miss Flower

Flowers, in Japan, can have meanings: pine branches are for strength; plum blossom means new hope; irises are used for ceremony; while the peony is the King of Flowers.

'Irises and peonies are too big for a dolls' house,' said Anne.

Of course they were too big, but now, in April and May, as Mother and Anne had told Nona, there were wild flowers everywhere in the grass and along the hedges and in the fields and woods just outside the town. Nona had never seen anything as lovely and every day she discovered something else; wild violets did for irises and wood sorrel or anemones made white peonies, while eyebright looked like dolls'-house lilies. In front of the Japanese dolls' house she made a path of sand and bordered it with cowries, tiny shells she had brought from Coimbatore. At the foot of the steps she put two little china-blue egg-cups, the kind that are like tubs, and filled them with lady's-slipper. Then she begged a big old meat tin from Mother and put it on the window-sill beside the house; she covered it with a layer of earth and moss. Following the pictures of Japanese gardens in Mr Twilfit's big book, she arranged a path with flat stones, and a little heap of pebbles to hold the shell that Anne had given her. The shell was filled with water and made a pool, and by it Nona planted some tufts of grass to look like bamboos, and tiny flowers to look like bushes. 'Japanese gardens have

197

to look natural, like hills and lakes and streams,' she said, and she made a stream of bits of broken looking-glass set in the moss, and by it she set the clay lantern she had modelled. Miss Lane had let her fire it in the school kiln and it had a gloss on it like stone. It looked like a toadstool with a hole in the hood. When a bit of birthday cake candle was put in, it shone over the garden at night, 'and it's quite safe,' said Nona. 'The clay won't catch on fire.' The garden was beautiful, 'but I do wish I had some trees,' said Nona.

'There aren't trees as small as that,' said Belinda.

There was no scroll yet, but in the niche Nona put a vase of flowers. For the vase she used her ivory thimble, and for flowers she chose a scarlet pimpernel – 'That's a peony, the King of Flowers' – and with it were stalks of grass – 'Dolls'-house bamboo,' said Nona. 'Bamboo means luck.'

'Yes. Yes!' breathed Miss Flower.

It was finished. 'They can move in tomorrow,' said Nona.

'Tomorrow!' Miss Happiness felt as if all of her were warmed by the firebox, but Miss Flower felt as if she might crack. 'I shan't close my eyes all night,' she said. They could not close in any case, but she meant that she would not sleep.

'Our house!' said Miss Happiness. 'Tomorrow we move into our house.'

'Yes!' Then Miss Flower stopped. 'We haven't

moved in yet. Suppose . . . suppose something were to happen and prevent . . .'

'But what could?' asked Miss Happiness.

Miss Flower did not know, but all at once she felt cold.

'Can I have a feast?' Nona was asking.

'You can ask some people to tea,' said Mother.

'Can I ask Mr Twilfit and Miss Lane and Mrs Ashton and Melly? And you and Father and Anne and Tom – and Belinda of course?'

'I'm not coming,' said Belinda.

'Why should Nona have people to tea?' asked Belinda, and kicked the corner of the table leg. 'It's not her birthday.'

'Now, Belinda . . .'

Belinda kicked the corner of the table leg again.

'If you do that,' said Mother, 'you can go upstairs at once.' Then she put her hand on Belinda's shoulder and said gently, 'Belinda. Nona has worked so hard. Don't spoil it'; but Belinda shook Mother's hand off, kicked the table leg harder than ever, and ran upstairs.

It was no wonder that Miss Flower trembled.

Chapter 6

The dolls were to have a feast too. 'A tea party,' said Nona.

'A tea ceremony,' said Miss Flower.

Belinda's dolls'-house food was a cardboard ham glued on a plate, some plaster fish glued on another and a plaster pink and white cake. 'That won't do at all,' said Nona, and she went to see Mr Twilfit to find out about a Japanese feast. In the end a beautiful little feast was set out on the low table: a bowl of rice made of snipped-up white thread – nothing else was fine enough; a saucer of bamboo shoots made of finely chopped grass; a saucer of pink and white sugar cakes made from crumbs of meringue cut round; and some paint-water tea. '*Green* tea?' asked Belinda.

'Japanese people drink green tea.'

'Huh! You know everything,' said Belinda, who was in a very bad temper. 'Everything!' she said. 'But there's one thing you don't know.'

'What is that?'

'Wait and see,' said Belinda, and she looked angry and pleased at the same time.

The dolls were dressed in new kimonos; Father had given Nona an empty cigar box and she kept their clothes in that. Mrs Ashton had made Miss Happiness a white kimono embroidered with a tiny pattern of leaves, over an under-dress of pale yellow silk, and with a sash of blue. Miss Flower's was coral pink over an under-dress of delicate violet colour, and her sash was pale green. Their hair was brushed and their socks and sandals had been painted. Tom had carefully patched the chip on Miss Flower's ear with some white paint and repainted Miss Happiness's shoe. 'We look quite new,' said Miss Happiness.

'Is it really going to happen?' asked Miss Flower. Even though she was dressed she could not quite believe it.

'It really is,' said Miss Happiness.

In the dolls' house the house lamp and the firebox were switched on, and the lantern was lit. In the real house the front door bell rang, and 'It really is,' said Miss Flower.

Everyone brought presents. Melly had a packet of water flowers, the Japanese paper flowers that uncurl into brightly coloured patterns when you drop them into water. 'You can put one or two in the shell for water lilies,' said Melly.

Mrs Ashton brought a tiny paper sunshade she had once found in a cracker. 'It's from Japan,' she said.

'Quite right,' said Miss Happiness and Miss Flower.

Miss Lane had brought her present in a matchbox; it was a length of paper three inches long and an inch and a quarter wide – if you measure with your ruler you will see how big it was. Top and bottom it was held on two matchsticks that Miss Lane had sandpapered smooth and fine; the paper could roll up on them, and on the paper, in fine, fine painting, was some white plum blossom and a bird; the bird was no bigger than a pea. There was some writing too, but so small that to read it you almost needed a magnifying glass, and Nona cried, 'It's my poem!'

> My two plum trees are
> So gracious . . .
> See, they flower
> One now, one later.

'Who could have done it?' asked Belinda.

'It looks like a fairy but I think it was Miss Lane,' said Nona.

'A scroll! A right size Japanese scroll!' said Miss Happiness.

'But shouldn't the writing have been Japanese?' asked Miss Flower doubtfully.

'Not in England. That wouldn't have been polite,' said Miss Happiness, and Miss Flower was satisfied.

Nona hung the scroll in the niche. 'Soon I must make you a new one,' said Miss Lane. 'This one is for spring but you should change them with the seasons.' Miss Happiness and Miss Flower gave two doll's nods, which means they nodded though you could not see them, and said, 'Quite right.'

Anne had made two pleated fans, no bigger than your finger nail. 'It says they should wear fans for the tea ceremony,' said Anne.

'Very right,' and Miss Happiness and Miss Flower were glad when the fans were tucked into their sashes.

Tom had made two tiny pairs of wooden clogs of the kind Japanese ladies use to walk in in the mud, fastened with a loop of scarlet cotton. 'O Honourable Tom!' said the dolls.

All the presents were beautiful but the best of all was Mr Twilfit's. He had brought two trees. 'Are those *trees?*' asked Belinda. 'Real *trees?*'

'A pine and a willow,' said Nona looking at the labels. She sounded dizzy, as indeed she was, for how many people have heard of or seen a pine tree ten inches high and a willow only seven? 'But – they're real, alive!' cried Nona.

'Quite real,' said Mr Twilfit, his eyebrows going up and down.

'I didn't know,' said Miss Flower with great respect, 'that there was anything like that in England.'

'England is indeed a most honourable country,' said Miss Happiness.

'They are grown for people who make sink gardens,' said Mr Twilfit. 'Dwarf gardens in sinks or basins.' Everyone was so enchanted that he was beginning to feel shy and his eyebrows grew still. 'Better plant 'em,' said Mr Twilfit abruptly, and he turned away to look at the house. As he looked he forgot to be shy and his eyebrows began to go up and down again. 'The President couldn't have made it any better,' he said to Tom.

The best of a dolls'-house garden is that it takes only five minutes to plant a tree. Nona planted the pine by the shell, the willow by the stream. They made the garden look exactly like the gardens in the book.

Then Nona turned to the dolls. She made them bow to the company – which means all the people there – and said, 'Miss Happiness and Miss Flower, will you come into your home?' but before they could be made to walk up the path bordered with shells and past the tubs of lady's-slipper, Belinda spoke:

'Not Miss Flower,' said Belinda. 'She's mine.'

'Belinda! Belinda! You're not going to spoil it?'

'Yes I am,' said Belinda.

Mother had taken Belinda to the playroom to talk to her. Belinda stood hard and angry by the table; her cheeks were red and her eyes very blue and bright. She argued with Mother.

'On the parcel it said "The *Misses* Fell". You said Anne was too old for dolls and we could have one each. You *said* so,' argued Belinda.

'But that was long ago,' said Mother.

204

'Miss Flower's mine,' said Belinda. 'You can't take her away from me.'

'It's just that you don't want Nona to have her,' said Mother sadly. 'Oh, Belinda! Belinda!'

'I don't care,' said Belinda.

'That's true,' said Mother. 'You never cared or thought about Miss Flower or wanted her.'

'I want her now,' said Belinda, and she took Miss Flower and threw her into her own dolls' house and slammed the door.

Belinda ate her tea very quickly. Her cheeks were still red, her eyes an even brighter blue. She talked a great deal and said funny things to make everyone laugh, but it was an odd thing that nobody laughed at them except Belinda. No one else really talked and nobody ate very much. Nona ate nothing at all and her face looked white and sick with disappointment; Belinda saw Melly steal a hand into hers, and 'Can I have another meringue?' asked Belinda; and when she put it into her mouth she laughed and blew the sugar crumbs all over the table.

'I think we will go into the drawing-room,' said Mother. 'Belinda, you had better finish your tea alone.'

In the dolls' house the lantern threw a soft light into the house where the front was open and the screens had been slid back to show the garden; the lantern made a reflection in the looking-glass stream and gave the tiny trees real shadows.

Miss Happiness knelt on her cushion in front of the table set ready for the tea ceremony, but she did not touch any of the tea; opposite her was the blue cushion, empty, and a little empty bowl.

'Oh, why couldn't Miss Belinda have taken me?' mourned Miss Happiness. That would have been dreadful enough, but she was stuffed fuller than Miss Flower and her plaster had not been chipped. 'Miss Flower wanted the house even more than I did,' mourned Miss Happiness. 'She was always frightened.' If dolls could have tears I am sure they would have rolled down Miss Happiness's plaster cheeks. 'Oh, I'm afraid!' cried Miss Happiness. 'I'm afraid that Miss Flower will not be able to bear it. I'm afraid she will break.'

There was certainly not a sound or movement in Belinda's dolls' house; not the smallest doll rustle.

When tea was over the guests quietly went home. 'Shan't we play any games?' asked Belinda, astonished.

'We would rather not play with you,' said Anne.

'Because you're a little rotter,' said Tom.

Belinda put out her tongue at him, which was not at all pretty for it still had crumbs of meringue sticking to it.

'You had better go upstairs,' said Mother.

Miss Happiness and Miss Flower

*

Nona put out the lantern, and switched off the lamp and the firebox. She washed the bowls and platters and put them away. Then she unrolled the blue quilts – the pink ones stayed in the pencil box cupboard – and gently she laid Miss Happiness down and covered her up. Miss Happiness looked very small and lonely in the big room and when Nona slid the paper screens shut they made a s-s-ssh like a sigh.

Belinda sang and danced all the time she was going to bed; it was odd then that the house should have felt so silent. Tom and Anne had gone to their rooms to do their homework; usually they did it with friendly calls from room to room, but now they shut their doors. Nona had got into bed without a word and lay with her face turned to the wall. Downstairs in the drawing-room Father and Mother talked in low tones. 'What a fuss about a doll,' said Belinda.

No one answered. She half thought of going to the dolls' house and taking Miss Flower out and throwing her at Nona, but 'I'll be darned if I will,' said Belinda.

Saying 'be darned' like Tom made her feel very big and important and she shouted and gargled as she did her teeth.

The house still stayed quite silent.

*

Belinda always went to sleep as soon as her head touched the pillow; only once, long ago, when she had had a cold, she had woken up in the night with a sore throat and stuffy nose. She had not got a cold now but there seemed to be something the matter.

She tossed and turned and twisted. She heard Anne and Tom go to bed, and then later – hours and hours, thought Belinda – Mother and Father came up.

'I can't go to slee-ep,' called Belinda. It did not sound loud, it sounded like a bleat, but Mother did not come in or give Belinda a glass of hot milk as she had that other night. Mother went into her room and shut the door.

Belinda was so surprised that she got out of bed and padded in her bare feet to Mother's door and knocked. Mother opened it a crack. 'I can't go to slee-ep,' wailed Belinda.

'I'm not surprised,' said Mother and shut the door.

Then Belinda felt something queer in her eyes and in her chest, as if something hot and aching were gathering and coming up. Quietly she went back to bed and burrowed under the clothes, but up the aching came until it spilled over; it was wet and splashed down on her pillow. It was tears.

'It's no good crying.' How often Belinda had said that to Nona, but sometimes it is good. As the tears soaked into Belinda's pillow the hard angry feeling seemed to melt away, and 'I'm sorry,' sobbed Belinda, 'sorry.' But she did not cry herself to sleep, she cried herself awake, perhaps more awake than she had ever been in her life.

It is lonely for a little girl to lie awake in the dark when everyone is sleeping, and then Belinda remembered she was not the only one who was alone.

Miss Happiness was alone in the Japanese dolls' house, and what of Miss Flower? Miss Flower was worse than alone in Belinda's dolls' house. Belinda had thrown her in and slammed the door. I threw her quite hard, thought Belinda. Did she break? And suddenly Belinda was more miserable than ever, so miserable that she could not stay in bed any longer; she had to see what had happened to Miss Flower. 'What did I do to Miss Flower?' asked Belinda, and more tears ran down her face. She got out of bed and tiptoed into the playroom.

When the dolls'-house door banged shut on Miss Flower I think she fainted. That was just as well, for when Belinda found her she was lying on her back with one foot in the air, her head under a broken chair and her hand in the dolls'-house wastepaper basket in which there was an earwig. Her kimono and hair were covered with dust, and the chip had opened again under the white paint into a trickle of plaster, but Miss Flower knew nothing until she felt a gentle hand come in and lift her. It was so gentle that she thought it was

Nona's; she never dreamed it could be Belinda.

Very gently Belinda lifted Miss Flower, put her leg straight, dusted her hair and clothes and shook the earwig off on to the carpet. Then she stood holding Miss Flower in her hand and wondering what to do next. Suddenly she tiptoed into Nona's room, where the Japanese dolls' house was shut and dark on the window-sill.

As Belinda slid the screen walls back they did not make a s-s-sh like a sigh, but a s-s-sh as if there were a secret – as indeed there was; for carefully, with two fingers, Belinda opened the pencil box cupboard and took out the pink quilts; carefully she unrolled them – and how clumsy her fingers were, though she tried to be careful. She unrolled the quilts beside Miss Happiness, and carefully put Miss Flower in and covered her. Then she slid the screens shut and tiptoed back to bed.

She was quite comfortable now and she went to sleep at once.

Chapter 7

It was a very strange thing. When Belinda had gone to bed nobody had seemed to like her. Now in the morning everybody liked her very much.

Nona came running into her room. She looked a new Nona now with her eyes shining and her hair flying, her cheeks pink. She jumped on Belinda's bed and in a moment they were hugging one another. 'I never thought we would do that!' said Belinda.

Mother came and gave her a kiss. Father ruffled her hair on his way to the bathroom and at breakfast everyone seemed to take her part.

'I had Miss Happiness *and* Miss Flower. It wasn't fair,' said Nona.

'We should have seen Belinda wasn't left out,' said Anne.

'I'll make you a Japanese dolls' house if you like,' said Tom, but as the days went on Belinda did not really want a Japanese dolls' house, though she liked playing now and then with Nona's. 'But I wish there were something for me,' said Belinda.

It was summer now. They all wore thin clothes and sun hats, went bathing and ate ice cream. The shops were full of cherries, then of peaches; perhaps it was the peaches that gave Nona her idea.

Miss Happiness and Miss Flower spent much of their time in the garden and took it in turns to carry the paper sunshade. Nona put clover for chrysanthemums in the flower vase in the niche – chrysanthemums are Japan's own flowers – and planted them in the egg-cups by the steps. The tiny willow tree blossomed.

Miss Happiness and Miss Flower had summer kimonos of pale blue, and Anne wove them two flat hats of yellow straw. Mr Twilfit, Mrs Ashton and Melly often came to visit them. Miss Lane sent a scroll for summer, with a lotus flower and a butterfly. In the evenings the garden lantern shone pale in the dusk. 'How beautiful it is,' said Miss Happiness, and Miss Flower had a moment of being frightened; her chip had been painted over again but she still could not forget the night in the dusty dolls' house. 'Miss Nona has opened our travelling box again. Why? Why?' she asked; but Nona was only studying the piece of paper that said 'I send you Miss Happiness, Miss Flower and Little Peach.'

'Mother, did you ever write to Great-Aunt Lucy Dickinson?' asked Nona.

'Why! I forgot!' said Mother.

'Could a letter get to America fast?' asked Nona.

'Of course it could, by air.'

'If I write to Great-Aunt Lucy Dickinson, will you help me to buy the stamp? It's a secret,' said Nona.

Miss Happiness and Miss Flower

The stamp cost one shilling and threepence, nearly two whole ninepences. This is the letter Nona sent:

'Dear Great-Aunt Lucy Dickinson,
    Miss Happiness and Miss Flower are well. We have made them a new house, but where is Little Peach? He wasn't in the box. Please send him.
    From your loving niece, Nona Fell.
    P.S. When you answer please put "Privit".'

That was how she spelt 'private'; as you know, she had not been at school very long. She wanted the answer marked 'private' so that no one else would open it. Then she added something else:

    'P.P.S. Please send him quickly.'

After Nona had posted the letter she began to look in the shops to see how big the peaches were.

It was three weeks later, a hot sunny morning, and they all had peaches for breakfast.

    'Christopher Columbus!' said Tom. 'Is it someone's birthday?'

    'Yes,' said Mother, and Nona giggled.

    Miss Happiness and Miss Flower were at breakfast too. They had paint-water tea on their table, tomatoes which were berries and white cotton rice;

213

they ate with new pine needle chopsticks. There were fresh trefoil flowers in the vase – trefoil looks like dolls'-house yellow chrysanthemums – and everything was extra fresh and tidy. '*Is* it a birthday?' asked Tom.

Miss Happiness and Miss Flower had their heads bent over their rice, but their glass eyes looked as if they were twinkling.

The biggest peach was Belinda's. It was so big that it looked as if it were spilling over her plate. 'Hey, I ought to have that one!' said Father.

'It's Belinda's,' said Mother, and Nona gave another giggle.

Mother showed Belinda how to slip her knife in to slit it, but as Belinda touched it, the peach seemed to wobble, then came in half. Belinda's eyes grew rounder and rounder; for there, in the middle of the peach, was a boy doll baby.

'A *Japanese* boy doll baby,' said Miss Happiness and Miss Flower.

He was little and fat, perhaps two inches high, wearing nothing at all, but with black hair – there was a piece of paper over it to protect it from the peach juice but Belinda snatched it off. His eyes were black glass slits and he had a smile just like Miss Happiness.

Belinda stared and stared. Then, 'How?' she cried. 'How?'

214

Miss Happiness and Miss Flower

'Never mind how,' said Mother, and Nona said, 'Who is it?'

With her eyes like bright blue saucers Belinda whispered, 'It's . . . It's Little Peach.'

Notes

Names. The names of Japanese girls always end in 'ko'.

'Happiness' can be translated as 'Sachi', so her name in Japanese would be 'Sachiko'.

'Flower' is 'Hano', so Miss Flower's name would be 'Hanoko', or, with the title 'Miss', 'Hanoko san'.

Star Festival. In Japanese this is called 'Panabapar' and is held in the evening of the seventh day of the seventh month.

As Nona said, it is in memory of two lovers separated on earth. Their spirits are in two stars and on this night they are allowed to meet across the Milky Way.

The wish papers are sold in the shops; they are of soft paper coloured yellow or red or green and are twisted up and hung on the good luck bamboos. Often children just brush the words 'River of Heaven'.

Kneeling. No Japanese girl of good manners would remain standing when there were elders or guests present. She would also kneel to serve tea or food.

The cushions are flat, stuffed with wadded cotton, almost like little eiderdowns.

Haiku. The haiku is a tiny verse form in which

216

Miss Happiness and Miss Flower

Japanese poets have been working for hundreds of years. They have only seventeen syllables (a syllable is a word or part of a word that makes one sound: for instance, 'shut' is one syllable, 'sha-dow' is two); as you can imagine they are very difficult to write and to translate.

As Miss Lane said, there are different haiku for different times of year (though on the scrolls a proverb or a single word is often used instead of a poem). In case you want to make up haiku or use them on scrolls, I give four different ones for Spring, Summer, Autumn and Winter:

> Spring: My two plum trees are
> So gracious . . .
> See, they flower
> One now, one later.

> Summer: What a peony . . .
> Demanding to be
> Measured
> By my little fan!

> Autumn: Cruel autumn wind
> Cutting to the
> Very bones . . .
> Of my poor scarecrow.

Tales from the Dolls' House

>   Winter: Three loveliest things
>   Moonlight . . . cherry-
>   Bloom . . . Now I go
>   To see silent snow.

But you may like to make up your own.

Firebox. Each Japanese room has one of these, called a hibachi. They are lacquered wood outside, earthenware lined, and they glow with a few pieces of charcoal in a bed of ashes. The doors slide open and you can warm your hands or boil a kettle for tea or rice. Very often in real houses the fireboxes are sunk in the floor.

Flower Arranging. Japanese girls of good family spend some months in learning how to arrange flowers, for Japanese flower arrangement – Ikebana – is an art.

In one side of every room is the tokonoma or niche. It is a place of honour as the fireplace is in Western homes. Its floor is raised higher than the rest of the room and it is here that the flowers are placed, only one or two, with twigs and leaves arranged in a pattern . . . and every flower or branch has its meaning.

The Lamp. The house lamp was made from a cotton reel. Tom stained the empty reel dark brown to make the stand, then ran a flex up through the hole in the

218

reel; a small size bulb fitted into the top, and Nona made a shade of tracing paper and joined it into a circle with sticky-tape. Tom cut a groove round the top of the cotton reel on which it could stand, and the lamp was done.

Little Plum

Chapter 1

Once upon a time there were two little Japanese dolls whose names were Miss Happiness and Miss Flower. They belonged to a girl called Nona Fell and they were her dearest possessions. Long ago – 'Nearly a year ago,' said Nona – when she had first come from India to live in Topmeadow with her cousins, the dolls had arrived too in a Christmas parcel from Great-Aunt Lucy Dickinson. No one knew anything about them but their names, which were written on a piece of paper in Great-Aunt Lucy Dickinson's spidery handwriting, but the two foreign little dolls had looked as forlorn, cold and homesick as Nona herself. In settling them in she had somehow settled herself.

Miss Happiness and Miss Flower were only five inches high; they were made of white plaster, their bodies of rag but, as Nona said, they were people. Even Nona's cousin Tom admitted that. Their eyes were slits of black glass, they had delicate plaster noses and red painted mouths. Their hair was real, black and straight, cut in a fringe. Miss Flower was a little taller and thinner, Miss Happiness's cheeks were fatter and her red mouth was painted in a smile. Both of them wore kimonos and had a sash high under their arms, folded over into a heavy pad at the back. On their feet were painted sandals. When this story begins they had not met Little Plum. In any case her story begins with the children – Nona and her cousins, Anne, Tom and Belinda – their surname was Fell too – it begins with the children and the House Next Door.

Nona and Belinda's bedroom windows looked straight into the House Next Door. The children always called it that because it had no name, besides it was so very much next door that its windows and the Fells' had only a few yards between them. That was the Fells' fault, as Father said. Two years ago they had to build on to their house. 'When we bought it,' said Father – long, long ago when Anne was a baby – 'we didn't know we were going to have all of you!' A playroom had been built and over it two bedrooms for Nona and Belinda to have as their own, and it was this that brought the two houses so close. There was a hedge between them, though it was not very high, and there was, of course, the ilex tree. It was the only ilex in the road and the Fells were proud of it – a great old tree that was almost evergreen because the old leaves only dropped when the next ones were ready to take their place in August. It grew between the back corner of the Fells' house and the House Next Door. Its trunk was in the Fells' garden but its roots and its branches had spread; indeed, some of these almost tapped the next-door upstairs windows. 'But it belongs to us,' said Belinda jealously. Father had wanted to lop its branches, or even to cut it down, but Mother would not let him. 'It's beautiful,' she said, 'and it does give both houses a little privacy.'

Mother and Father did not really like the House Next Door being so close, but Belinda and Nona liked to look into the rooms over the way. 'But I wish there was somebody in them,' said Belinda. It had been empty for a long, long time and the windows had slowly become so dirty that the children could not see past them, while the roses that grew up the wall had twined right over them. 'It's getting derelict,' said Mother. Derelict means shabby, forgotten, falling to bits, and it was sad that the House Next Door must become that. 'Why doesn't somebody buy it?' asked Belinda.

'I expect the price is too high,' said Father.

'And I expect it would take a lot of money,' said Mother, 'to keep up a house like that.'

It was true that the Fells' house and garden would have fitted into half of the gracious white house that had a garden in front with a lawn and flower beds and a gravel drive round them, and a big garden behind.

'There are eighteen windows just in its front – I counted,' said Belinda. 'And in our house live Mother and Father, Anne, Tom, Nona and me – six people,' which was not counting Mrs Bodger who came to clean every day, while in the House Next Door lived no one at all.

Tales from the Dolls' House

'Poor house, becoming derelict,' said Nona.

Nona was nine years old, a dark, thin child. Belinda was eight, a rough, tough little girl with curly fair hair. Anne was fifteen, Tom twelve. Anne, Tom and Belinda had lived in Topmeadow all their lives. It was the suburb of a country market town, not far from London, and it was pretty, with wide streets, houses with gardens, old cottages. It still had its village High Street and its great park, as English villages have, though the park belonged to the town now. The children thought it the best place in the world to live in and it seemed a waste that the House Next Door should be empty.

Then one September morning Belinda was late. That was not uncommon; she by no means always got up when she was told, and this morning, leaving out washing, not doing up her zip, or tying her shoe laces, she had just pulled her jersey over her head and was giving a hasty brush to her hair when she stopped, the brush still in her hand; a lorry had drawn up at the gate of the House Next Door and men in overalls with ladders, planks and buckets were getting out. Belinda watched while the men came up the path and one of them took a key out of his pocket and opened the front door. Then she saw another thing. A second man had planted a notice board by the hedge. Belinda read it and then, with the brush still in her hand, she tumbled down the stairs and burst into the dining room.

'Guess what?' she shouted. 'The House Next Door is sold.'

Mother, Anne, Tom, Nona all looked up at her but Father only turned over a page of his newspaper, and said, 'Didn't I tell you? It was sold a month ago.'

'Father!' said Belinda, and they all bombarded him with questions.

'What's their name?'

'Who are they?'

'When are they coming?'

'Where do they come from?'

And Belinda beseeched, 'Have they any children? Have they?'

Father read a little more, ate another piece of toast, drank a little coffee, while Belinda danced in her chair with impatience. When at last he did speak, all he said was: 'I suggest, Belinda, you do up your zip.'

Belinda did up her zip.

'And your shoe laces.'

Belinda tied her laces.

'And go upstairs and finish brushing your hair. Yes, and you might wash your face,' Father called up after her. 'I can see you had cocoa last night for supper.'

When Belinda came down, neat and tidy, Father had turned another page. She had to wait, but at last he said, 'I believe their name is Jones.'

'That's a good ordinary name,' said Mother.

'Ah, but they are not ordinary Joneses, they are Tiffany Joneses.'

A double-barrelled name, but it sounded most impressive; in fact, she could hardly say it. 'Stiffany Jones,' she said the first time.

'Tiffany Jones,' Nona corrected her, and then said thoughtfully, 'It makes Fell seem very plain.'

'He has mines in the Far East; firms in Burma and Japan,' said Father.

'It sounds rich,' said Nona.

'They must be rich,' said Belinda, 'to pay the high price.'

'We don't think about whether people are rich or not,' said Mother, which was not entirely true. Nona and Belinda were to think about it a great deal in the weeks to come, but now there was something else in which they were far more interested.

'Have they any children?' Belinda asked again.

Chapter 2

The House Next Door was made new. 'And how new!' said Belinda. All that autumn other boards appeared: Mason and Perry Ltd, Builders; Goss and Gomm, Central Heating; Palmer Green Ltd, Electrical Engineers. Men swarmed in and over the house from the garden to the roof, and the whole road was filled with the sound of knocking and hammering. A concrete mixer turned. Rubble and old wood, pulled-out fireplaces, pipes, cooking stove and cisterns were dumped on the lawn. Lorries came and went; the gas people arrived and a telephone van; and the pavement was taken up. Soon the ilex was covered with dust, and more dust with smells and noise came over the hedge into the Fells' house. Mother said it was almost unbearable, but Belinda loved it. She and Nona watched all day, every day, and every day they had something new to report.

'It gets intresinger and intresinger,' said Belinda.

A fireplace with a white mantel went in; 'Marble,' Nona told Belinda. The floors were sanded with a machine that made the worst noise and dust of all. Then they were repolished. Doors and windows, skirting and banisters were painted white. 'The House Next Door has two staircases,' said Belinda. She went in and out and had made friends with the workmen, but Nona was too shy; she only watched.

Then other new boards appeared: Martin Moresby, Decorators, and Hall, Jones and Hall, Perfect Landscape Gardeners. Belinda was not allowed in any more; pale satined wallpapers went up, new carpets were laid in every room and on the stairs.

'Must have cost a fortune,' said Belinda.

'Not a *fortune*,' Anne corrected her, but Belinda nodded her head.

'I heard the men say so.' Belinda might not be able to go in but she could still look and listen. 'Saucers and pitchers', Father called Belinda's eyes and ears.

The landscape gardeners tidied the garden, pruned, cleared and weeded; made new paved walks where the old brick paths had been and dug new flower-beds. The lawns were dug up too, smoothed and turfed and rolled, their edges trimmed. The roses round the windows were cut back, and the flower-beds were filled with new plants bearing labels with strange sounding names: 'Cystisus albus?' asked Belinda; 'Viburnum sterile?' Nona wrote them down and took them to her friend, old Mr Twilfit who kept the bookshop.

Nona was often in and out of the bookshop, and sometimes she took Miss Happiness and Miss Flower to visit Mr Twilfit. 'You see, he helped to establish them,' she said. He had lent her books on Japan so that she could learn to play with them properly, he had helped design the dolls' house, 'and he has given me all sorts of things,' said Nona.

He was a surprising friend of Nona, who was a timid child. 'She was brought up in India away from people, and that made her shy,' Belinda often explained. Most children were afraid of Mr Twilfit; he had a bad temper, a habit of roaring in his deep voice and his eyebrows looked ferocious; 'grey caterpillars', Belinda called them. Even she was quiet when she went with Nona to the bookshop, quiet and very respectful; 'Mr Twilfit must be very wise, with all those books,' she said.

'Silly, he doesn't read them,' said Tom. 'He sells them.'

'He reads a lot of them,' said Nona, 'and Belinda's right. He is wise; the wisest man I know.' When there was anything Nona wanted to know she always went and asked Mr Twilfit.

'Cystisus albus?' he said now. 'That's a pearly white broom. Viburnum sterile? That's a snowball tree.'

'Why couldn't they say so?' asked Belinda.

Even the garage was made new, big enough for three cars, and given doors that opened by themselves if you pressed a button, which seemed magical to Belinda; the garage had a new glass roof too, over its courtyard.

'That's for the chauffeur to wash the cars under when it rains,' said Tom.

'Will they have a chauffeur?' asked Belinda, impressed.

'Sure to; and I expect he will live in the flat over the garage. It's being made new too,' said Tom.

The Tiffany Joneses, it seemed, left nothing to chance. Burglar alarms were fitted to all the doors and the downstairs windows.

'Well, they probably have valuable things,' said Anne. Then the fire escapes with curly iron steps were built each side of the house; the one on the Fells' side was close beside the ilex tree, almost touched by its branches.

'I hope they won't ask us to lop it,' said Anne.

'They will probably like the way it screens their garden from us,' said Mother.

At last, just at Christmas time, the House Next Door was ready, spick and span, in fact so spick and span it made one catch one's breath.

'Just imagine if you left finger marks on that white paint,' said Anne.

'If you brought in a bit of mud on those floors,' said Tom, while Mother said she would hardly dare to cook in the white tiled, blue and white kitchen. The garden too was uncomfortably tidy.

'Suppose a ball went into one of those shrubs,' said Tom.

'If you fell off your scooter into one of the beds,' said Belinda, 'or rode your bicycle on the paths and went on to the new grass.'

'You couldn't ride your bicycle in that garden,' said Nona, 'or scooter.'

'I don't think there *can* be any children,' said Belinda, but when two days after Christmas the furniture arrived, Belinda and Nona saw what was unmistakably children's furniture – and what beautiful furniture it was. There was a pale blue bed with poles, like a four-poster, with a pale blue dressing table, chest of drawers and chairs to match. There was furniture too, for a sitting room: a school desk, a blackboard, small armchairs, bookcases and, delivered in a special van, a miniature white piano. There were toys: a big dolls' house, dolls' beds, a doll's perambulator almost as large as a real one, a cooking stove, a pale blue bicycle, and all of them were obviously for a girl.

Tom groaned. 'We have enough girls already.'

'I think,' said Belinda, 'there must be four or five, there are so many toys.'

'But there's only one bed,' said Nona.

To their great excitement, all these were carried into the two rooms that were opposite Nona and Belinda's bedrooms.

'That's where the girl is going to sleep and play,' said Belinda. 'What fun! We shall be able to watch her and wave to her.'

'If she will wave to us,' said Nona, but such a doubt never entered Belinda's head.

Not long after the furniture, a lady and gentleman arrived.

'In . . . is it a Rolls-Royce?' whispered Belinda.

'A Phantom Silver Cloud II,' said Tom, 'and brand new.'

It was grey and black with dark grey leather. A gentleman was driving with a lady beside him, and a chauffeur in a grey uniform was sitting behind.

The big car stopped at the gate: the chauffeur sprang out to open the door, but the gentleman was already out and, 'Is that the father?' whispered Belinda. 'He doesn't look like a father.'

He was certainly not like any of the fathers she had ever seen: he was young, tall, thin, pale and far more . . . 'elegant,' said Nona. She and Belinda, little girls as they were, could see he was beautifully dressed. 'I never thought of a man's clothes being beautiful before,' said Nona afterwards. 'His trousers had edges,' whispered Belinda. She meant their creases were sharply pressed. His shirt seemed to be cream coloured silk, his shoes shone, his dark overcoat looked warm and rich, and Nona thought with a pang of her uncle's raincoat, his office suit, his old tweed coat and flannels. Mr Tiffany Jones was wearing what Belinda called a city hat, from seeing men who wore them catching the morning train to London. 'It's a bowler hat,' said Nona.

The lady looked older than he; tall too, but large, in

234

a large fur coat, high-heeled fur boots and a red velvet hat. Her face was red too, 'red and white,' said Belinda.

'Hush! That's rouge and powder,' said Nona.

'Does she think it looks nice?' asked Belinda.

The lady had a string of pearls, and a diamond watch over her glove. Belinda and Nona saw it sparkle as she lifted her hand and, 'I can smell her from here,' said Belinda.

After the Rolls-Royce came another, smaller car and in it were two women who wore white overalls under their coats; it was driven by a man who soon afterward appeared in a striped jacket. 'A butler,' said Nona, but Mother said he was more likely to be a house-man. The children could see them through the windows, hurrying about, moving furniture, carrying things, while the lady stood in the middle of each room in turn, ordering everyone about.

The gentleman stayed out in the garden, walking about the lawn, looking at the flower-beds as if he did not like them very much. Every now and again he read one of the labels, and seemed as surprised as Nona and Belinda had been at their names.

He heard Belinda's loud voice and looked up, saw them behind the hedge and smiled. Even to the children it seemed a sad and absent-minded smile and, I wonder what's the matter with him, thought Nona.

The front door opened. 'Harold! Harold!' the lady called in an imperious voice that was louder even than

Belinda's. 'Harold! You might come and help.'

'My dear Agnes, I thought I should only be in the way.'

'It's your house!' said the lady.

'Then isn't it hers? Isn't she Mrs Tiffany Jones?' asked Belinda.

It seemed that she was not. The new cook had made friends with Mrs Bodger and soon the Fells knew all about the Tiffany Joneses. 'With Mrs Bodger and Belinda, who could help it?' as Father said. The real Mrs Tiffany Jones, it seemed, was in hospital because two years ago she had caught polio.

'Polio . . . that's the illness when you can't move, isn't it?' asked Belinda. She tried to imagine what that would be like. 'It would be terrible,' said Belinda, awed.

'Polio often does paralyse,' said Mother. 'How very, very sad.'

'She got it in London,' Belinda reported, 'and Miss Tiffany Jones had to come and look after the house there, and look after the girl.' Mrs Bodger had said there was one little girl. 'Look after her,' said Belinda, 'because Mr often goes travelling, but now Mrs Tiffany Jones had been sent to . . . to . . .' Belinda could not remember the name and said, 'to a famous hospital there.'

'Of course, Stoke Mandeville,' said Mother, which was not far from Topmeadow. 'That's where they teach people to move again; walk and swim and use wheelchairs. Perhaps it means she is getting better.'

'He bought the House Next Door just to be near her – this great big house,' said Belinda. 'Miss Tiffany Jones has come here too, and will look after it. She's his sister, his much older sister. She used to look after him when he was a little boy. That's why he can't say "boo!" to her.'

'Belinda, you are not to repeat gossip,' said Mother.

'It isn't gossip. He can't,' said Belinda. 'Their cook told Mrs Bodger.'

'Then Miss Tiffany Jones is the little girl's aunt,' said Nona. 'I don't think I would like her for my aunt.'

'She's a proper old cat,' said Belinda.

'*Belinda!*' Mother was horrified.

'But she is, Cook told Mrs Bodger so.'

The cook's name was Mrs Mount; the other maid was Eileen. The house-man was called Selwyn, 'and you don't call him Mister,' said Belinda. The chauffeur was Benson; 'you don't call him Mister, either.' They were all complete except for the little girl.

Then, on a bitter January day, the Rolls drew up at the next-door gate and out got a girl and a woman. Belinda and Nona, who were just coming back from the shops, clutched one another.

The girl walking up the path looked about the same age as Nona. She was wearing a green velvet coat and hat, white boots, fur-topped, and white fur tippet, white gloves and a white shawl wound round her neck and over her mouth. 'As well as the tippet!' said Belinda.

The girl was as pale as Mr Tiffany Jones, and down her back hung a long fall of fair hair. It gave her the look of being drowned, thought Nona.

She and Belinda looked to where the woman was taking a rug and parcels from the chauffeur. She was a big solid-looking woman with a big face and iron-grey hair, and she was dressed in an iron-grey coat and hat. 'She looks iron all over,' said Nona.

'Is she the nurse?' asked Belinda in a whisper. 'That girl's too old to have a nurse. That must be a governess.'

'She doesn't look like a governess,' said Nona uncertainly. 'Perhaps she's a kind of maid.'

Miss Tiffany Jones had come out on the steps to meet them. 'Come in! Come in! Come along in!' she called in her imperious voice. 'Hurry up, Matson,' she called to the woman. As with Selwyn and Benson, Miss Tiffany Jones did not say Mrs or Miss. It seemed rude to Belinda to call people by their surnames, but 'Come along, Matson. Hurry up out of the cold,' called Miss Tiffany Jones.

'They are coming as fast as they can,' murmured Belinda. She and Nona had gone into their own garden and were looking through the hedge.

Selwyn came out to carry the suitcases. 'Welcome home, Miss Gem,' he said respectfully as if he were talking to a grown-up.

'Jem; that's a boy's name,' said Belinda.

238

'Not J-E-M, silly; G-E-M,' said Tom, who had come up behind them.

'Never heard of it,' said Belinda, as if she had heard of everything.

'It certainly goes well with Tiffany,' said Mr Twilfit when he heard it. Nona and Belinda had gone down to the bookshop to tell him that Gem had arrived. Tiffany's, he explained to them, was a famous jeweller's and goldsmith's in New York. 'Does it belong to Gem's father?' asked Belinda, her eyes round.

'Hardly probable,' said Mr Twilfit; 'might be some connection, though.'

'I think "Gem" is a pretty name,' said Nona.

'Gem Tiffany Jones. It's the richest name I ever heard.'

'Belinda,' said Mother a day or two later. 'Belinda, you are not to go next door.'

'Oh Mother, why not? Mr Tiffany Jones smiles at us.'

'I know,' said Mother, 'But Miss Tiffany Jones doesn't.'

Mother had spoken to Miss Tiffany Jones when she met her in the road. 'I hope you are going to like living in Topmeadow.'

'After London?' Miss Tiffany Jones gave a queer little laugh that did not sound amused. 'Like living in a *suburb*, and not even a London suburb?'

'But Topmeadow's a lovely place,' said Belinda.

Miss Tiffany Jones did not speak to Mother again, nor nod to any of them or smile, and, 'You are not to go next door,' said Mother to Belinda.

'Which means not hanging round the gate,' said Anne, and Belinda blushed.

'I want to make friends,' said Belinda.

Belinda was friends with everyone: with the shop people, the postman, the laundryman, the Vicar; with Sir William Mortimer who was Topmeadow's Member of Parliament and with the old chestnut seller who had his stand in winter at the corner of the road.

Nona had only three friends, and she had made them through Miss Happiness and Miss Flower. Nona was friends with Melly, the girl she sat next to at school, Miss Lane who taught there, and Mr Twilfit.

These were Nona's friends, but to Belinda everyone was a friend, and it was an astonishing idea to her for the Fells not to make friends at once with the Tiffany Joneses, but Mother was quite firm.

'You are not to go next door, Belinda.'

'What? Never?' asked Belinda.

'Not unless you are asked,' said Mother.

'But suppose they never ask me?'

'Then you can never go,' said Tom.

Chapter 3

The weather grew colder and colder, until one day snow began to fall. It fell all the morning and by the afternoon the road, the roofs and gardens, the whole of Topmeadow, was white with snow. Then the sky cleared, the sun came out, the frost sparkled and Nona brought Miss Happiness and Miss Flower out to see the snowy world. The dolls wore warm coats over their kimonos, coats wadded and quilted with cotton wool. Over their painted sandals they had warm white socks and Tom had made them tiny clogs, cut from a cork and tied on with cords of embroidery cotton. Their heads were protected by round flat hats tied under their chins. Nona brought them down as far as the low wall that bounded the Fells' garden from the road; she made them walk up and down along the wall; their feet left footprints in the snow, smaller than a bird's.

Belinda came to look. 'What are you doing, Nona?'

'Miss Happiness and Miss Flower have come out to admire the snow.'

'Is that what they do in Japan?'

'My book says so.'

'You might have told me,' said Belinda. 'I would have brought Little Peach.'

Little Peach was a Japanese boy baby doll, no bigger

than my thumb. He had come to Belinda in a peach as Peach Boy in the Japanese fairy tale had come (the fairy tale of Little Peach or Peach Boy can be found in every Japanese fairy-story book). Now Belinda ran up to her bedroom and fetched him. Little Peach's hair was cut round, his legs were curved like a baby's and he had no clothes; Belinda had lost his coat and trousers and had not had time to make him any more – Belinda never had enough time – but she had wrapped him in a handkerchief. Now, 'You keep him,' she said to Nona.

Nona was used to keeping Little Peach – Belinda always had so many other things to do – and now Nona tied him on Miss Flower's back in the way that Japanese girls often carry their baby brothers. She had just begun to make them walk up and down the wall again, when the next door gate opened and out came Mr Tiffany Jones. He stopped when he saw them, then came closer, bending his height down to look. 'How very pretty,' said Mr Tiffany Jones, gazing down at Miss Happiness, Miss Flower and Little Peach. 'May I touch?' And when Nona shyly nodded, he picked up Miss Happiness.

'Why, you have made them tanzen – proper Japanese coats – and tabi,' he said, touching the socks. Tabi means 'footbag' in Japanese and tabi are like bags with one toe for the big toe. Nona, of course, had not been able to separate the dolls' toes but their warm white socks did look like tiny bags.

'Lucky little dolls, they are beautifully warm,' said Mr Tiffany Jones, gently putting Miss Happiness down. 'What are they called?'

Nona told him their names and, 'They have come out to admire the snow,' Belinda explained. 'Japanese people do.'

'So they do,' said Mr Tiffany Jones. 'And I believe they make up poems about it – or say one,' and, standing in the road in all his elegance, Mr Tiffany Jones recited:

> 'All heaven and earth
> is flowered white,
> hidden in snow,
> unceasing snow.'

'Why, that's a haiku!' cried Nona, delighted. A haiku is one of the smallest Japanese poems, only seventeen syllables long, just right for dolls, and if Miss Happiness's and Miss Flower's little plaster faces could have smiled, they would have given the honourable gentleman a smile and they would have bowed to him – Japanese people bow a great deal, and they speak of people as 'honourable'.

'How do *you* know about Japanese things?' said Belinda to Mr Tiffany Jones. 'Nona knows, and Mr Twilfit, but how do you?'

'Well, I go to Japan sometimes,' said Mr Tiffany

Jones. 'As a matter of fact, I'm going there tomorrow for three or four days.'

'Did he say three or four days?' asked Belinda, when he had gone on down the road. 'But . . . Japan's on the other side of the world.'

'Nowadays people fly all over the world very quickly,' Nona told her, and Father said that too. Mr Tiffany Jones, Father said, was an important person in business. 'He might very well fly to Japan for just one meeting,' said Father.

Before Mr Tiffany Jones had walked away, he had bent down and picked Miss Flower up to look at her. 'Charming,' he said, touching Miss Flower's red hat with a gentle finger, and, 'I wish my little girl could play like this,' he said, and he had not sounded important, only wistful.

'You know,' said Mother a few days afterwards, 'I am beginning to feel sorry for that little girl.'

'What little girl?' Nona and Belinda did not quite follow Mother. 'What little girl?'

'Gem; I'm sorry for her.'

'*Sorry!* For *Gem?*'

'Yes,' said Mother.

'But . . . she has *everything*,' said Nona.

'*Look* at the things she has,' said Belinda.

One thing that particularly filled Belinda with envy was Gem's pony. Almost every day the riding master from the stables near the Park would ride up to the

House Next Door, and beside his horse trotted a white pony, glossy white, with a long white mane and tail, the daintiest pony imaginable. 'Half Arab, he told me so,' said Belinda.

The pony had a new saddle and bridle with a scarlet headband, a white sheepskin under the saddle; 'And he's Gem's *own*. They just keep him at the stables. If I had a pony like that,' said Belinda, 'I would be happy forever.'

'Would you, I wonder,' said Mother, 'if you had to be Gem?'

When Nona and Belinda came to think of it, Gem did lead a queer restricted life. Belinda tried to imagine what it would be like not to be free to run in and out of the house and garden. Gem was older than Belinda, but she was not even allowed to run as far as the pillar-box at the corner to post a letter; Selwyn posted the letters. She never went on errands to the shops as Belinda loved to go. 'They give me sweets and apples,' said Belinda, and Mr Hancock, the fishmonger, sometimes let her ring up the cash register for him. Gem never went to the Park to meet other children for games – she walked there beside Matson – and Mr Tiffany Jones was right, she never seemed to play. 'Why doesn't she play?' asked Belinda. 'He said he wished she could. Why doesn't she?'

Nona did not know but, 'Perhaps she needs a Japanese doll,' said Miss Happiness and Miss Flower.

Tales from the Dolls' House

They could talk to one another but, of course, nobody else could hear.

The children had discovered that Matson was Gem's especial maid. 'A maid for what?' asked Belinda.

'To keep her rooms tidy,' suggested Anne.

'Doesn't she have to tidy them herself?'

That made Belinda envious.

'And to look after her clothes,' said Anne.

'Does she have so many clothes?'

That was another thing: Gem never seemed to wear the comfortable, ordinary clothes Nona and Belinda wore – jeans, or shorts and jerseys, an anorak with a hood, a kilted skirt, hair tied up in a ponytail. 'She's always dressed up,' said Belinda; dressed in elaborate dresses with ruffled petticoats, in coats with white collars or trimmed with fur, in tailored suits. For riding, Gem wore jodhpurs, a white silk shirt, yellow waistcoat, smart tweed jacket, velvet cap and dear little jodhpur boots. She had fur-trimmed boots and hats, spotless white gloves, and she had a real fur coat, 'like a lady's, only little,' reported Belinda.

More and more Gem seemed like a girl in a book, 'and not a very truthful book,' said Nona, because nowadays not even princes and princesses were treated like this. 'Princesses have to be friendly and smile and wave,' said Belinda. Gem never smiled or waved; like her aunt, she did not seem to want to know the Fells. They never saw her stand at her windows and watch

Little Plum

Nona's and Belinda's or peer through the hedge as they did. If she met them on the road she looked the other way. Of course, she may not have been free to wave or smile; everywhere she went Matson followed her, 'like a policeman,' said Belinda. 'Only, policemen are nice,' said Nona. Soon Nona and Belinda found themselves saying, 'Poor Gem.' How odd it was that Gem should be poor when she was so very rich.

Mr Tiffany Jones came back from Japan and, 'Did he bring the little Miss a Japanese doll?' Miss Happiness and Miss Flower asked anxiously. No, it seemed he had only brought Gem a Japanese lantern. It was a beautiful lantern, big, of misty white paper with a black band top and bottom; when it was lit it glowed yellow. Nona, Belinda and the dolls could see it hanging up in Gem's sitting-room window; it looked most poetical – but Miss Happiness and Miss Flower were curiously disappointed.

Belinda's best present at Christmas had been a pair of roller skates. Up till then she had used Tom's old ones, dreadful ones that had the old kind of steel wheels, 'horribly noisy,' said Anne, and were rigid, without ball bearings, the grips worn out. They were always coming off and bringing Belinda down. The new ones were beautiful, with leather heel grips, ball bearings and hard rubber rollers; they were swift, almost noiseless, and on them Belinda felt she flew.

'But if they are fast, they can be dangerous,' Mother told her. 'You can go as fast as you like in the Park or round the tennis court, but you are not to go fast on the road.' She let the children skate on the pavement of their own road because it was quiet, but they were not allowed to go up to the shops at its end; Mother did not know that they often skated round the corner into the next road that led to the Park. 'You may skate slowly, on our pavement, but if you go fast, I shall have to stop it,' said Mother.

On those new skates, Belinda could not help going fast – at least, she could not resist it. Besides, she and Tom had a secret game: they raced on opposite pavements, each side of the road. Tom gave Belinda a start and they skated to the far end, away from the shops, and back again to the house. Tom had to turn round a pillar-box at the corner of his pavement, Belinda round a lamppost. They both went furiously fast. 'But only when we see the road is empty,' said Tom. 'Or almost empty,' said Belinda, who was not as careful as Tom. 'One or two people don't matter.'

Sometimes they did matter. Once one of the people was Miss Tiffany Jones. Belinda had not realized who she was, and shot past her, making Miss Tiffany Jones almost jump out of her skin. 'Child! You must not skate like that, on a public road,' she cried. Belinda, dragging her skate sideways, had managed to stop.

'How dare you!' scolded Miss Tiffany Jones. 'I don't

know where you come from – ' she seemed curiously blind to the Fells next door – 'but if I see you again, I shall tell the police. Why! You might give someone a heart attack!'

Scarlet in the face, her head sheepishly down, Belinda skated slowly away and stole in at her own gate, and for two whole days she did not skate on the road at all. She even carried her skates to the Park, but Belinda was not very old, and when you are young, you forget. Besides, by far the most exciting place for skating was the road. On the third day she was back again, but she kept a wary eye out for Miss Tiffany Jones.

'There's ice on the roads,' said Father next morning at breakfast. 'Be careful how you walk.'

'And how you skate,' said Mother. 'Better keep off the road, Belinda. If you get a patch of ice, you might skid and not be able to stop.'

'I can always stop,' said Belinda, 'and if I can't, it's more fun.'

'Not fun for other people,' said Anne.

'Oh, I can always dodge them,' said Belinda airily.

It was wonderful skating that day. Tom and Belinda stayed in the Park all the morning; it was almost lunchtime when they came back, and the pavements were empty. They were on the road leading to their own, and 'Let's race home,' said Belinda.

'What about the corner?' asked Tom. The corner to their own road was sharp.

'Oh, there won't be anybody there,' said Belinda. 'We can swing round the lamppost.'

'All right. Give you forty yards to start,' said Tom, and when they were stationed, 'Ready! Steady! GO!' called Tom.

Belinda's skates were so good and she was skating so well, that she was able to keep well ahead of Tom. She could hear him, though, coming behind her and, 'I'm going to get there first,' she said through her teeth. The air was so cold and she was going so fast that her cheeks stung and her eyes were watering, but – faster – faster – faster – thought Belinda.

She reached the corner, swung round the lamppost to turn, but did not really look as she gathered speed again; nor did she listen or she would have heard Tom grinding to a halt and shout, 'Look out! Belinda, look out!'

Then suddenly in front of her she saw the Tiffany Joneses, Mr, Miss and Gem, their backs towards her, walking towards their front gate. They were strung so much across the pavement, that there was no room for Belinda to pass. She tried to brake, but she was going too fast; she tried to steer towards the wall, and met exactly what Mother had warned her about, a patch of ice. The skates flew sideways, she spun round twice and, pell-mell, crash, went into the back of Gem and sent her flying. Worse than that, skidding after her, Belinda lost her own balance, veered backwards and forwards, clutching Gem; the skates flew up, one roller catching Mr Tiffany Jones on the shin where he had whipped round to look. Then Belinda fell flat on her back on the ice, bringing Gem down on top of her.

What a to-do there was! Mr Tiffany Jones was hopping on one leg, swearing with pain; his black striped trousers had a great rip. Miss Tiffany Jones was half crying with shock and scolding in her high, loud voice. Tom, who had rushed up, was picking up Gem as well as he could with his skates on, trying to clean her coat from mud and ice, while he told Belinda under his breath what he thought of her. Gem's white fur hat was lying in the road, her muff was dangling on one string, the gold-green hair was draggled with ice and mud, and she was silent and white. 'She might have said something,' said Belinda afterwards. 'Well, you knocked the breath out of her,' said Tom.

He left Gem to Miss Tiffany Jones and dragged Belinda to her feet. Belinda was too ashamed and shocked to say a word then, but Tom apologized, though Miss Tiffany Jones hardly paused long enough to hear him. 'A perfect little hooligan,' she was saying. 'I told her only the other day not to skate like this; she must be severely punished,' she told Tom.

'It was partly my fault,' said Tom. 'I let her race.'

'Then you should be thoroughly ashamed of yourself.'

'Oh come, Agnes! It was an accident,' said Mr Tiffany Jones, who was beginning to recover, 'and Gem isn't hurt.'

'Accident! Not hurt! The child looks stunned and sick.' Then Miss Tiffany Jones turned again on Belinda. 'Using the streets as a skating rink! You are a public danger. I would telephone your mother, but as she lets you play in the streets, I doubt it would do much good.'

She swept Gem in at the gate; Mr Tiffany Jones said, 'She will calm down by and by,' and smiled and followed her. Tom took Belinda home. He was given a good talking to and both their skates were confiscated for a week.

Mother wrote a note of apology to Miss Tiffany Jones and made Belinda, who could not bear writing letters, write one to Gem. This was a real punishment for Belinda, and even when she had written it three times there were still blots. 'I bet Gem writes *beautifully*,' she said, but that they could not know, because Gem did not answer; nor did Miss Tiffany Jones.

'That's not very gracious of them,' said Father.

Mr Tiffany Jones still lifted his hat when he met Mother in the street – 'And he lifts it to me,' said Anne – he still smiled with his wistful smile, and said, 'Hullo Tornado,' in a most friendly way when he met Belinda, but Miss Tiffany Jones swept by with her head in the air. As for Gem, she walked straight past. 'She thinks I did it on purpose,' said Belinda resentfully.

'I'm sure she doesn't,' said Mother.

'Then she might at least smile,' said Belinda. 'Anyone can smile.'

'Do you smile at her?' asked Mother.

'Certainly not,' said Belinda. 'But why are the Tiffany Joneses like this? Why?' she asked Mother.

'Different people have different ideas,' said Mother, 'and bring their children up differently.'

'Not as differently as this,' said Belinda.

'Remember Topmeadow is a new place for them,' said Nona. 'Remember how silly I was when I first came.'

'You were miserable,' said Belinda, 'but you weren't stuck up.' Then a thought struck her. The holidays were almost over. 'Soon it will be time for school,' said Belinda. 'Gem will have to go to school. *That* will unstick her.'

But when term time came Gem did not go to school.

Instead, a number of new people came to the House Next Door. A lady came every day from half past nine until one; she was a proper governess and her name, the children discovered, was Miss Berryman. The Mademoiselle from their own school came twice a week to teach Gem French privately. 'But she knows French already,' said Belinda. 'She can talk it.' This was a mystery to Belinda, who was still struggling with 'avoir' and 'être'. A gentleman came on three afternoons at half past four to teach Gem the piano. 'And she has to practise a whole hour every day,' said Belinda. They could hear her on the little white piano and, 'She's very good,' said Anne, 'better than I am and I'm twice her age.' Gem learned elocution and had private dancing lessons, 'ballet, twice a week,' said Nona, longingly.

There seemed a great many lessons for one small girl. 'Chivvied from morning to night – that's what she is,' Belinda reported in the words of Mrs Bodger. 'Nothing but putting clothes on and taking them off, and practising and lessons, lessons, lessons.'

Mother was disturbed by this. 'Every child should have some private time,' she said, 'time of her own and time for play.' Perhaps Mr Tiffany Jones felt this too. When Mother took Belinda to buy a new satchel – Belinda's first grown-up satchel; before she had only had an old one of Anne's – and they met Mr and Miss Tiffany Jones, 'Getting ready for school?' he asked pleasantly.

'School has started,' said Belinda, who was amazed that anyone living in Topmeadow should not know that.

'I didn't know,' said Mr Tiffany Jones as if he had guessed what Belinda was thinking. 'You see,' he said, 'Gem doesn't go to school.'

Little Plum

'Not at Topmeadow,'Miss Tiffany Jones broke in. 'Gem is a very gifted child,' she said; 'she couldn't go to an *ordinary* school. Come, Harold,' and she put her hand on Mr Tiffany Jones's arm and marched him away.

Nona had made Miss Happiness and Miss Flower go to school too. 'A school by themselves', and she said, 'I wish they knew another Japanese child.' She had made tiny writing books for the dolls, bound in the Japanese way, pleated into pages that can be opened out into one long scroll; you begin on the last page and work back to the first. Japanese characters are written with a brush and not a pen; Nona made the smallest possible brushes from a splinter of a match and a piece of feather, and copied some Japanese characters on to a dolls'- house blackboard for the dolls to copy and write. Japanese is such a different language that in Japan children spend all their time learning to read and write, but she made each of the dolls learn a haiku too. 'One day you shall say them to honourable Mr Tiffany Jones,' she told them, and the dolls felt pleased. Miss Happiness's haiku was:

> 'You stupid scarecrow!
> Under your very
> stick feet
> Birds are stealing beans.'

While Miss Flower's was this:

> 'Gay butterflies
> be careful of
> pine needle points
> in this gusty wind.'

When Mother saw Mr Tiffany Jones on the road she always stopped and asked, 'How is your wife?'

'Getting on; getting on, I hope,' said Mr Tiffany Jones, but he did not sound at all hopeful; he sounded wistful. He seemed to like watching Belinda and Nona with Mother, though when he saw the way Nona hung on her arm, and heard Belinda's chatter, his face would grow more wistful than ever. 'I wish Gem could be with her mother like this,' he said one day. 'When she does see her, she treats her as a stranger.'

'But you take Gem to see her often?' said Mother.

'Well, no,' said Mr Tiffany Jones. 'Agnes, my sister, says it would be too distressing. You don't think so?' he added, looking at Mother's face.

'It is distressing for a little girl *not* to see her mother,' said Mother. 'But perhaps Mrs Tiffany Jones will be coming home soon.'

'I should like her to, but Agnes says it would be too difficult,' and he sighed.

'Difficult! With all those servants,' said Anne when he had walked on. 'If you ask me, Miss Tiffany Jones likes bossing that lovely house and doesn't want to give it up,' but, 'You are not to gossip about things you cannot know,' said Mother.

'We do know,' said Anne. 'Anyone can see it and she likes bossing Gem too. Why doesn't he tell her not to? "Agnes says . . . ! Agnes says . . . !"' mocked Anne.

'Don't, Anne,' said Mother. 'You mustn't criticize the poor man. He is driven half out of his senses with worry.'

Chapter 4

'I'm going to spring-clean the dolls' house from top to bottom,' said Nona one wintry afternoon when the children could not go out.

'It isn't spring,' said Belinda.

'I mean clean it thoroughly,' said Nona, and before Belinda could argue about anything else, Nona ran out of the playroom and upstairs to her own room. Because it was such a dark and dismal afternoon, she turned on the light; she forgot to draw the curtains.

In Japan, houses are more simple and empty than ours. Walls are usually paper screens called *shoji* that slide backwards and forwards to let in the light, or to make doors and windows. The floors are covered with matting and Japanese people do not often use chairs, but have cushions to sit on; they have a low table or two, and a warm charcoal stove or firebox sunk in the floor round which all the family gathers. In the chief room is a niche called a *tokonoma* which has one picture hanging in it – a picture on a scroll that is changed to match the season; in winter, snowflakes perhaps; in spring, perhaps blossom; in summer a peony or a spray of morning glory or a bird; in autumn maple leaves that have turned red or yellow. A Japanese garden is part of the house, with trees and stones, perhaps a

Little Plum

stone lantern, perhaps a curved bridge over a stream; often the bridges are so curved that they make a half hoop or crescent moon.

Nona's dolls' house was a dolls' house like that – a Japanese dolls' house. Tom had made it for her and, 'It must be the only one in England,' she often said proudly. It was raised on a plinth and had a flight of steps leading up to it. The walls were wooden with paper lattices that, in the front of the house, opened out into a pair of windows, while at the back, they were miniature shoji. Tom had made the screens for the shoji slide in the smallest possible grooves so that when they slid back, the house could be open to the garden. The lattices were of narrow strips of stiff white paper that criss-crossed. There was only one room in the dolls' house, but a hall led off it, divided by sliding screens of pale green paper. Japanese people call a hall the 'shoes-off' place, and Miss Happiness and Miss Flower kept their tiny clogs there. The floor was covered with matting – it was really a straw luncheon mat. There was a cupboard that was really a roll-top pencil box standing on its side: being a Japanese pencil box, a mountain – Fumi-Yama – was painted on its rollers. In it, in the daytime, the dolls' bed quilts and pillows were kept, and on its top were dolls'-house-size books and tiny bowls and platters. There was a firebox, the size of a matchbox, in which a bulb under red paper made a warm glow, a low table on which was a teapot and tea bowls, and beside it cushions in red and blue. The lamp was a cotton reel with a bulb fixed in its hole, and a painted paper shade; and the dolls had a dolls'-house television set. At the end of the room was the dolls'-house tokonoma, painted in pale green, with a polished black wood floor, and in it Nona always kept a scroll, a three-inch-long slip of paper with a shaved match each end to weight it. On this winter day, the scroll picture was of snowflakes and bamboos painted on brown paper. In a tiny yellow vase Nona arranged green pine needles and a single winter jasmine flower.

The dolls'-house garden lay behind the house; it had a looking-glass stream bridged with a half-moon wooden bridge that Tom had carved; there was a stone lantern too, that Nona had modelled in clay and fired in the school kiln; being up to date, the lantern was fitted with an electric bulb and could be switched on with the house lamp. Best of all, the garden had miniature trees, real ones, growing in the earth, a nine-inch-high cedar and an even smaller willow tree; they had been given to Nona by Mr Twilfit when the dolls'-house garden was made. The Christmas present she had liked best were some real miniature irises – not three inches high. 'They will flower in the summer,' said Nona.

Now she was arranging and dusting the house as she loved to do, and the dolls were helping her.

Little Plum

Miss Happiness had an apron over her kimono, a handkerchief tied over her black hair; Nona had given her a duster the size of a postage stamp. In the garden Miss Flower was looking after Little Peach. Tom had made him a swing that hung from a branch of the cedar tree. Little Peach sat in it and every now and then, Nona gave it a gentle tap; it looked as if Miss Flower were really swinging him.

Nona was so busy playing that she never thought of looking up, of glancing across the way; if she had, she would have seen a small pale face pressed against the glass, fair hair falling each side of it – a book forgotten on the sill; someone was watching every move she made.

Perhaps you have been to the theatre and seen a stage lighted up; when the audience sits in darkness, the stage seems to come close, everything on it shows clearly. Gem's sitting room was in darkness and from it, that dark winter afternoon, Nona's windowsill, the dolls' house and its garden seemed lighted liked a stage. You must remember how close the houses were. The ilex branches came a little across, but it was possible to look through the leaves.

Miss Flower looked across and saw Gem. In her silent, doll way she told Miss Happiness, 'Honourable little Miss Next Door is watching us.' Miss Happiness looked too, but Nona never even glanced across the way.

Gem stayed there until Matson came in, switching

on the light, when she jumped and picked up the book she had forgotten and pretended she was learning her French verbs.

You may wonder why, if Gem watched Nona so carefully, she always looked away when she met her or Belinda in the street and why she never smiled. I am afraid there was a reason.

Every Tuesday and Thursday afternoon, Belinda's class at school went to the Park to play netball, and when they were coming back, at four o'clock, they met Gem going to her dancing lesson. They walked two and two down the road, fourteen little girls, all fourteen of them dressed alike, in dark blue coats and berets, blue and yellow striped mufflers; this uniform made Gem seem more than ever conspicuous; she looked such a dressed-up little girl in her velvet coat, white fur cap and muff, white boots. Belinda and the others had short hair or plaits or ponytails; Gem's hair flowed down her back, and always beside her walked Matson, carrying her shoes, her dressing case and a shawl.

'That's her Nanny,' Belinda told the girls at school. She had told them many things about Gem, in fact they knew all about her, and each time Gem passed, fourteen pairs of eyes looked her up and down, and there were fourteen sniggers. Presently there began to be little flipped remarks, not loud enough for the mistress at the back to hear, but quite loud enough for Gem:

Little Plum

'Here comes the snow queen.'

'Here comes the ballerina.'

'Don't catch cold, will you dear?'

'Nanny! Nanny! where's my handkerchief?'

Sometimes the mistress in charge of them was Mademoiselle and she would greet Gem in French so that Gem had to answer her, and 'Swank pot!' hissed the girls, or 'Parlez-vous français, s'il vous plaît.'

One of the girls had a rhyme:

'Gem T.J. tall and slender,
She's got legs like a crooked fender.'

Which was quite untrue; Gem's legs were perfectly straight. The only sign she gave that she had heard was that, as she walked past them with that stony face, she walked faster, while white patches came round her nostrils and she seemed to breathe quickly through them, her lips held tightly together. If Mademoiselle were there she would hurry even more.

Belinda thought it funny until she told about it at home. She told it shaking with laughter but, 'Belinda. Belinda. Belinda,' said Mother.

'You set them all on,' said Anne; 'I have a good mind to report you.'

'Fourteen against one,' said Tom. 'You little rotters.'

'It must have felt like whips,' said Nona.

263

Belinda felt ashamed, so much so that she began to whistle very loudly.

'No wonder Gem hates us,' said Nona.

'Well, I hate her,' said Belinda, but it is odd; when you have done something that is unfair to someone, you cannot get them out of your mind, and 'I do *wish* I could go next door,' said Belinda.

There were ways and ways of being disobedient and I think Belinda knew them all. 'You are not to go next door,' Mother had said but, 'If I am in the ilex tree,' said Belinda, 'how can I be next door?'

'You can't get up into the ilex tree,' said Nona. 'It's too high. Besides, the ilex tree is Tom's.'

The children all had their private and particular places in the garden where it was understood no other child trespassed. Anne had had the old white bench half hidden under the apple trees; now Nona had inherited it from her and often took Miss Happiness, Miss Flower and Little Peach there for secret picnics. Belinda had a cave at the back of the woodshed; Tom had the ilex. For two years running he and his friends, Stephen and Ronnie, had built a Swiss Family Robinson house up in the branches. None of the others had seen it, not even Belinda. Though Belinda very often took no notice of Mother or even of Father, she always did what Tom told her, and 'You keep OUT,' Tom had said, and Belinda kept out. 'But that was last year,' she said now.

Little Plum

There came a half holiday at the beginning of February, one of those still, sunny February days that seem as if spring had come. The snow had melted, there were snowdrops in the garden beds, and a bee buzzed round the catkins. Belinda was in the garden quite alone.

Father was, of course, at his office; Mother had taken Anne and Nona shopping, but Belinda had not wanted to go. 'Very well, you may stay here with Tom,' Mother had said.

Tom was in the garage, where he had his carpenter's bench. He was clever at making things; it was he who had made the Japanese dolls' house for Nona, and now he was making an oak bookshelf for Mother's birthday. He was trying to get it finished and was very busy. On the Tiffany Joneses' side of the hedge all was quiet too. They were all out. Mr Tiffany Jones was usually out all day, and Gem had gone riding. Belinda had watched her being put up on the white pony by the riding master; then they had trotted away. Matson, in her grey coat, had gone off in the direction of the shops. Presently Selwyn, looking unfamiliar in a greatcoat, had followed her. Miss Tiffany Jones had been driven away in the Rolls-Royce. 'Phantom Silver Cloud II,' murmured Belinda. She could hear television sounding from the maids' sitting room on the other side of the House Next Door. That meant Cook and Eileen were watching it. The gardener was in the potting shed; there was no one to watch Belinda or hear her, and – NOW, she thought, NOW.

'Tom, are you going to use the ilex house this year?'

Tom was busily planing a board and at first he could not hear her. She had to wait until he stopped to rest.

'This year are you going to use the ilex house?' she asked again.

'The ilex house?' asked Tom, as if he had never heard of it.

'The ilex house, up in the ilex, that you made with Stephen and Ronnie.'

'Oh that!' said Tom, and he asked, 'What do you think we are? Kids?'

That was what Belinda wanted to hear and her face beamed as she asked, 'Then can I have it? Can I?'

'If you like,' said Tom indifferently, and went back to his planing.

Belinda ran pell-mell off to the ilex, but Nona was quite right; when she stood close under it, the lowest branch was high out of her reach, while the house was higher up still. Looking up she could see planks, ropes, a ladder going up into the higher branches, a chair, a saucepan; it looked exciting, but how was it reached? She went back to Tom.

Once more she had to wait until he broke off from his planing. 'Tom, how did you get up?'

'Up where?'

'Up into the ilex.'

Little Plum

'We made a rope ladder,' said Tom, feeling down the board to see if it were smooth.

'I saw a ladder up there . . .'

'A *rope* ladder.'

'Where – is it?'

'Lashed to the first branch. We kept it rolled up there; that's how we stopped anybody getting up.'

'But how did *you* get up? To . . . to unroll it?' in her earnestness Belinda stammered.

'One of us got on the other chap's shoulders.'

'I haven't a chap,' said Belinda. 'Could I get on your shoulders? Would you let me? Oh Tom, will you come?'

'Sometime I will,' said Tom. 'Not now. I'm busy.'

'But I want it *now*. Please, dear darling Tom.'

'I'm not your dear darling Tom,' said Tom. 'You kicked me at breakfast this morning. Look,' and he showed a blue bruise on his shin.

Belinda had kicked him under the table because he had laughed at her. She was sorry now – Belinda was often sorry for things she did – but it was too late. He had already gone back to his planing. 'Hop it,' said Tom, and Belinda had to hop it.

The garden steps were too heavy for her to carry, as was the garden table, and if she had dragged it to the tree it would have left telltale marks on the grass. The garden chairs were flimsy and not high enough. Then what . . . ? Belinda looked round the garden and saw where Father, as soon as the snow had cleared, had begun hoeing the ground between the wallflowers in the long bed, raking the old dead leaves off. His wheelbarrow, half full of leaves, stood on the path, a big, heavy, wooden wheelbarrow.

Belinda emptied the leaves on the path; it was a struggle because the barrow was almost too heavy for her to tip and get upright again, but at last she was able to wheel it round the edge of the lawn until it stood under the ilex. The barrow was steady and firm; it needed to be that because in it Belinda began to build a tower. The barrow was just wide enough to hold a kitchen chair, a wooden one without arms. Then she found a box in the tool shed, an oblong wooden one that had once held sherry bottles; she stood it on the chair and on top of it put a big flowerpot, upside down. Then she climbed into the barrow and up on to the chair. The box left only a narrowest edge of chair seat around it, almost too narrow to stand on, but Belinda steadied herself against the ilex trunk, and managed to fit a foot each side of the box. Then, with a huge stretch, she got one foot on the box itself. It wobbled a little as she stood on it and she quickly levered herself further up against the ilex trunk and brought her other foot up to balance a foot each side of the flowerpot. Now she could reach the branch with her hand and could see a tied-up bundle of rope that must be the rope ladder, but she needed to be higher to untie it. Holding on to the branch with one hand, she stepped cautiously right up on the flowerpot. It was not very safe as she had to stand on one foot – there was no room for the other – but, feeling with her toe, she found a small hollow in the bole of the tree in which she could rest her second foot. Now she could almost stand square with her chest against the branch and she could use both hands to untie the ladder. That was hard work; Tom's knots were undone and she was struggling with the others when, pulling on the obstinate rope, she jerked. It was a small jerk but it was enough! The flowerpot skidded away from her foot, the box shot sideways and the chair over-balanced and, crash, Belinda, flowerpot, box and chair toppled out of the wheelbarrow. The chair and the box landed with a thwack, Belinda fell on her head, hitting her eye on the wooden wheelbarrow wheel, and the flowerpot bounced and caught her on the mouth.

For a moment tree, houses, sky seemed whirling round in front of her. She had a stinging pain in her eye, a hot wetness in her mouth, worse pain in her arm, and a burning in one of her knees.

'Ouch!' said Belinda. 'Ouch!' The pain was so bad that it made her feel sick, but she sat up on the grass while blood ran down her anorak jacket. Exploring with her tongue, she felt something in her mouth and spat; with the blood she spat out came something small and hard and white. It lay on the path and with her good eye she peered down at it. It was a tooth. 'Gosh!'

said Belinda in awe. There was a rent in the knee of her trousers and through it showed a graze, dark red with swelling coming up around it. The sleeve of her anorak was ripped too, and her elbow hurt. Belinda was only just eight; she could not help two tears squeezing out of her eyes and she sniffled.

She spat out more blood, then slowly, painfully picked herself off the grass. She had thought she must go to Tom, but though the graze stung her and her elbow hurt, nothing seemed to be broken. The tree and the houses were steady again; from the ilex branch the ladder dangled, one side half-free, and, I had nearly done it – nearly, thought Belinda.

She had no handkerchief, 'as usual', Tom would have said, but she went round to the kitchen, hobbling because of her knee. Mrs Bodger had put some dusters on the windowsill to dry and Belinda took one to staunch her bleeding mouth. When she put her hand up to her eye, the hand came away red; she looked in the mirror Mrs Bodger kept over the sink, but though the eye was closing up, puffed and purple looking, the cut was more like a slit and not deep enough to bleed.

'Ouch! Ouch!' said Belinda, looking at it. Her lip was swelling too, and there was a dark gap where the tooth had been. It was altogether a piteous looking face that gazed back at her from the mirror – wait till Mother sees my trousers and anorak, thought Belinda.

The thought of Mother made Belinda cry a little

more. What will she say? what will she? she thought, but it was no use thinking about it now. If you are obstinate you have also to be brave, and Belinda had a drink of water to help her stop crying and limped back to the ilex tree. She put the chair back in the barrow, the box on the chair, the flowerpot on the box, then painfully and much more carefully climbed up her tower again. She was not as agile now, and the pain made her more clumsy; she fell twice more. Once the box gave way, but she managed to hold to the branch and drop gently on to the grass, missing the path. Once she and the tower fell right down, but this time she was wary and managed to fall on her back. It made her mouth bleed again, which hurt, and her sleeve was ripped even more, but at last the ladder hung free from the branch, she was able to climb down and, 'After this, if I stand on the box – only the box – I can reach the ladder *easily*,' said Belinda. Yes, she could get up the ilex without Tom and, though it hurt to move her lip or eye, Belinda smiled.

She hid the box, put the chair back in the kitchen, the flowerpot back in the shed, and wheeled the barrow to where it had been left by the wallflower bed, and filled it with the leaves again as well as she could. Then painfully she straightened herself up.

Belinda was triumphant, but she was very sore and there was no sign of Mother, Anne and Nona coming in. It would be a long time before Father came back from the office and, I need a grown-up, thought Belinda. Tom was not grown-up, besides he would be cross with her. School was closed; Mrs Bodger lived at the other end of town but, 'I believe,' Belinda said to herself, 'I believe I shall go and see Mr Twilfit. He's so kind to Nona, perhaps he will be kind to me.'

She limped to the gate; her knee was beginning to stiffen up and hurt hideously, but she went on, out into the road. Then, as she turned to go down towards the shops, she found herself face to face with Miss Tiffany Jones.

Miss Tiffany Jones had just got out of the Rolls-Royce; the chauffeur, his arms full of parcels, was handing her a bunch of roses – 'Roses in February!' said Anne afterwards – but at the sight of Belinda the roses were left almost midair and, 'Good gracious!' said Miss Tiffany Jones. 'Good *gracious*!' She looked at Belinda's face, swollen and marked with tears and blood, at her puffed lip and closed-up eye; her torn anorak and trousers stained with grass and blood. '*Good gracious!*' said Miss Tiffany Jones again.

'It's the little girl from next door, Miss,' said the chauffeur.

'I know that,' snapped Miss Tiffany Jones.

'She seems to be hurt, Miss. Shouldn't we . . .' but Miss Tiffany Jones cut him short.

'You have been fighting,' she said to Belinda.

Belinda was offended. She was eight years old, and

knew perfectly well that girls should not fight. 'Not with fists,' Tom had taught her; 'or kicking.' Belinda pulled people's hair – sometimes; she had been known to pinch, 'and scratch', Tom would have said; a year ago she might have kicked a table; she had kicked Tom that morning, but she would not have been in a fight that hurt people like this.

'Just playing,' said Belinda.

'Playing!' said Miss Tiffany Jones. 'Well, I certainly hope you confine that kind of playing to your own garden.'

'We will see that she does.' It was Mother's voice; she, Anne and Nona had come up behind them, and in a moment Belinda was sobbing against Mother's coat. A cool handkerchief was in her hand and Mother's cool, careful fingers were examining the cut eye and the swollen lip, while Anne tenderly looked at the grazed knee. Nor did Mother say one word about Belinda's clothes. She merely said, 'Good afternoon, Miss Tiffany Jones.'

'I advise you to get your doctor,' said Miss Tiffany Jones; her voice sounded as if she were speaking to Mother twenty yards off instead of being just beside her. 'That cut looks dirty to me; you should certainly get the doctor.'

'I think I can deal with it,' said Mother quietly. 'Come, Anne and Nona,' and she led Belinda indoors. Soon Belinda was tucked up in bed, her cuts washed and dressed, her eye covered with ointment. Anne brought her a special supper on a tray; a bowl of soup, a roll of crusty bread, a private pat of butter, a plate of orange jelly, all laid on a pretty green cloth with a little vase of snowdrops. Belinda, leaning back on her pillows, felt a heroine.

Chapter 5

Sunday, Monday, Tuesday, Wednesday went by before Belinda could climb the ilex tree again. 'Days and days,' sighed Belinda. She was too sore and stiff to do more than hobble. Though her lip was better, her eye was so purple and swollen that Mother kept her back from school. She seemed, too, a little suspicious of what Belinda had been doing when she hurt herself and would not let her out of her sight. Mother had never once asked what happened to Belinda when she hurt herself so badly, though all the others had said, 'What were you *doing?*'

'I fell over the wheelbarrow,' said Belinda, which was true. She, the chair, the box and the flowerpot had fallen over the side.

'*Over* the wheelbarrow? How could you?'

'I did,' said Belinda.

'But how did you hurt yourself like that?' said Anne, and Tom shrugged and said, 'Très rum.' Nona was wiser. 'I know what you were doing,' she said. 'Trying to reach the ilex branch.'

Mother asked no questions, but when Belinda was better Mother looked at her closely and said, 'Belinda, if I were you, I should try to put the Tiffany Joneses right out of your head.'

Tales from the Dolls' House

'Yes, Mother,' said Belinda, but how could she do that when the Tiffany Joneses were next door?

Then came another half-holiday, a Thursday, when Nona had a friend, Melly Ashton, to tea. Mrs Ashton brought Melly and was to have tea in the drawing room with Mother while the children had theirs in the playroom. Melly and Nona were there now, making a set of clothes for Peach Boy. Belinda knew what they were doing but as it was supposed to be a surprise, she had to keep out of the way. Anne and Tom were out; there was nothing for Belinda to do, and 'I believe,' said Belinda, 'even if I am still stiff and can only see out of one eye, I believe I will go up the ilex tree.'

As she let herself quietly out of the garden door, she could hear Mother's and Mrs Ashton's voices in the drawing room, Nona and Melly laughing in the playroom. Belinda quietly shut the door, went round to the tree, and – though it hurt her leg – pulled the box out of the bushes. She got up on it and, holding on to the rope, stretched her foot up to the lowest rung of Tom's ladder. It could just reach and though she said 'Ouch!' when her weight came on her wrenched shoulder, she pulled herself up by her hands, then went up rung by rung until she reached the first branch. After that it was easy. She could climb from one branch to another until she came to the platform the boys had built for the floor of their house. It was not large; there was just room enough for a chair, two stools made of logs sawn off so that they stood levelly, and a rusty spirit stove. Then did they cook up here? Belinda wondered in admiration. It seemed they had; a packing-case cupboard was nailed to the tree and in it was what looked like a packet of dried-up sausages, a few old potatoes and a loaf, green with mould. Belinda threw them down the tree. There was also a spoon, a bottle opener, a plastic cup and a notebook in the cupboard. Belinda tried to read the notebook, but it was so soaked that the pages had stuck together and the ink had run. From the platform a ladder led up to the branches above, on which she could see three doormats tied. Were those their bedrooms, she wondered. The ladder, she could see now, was only a bit of a ladder, perhaps a cherry ladder that had broken off short, or Tom had sawn it, but it was high enough to reach the bedroom branches – about six feet long.

Now that she had seen it at last, Belinda did not think the house so very exciting; of course, it had been deserted long ago, but even then, thought Belinda. What did excite her was that from where the platform had been built against the ilex trunk, a pair of branches went across the hedge so far that they almost touched the fire escape to Gem's sitting room window. The lower branch was big, ending in a fork with a spread of dark green leaves; the upper branch was thin and leafy so that it made what Belinda called a roof over the lower one. I could sit on the big one, and wriggle to the fork, thought Belinda, and nobody would see me. Belinda never waited; in a second she had lowered herself from the platform to sit astride a branch; then she began to work herself forward.

It was perilous; the hedge, with the garden path on the Fells' side, and one of the Tiffany Joneses' new paved paths on the side of the House Next Door, was below her, the paths at least fourteen feet below, but it never occurred to Belinda to look down, and quite happily she worked her way along the branch, her hands holding it, her legs dangling. She was holding her breath too, with excitement, and her cheeks were crimson. Every now and then the big branch had small side ones, so that she had to slide her leg over them.

Now – though almost hidden by the ilex leaves – she was really close to Gem's sitting room window with the rose creeper round it; she could see right into the beautiful room with its desk and small white piano, the pale walls and flowered rugs; she could see the big dolls' house, dolls' beds and dolls' furniture; there were pictures, and the bookcases were filled with – dozens of books – thought Belinda. If she turned her head and bent sideways, she could see into the bedroom too, with its pale blue four-poster bed, the dressing table that matched it and on which were small-sized silver brushes and combs and clothes brushes. A little armchair covered in rosy chintz had a dress laid on it ready for Gem to change into, a velvet dress with a ruffle round the neck. A book was thrown down by the bed.

We're not allowed to throw books down like that, thought Belinda virtuously, but on the other hand, Gem's shoes were not left all anyhow as Belinda's often were, but set neatly side by side . . . but Matson did that, I expect, thought Belinda.

Both rooms were more beautiful than any Belinda had seen but suddenly she was not looking at the rooms; she had seen something else. She looked, blinked, looked again, then quickly, far more quickly than she had come forwards, she wriggled backwards along the branch to the platform, where she turned herself round and, forgetting all about soreness and stiffness, almost tumbled down the branches. When she reached the ladder, she swung herself down it, dropped and landed on the grass and, not stopping to hide the box, ran limping and hopping into the house, where she burst into the playroom. 'What do you think?' panted Belinda, only she was so out of breath that the words all rang together; 'Whaddya think?'

Nona and Melly looked up in astonishment – Melly had hastily hidden their work under her dress. They looked astonished as, 'Whaddya think?' panted Belinda.

They did not know what to think, because they could not understand her. They had to wait until Belinda recovered her breath. 'Nona, Melly, what do you think?' Now the words were a little clearer. 'What *do* you think? She – Gem – *she* has a Japanese doll.'

Miss Happiness and Miss Flower were kneeling close beside Nona on their red and blue cushions while Peach Boy had a cotton reel as a stool; they too heard Belinda's announcement and, 'Then the Honourable Gentleman didn't only bring the lantern,' said Miss Happiness, and Miss Flower said, 'Another new person has come to live at the House Next Door!' Together they softly whispered, 'Aisatsu suru,' which is the Japanese for 'Welcome'.

Three people were on the big branch of the ilex tree; Nona behind Belinda, Melly behind Nona. They had both been frightened to leave the platform and go out along the branch; in fact Melly had had to shut her eyes and wriggle blindly forward holding on to Nona, but Belinda encouraged them in whispers, and now they were all far out on it, looking over one another's shoulders into Gem's sitting room and, 'There! I told you . . . look!' whispered Belinda. 'Look on Gem's windowsill.'

Nona and Melly looked in and, 'She *is* a Japanese doll,' said Nona, marvelling.

The doll was little, perhaps three inches high. 'Almost as small as Little Peach,' whispered Belinda, but she was unmistakably Japanese. She seemed to be made of the same plaster as the others, and perhaps had the same rag body, with a plaster face and little plaster hands and feet. Her feet were bare and, as if she were not much more than a baby, her legs were curved to sit down. 'Like Peach Boy's,' said Belinda. Her eyes were black glass, and she too had little painted eyebrows; her mouth was painted in red and looked like a half open rosebud. Her hair was black with a fringe, but she had a topknot wreathed with white blossom and pinned with a tiny silver pin. She was dressed in a pale blue kimono, the colour of a pale blue winter sky, patterned with sprays of white flowers, and her sash was pink.

'Look at her hair! Her topknot with the blossom!' whispered Melly.

'Look at her kimono, that's plum blossom on it,' whispered Nona.

'She looks like a girl Little Peach – Peach Blossom,' said Belinda. 'Only she's not peach, she's plum. Little Plum! That's her name.' In her excitement Belinda raised her voice. 'We will call her Little Plum.'

Nona hushed her, then objected, 'You can't give a name to somebody else's doll.'

Belinda's eyes grew bright and determined. 'She is Little Plum,' said Belinda in a very loud whisper.

I wish I could go over and touch her, thought Belinda. I wish the big branch stretched that far. I wish our dolls could play with Little Plum. I wish, oh how I wish, thought Belinda, that I could go next door.

*

On the way back from school next afternoon, Nona and Belinda met Miss Tiffany Jones, and, to their surprise, she stopped them. Then she looked them over in her condescending way. They were certainly very different, in fact you could not imagine two more different girls. Nona – in her dark blue coat and beret – was neat, her striped school muffler was wound round her throat, the two ends crossed tidily on her back and held by a belt. Her long socks were straight, her shoes clean and she had on her gloves. Belinda had been in a hurry when she put on her things to go home: her beret was crooked, her coat buttoned wrongly, her muffler dangling anyhow. Her socks were falling down and her shoes were muddied where she had carefully stepped in all the puddles. 'Well, I like puddles,' said Belinda.

As Miss Tiffany Jones's eyes came to Belinda, her eyebrows went up, and her mouth turned down. Then she turned back to Nona. 'You seem a nice quiet child,' she said.

'Thank you,' said Nona. She did not know what else to say. She could not really believe she was talking to Miss Tiffany Jones.

'What's your name?'

'I am Nona. This is Belinda.' Nona tried to bring Belinda in, but Miss Tiffany Jones ignored her.

'You are . . . how old?'

'Nine,' said Nona. 'Belinda is eight.'

'Gem is nine too,' said Miss Tiffany Jones; 'my

brother wants her to make friends with you and . . . yes, I should like her to have a nicely mannered little friend. I will write your mother a note.'

'She isn't my mother,' said Nona. 'She's my aunt.'

'Your aunt, to ask if you may come to tea.'

'*And* Belinda?' asked Nona.

Miss Tiffany Jones's gaze came back to Belinda; once more it went over the crooked beret, the wrong buttons, the trailing muffler, wrinkled socks and muddy shoes. 'Belinda?' she repeated; 'I'm afraid not Belinda; she is impossibly rough. I'm afraid I couldn't allow Gem to play with her.'

Belinda's face went as scarlet as if it had been slapped. She had to bite her lip to keep it from shaking, and she scuffed the pavement with the toe of her shoe. Colour came into Nona's face too, a bright pink spot on each cheek. Her head went up and she said, 'Thank you, but I don't go out to tea without Belinda.' She took Belinda's hand, and they walked away up the road. When they got into their own garden and the gate was shut, Belinda said through clenched teeth, 'I hate . . . I hate *all* Tiffany Joneses.'

Nona and Melly refused to go up the ilex tree again; indeed the children had had great difficulty in getting down it, but Belinda went up every day. 'Because I'm sorry for Little Plum,' she said.

Belinda, as you may have guessed, was not fond of dolls. She liked ponies, boats, balls, roller skates, helping Tom with his carpentry. She was glad to let Nona – and Miss Happiness and Miss Flower, of course – look after Peach Boy; then why should she suddenly have such an interest in a little doll – and one that did not even belong to her.

'Gem doesn't play with her,' she told Nona.

'I expect she thinks she is an ornament,' said Nona.

'A doll an ornament!' Miss Happiness and Miss Flower were shocked but, 'I have seen Matson dust her,' said Nona.

'Dolls wouldn't need to be dusted if they were played with!' said Miss Happiness, and Miss Flower wished that her plaster neck would have let her shake her head in dismay. Nothing is worse for a doll than not to be played with. Perhaps Belinda caught their serious thoughts. '*Why* doesn't Gem play with her?' she asked.

Perhaps she doesn't know how,' said Nona.

'H'm!' said Belinda. She was silent a moment and then she said, 'It would be fun to teach her.'

'Nona,' she asked a day or two later, 'could you make a little padded coat?'

'A tanzen?'

'Yes, like Miss Happiness's and Miss Flower's, only smaller. Poor Little Plum looks so cold.'

Miss Happiness and Miss Flower were charmed. They had not ceased to talk and wonder about the little doll over the way. 'Miss Belinda wants to make

Little Plum warm. Little Miss has a heart of gold,' they said but, 'You are not teasing Gem *again*?' asked Nona.

Belinda opened her eyes wide so that they looked very innocent. 'How could I tease her?' she asked. 'How could I when I never see her – and she will never see me?' said Belinda, and chuckled. 'Please make a little tanzen,' she begged.

In a day or two the coat was made; it was short, of scarlet silk wadded with cotton wool, with scarlet cords to tie it. Nona had learned the shape of a tanzen from the books Mr Twilfit had lent her. Nona was getting very clever with her fingers. 'Really, I think you sew better than Anne,' said Mother. To go with the coat was a pair of tabi, so small that they fitted the top of Nona's little finger. They too were soft and warm, 'and they should just fit,' she said. Then she, who hardly ever asked questions, did ask one. 'Belinda,' asked Nona; 'how will you get the socks and coat to Little Plum?'

That was the question.

'You could post them,' said Nona.

'Miss Tiffany Jones might open the parcel, or Matson,' said Belinda, and she said thoughtfully, 'Matson doesn't go near the windowsill after she has dusted, but Gem does now, two or three times a day. She stands there; I have seen her though she doesn't look at us.'

'She does,' said Miss Happiness, and Miss Flower could have said, 'Indeed she does. Little Miss often looks across at us,' but Belinda was too busy thinking to pay attention to the dolls. 'I must put the coat and socks on the windowsill,' she said.

'But how?' asked Nona.

'Somehow,' and Belinda went up the ilex tree to think.

She thought of getting Tom's fishing rod and dropping a parcel on Gem's windowsill, but how would she get the parcel off the hook? She was a good thrower but she could not be sure of throwing a parcel so that it would go in through the window or else lie on the window-ledge. It might drop down into the garden, the gardener finds it and takes it in to Miss Tiffany Jones.

'No, I must take it myself,' decided Belinda.

Even if she could have reached it, she could not climb up the rose; its stem was too slender, besides, it was prickly. She wondered if she could jump across on to the fire escape, but even holding on to the upper branch it would be difficult to jump off the fork and how could she jump back? She could perhaps have swung on the upper branch across on to the fire escape, then run down it to slip out through the garden . . . but I'm not allowed in the Next Door Garden, thought Belinda. She thought and brooded, and each time her eyes and her thoughts came back to the fire escape.

It was elaborate as everything belonging to the Tiffany Joneses, a twisting spiral of iron with railings and a small landing on each floor; one of these landings was just by Gem's window. From the fork to that landing was not very far and suddenly . . . I believe I could make a bridge to it, thought Belinda. If I could slide, say a plank, or something, across until one end was on the fire escape, the other on the fork, then I could stand on the landing on one foot, put my other foot on that drainpipe; I could hold on to the fire escape railing with one hand and 'I believe,' said Belinda to herself, 'I believe I could just, just reach the window-ledge. If Matson had left the window open, I could put a hand inside.'

Most people, even children, would have thought of the danger of going across that space on a plank which would be narrower, not half as firm as the ilex branch. It would be high above the ground, and not protected or screened by other branches or leaves; most children would have thought of turning giddy, or of the plank wobbling, or falling, but Belinda did not give a single thought to any of these things. A plank, she was thinking, a plank. How can I get a plank, and if I get it, how can I get it up the ilex tree? It was then that her eye fell on the ladder.

There it was, already in the tree, the ladder Tom and the boys had brought up – one end resting on the platform, the other up the tree. It looked as if it might be the right length, not too long to manage, not too short to reach and, it's better than a plank, thought Belinda, if I can tilt it forwards, tilt it so that it will come down slowly until it is resting flat on the branch . . . No sooner had Belinda thought these things than she jumped up to try.

She managed to ease the ladder forward a little so that she could stand behind it, and, I must push its top forward among the branches and see if I can bring it forward and down, thought Belinda and, standing with her feet apart and firmly planted, she gripped the ladder with both hands and pushed. The top came forward, then forward a little more. It caught on a small branch full of leaves and she had to shake it free; it scraped against big branches and she had to juggle it; then, suddenly, it became heavier, too heavy for Belinda; she tried to hold it but it came down with a rush that almost took her off her feet. Instinctively she let it go and, with a rending of leaves and branches, the ladder fell with such a thwack that it shook the whole tree. Belinda just missed being hit by the bottom of the ladder as it sprang up and bounced off the platform.

The spirit stove, saucepan, and chair went flying. It was a good thing no one was walking underneath, as Tom said afterwards. For Belinda, the thwack sounded as loud as a clap of thunder. She expected that heads would appear at all the Tiffany Joneses' windows; that on the Fells' side Mother and Tom, Anne and Nona would run out, calling, 'Goodness! What happened?' Belinda waited on the platform, making herself as flat as possible against the tree, shutting her eyes and holding her breath, but no one appeared, nobody called and soon the ilex leaves stopped shaking and she could dare to look. Luck was with her; the ladder had been caught by the smaller branches, and was lying just where she had wanted it to lie – along the big branch.

It was a little too sideways on but, with its weight on the branch, it was easy for her to guide it into position and soon it was lying across the branch, one end resting on the fork. I can push it forward as I come forward myself, thought Belinda, push it right out until the far end lies on the fire escape. She was delighted. It's wider than a plank, she thought. Wider – nice and safe! The ladder was perhaps a foot wide, the drop to the path below was, as you know, all of fourteen feet, but Belinda did not think of that. She had her bridge.

When she had it in position, Belinda knew she must tie its near end firmly to the fork. She had that much sense. If I didn't it might slip sideways, she thought. She knew too she must be quick or somebody might see her. She cut a length of rope from the boys' store with Anne's Girl Guide knife that she was not supposed to touch. Little Plum's coat and socks were ready, pinned to a notice that Belinda had written; she had them in the pocket of her anorak. Now she sat down astride the branch behind the ladder, pushing it in front of her, and began to wriggle forward.

The ladder, polished and smooth with age, slid along the branch quite easily, more easily than Belinda – who

289

had to keep stopping to slide a leg over a side branch. When she reached the fork, leaning forward she pushed the ladder on ahead. Will it be long enough, she asked, oh, will it? But it was just long enough. When one end rested on the fire escape, the other just lay on the fork. Belinda pulled her rope through the last rung, which was resting on the fork, and quickly lashed it until it was firm. When it was lashed, it did not wobble – very much, thought Belinda; but it wobbled a bit, and she breathed hard as she put first one leg, then the other, across the fork and levered herself forward until she was sitting on the ladder, a leg each side. It did not feel wide or safe; it felt thin and flimsy after the big branch, and Belinda almost went back but, 'It's only a little way,' she told herself.

It was certainly not as easy to wriggle forwards along the ladder as it had been along the branch; her trousers kept on catching; she was afraid too that the end on the fire escape would tip up and she wished she could have lashed that end as well, but still she went forward, bit by bit, holding firmly with her hands, slipping them along in front of her. She did not once look down, which was as well, and in a minute her hand went out and caught the fire escape; then she was standing on the landing. With a beating heart she unpinned the notice and, facing the house wall, put her left foot on the drainpipe and, holding firmly to the railing with her right hand, she stretched out her left, being careful not to catch her sleeve on the rose thorns. The sitting room window was open a crack and, though this first time Belinda did not dare crane forward too far, she was able to stick the notice with the coat and socks through the crack. In two minutes more she had wriggled back along the ladder and was over the fork back in the ilex tree.

She could not turn round on the branch to unlash the rope; and she had first to go right back along it to the platform, where she turned round and wriggled forward again. Then she had to work herself backwards, pulling the ladder back along the branch, until it lay safely hidden among the leaves. Only then was she able to rest, sitting on the platform, but still breathing very hard and waiting for her heart to stop its pounding. She felt as if she had taken an hour but no, it was only minutes; nobody had come running, nobody had seen or heard, and Little Plum's coat, her socks, and the notice were safely on Gem's windowsill.

From the dolls' house, Miss Happiness and Miss Flower had seen the ilex shaking; they could just see the end of the ladder as it slid out to rest on the fire escape across the way and, 'Is it a bridge?' asked Miss Flower. If it were a bridge it looked exceedingly narrow and when they saw Belinda working her way to the end of it, their plaster seemed to creep with fear. Miss Flower especially felt as if she trembled. 'Little Miss is as brave as a dragon!' she said.

Tales from the Dolls' House

When Belinda reached the fire escape she was lost from their sight in ilex leaves but they saw her hand reach up to Gem's window. 'The new little doll has her coat and socks,' they told one another and, 'How pleased her little Miss will be with what our little Misses have done.' But of course, neither Miss Happiness nor Miss Flower knew what Belinda had printed in big letters on the notice: 'CAN'T YOU KEEP YOUR DOLL WORME?' Belinda had printed.

She had not been able to wait for Gem to come in because it was time for tea, but as soon as tea was over she slipped out again, ran to her ladder and climbed up. It was beginning to be dusk but she could see that her notice was gone. Little Plum was in her usual place on the sill opposite and she was not wearing the coat or socks. On the window-ledge outside was propped a notice, larger than Belinda's – Gem had used one of her expensive painting blocks. On it was printed in big letters: 'MIND YOUR OWN BUSINESS'. And underneath was written: 'And it's "warm", not "worme".' Next day Belinda found the scarlet jacket and the socks; they had been wrapped round a pebble and thrown over the hedge into the Fells' garden.

Chapter 6

'MIND YOUR OWN BUSINESS'. Nona would have minded hers at once but, 'Huh!' said Belinda, as if she were delighted, and next afternoon, 'Nona, haven't you another paper sunshade like the dolls' house one?' she asked.

Nona had found two sunshades in crackers at a party that Christmas. They matched the one that stood in the dolls' house 'shoes off' place and Nona had kept them carefully. Now reluctantly she took one out – it was pink with blossoms on it – and gave it to Belinda. 'I was keeping it in case . . .' she said, but Belinda was already writing. 'How do you spell "umbrella"?' she asked.

Gem almost caught Belinda that afternoon. Belinda had hardly got back to the platform and turned to draw back the ladder when Gem and Matson came up the garden path. Belinda was almost hidden by the top branch but not quite, and she froze as a rabbit does when it scents danger. 'Oh, don't look up! Don't!' prayed Belinda, and held her breath until Gem and Matson had passed safely into the house. Then she had to hurry and untie the ladder from the fork, but she tried so hard to be quick that her hands fumbled and she had only just time to draw back when Gem came into the sitting room. As fast as she could Belinda wriggled back to the platform and flattened herself against it and, 'What will Gem do when she sees the sunshade?' asked Belinda. She had put it on the windowsill with a message: 'We take our dolls OUT. Why don't you? If you're afraid of rane, here's an umbrella.' The sunshade was not an umbrella, but Miss Happiness and Miss Flower could use theirs in the rain because Nona had painted it on the outside with oil.

Belinda had not long to wait. In what seemed a minute the window opened wide and the sunshade was thrown out, thrown by Gem's hand, and hard. It was open, and like a little parachute, it caught the wind and floated, eddying towards the Fells' garden, and Belinda saw that it went so well because it was weighted by a screwed-up paper. A message, thought Belinda. It eddied over the Fells' garden, coming lower and lower.

Belinda ached to go and catch it, but with Gem at the window she had to stay where she was – and as still as that frozen rabbit. Suppose I sneeze, thought Belinda, and at once she wanted to sneeze. Luckily Tom had taught her a trick of rubbing her finger hard under her nose and she just managed not to sneeze.

The sunshade came down, caught in a forsythia bush in the Fells' border, but still Gem stayed watching at the window, while Belinda grew colder and colder; she could not feel her feet at all, her hands ached with

Little Plum

cold and her nose was running but, she's trying to trap me, thought Belinda. Nothing would have made her move.

It was growing dark; soon Mother would miss her; people would be set to search: Tom, Anne, Nona, presently Father; then Mother must find out what she was doing. Belinda knew without telling that Mother would be very annoyed. She began to think she should have to move when the Tiffany Jones's gate opened, and there was Gem's music master coming as he did every Monday, Wednesday and Friday. Belinda had forgotten it was Friday and, it must be half past four, she thought. At the same moment the lights in Gem's sitting room went on and Matson stood there in the doorway, telling Gem to come down. Gem had her lessons on the grand piano in the drawing room; she only used the little white piano for practising.

Because the window was shut, Belinda could not catch words, but she could hear their voices – Matson's expostulating, Gem's curt – and see their gestures. 'I won't come down,' Gem seemed to be saying. 'You must, Miss Gem,' Matson was answering and, 'I won't move,' said Gem. Matson must have gone to get Miss Tiffany Jones, for that large lady appeared in the doorway. At the sound of her loud voice Gem left the window quickly and, she doesn't want Miss Tiffany Jones to know, thought Belinda. At least Gem was not a sneak. Miss Tiffany Jones spoke so peremptorily, that slowly, reluctantly, Gem went out of the door. Belinda had almost moved when Gem suddenly whipped back again, ran to the window and took a hasty peep.

'Ha! ha! You thought you would catch me,' said Belinda under her breath and, cold, as she was – shivering, thought Belinda – she made herself stay quite still until she heard Gem's scales going up and down and was sure that it was safe to come down.

She was chilled to the bones but it was just light enough in the garden to find the sunshade parachute. She had to take it indoors before she could read the message, which was written in small clear writing; what it said was clear too: 'Trespassers will be prosecuted', Gem had written. 'If I find you in our garden, I shall call the POLICE.'

When they saw the pink sunshade thrown out of the window, Miss Happiness and Miss Flower were grieved. 'But why?' they asked. 'Why? We had hoped Little Plum would go out into the world and perhaps come and visit us.' Something was going on that they did not understand, but it was certainly exciting. 'What will little Miss Belinda think of next?' they asked.

'Nona, can you make a Japanese dinner on a tray?'

'Yes, but you will have to buy a dolls'-house tea set,' said Nona.

'Buy it with my own money?'

'If you want a Japanese dinner,' said Nona.

Little Plum

Belinda had not told Nona how the jacket and socks had come back, the sunshade been thrown out, nor told her of Gem's messages, but Nona seemed to have a shrewd idea of what was happening. 'If I lend Miss Happiness's and Miss Flower's bowls and tea things, anything might happen to them,' she said. 'You can buy one of those painted metal tea-sets; Tom would file the handles off the cups to make the bowls. There is a pretty pink set in the window at Merrow's shop and they only cost nine pence.'

'Nine pence! That's heaps of money,' said Belinda. 'I can't spend nine pence on Gem.'

'Then you can't have a Japanese dinner.'

'And why a teapot for dinner?' Belinda was trying to argue, but Nona was firm.

'Japanese people seem to have tea with everything – green tea – I can make that with paint water.'

Belinda hated to spend her pocket money, but Gem's last message had been really rude and, 'I'll show her who's trespassing,' said Belinda.

Nona had never made anything prettier than that tray. She made it from the lid of an old pillbox, and painted it shiny black outside, scarlet inside for lacquer. She gummed the pink bowls on to it in case Belinda spilled them, and gummed the food on as well, but dolls are used to having dolls' house food fixed on with gum. There were notices the size of half your little finger-nail, to say what each bowl held:

'rice', said one – that was snipped-up white cotton; 'fish' – they were cardboard fish as small as ants, painted silver in a red sauce ('Japanese people are very fond of fish,' said Nona); 'vegetable' – ground up green parsley in another sauce; 'cake' – pink and white meringue sugar crumbs. There were chopsticks made from pine needles and, what was most wonderful of all, the tea was hot. Tom had filed the teapot handle off as well as the cup handles and bored two tiny holes, through which Nona threaded a loop of brown cotton and buttonhole-stitched it so that it looked like a wicker handle such as real Japanese teapots have. Belinda had taken the tea over in an old aspirin bottle, keeping it in her pocket so that it should not get cold. 'It was boiling when I put it in,' she told Nona.

Miss Happiness and Miss Flower hoped Gem, when she found the tray, would play with it. 'Pour out a bowl of tea,' Miss Happiness and Miss Flower tried to tell her when they saw her at the window. 'Make Little Plum use those chopsticks.' But again Miss Happiness and Miss Flower had not seen the message that had come with the tray: 'Why don't you give your poor starving doll some FOOD?'

Gem read it and next moment tray, food, bowls, saucers, teapot, chopsticks, everything had gone out of the window.

As soon as Gem was out of the way next day – gone for a walk in the Park with Matson – Belinda went up in the ilex tree to see how Gem had liked the dinner. She soon saw! Down below on the path was something scarlet, black and pink, a thrown-down tray, its food all scattered, while, on Gem's windowsill, close by the ledge, was a small china pot with a cover. By it was a notice printed: 'FOOD FOR YOU.' When Belinda had spied round to see both gardens were empty she went across to get it. Whatever can it be? thought Belinda.

When she was safely down again, she took the cover off the pot; inside was something that looked like dreadfully smelling, dreadfully coloured jam – covered by a piece of paper that said: 'My own recipe.' The recipe was written out in Gem's pretty handwriting:

> 'Vinegar
> Mustard
> Castor oil
> Toadstools
> Frogs' eggs
> Crushed cockroach
> Worms.'

At the bottom was written: 'Take it.'

'Good heavens gracious me!' said Belinda, her eyes round. After the first minute, she thought it was funny but when she showed it to Nona, Nona was not as sure. 'I don't like it,' said Nona.

'We're not meant to like it,' said Belinda.

'You're teasing Gem,' said Nona; 'don't go on.'

But Belinda said, 'We're not teasing now. We're fighting.'

The war had now been on for three weeks and, 'Little Plum needs a bed,' said Belinda. 'Nona, can you and Melly make her some quilts and pillows?'

Japanese people do not have bedsteads – only those who copy Western habits. Most sleep on the floor on thick quilts piled one on top of the other, with more quilt coverings and a hard pillow for their heads. 'They used once to have wooden pillows,' said Nona, but all the same Japanese quilt beds are very comfortable. Miss Happiness and Miss Flower could have told you that. They each had sets of quilts, one all in blue, the other in pale pink. Peach Boy had a scarlet set but he usually slept in the pocket of Belinda's dressing gown, which was flung down on the end of her bed, or on the floor.

Nona chose some flowered stuff, palest blue, to match Little Plum's kimono, with a pattern of blossom, and made two quilts for Little Plum to lie on, wadded with cotton wool, a pillow with tassels at the corners and an overquilt, thinner but wadded too. It was the prettiest set she had made. 'I think Gem will like it,' she said.

'I believe, if the window was open, I could put Little

Little Plum

Plum into the quilts,' said Belinda. 'I believe I could reach; if *I* don't put her into them, I'm sure Gem won't. Poor Little Plum!' said Belinda.

It is certainly tiring for a little doll to have to sit all the time. 'Never to lie down,' said Miss Flower. 'Never to be moved,' said Miss Happiness. They were pleased that now Little Plum could go to bed – but could she?

You may wonder, if Gem wanted Belinda – she was sure the trespasser was Belinda – to mind her own business, why she did not put Little Plum out of reach, or out of sight.

'Perhaps she likes the things we sent,' said Nona. Remember that Belinda had not told Nona how Gem had thrown the jacket and socks over the hedge; how she had cast out the sunshade and smashed the dinner tray and, 'I think Gem's pleased,' said Nona, but Belinda shook her head.

'She just wants to catch me,' said Belinda.

Belinda had to take Little Plum off Gem's windowsill to put her into the quilts.

'Where is she going?' cried Miss Happiness and Miss Flower as they saw a topknot and a flowery kimono in Belinda's hand up in the air: but, in a moment, Little Plum's legs were straightened and she was slid between covers much warmer and more silken soft than anything she had ever known: a pillow was tucked under her head and a minute later she was back on the windowsill, but lying down with the quilts all around her. Beside the bed was one of Belinda's notices: 'It's crool to make children sit up all night. *Our* Japanese dolls have Japanese BEDS.'

Next day a paper bag was hanging from Gem's windowsill. When Belinda went over and got it, she found there was no message inside; no message was needed; in the bag were the pretty quilts and pillow snipped to bits.

Even Belinda was a little dismayed. She showed the bag to Nona and Nona could have cried. 'But why?' she asked. 'Why? It took me *hours* to sew those quilts,' and she said, touching the snippets, 'Belinda, what are you trying to do? Make Gem like Little Plum or make her hate you?'

'Make her like Little Plum, of course,' said Belinda.

'You would do it better without insulting messages,' said Nona.

'Are they insulting?' asked Belinda with great satisfaction.

'You know they are.'

'Well, she insults back,' and, 'Gem's a good fighter,' said Belinda.

Gem was. Next time Belinda went over the ladder, on one of Gem's ballet lesson days, the window was open wider than usual. Before Nona had seen the quilts snipped up, she had made Little Plum a cushion to match them, and Belinda had determined to sit

Little Plum on it. She had written a notice: 'Our dolls have coochons to sit on.' She was in a hurry because she only got back from school a few minutes before Gem was due in and she was perhaps not as careful as usual; as she reached up for Little Plum her hand knocked the window frame.

There was a blinding icy cold splash, something hit Belinda on the head and nearly sent her spinning off the drainpipe. How she kept her foot on it and clung to the fire-escape railing she did not know, because she was gasping for breath and spluttering; then she saw that the window was streaming with water while far below where she might have fallen was a small white plastic bucket, still rolling a little from its fall. It lay beside the cushion that had been knocked out of Belinda's hand, and 'Sh-she s-set a b-booby trap for me,' said Belinda through her chattering teeth.

It was a successful trap. How Gem had put the bucket up without Matson knowing, the children never knew; as the bucket was white and hidden a little in the rose creeper Belinda, in her hurry, had not seen it against the white house wall; nor had she noticed that the window was open wider than usual, and unfastened so that it swung at a touch. There had not been a great deal of water in the bucket – if there had been Gem could not have lifted it to balance it on the open window – but there was enough to soak Belinda's head and shoulders; water had run down her neck so that she was wet to the skin and so cold that she could hardly struggle back along the ladder, and her numbed hands found it hard to untie the ropes. She took a long time to turn round, come back for the ladder, draw it in, and climb down the ilex tree again. Fortunately Gem was late, but by the time Belinda got back to the house she was shivering from head to foot.

The first person she ran into was Mother. 'Belinda!' cried Mother. '*Belinda!* Where *have* you been?'

'Into a bucket of water,' said Belinda truthfully.

'But how . . . ?'

'It fell on me,' Belinda was just going to say, but Mother had seen how she was shivering and she wasted no more words. In a few minutes Belinda was in a hot bath. Mother was rubbing her hair dry with warm towels and had called to Nona to make a hot milk drink.

'She might have killed me,' Belinda whispered to Nona when she was dressed again in dry clothes and Nona had brought the milk, into which she had put some honey. 'I might have been dead!' Belinda sounded thrilled but Nona was remembering the snipped up quilts and, 'Belinda, give this up,' she begged.

'What! Now?' said Belinda. 'Let her win now? Wait . . .' said Belinda, and her eyes were bright blue over the top of the glass of milk. 'Wait and see what *I'm* going to do to *her*!'

When the bucket fell on Belinda, Miss Happiness

and Miss Flower had been shocked, almost as shocked as Belinda herself. Japanese are courteous people and, 'Little Misses to do that to one another!' they said. They were not only shocked, they were worried about Little Plum, because some of the water had surely splashed on her. 'And Little Plum has no mother to put her into a hot bath,' said Miss Flower, 'to rub her hair dry.'

'No Miss Nona to make her a hot drink,' said Miss Happiness. They knew that Gem would not think of a little doll being cold, her plaster almost frozen, on the windowsill.

Miss Happiness and Miss Flower were beginning to understand that Little Plum was in the middle of some sort of quarrel, and they did not know what to wish for: that Belinda would stop climbing the ilex tree; that Gem could learn to play; 'That we should all be peaceful and happy together,' said Miss Happiness. The two little dolls were still talking it over that late afternoon when there came a sudden and determined shaking in the ilex tree.

Chapter 7

Gem walked out of the Tiffany Joneses' gate and in at the Fells'. Matson was not with her, nor Miss Berryman. She wore her velvet dress with the net ruffle and had only a coat put round her; no gloves or white boots, only bronze house shoes. Her head was bare and she had no shawl. She went to the front door and rang the bell. Mother came to answer it and, 'Why, Gem!' cried Mother.

'Will you please,' said Gem in a strange high tone – it was the first time Mother had heard her speak – 'Will you please tell your child, Belinda, to give me back my doll?'

Mother opened the door wider and said, 'Come inside, out of the cold.'

When Gem was in and the door was shut Mother asked, 'Does your aunt, does Matson, know you are here?'

'No, they don't,' said Gem. 'But it doesn't matter. I have only come to get my doll.'

'Your doll?'

'Yes, my doll.' Gem spoke as if Mother was her enemy.

'But what makes you think she is here?'

'I know she is,' said Gem. 'That's why. Please give her back.'

306

'But how could she be?' asked Mother. 'How could a doll of yours be here?'

'I don't know how,' said Gem, 'but she is here. She was on my windowsill – a little Japanese doll – and she's gone.'

'A *Japanese* doll,' said Mother, and she asked, 'When did she go?'

'This afternoon.'

Mother suddenly looked at Gem in a different way. 'It wouldn't by any chance have something to do with a bucket of water?'

Gem's eyelids came down over her eyes like seals and she shut her lips.

'Come into the sitting room,' said Mother, and she called down the passage to the playroom, 'Belinda, come here. I want you.'

Belinda came. When she saw Gem, though she tried not to let her face show anything, she could not help a smile.

'Belinda, answer me truthfully. Have you got Gem's doll?'

'No, I haven't,' said Belinda, but Mother was not satisfied.

'Do you know who has?'

'No,' said Belinda, but Mother seemed to guess she might have said more.

'Do you know anything about her?'

'Of course I do,' said Belinda. 'We all do. Gem has

a dear, sweet little Japanese doll called Little Plum –
such a pretty little doll with a topknot – and she takes
no care of her. I'm not surprised to hear she's lost,'
said Belinda.

Before Mother or Gem could say anything to that
there were sounds from the garden next door; agitated
sounds of, 'Gem! Miss Gem! Miss Gem, where have
you got to? Gem, are you hiding? Miss Gem! Gem!'

'They have missed you,' said Mother, but Gem did
not seem to have heard. She was glaring at Belinda,
and Belinda glared back.

'I had better tell them where you are,' said Mother.
'Stay here, Belinda. We will sort this out when I come
back.'

Gem and Belinda were left alone. Belinda was
slightly afraid of Gem; she looked so fierce with her
face set, her green eyes blazing. Belinda had never seen
anyone in such a towering temper.

'How dare you take my doll?' said Gem.

'I didn't take her; I rescued her . . . for her own
good,' said Belinda, who had heard her headmistress
say that. 'You were cruel to her.'

'I was not,' said Gem.

'You were,' said Belinda.

'You took her. You're a thief.' Gem came one step
nearer, Belinda instinctively took one back. 'Thief!
Trespasser! Liar!'

'I'm not a liar.'

308

Little Plum

'You were telling lies to your mother just now.'

'I was not,' but Belinda's voice was uncertain. 'I was *not*. I haven't got your doll, see; I don't know who has her because nobody has her. She's by herself in a safe place. So bah!' said Belinda, as they said at school. 'So bah! Squish squash, flat on the floor.'

'*You'll* be flat on the floor.' Belinda backed away as Gem came closer, breathing in an alarming way through her nostrils. Her words came out through set lips. 'Thief!'

'Cruel!' Belinda retorted. 'Cruel beast.'

'Thief! Liar! Trespasser!'

'Beast! Beast! Beast!'

Then Gem sprang at Belinda and Belinda forgot all Tom's teaching, and hit out with both fists. She pulled Gem's hair. Gem screamed and hammered Belinda with her fists, and in a moment they were locked together, rolling, thumping, scratching and kicking, on the floor.

'Good gracious! Gracious! Help!'

'Miss Gem! Miss Gem!'

Miss Tiffany Jones and Matson were in the doorway. When they stood together they could not get in, and you could hardly see Mother behind them.

'Belinda! Belinda!' screamed Nona from under Matson's arm. She dodged under it, squeezed past Miss Tiffany Jones and jumped in to help Belinda but, '*Belinda!*' Mother had thundered in such a voice that Belinda let go of Gem. Matson, with surprising quickness, ran in, caught Gem and held her, while Nona pulled Belinda away.

Both children were panting. Belinda had a scratch right down her cheek, more scratches on her hands and her hair was tousled, while Gem's was hanging over her face. The beautiful velvet dress was torn, its net ruffle hanging down. Belinda stared at it aghast. One of Gem's high white silk socks was torn, her cheek was cut where it had hit a chair, and her face was beginning to swell.

Miss Tiffany Jones was silent now; she seemed too appalled to speak. Matson gave grunts of consternation and began dabbing at Gem's cheek with her handkerchief. Nona stroked Belinda's shoulder in silent sympathy. 'It wasn't meant for a fight,' said Nona, trying to explain. 'It was just that it turned into a fight.'

'A fight about what?' asked Miss Tiffany Jones faintly.

'About Little Plum,' said Nona.

'Little Plum? Little Plum? Who is Little Plum?'

As Miss Tiffany Jones said that Gem began to laugh.

'Belinda, go up to your room *at once*,' commanded Mother. Belinda went, but Gem still went on laughing – it was a horrible high laughing that Nona did not like to hear. Matson picked up Gem's coat, wrapped it round her and took her away, still laughing.

Little Plum

'But . . . but it's nothing to laugh at,' said Miss Tiffany Jones in bewilderment.

Gem and Belinda were both in their rooms, Belinda because she was punished, Gem because she would not come out. Nona had seen how, in the garden, she had torn herself away from Matson and run into the house.

She must have run upstairs because when Nona went into her own room, she could hear knockings, and voices calling over the way, 'Miss Gem! Miss Gem! Open the door.' It seemed that Gem took not the faintest notice. Uneasy and unhappy, Nona watched and listened. Presently, Matson and Miss Tiffany Jones gave up and there was silence and, with a sigh, Nona turned away from her own window but, before she left it, she bent as she often did to look in the dolls' house. It always comforted her to see Miss Happiness and Miss Flower. She bent down, and stopped. She had caught sight of Miss Flower's pale blue bed, quilts and pillow, lying out on the matting. In the daytime? thought Nona, puzzled. I didn't put them there. She bent right down to look into the house properly, and there, on Miss Flower's blue pillow lay an unmistakable topknot. 'Little Plum!' cried Nona. 'Little Plum!'

The dolls had been astonished when Little Plum had suddenly appeared in their house; astonished, although, 'Of course she is very welcome,' they said courteously.

'But it seems strange,' Miss Flower could not help saying, 'that a guest should go straight to bed.'

'It was Miss Belinda's idea,' said Miss Happiness. 'If Miss Nona had been here, she would at least have let us offer her some tea.'

'That would have been more polite,' and Miss Flower could not help feeling that when things were not polite they were somehow wrong.

'We should have bowed to her and she to us,' and then Miss Flower sank her voice. 'Is she a refugee?' she asked.

'I don't think so,' said Miss Happiness. 'Refugees are people who have run away or been driven out. I think Little Plum was brought here,' said Miss Happiness.

'Kidnapped?' asked Miss Flower in alarm. 'Would our Miss Belinda do that?'

'I hope not, but I think so,' said Miss Happiness.

Meanwhile Little Plum's topknot looked so comfortable on Miss Flower's pillow, she seemed so content lying there in the pale blue quilts, that it was as if she were saying, 'Let me lie here for ever.' But Little Plum was still in the middle of a quarrel. Nona's face had filled with consternation and the next minute her hand had taken Little Plum out.

*

Little Plum

'You must give her back *at once*,' said Nona.

Belinda knew she was on losing ground. Nona's scandalized face and wrathful eyes made her feel uncomfortable.

'At once!' said Nona.

'Mother says I mustn't come out of my room,' said Belinda, but feebly.

'She would want you to come out for this. She has gone to Miss Tiffany Jones, to explain,' said Nona, but how could Mother explain that . . . Nona hated to say it but she had to . . . that Belinda had stolen Little Plum. 'Oh Belinda!' said Nona. 'How can you be so bad?'

'Gem was unkind to Little Plum.'

'She wasn't unkind – she was just not kind; but that doesn't matter. You must put Little Plum back where you found her – at once.'

'Then Gem will win,' said Belinda sulkily.

'She deserves to win,' said Nona, and like a policeman she put Little Plum into the pocket of Belinda's anorak, which she fetched from the cloakroom, and chivvied Belinda down the stairs. There she turned across the garden towards the gate, but Belinda stopped. 'I have to go up the ilex tree,' said Belinda.

'The ilex? To get up to Gem's window? But . . . I thought you went up the fire escape; you can't reach from the ilex tree.'

'I can. Wait. You'll see.'

313

Slowly, sullenly, Belinda went up the tree. Nona stood at the bottom of the ladder, looking up, mystified as to what Belinda was doing, but when Belinda reached the big branch, she stopped. The light was on in Gem's sitting room and Belinda could see in. Gem was sitting at her desk, her face down on her arms, her shoulders shaking and, 'Nona,' Belinda whispered urgently, 'Nona, Gem's crying.'

'Crying? She was laughing.'

'She's crying now.' Belinda saw how Gem's shoulders shook, how great sobs shook all of her and, 'She's crying terribly,' whispered Belinda.

Nona climbed up the ladder on to the platform and looked in too. 'Oh Belinda, what have you done to her?' said Nona.

'Did I do that?' asked Belinda, startled. She was a rough, tough little girl but she had a tender heart and now, at the sight of Gem so hopelessly crying, a lump began to gather in her own throat and she had a miserable, guilty feeling.

'What can I do?' she whispered to Nona.

'I don't know how you got up to the window,' said Nona, 'but do as you did before. Then tap on it and give Little Plum to Gem.' Nona still thought Belinda would come down, slip across the two gardens and go up the fire escape. It had not occurred to her there was any other way to the House Next Door, and she turned to lead the way, climbing off the platform and from branch to branch down the tree, then down the rope ladder. At the foot of the ilex she stood and waited for Belinda, but Belinda did not come. Instead there were queer sounds up above and, 'What are you doing?' Nona called up.

'Getting the ladder ready,' said Belinda calmly.

'What ladder?' Then Nona saw the wooden ladder sliding into position, one end on the fire escape, the other on the fork. In a moment Belinda was lashing it firm. 'You're not . . . you're not going across *that*!' cried Nona in horror.

'Why not?' said Belinda. 'I often do.'

'No! No! Belinda, no!' Nona almost screamed, but Belinda was already astride the ladder, her legs dangling, her hands in front of her as she wriggled forward. Nona, looking up, saw the sickening drop from the ladder to the path and she could not look any more. She cowered against the ilex tree and hid her eyes.

That was why she did not see Mother come back from the House Next Door. Mother had met Tom outside the gate. Now, from the path, they saw Belinda. Mother stood still. Tom was just going to shout when Mother's hand came down on his shoulder. 'Hush! don't shout; don't move,' she said. 'If you make her look down she will fall.' All the colour had drained out of Mother's face, her eyes were wide with terror. As they stood there, Mr Tiffany Jones came walking up to the gate of the House Next Door. He had his hand on the latch to open it when from the Tiffany Joneses' garden came a piercing scream.

It was Matson. Thinking that perhaps Little Plum had been dropped in the garden, Matson had gone to look. 'Children beat me,' Matson had said to Selwyn. 'Gem didn't care at all about that doll, and now suddenly . . .' Matson was beating the bushes when she happened to look up. At her scream Mr Tiffany Jones looked up too. Then he flung open the gate and ran in. Miss Tiffany Jones, Selwyn, Cook, Eileen all rushed out of the house; the gardener threw down his broom and ran too, and all the while Matson pointed and screamed. In her room Gem lifted her head from her desk and listened, then came to the window to look.

Mother and Tom ran from their side of the garden; Nona stood, pressed back against the trunk of the ilex tree, and high above them all, halfway across the ladder, Belinda heard.

She heard and looked down. She saw faces staring up at her, the pointing hands and, as if their fear had come up to her, suddenly Belinda was afraid. She had never looked down before. Now, her feet below her, she saw the path; there was nothing each side of her but the empty air and she felt how narrow the ladder was, how her legs were dangling in nothing – and all at once she felt giddy and sick. Cold drops came out on her forehead, and the backs of her knees. Her hands felt damp. She swayed. Below, on the lawn, Miss Tiffany Jones fainted away.

By now Tom was past Nona, up the ilex tree and out along the branch. 'Hold on,' called Tom, 'I'm coming.' But, big boy that he was, when he reached the fork and the ladder Tom could not make himself get on it.

'Don't go, Tom. Don't go,' Nona whispered up frantically. She need not have said it. Tom could not make himself go. He lay along the branch and tried to reach Belinda, but he could not. 'Come back, Bel,' he said. 'Come back towards me.' But, 'I can't,' gasped Belinda, 'I can't.'

She who had gone across the ladder so many times could not move now; she could only sit and shut her eyes and cling with her hands.

'Don't look down. Don't,' came Mother's even voice, but Belinda could not look anywhere. Matson's noise had been joined by Cook and Eileen, Selwyn had run in again to telephone the fire brigade, while a crowd began to gather in the road. A woman screamed louder than Matson. A whole tumult of sound was gathering, beating in Belinda's ears, when a voice spoke close beside her. 'Open your eyes,' it said, 'and look at me.'

It was such a quiet voice in the hubbub that it reached Belinda. She opened her eyes and there, on the fire escape, just in front of her, was Mr Tiffany Jones. His brief case, his bowler and his beautiful greatcoat were cast down on the landing, and he was holding the end of the ladder, speaking to her. 'Brave girl,' came that quiet voice. 'Look at me.' It was wise to keep on saying it.

Below, on the path, Selwyn and the maids had spread a blanket and were holding it to catch Belinda if she fell but, 'You won't fall,' said Mr Tiffany Jones steadily. 'Look straight at me. Now move your right hand forward.'

'I – can't,' said Belinda through stiff lips.

'You can.'

'I – can't,' and to everyone's horror, Belinda swayed again. 'I'm – I'm going to fall,' she said in a rush.

'Fall? With Gem looking?'

'Gem?' Belinda stiffened.

'Gem's watching you,' said Mr Tiffany Jones. 'Watching you from the window.'

Belinda looked up and there was Gem's face pressed against the glass, pressed tightly, looking at Belinda.

'Do you want her to think you're a coward?' came Mr Tiffany Jones's voice. 'Do you want her to laugh at you and think you're afraid?'

'I'm not afraid.' The words were jerked out of Belinda.

'Then move your right hand,' and suddenly Belinda was able to obey. 'Come forward an inch. Move your right hand . . . now your left. Come forward,' said Mr Tiffany Jones. 'Come or she'll think you are afraid.'

Little Plum

His face was oddly pale and he too had wet drops on his forehead. Belinda could see them running down his cheeks but he was smiling at her and he still held her in his eyes. 'Your right hand forward. Now your left . . . come forward. That's right. You show Gem you're not a coward.'

A hush had fallen on the garden and the street as Belinda began to move. Mother stayed silent down below, Tom silent in the tree, Nona silent at its foot. Gem was silent at the window, her hands clutching the sill. Slowly, as Mr Tiffany Jones commanded her, Belinda moved along the ladder towards the fire escape. She had been perhaps only two feet out of Mr Tiffany Jones's reach, but it seemed a long way to the people who were watching, and Mother's hands were pressed together, while Nona pressed hers against the ilex trunk. Then, as Belinda, still looking at him, came that two feet nearer, Mr Tiffany Jones's hands shot forward, caught her in a strong grasp and in a moment she was on the fire escape with him.

Chapter 8

'No sweets for a week; bed every night at six and you are not to go out anywhere unless someone is with you. I can't trust you any more,' said Mother.

Belinda hung her head. She was very much ashamed.

'She has had a terrible fright. Must she be punished?' asked Mr Tiffany Jones.

'I'm afraid she must,' Mother said. 'Belinda has been very naughty for a long time.' And Mother doesn't know half of it, thought Belinda.

Mr Tiffany Jones was right; she had had a terrible fright.

'Perhaps this will teach you,' said Mother. 'Teach you that when you want to do things you must use a little sense.'

As long as she lived Belinda would not forget this moment when she had turned giddy on the ladder and felt herself sway. Over and over again she woke in the night and thought it was happening again, and her hands and the backs of her knees were always wet. I might have fallen and been dead, thought Belinda. One of the worst parts was that it was all of it public; everybody, everywhere she went knew how foolhardy she had been, yet it was what people did not know that tormented Belinda. Nobody knew but Nona, though

Mother seemed to have guessed.

'You have told lies,' said Mother. 'Yes, even if you did not tell direct ones, you did not tell the truth and that amounts to lying. You took Little Plum, who wasn't yours; and I can guess,' said Mother, looking even sterner, 'I can guess that you have been unkind.'

Mr Tiffany Jones was beginning to guess too, yet it seemed that he still liked Belinda. 'Even after I have been such a trouble!' said Belinda. He seemed to like her – and to be a little cross with Miss Tiffany Jones. 'What I don't understand,' he said, 'What I don't understand, Belinda, is why you couldn't come and see Gem in the ordinary way.'

'Because I'm impossibly rough,' said Belinda.

'Who said so?'

'Miss Tiffany Jones.'

'Agnes? She did, did she?' said Mr Tiffany Jones.

'I try to be gentle,' Belinda explained, 'but I'm not. Nona is; she doesn't even try, because she *is* gentle. I do try but . . .' and here she was remembering knocking Gem over with her skates, and fighting, kicking and scratching on the sitting-room floor. 'Sometimes,' said Belinda in a low shamed voice, 'I'm not.'

'Well, Gem was pretty fierce,' said Mr Tiffany Jones. 'That's quite a nasty scratch you have on your cheek; and I think that I should like you to come – and so would Gem.'

321

But she wouldn't, thought Belinda sadly, and that was true; for all Mr Tiffany Jones's friendliness, Gem still kept her face turned away, still walked past with set lips, would not answer the most friendly smiles. Mother asked her to tea, and she would not come. Mr Tiffany Jones, they knew, had suggested they come to the House Next Door. Gem would not have them.

'You can't be surprised,' said Nona. Belinda was not surprised, and she could not forget the sight of Gem with her head down on her desk, sobbing her heart out. These things were like thorns in her mind and, 'I don't know what to do,' said Belinda. 'I would do anything if I could think of a way to make friends.'

Sometimes, when one is truly sorry and trying to make amends, a way seems to come. 'How can I tell Gem I'm sorry when she won't speak to me?' said Belinda in despair. 'How can I show her when she won't come near us? What can I do? What can I do?' asked Belinda, and then the thought came: if I were Nona, I should ask Mr Twilfit what to do.

As you know, when an idea came to Belinda, she acted on it at once, forgetting everything else. Now she forgot about not going out alone, forgot about not skating in the road near the shops and . . . I'll go at once on my roller skates and then I shall be quicker, thought Belinda. In five minutes she was standing breathless in front of Mr Twilfit at a counter piled high with books – she had left her skates outside –

without waiting to say good morning, or give a word of explanation, she began: 'Mr Twilfit, you made friends with Nona when nobody else could. You understood about Miss Happiness and Miss Flower when they needed a Japanese house. You showed Nona how to make it.' The words tumbled out breathlessly. 'It was you who gave us the Japanese fairy-tale book that gave Nona the idea of Little Peach. It was you all the time, and *please* can you help me what to do about Gem and Little Plum?'

'What in thunder are you talking about?' asked Mr Twilfit.

'I'll tell you.' Belinda stood on tiptoe to lean nearer to him across the counter, and her hands happened to come down on a book that was lying there open.

'*Look* at your hands,' roared Mr Twilfit. 'Look – at – your hands!'

Belinda was too stalwart a child to be afraid of Mr Twilfit; besides she was quite used to being scolded and she knew her hands were grubby. She remembered now that Nona always washed hers before she went to the bookshop.

'You keep your hands behind you when you come into this shop,' said Mr Twilfit, and Belinda obediently put her hands behind her. 'And talk slowly,' said Mr Twilfit, 'and don't shout.'

'Yes, Mr Twilfit,' said Belinda.

'Now you can tell me,' and Belinda began again. She

began with the House Next Door, Mr Tiffany Jones and Miss Tiffany Jones, but Mr Twilfit interrupted her. 'I know the woman,' he said. 'She's a fool – wanted me to teach that poor child Latin. Go on.'

Belinda told about Gem coming and about Matson, about Gem's beautiful rooms and clothes and the pony; about how she had knocked Gem down with her roller skates, and – shamefacedly – about meeting her on the road with the class and teasing.

'Fourteen against one,' said Mr Twilfit, just as Tom had done, and Belinda hung her head. She told about Little Plum and how she had seen her from the ilex tree; about taking over the coat and socks, the sunshade, the Japanese dinner, the quilts; reluctantly she told about the insulting messages. She grew red as she told about them, but she told. 'I think I was teasing.' She said 'I *think*' because she was not quite sure now that it was only teasing. She told about Gem's dreadful recipe and the snipped quilts and, 'H'm . . . getting fiercer,' said Mr Twilfit. When she came to the bucket of water, he said, 'Good for her,' and then Belinda's voice tailed away. She did not like to tell about the end but, 'Go on,' said Mr Twilfit. 'Let's have it all.' And in a small voice, her head bent over the counter, Belinda told.

She forgot to keep her hands behind her and one finger traced a pattern on the book she had been told not to touch, but Mr Twilfit did not interrupt her. She told about stealing Little Plum – Belinda called it stealing now – about Gem's coming and Belinda's lies – she called them lies now – of the fight and the frightening way Gem had laughed, then of how she had cried. She told of how she herself had suddenly been afraid on the ladder but of the danger she hardly said a word; it was all about Gem, and when she had finished Belinda's head was bowed low over the counter and tears were spattering down on the book. Mr Twilfit did not say a word; he only leaned forward and very gently lifted it out of the way, wiped the tears off its page with a large and yellow handkerchief, which he then passed to Belinda. 'Blow your nose,' said Mr Twilfit, and only when Belinda had blown, and wiped her eyes, did he say, 'H'm. You have got yourself into a pretty pickle, haven't you?'

The shop door opened, twanging the bell. Belinda hastily turned away to hide her face but it was only Nona. Nona had guessed that Belinda had forgotten what Mother had said about not going out alone, and had come running after her. She had seen Belinda's skates outside the bookshop and had been surprised, but now when she saw Belinda crying into Mr Twilfit's handkerchief, she guessed what had happened and quickly came to stand beside her. 'She's sorry. Terribly sorry,' Nona told Mr Twilfit.

'Yes, but I don't know how to say it,' sobbed Belinda.

Mr Twilfit cleared his throat and blew his nose on a second handkerchief that came out of his other pocket;

this one had green and brown checks. The blow made a noise rather like a whale spouting, if you have ever heard such a thing. He put the handkerchief away and his eyebrows worked up and down which, as Nona could have told Belinda, meant that he was pleased, not angry. Then, 'It's always difficult to say you are sorry,' he said gently to Belinda, 'but you are lucky.'

'Lucky?' Belinda was so astonished he should say lucky that she stopped crying. 'Lucky?' she asked.

'Yes. Do you know the date?'

'The date?' This too was such a surprising remark that Nona and Belinda spoke together.

'Yes, the date.'

'It's the end of February,' said Nona and, 'Is it something to do with Leap Year?' she asked. 'But it can't be; this isn't Leap Year.'

'I'm talking about the Japanese calendar,' said Mr Twilfit. 'You say this Little Plum is a Japanese doll?'

They nodded.

'Well then, this is a quarrel about dolls, a Japanese doll,' said Mr Twilfit, 'and what better day could you have to make it up on than the Japanese Feast of Dolls?'

Belinda's head came up. Nona's face began to shine.

'Wait,' said Mr Twilfit. 'I can find you a book about it. *Japanese Festivals and Ceremonies*. It's somewhere in the office. I had meant to give it to Nona for her birthday but you had better have it now.'

Mr Twilfit rummaged in his office, then, 'Here it

is,' he said and came out carrying a book that had a lantern like Gem's on the cover. He turned the leaves over until he found the right place and then began to read. 'Every year, throughout Japan,' he read, 'girls have a festival of their own. It is a Doll Festival, when big and little girls arrange ceremonial dolls in a display.'

'What are cer . . . cerry . . . dolls?' asked Belinda.

'Ceremonial dolls; grandly dressed dolls kept for special occasions. "Often they are handed down from mother to daughter for a hundred years or more,"' read Mr Twilfit from the book, '"and used only on this especial day. There should be about fifteen dolls, set out on steps covered with red cloth . . ."' and he went on to read to Nona and Belinda all about the Emperor and Empress dolls, the court on the steps below them and the delicate and beautiful things that were put round them. '"Tea things, musical instruments, fans, chairs, palanquins . . . all miniature and exquisitely made of lacquer, silver or ivory, while in vases around,"' read Mr Twilfit, '"are sprays of peach blossom, the special flower of this day."'

'Blossom. That would suit Little Plum,' said Nona.

'"The Festival,"' read Mr Twilfit, '"is held on the third day of the third month." That is the third of March,' he said looking up. 'Today is the 27th of February so that is in four days' time, which would give you just time to get it all ready. I suggest,' said Mr

Twilfit, 'that you keep the Festival of Dolls and that you invite Miss Gem Tiffany Jones and her Little Plum to keep it with you.'

There was a moment's amazed silence then, 'If we only could . . .' said Belinda.

'We haven't any ceremonial dolls,' said Nona.

'No emperor or empress,' said Belinda.

'We could make the steps and cover them with red but . . . even if we could find dolls they would be terribly expensive.'

'Dolls' tables with dinners and . . . what are palanquins?' asked Belinda.

'Sedan chairs and lacquer,' Nona was saying, 'and there's no peach blossom now. Anne can make blossom with paper but would she? It's a beautiful idea,' said Nona, 'but in our house . . .'

'Your house wouldn't be suitable,' said Mr Twilfit. 'It isn't a Japanese house.'

'Then . . . ?'

'Gordon's Ghost!' said Mr Twilfit, losing patience. 'Haven't you a Japanese dolls' house?'

'Of course, but . . .' Then light broke. 'You mean . . . we should have a dolls' Doll Festival,' cried Nona and Belinda.

It was the smallest envelope Gem had ever seen; not more than an inch square, of red paper and written in writing as small as fly marks. Where the stamp might

328

have been a white flower was painted. At the back was a gold seal, the size of a pin's head. The fly mark writing said:

'To Honourable Little Plum,
The House Next Door.'

Gem looked at it as if it might hurt her.

'Open it,' said Mr Tiffany Jones.

'It's a trick,' said Gem.

'I don't think it is,' said Mr Tiffany Jones, 'but you can't tell until you look; and it's for Little Plum, not for you,' said Mr Tiffany Jones, putting his arm round Gem. 'She can't open it herself. You must open it for her.'

Slowly Gem took the envelope up and broke the seal, which was a pity because it was so pretty; she opened the envelope flap and took out the letter, folded and about one and a half inches long. It was written in the same microscopic writing, painted with the same flower.

'"On the third day of the third month,"' read Gem in a shaking voice, '"at four o'clock in the Japanese dolls' house, Miss Happiness and Miss Flower are keeping the Doll Festival. Please, Honourable Little Plum, come and keep it with them."' Below was written 'Refreshments. Ceremonial Dress (fans should be worn). R.S.V.P.' which is what formal invitations have written on them.

'It means "Please answer",' said Mr Tiffany Jones.

Below that again was written clearly: 'Please bring your most Honourable Girl.'

Gem stared at it, her eyes wide; then a flush ran up her neck to her face and glowed in her cheeks. 'Most honourable girl,' she whispered.

Chapter 9

The dolls' house had been brought down into the playroom. Nona and Belinda had cleaned it from roof to floor; clean new matting had been laid down on the floor. Nona and Melly had made new cushions and there was a third one in pale blue silk for Little Plum.

A vase of peach blossom stood in the niche. Anne had made the blossom, not of paper – that had looked too clumsy – but of peach-coloured embroidery silk in knots on the smallest of stems from a rosebush. Two other vases stood each side of red shelves, shelves like steps covered in red paper.

'What are they made of?' asked Gem, wondering.

'You will never guess,' said Belinda.

'I made them a cake,' said Nona. 'Cake cut into shapes so that I could stick the match people in.' The match dolls looked so real that from the beginning she had called them the match people.

'How could we get the dolls?' Belinda had asked Mr Twilfit at the bookshop. 'Those cere . . .' again Belinda could not manage the word, but Nona finished it for her. 'Dolls' ceremonial dolls would have to be *teeny*.'

'Perhaps I could model them,' Nona said, but had broken off. 'No, I couldn't model dolls as small as that and then there are all the clothes . . .'

'When I was a boy,' said Mr Twilfit, 'my sisters made dolls of clothes' pegs; peg dolls we used to call them.'

'Pegs would be too big,' said Belinda.

'What do your dolls use for pegs?'

'Bits of split-up matches.'

'Well then?' said Mr Twilfit and, 'Matches would do,' Nona had cried.

Mr Twilfit had been right; matches made perfect dolls'-house dolls' dolls. 'But you must be careful if you use matches,' Mother had said, 'careful not to strike them.'

'I'm not going to strike them,' said Nona. 'I need their heads.' She had pointed the other end of each match so that, stuck in the cake, they stood upright. Then she dressed them. They looked very real. On the top step, in front of the gold paper screen, were the Emperor and Empress in robes made of gold and silver paper that stood stiffly out round them. On the Emperor's black head, for a hat, Nona had stuck a crumb of gold tinsel, while the Empress had a fuzz of gold thread. Their faces she made from the smallest blob of pinkish yellow paint. Each side of them sat a fat little dog. Nona had moulded them from a blob of plasticine and had painted faces. 'Those dogs are called "chins",' said Belinda.

The shelf below was for the court ladies, more matches dressed in papers of ruby red, blue, purple and green. 'You know those toffees wrapped in colours – Nona used those,' Belinda explained to Gem.

On the third shelf were five musicians and here

Nona had been especially clever, though Anne had had to help her. To make instruments for match people had been almost impossible, 'But Nona made them,' said Belinda proudly.

Japanese instruments are different from ours; Nona had made bamboo flutes from pine needles and fastened them to the musicians' sleeves with a drop of glue. The drum was made entirely of silver sixpences, five of them, glued one on the top of the other. 'A very expensive drum,' said Nona, 'but I'll unglue the sixpences and give them back to Mother.' The drumsticks were two pins. Mr Twilfit had shown Nona pictures of a *samisen*, which is like a banjo, and she had made two of cut-out card, painted silver with painted strings.

On one of the lowest shelves were gardeners dressed in plain red paper, tiny trees covered with more blossom, and chairs and tables cut from fine white card and painted in shining black to look like lacquer. On the tables were twisted gold paper cups and plates holding dolls'-house rice and hundreds and thousands, 'Which are the right size for dolls'-house dolls' doll's cakes,' said Belinda. They had not any sedan chairs or palanquins but they had made tiny fans and dolls'-house pots of peach blossom. It really looked like the photographs of the Doll Festival; and, 'I have never seen anything as beautiful,' said Gem.

She was a different Gem. She had come quite alone, no Matson and no shawl, though it was sleeting, and she had made Little Plum as pretty and as cared for as Miss Happiness and Miss Flower, better cared for than Little Peach. Little Plum had a new silk sash and a tiny fan, pleated with stiffened gold net. 'I pleated it myself with my doll's iron,' said Gem. She had never thought before of ironing herself.

'I think,' whispered Miss Flower to Miss Happiness, 'Miss Gem is going to be nearly as clever as our Miss Nona.'

Little Peach was allowed to come; 'Though he's a boy, he's only a baby,' Belinda had said, but they had sent Tom out.

'In Japan, boys have their own festival,' Nona had explained. 'Then they have big fish made of thin cotton or silk, lucky fish called carp. They fill with air like a balloon and the fish are hung outside the houses on tall poles. One day we'll make that festival for Little Peach,' said Nona.

There were presents for Little Plum, a new wadded scarlet jacket hanging in the shoes-off place and a pair of white socks. 'Her tanzen and her tabi,' said Nona with a shy smile. Then Belinda brought out a new sunshade, not pink with blossoms, 'We hadn't another,' said Nona. This was blue with white birds flying on it, but Gem thought it even prettier. Nona had made a second dinner tray, a black tray with red edges that held a teapot, bowls and plates, a complete dinner for Little Plum to have next day. Belinda had paid another nine pence for the tea set and Nona herself had bought a low table like the dolls'-house one, and made the cushion on which Little Plum was sitting now. Finally Nona went to the pencil-box cupboard and brought out a roll of quilts, not flowered this time but in colours of blue and white, a set of quilts and a pillow. 'A new bed for Honourable Little Plum,' said Belinda.

Melly had been asked to come and some of the girls in Belinda's class at school. Gem flinched when she first saw them but you would not have known they were the same little girls, they were serious and polite. 'We can't think what there was to laugh about now that we know Gem,' they said. Mr Twilfit came in, 'Just to look,' he said, but stayed to tea. He sat and watched them all, his eyebrows working furiously up and down. Father could not be back in time but he had given Mother 'a whole pound' said Belinda, to spend on food.

Mother had made Japanese food. It was odd how Mother suddenly seemed to know about that. She made *sushi*, which are slices of pressed rice with all kinds of surprises in the middle – meat, shrimps, or a slice of crystallized orange, or a dab of custard with seaweed on top. 'Seaweed you can eat,' said Belinda. There were bowls of fish in sauce, bamboo shoots in syrup, rice-flower cakes in pink and white. 'Where did she buy bamboo shoots in Topmeadow?' asked Nona.

'Father must have bought them in London,' said Belinda.

'As well as the pound?' That seemed extravagant, and Father certainly could not have paid for the chopsticks Mother suddenly produced, with little tea bowls in fine china that had flowers painted on it. 'Those must have been terribly expensive. Too expensive for us,' said Nona.

'I believe,' said Belinda suddenly, 'I believe it's Mr Tiffany Jones.'

Certainly Nona had seen him talking to Mother in the road, and once, when the children were all in bed, she had been certain she had heard Mr Tiffany Jones's voice downstairs and, something is going on, thought Nona.

Just in case anyone got tired of Japanese food, there were sausages on sticks, little chocolate tarts, fruit salad, banana sandwiches and cola and lemonade to drink. 'Just in case,' said Mother.

The dolls had a feast too, in which Nona had tried to copy all the things Mother had made and filled the dolls' bowls and plates with them, and she made hot green paint-water tea to pour out of the dolls'-house teapot. Miss Happiness and Miss Flower knelt on their cushions by the tea table; Little Plum with her curved legs could only sit on hers, and Little Peach was put to crawl on the floor.

*

Little Plum

In the midst of the happiness and excitement there was a loud knock on the door and, 'Gem, will you answer it?' asked Mother.

This immediately struck Nona as odd. Belinda was too busy handing round plates of sushi, seeing everyone had a bowl of tea, or a cola or a lemonade, to pay much attention but Nona stood still, a plate of sausage sticks in her hand; she was watching and listening. 'Gem, will you answer it?' Gem only thought Mother was making her one of the family and looked pleased and proud. She went to the door and a moment later, 'Mother!' shouted Gem in a voice as loud as Belinda's. 'Mother!'

So that's what they were planning, thought Nona, our Mother and Mr Tiffany Jones, and she, like everyone else, rushed to the door.

There was Mr Tiffany Jones, not looking sad any longer, but happy and laughing. He was pushing a wheelchair and in it, with a fur rug tucked round her knees, a deep blue coat with fur sleeves, a fur hat, sat a lady laughing. Pale green-gold hair showed under the fur of her hat, she had Gem's straight nose and grey-green eyes; her skin was pale too, but flushed now with laughing. 'May we come in?' she said, but, 'Mother!' cried Gem again and half strangled her with a big hug.

'That isn't treating her mother as a stranger,' said Anne.

Mr Tiffany Jones wheeled the chair in, and in a moment Gem's mother was surrounded by little girls.

337

Nona, Belinda, Miss Happiness and Miss Flower were introduced: 'We made our best and ceremonial bows,' said Miss Flower, satisfied. Gem's mother was shown Little Peach, but Little Plum did not have to be introduced or shown; she was sitting on Mrs Tiffany Jones's lap.

Neither Mr nor Mrs Tiffany Jones would have known Gem; Gem with her hair flying, her cheeks pink, her eyes bright; Gem talking, snapping out remarks as fast as the other girls, Gem . . . 'Happy!' said Mr Tiffany Jones.

'I can never be grateful enough . . .' he was just beginning to say to Mother, when there was another ring at the front door – a peremptory ring – and, 'Miss Tiffany Jones has come,' said Anne in a warning voice to Mother.

A silence fell as Miss Tiffany Jones came into the room. Mr Tiffany Jones looked worried while Gem became stiff and silent, and Belinda went and stood behind Nona. Miss Tiffany Jones's gaze went over them all, over Mr Tiffany Jones and Mrs in the wheelchair; over Mr Twilfit whom she seemed surprised to see; over Mother, Anne, the little girls, the dolls, the dolls' house and the dolls' festival, and 'Why was *I* not informed?' asked Miss Tiffany Jones.

'Informed of what, Agnes?' asked Mrs Tiffany Jones. Her voice went higher and higher. 'Gem came to this party,' said Miss Tiffany Jones, 'without my being consulted. She came without Matson or me.' But Gem had lifted her head; she was holding her mother's hand now and, 'I was asked to come with Little Plum,' she said. 'Only Little Plum.'

'Little Plum? Who is Little Plum?' asked Miss Tiffany Jones as she had asked before.

Miss Happiness and Miss Flower would dearly have loved Little Plum to sit up and tell Miss Tiffany Jones who she, Little Plum, was, but of course Little Plum had to be silent; yet Mrs Tiffany Jones seemed to understand how the dolls felt. Her finger was stroking Little Plum's topknot in a soothing way and, 'Little Plum is this little doll,' she said. 'A most important little doll who has been invited to this party with Gem – and only Gem,' said Mrs Tiffany Jones. 'We, Harold and I, came separately. It's a wonderful party and in half an hour, Agnes,' said Mrs Tiffany Jones, 'we are all coming next door for some ice cream and fruit punch. Will you be so kind as to tell Cook, Agnes? Ice cream, fruit punch in half an hour.'

Miss Tiffany Jones, Anne said afterwards, gasped like a fish, but Mrs Tiffany Jones took no notice. 'You see, you don't have to tell people when you come home,' she said. 'And I,' said Mrs Tiffany Jones, 'have come home.'

'Gem didn't smile at us because she thought we didn't smile at her. Think of that!' said Belinda. 'Gem *liked* my messages. She said they were interesting. I'm going to teach her to climb the ilex tree.'

'But not to go over the ladder, I hope,' said Anne.

'Of course not,' said Belinda scornfully.

'Gem's looking after Little Plum properly now. Tom says he will make another Japanese dolls' house for her. I'm going to teach Gem to roller skate; she can use my skates and she says I can ride her pony. Gem says I can go next door whenever I like.'

It would have been difficult to find in all Topmeadow, or the whole of England, two happier girls than Gem and Belinda. 'We're best friends,' said Belinda.

Nona was happy too. 'All the worries and badness and teasing have melted away,' said Nona.

Miss Tiffany Jones had packed her boxes and been driven away in the Rolls-Royce. 'For ever!' said Belinda.

Though Gem's mother still could not walk and had to live in her wheelchair or on a sofa or bed, the House Next Door was changed. Mr Tiffany Jones no longer looked worried or sad and Gem was a different girl; her hair was cut so that it fell just to her shoulders and in the daytime was tied in two bunches; she wore trousers, an anorak like Nona's and Belinda's and was allowed to run in and out as she liked. Matson had left. 'I don't need someone to look after *me*,' said Gem. 'I have to look after Mother.' Miss Berryman had gone away too. Gem was going to school. 'Next term?' asked Mother.

'Next term? She's coming tomorrow,' said Belinda.

Every Friday night before dinner Father and Mr Tiffany Jones played chess, one Friday at the Fells', the next

Little Plum

Friday at the House Next Door. Mother wheeled Mrs Tiffany Jones down to the shops; Mrs Tiffany Jones took Mother out in the Rolls-Royce. The children went to school together, spent their playtimes together, shared their friends. Gem still learned ballet, spoke French, was good at music – and had a pony; the Tiffany Joneses still had Selwyn, Cook, Eileen, a gardener and a chauffeur, while the Fells had only Mrs Bodger, but it made no difference. As for Miss Happiness, Miss Flower, Little Peach and Little Plum, they were hardly ever apart.

Each night before they went to bed they sent each other a signal. Nona would switch on the dolls' house lights; Gem would switch on her Japanese lantern. Miss Happiness and Miss Flower would come to the window and bow; Little Plum would come to hers and bow back. Belinda made Peach Boy give a little bob. 'He's too young to bow,' she said. Then she would tuck him up. Miss Happiness and Miss Flower went into their quilts, Little Plum into hers.

Then Nona and Belinda would wave their hands and put out the dolls'-house lights.

Gem would wave and put out her lantern.

'Sayonara,' was called from the Fells' house into the darkness past the ilex tree – 'Sayonara' is Japanese for goodbye. It was Miss Happiness and Miss Flower speaking, though it sounded like Belinda and Nona.

'Sayonara,' would come back from the House Next Door. It sounded like Gem's voice, but it was Little Plum.

The Fairy Doll

For Rose Mary because, once upon a time, I am afraid
we treated her as Christabel, Godfrey and Josie treated
Elizabeth before she had the fairy doll.

Chapter 1

Nobody knew where she came from.

'She must have belonged to Mother when Mother was a little girl,' said Father, but Mother did not remember it.

'She must have come from Father's house, with the Christmas decorations,' said Mother, but Father did not remember it.

As long as the children could remember, at Christmas every year, the fairy doll had been there at the top of the Christmas tree.

She was six inches high and dressed in a white gauze dress with beads that sparkled; she had silver wings, and a narrow silver crown on her dark hair, with a glass dewdrop in front that sparkled too; in one of her hands she had a silver wand, and on her feet were silver shoes – not painted, stitched. 'Fairies must have sewn those,' said Mother.

'Or mice,' said Christabel, who was the eldest.

Elizabeth, the youngest, was examining the stitches.

'Fairy mice,' said Elizabeth.

You may think it is a lucky thing to be the youngest, but for Elizabeth it was not lucky at all; she was told what to do – or what not to do – by her sisters and brother all day long, and she was always being left out or made to stay behind.

'You can't come, you're too young,' said Christabel.

'You can't reach. You're too small,' said Godfrey, who was the only boy.

'You can't play. You're too little,' said Josie. Josie was only two years older than Elizabeth, but she ordered her about most of all.

Christabel was eight, Godfrey was seven, Josie was six, but Elizabeth was only four and she was different from the others: they were thin, she was fat; their legs were long, hers were short; their hair was curly, hers was straight; their eyes were blue, hers were grey and easily filled with tears. They rode bicycles; Christabel's was green, Godfrey's was red, Josie's dark blue. Elizabeth rode the old tricycle; the paint had come off, and its wheels went 'Wh-ee-ze, wh-ee-ze, wh-ee-ze.'

'Slowpoke,' said Christabel, whizzing past.

'Tortoise,' said Godfrey.

'Baby,' said Josie.

'Not a slowpoke, tortoise, baby,' said Elizabeth but they did not hear; they were far away, spinning down the hill. 'Wh-ee-ze, wh-ee-ze, wh-ee-ze,' went the tricycle, and Elizabeth's eyes filled with tears.

'Cry-baby,' said Josie, who had come pedalling back, and the tears spilled over. Then that Christmas, Elizabeth saw the fairy doll.

*

The Fairy Doll

She had seen her before, of course, but, 'Not really,' said Elizabeth; not properly, as you shall hear.

Every year there were wonderful things on the Christmas tree: tinsel and icicles of frosted glass that had been Father's when he was a little boy; witch balls in colours like jewels and a trumpet of golden glass – it had been Father's as well – and bells that were glass too but coloured silver and red. Have you ever rung a glass bell? Its clapper gives out a 'ting' that is like the clearest, smallest, sweetest voice.

There were silvered nuts and little net stockings filled with gold and silver coins. Can you guess what the coins were? They were chocolate. There were transparent boxes of rose petals and violets and mimosa. Can you guess what they were? They were sweets.

There were Christmas crackers and coloured lights and candles.

When the lights were lit, they shone in the dewdrop on the fairy doll's crown, making a bead of light; it twinkled when anybody walked across the room or touched the tree, and the wand stirred in the fairy doll's hand. 'She's alive!' said Elizabeth.

'Don't be silly,' said Christabel, and she said scornfully, '*What* a little silly you are!'

Thwack. A hard small box of sweets fell off the tree and hit Christabel on the head.

The fairy doll looked straight in front of her, but

349

the wand stirred gently, very gently, in her hand.

In the children's house, on the landing, was a big chest carved of cedar wood; blankets were stored in it, and spare clothes. The Christmas things were kept there too; the candles had burned down, of course, and the crackers had been snapped and the sweets and nuts eaten up, but after Christmas everything else was packed away; last of all the fairy doll was wrapped in blue tissue paper, put in a cotton-reel box, laid with the rest in the cedar chest, and the lid was shut.

When it was shut, the chest was still useful. Mother sent the children to sit on it when they were naughty.

The next Christmas Elizabeth was five. 'You can help to dress the tree,' said Mother and gave her some crackers to tie on. 'Put them on the bottom branches, and then people can pull them,' said Mother.

The crackers were doll-size, silver, with silver fringes; they were so pretty that Elizabeth did not want them pulled; she could not bear to think of them tattered and torn, and she hid them in the moss at the bottom of the tree.

'*What* are you doing?' said Godfrey in a terrible voice.

He had been kneeling on the floor with his stamp collection, for which he had a new valuable purple British Guiana stamp. He jumped up and jerked the crackers out.

'You're afraid of the bang so you hid them,' he said.

350

The Fairy Doll

Elizabeth began to stammer 'I – I wasn't –' But he was already jumping round her, singing, 'Cowardy, cowardy custard.'

'Cowardy, cowardy custard . . .'

A gust of wind came under the door, it lifted up the new valuable purple British Guiana stamp and blew it into the fire.

The fairy doll looked straight in front of her, but the wand stirred gently, very gently, in her hand.

Elizabeth was often naughty; she did not seem able to help it, and that year she spent a great deal of time sitting on the cedar chest.

As she sat, she would think down through the cedar wood, and the cotton-reel box, and the blue tissue paper, to the fairy doll inside.

Then she did not feel quite as miserable.

The Christmas after that she was six; she was allowed to tie the witch balls and the icicles on the tree but not to touch the trumpet or the bells. 'But I can help to light the candles, can't I?' asked Elizabeth.

Josie had been blowing up a balloon; it was a green balloon she had bought with her own money, and she had blown it to a bubble of emerald. You must have blown up balloons, so that you will know what hard work it is. Now Josie took her lips away for a moment and held the balloon carefully with her finger and thumb.

'Light the candles!' she said to Elizabeth. 'You? You're far too young.'

Bang went the balloon.

The fairy doll looked straight in front of her, but the wand stirred gently, very gently, in her hand.

Under the tree was a small pale blue bicycle, shining with paint and steel; it had a label that read: ELIZABETH.

'You lucky girl,' said Mother.

The old tricycle was given to a children's home; it would never go 'wh-ee-ze, wh-ee-ze' for Elizabeth again. She took the new bicycle and wheeled it carefully onto the road. 'You lucky girl,' said everyone who passed.

Elizabeth rang the bell and once or twice she put her foot on the pedal and took it off again. Then she wheeled the bicycle home.

That year Elizabeth was naughtier than ever and seemed able to help it less and less.

She spilled milk on the Sunday newspapers before Father had read them; she broke Mother's Wedgwood bowl, and by mistake she mixed the paints in Christabel's new paint box. 'Careless little idiot,' said Christabel. 'I told you not to touch.'

When Mother sent Elizabeth to the shop she forgot matches or flour or marmalade, and Godfrey had to go and get them. 'You're a perfect duffer,' said Godfrey, furious. Going to dancing, she dropped the penny for her bus fare, and Josie had to get off the bus with her.

The Fairy Doll

'I'll never forgive you. Never,' said Josie.

It grew worse and worse. Every morning when they were setting off to school, 'Elizabeth, you haven't brushed your teeth,' Christabel would say, and they had to wait while Elizabeth went back. Then they scolded her all the way to school.

At school it was no better. She seemed more silly and stupid every day. She could not say her tables, especially the seven-times; she could not keep up in reading, and when she sewed, the cloth was all over bloodspots from the pricks. The other children laughed at her.

'Oh Elizabeth, why are you such a stupid child?' asked Miss Thrupp, the teacher.

Sometimes, that year, Elizabeth got down behind the cedar chest, though it was dusty there, and lay on the floor. 'I wish it was Christmas,' she said to the fairy doll inside. Then she would remember something else and say, 'I wish it never had been Christmas,' because worst of all, Elizabeth could not learn to ride her bicycle.

Father taught her, and Mother taught her; Christabel never stopped teaching her. 'Push, pedal; pedal pedal pedal,' cried Christabel, but Elizabeth's legs were too short.

'Watch me,' said Godfrey, 'and you won't wobble.' But Elizabeth wobbled.

'Go fast,' said Josie. 'Then you won't fall.' But Elizabeth fell.

353

Tales from the Dolls' House

All January, February, March, April, May and June she tried to ride the bicycle. In July and August they went to the sea so that she had a little rest; in September, October, November she tried again, but when December came, I am sorry to tell you, Elizabeth still could not ride the bicycle.

'And you're seven years old!' said Christabel.

'More like seven months!' said Godfrey.

'Baby! Baby!' said Josie.

Great-Grandmother was to come that year for Christmas; none of the children had seen her before because she had been living in Canada. 'Where's Canada?' asked Elizabeth.

'Be quiet,' said Christabel.

Great-Grandmother was Mother's mother's mother. 'And very old,' said Mother.

'How old?' asked Elizabeth.

'Ssh,' said Godfrey.

There was to be a surprise, the children were to march into the drawing room and sing a carol, and when the carol was ended Great-Grandmother was to be given a basket of roses. But the basket was not a plain basket; it was made, Mother told them, of crystal.

'What's crystal?' asked Elizabeth.

'Shut up,' said Josie, but, 'It's the very finest glass,' said Mother.

The roses were not plain roses either; they were

The Fairy Doll

Christmas roses, snow-white. Elizabeth had expected them to be scarlet. '*Isn't she silly?*' said Josie.

Who was to carry the basket? Who was to give it? 'I'm the eldest,' said Christabel. 'It ought to be me.'

'I'm the boy,' said Godfrey. 'It ought to be me.'

'I'm Josephine after Great-Grandmother,' said Josie. 'It ought to be me.'

'Who is to give it? Who?' In the end they asked Mother, and Mother said 'Elizabeth.'

'*Elizabeth?*'

'*Elizabeth?*'

'*Elizabeth?*'

'Why?' They all wanted to know.

'Because she's the youngest,' said Mother.

None of them had heard that as a reason before, and –

'It's too heavy for her,' said Christabel.

'She'll drop it,' said Godfrey.

'You know what she is,' said Josie.

'I'll be very, very careful,' said Elizabeth.

How proud she was when Mother gave the handsome, shining basket into her hands outside the drawing-room door! It was so heavy that her arms ached, but she would not have given it up for anything in the world. Her heart beat under her velvet dress, her cheeks were red, as they marched in and stood in a row before Great-Grandmother. 'Noel, Noel,' they sang.

Great-Grandmother was sitting in the armchair; she had a white shawl over her knees and a white scarf patterned with silver over her shoulders; to Elizabeth she looked as if she were dressed in white and silver all over; she even had white hair, and in one hand she held a thin stick with a silver top. She had something else, and Elizabeth stopped in the middle of a note; at the end of Great-Grandmother's nose hung a dewdrop.

An older, cleverer child might have thought, Why doesn't Great-Grandmother blow her nose? But to Elizabeth that trembling, shining drop was beautiful; it caught the shine from the Christmas tree and, if Great-Grandmother moved, it twinkled; it reminded Elizabeth of something, she could not think what – can you? – and she gazed at it. She gazed so hard that she did not hear the carol end.

'. . . Born is the King of Is-ra-el.'

There was silence.

'Eliza*beth*!' hissed Christabel.

'Go *on*,' whispered Godfrey.

Josie gave Elizabeth a push.

Elizabeth jumped and dropped the basket.

The Christmas roses were scattered on the carpet, and the crystal basket was broken to bits.

Hours afterward – it was really one hour, but to Elizabeth it felt like hours – Mother came upstairs. 'Great-Grandmother wants to see you,' she said.

The Fairy Doll

Elizabeth was down behind the chest. The velvet dress was dusty now, but she did not care. She had not come out to have tea nor to see her presents. 'What's the use of giving Elizabeth presents?' she heard Father say. 'She doesn't ride the one she has.'

Elizabeth had made herself flatter and flatter behind the cedar chest; now she raised her head.

'Great-Grandmother *wants* to see me?' she asked.

Great-Grandmother looked at Elizabeth, at her face, which was red and swollen with tears, at her hands that had dropped the basket, at her legs that were too short to ride the bicycle, at her dusty dress.

'H'm,' said a voice. 'Something will have to be done.'

It must have been Great-Grandmother's voice; there was nobody else in the room; but it seemed to come from high up, a long way up, from the top of the tree, for instance; at the same moment there was a swishing sound as of something brushing through branches, wings perhaps, and the fairy doll came flying – it was falling, of course, but it sounded like flying – down from the tree to the carpet. She landed by Great-Grandmother's stick.

'Dear me! How fortunate,' said Great-Grandmother, and now her voice certainly came from her. 'I was just going to say you needed a good fairy.'

'Me?' asked Elizabeth.

357

Tales from the Dolls' House

'You,' said Great-Grandmother. 'You had better have this one.'

Elizabeth looked at the fairy doll, and the fairy doll looked at Elizabeth; the wand was still stirring with the rush of the fall.

'What about the others?' asked Elizabeth.

'You can leave the others to me,' said Great-Grandmother.

'What about next Christmas and the tree?'

'Next Christmas is a long way off,' said Great-Grandmother. 'We'll wait and see.'

Slowly Elizabeth knelt down on the floor and picked up the fairy doll.

Chapter 2

'How can I take care of her?' asked Elizabeth.

'She is to take care of you,' said Mother, but as you know if you have read any fairy stories, fairies have a way of doing things the wrong way round.

'Pooh! She's only an ordinary doll dressed up in fairy clothes,' said Josie, who was jealous.

'She's not ordinary,' said Elizabeth, and, as you will see, Elizabeth was right.

'What's her name?' asked Josie.

'She doesn't need a name. She's Fairy Doll,' said Elizabeth, and, 'How dare I take care of her?' she asked.

Fairy Doll looked straight in front of her, but Elizabeth must have touched the wand; it stirred gently, very gently, in Fairy Doll's hand.

'Where will she live?' asked Josie. 'She can't live in the dolls' house. Fairies don't live anywhere,' said Josie scornfully.

'They must,' said Elizabeth. 'Mother says some people think fairies were the first people, so they must have lived somewhere.' And she went and asked Father, 'Father, where did the first people live?'

'In caves, I expect,' said Father.

'Elizabeth can't make a cave,' said Josie.

Elizabeth had just opened her mouth to say, 'No,'

when 'Ting' went a sound in her head. It was as clear and small as one of the glass Christmas bells.

'Ting. Bicycle basket,' it said.

Elizabeth knew what a cave was like; there had been caves at the seaside; there was one in the big wood across the field, and this very Christmas there was a clay model cave, in the Crèche, at school. If she had been a clever child she would have argued, 'Bicycle basket? Not a *bicycle* basket?' but, not being clever, she went to look. She unstrapped the basket from her bicycle and put it on its side.

The 'ting' had been right; the bicycle basket, on its side, was exactly the shape of a cave.

The cave in the wood had grass on its top, brambles and bracken and trees and grass. 'What's fairy grass?' asked Elizabeth, and 'Ting,' a word rang in her head. The word was 'moss'.

She knew where moss was; they had gathered some from the wood for the Christmas-tree tub. A week ago Elizabeth would not have gone to the wood alone, but now she had Fairy Doll and she set out through the garden, across the road and fields; soon she was back with her skirt held up full of moss.

She covered the outside of the bicycle basket with the moss like a cosy green thatch; then she stood the basket on a box and made a moss lawn around it. 'Later on I'll have beds of tiny real flowers,' she said.

The Fairy Doll

It is odd how quickly you get used to things; Elizabeth asked, and the 'ting' answered; it was a little like a slot machine. 'What shall I put on the floor?' she asked.

'Ting. In the garage.'

A cleverer child would have said, 'In the *garage?*' Josie, for instance, would not have gone there at all, but Elizabeth went, and there, in the garage, Father was sawing up logs.

'What did they put on the cave floors?' asked Elizabeth.

'Sand, I expect,' said Father.

Sand was far, far away, at the seaside; Elizabeth was just going to say, with a sigh, that that was no good when she looked at the pile of sawdust that had fallen from the logs, and, 'Sawdust! Fairy sand,' said the 'ting'.

'What about a bed?' said Josie.

'A bed?' asked Elizabeth, and back came the 'ting'. 'Try a shell.'

'A coconut shell?' asked Elizabeth, watching the blue tits swinging on the bird table, but a coconut seemed coarse and rough for a little fairy doll. A shell? A shell? Why not a real shell? Elizabeth had brought one back from the seaside; she had not picked it up, the landlady had given it to her; it was big, deep pink inside, and if you held it to your ear you heard, far off, the sound of the sea; it sounded like a lullaby. Fairy

361

Doll could lie in the shell and listen; it made a little private radio.

The shell needed a mattress. 'Flowers,' said the 'ting'.

Josie would have answered that there were no flowers now, but, 'Is there a soft winter flower, like feathers?' asked Elizabeth. 'Ting' came the answer. 'Old man's beard.'

Do you know old man's beard that hangs on the trees and the hedges from autumn to winter? Its seeds hang in a soft fluff, and Elizabeth picked a handful of it; then she found a deep red leaf for a cover; it was from the Virginia creeper that grew up the front of the house.

Soon the cave was finished – 'and with fairy things,' said Elizabeth. She asked Father to cut her two bits from a round, smooth branch; they were three inches high and made a table and a writing desk. There were toadstools for stools; stuck in the sawdust, they stood upright. On the table were acorn cups and bowls, and small leaf plates. Over the writing desk was a piece of dried-out honeycomb; it was exactly like the rack of pigeonholes over Father's desk. Fairy Doll could keep her letters there, and she could write letters; Elizabeth found a tiny feather and asked Godfrey to cut its point to make a quill pen like the one Mother had, and for writing paper there were petals of a Christmas rose. If you scratch a petal with a pen, or, better still, a pin,

The Fairy Doll

it makes fairy marks. 'Later on there'll be all sorts of flower writing-paper,' said Elizabeth.

There was a broom made of a fir-twig, a burr for a doorscraper; a berry on a thread made a knocker. 'In summer I'll get you a dandelion clock,' she told Fairy Doll.

'You haven't got a bath,' said Josie.

'Fairies don't need baths,' said Elizabeth. 'They wash outside in the dew.'

It was odd; she was beginning to know about fairies.

'What does she eat?' asked Josie.

'Snow ice-cream,' said Elizabeth – it was snowing – 'holly baked apples, and hips off the rose trees.'

'Hips are too big for a little doll like that,' said Josie.

'They are fairy pineapples,' said Elizabeth with dignity.

'Look what Elizabeth has made,' cried Christabel, and she said in surprise, 'It's pretty!'

Godfrey came to look. 'Gosh!' said Godfrey.

Josie put out her hand to touch a toadstool, and a funny feeling stirred inside Elizabeth, a feeling like a hard little wand.

'Don't touch,' said Elizabeth to Josie.

Spring came, and Fairy Doll had a hat made out of crocus, and a pussywillow-fuzz powder puff; she ate fairy bananas, which were bunches of catkins – rather than large bananas – and fairy lettuces, which were hawthorn buds – rather small; she ate French rolls, the gold-brown beech-leaf buds, with primrose butter; the beds in the moss lawn were planted with violets out of the wood.

One morning, as they were all starting off to school, Christabel said, as usual, 'Elizabeth, you haven't brushed your teeth.'

Elizabeth was going back when she stopped. 'But I have,' she said. She had been in the bathroom, and 'Ting. Brush your teeth' had come in her head. 'I've brushed them,' said Elizabeth, amazed. Christabel was amazed as well.

A few days afterward Miss Thrupp said in school, 'Let's see what Elizabeth can do,' which meant, 'Let's see what Elizabeth can't do.' 'Stand up, Elizabeth, and say the seven-times table.'

'Seven times one are seven,' said Elizabeth, and there was a long, long pause.

'Seven times two?' Miss Thrupp said encouragingly.

Elizabeth stood dumb, and the class began to laugh.

'Hush, children. Seven times two . . .'

'Ting. Are fourteen.' And Elizabeth went on. 'Seven threes are twenty-one, seven fours are twenty-eight . . .' right up to 'Seven twelves are eighty-four.'

At the end Miss Thrupp and the children were staring. Then they clapped.

In reading they had come to 'The Sto-ry of the

The Fairy Doll

Sleep-ing Beau-ty.' Elizabeth looked hopelessly at all the difficult words; her eyes were just beginning to fill with tears when, 'Ting,' the words 'Lilac Fairy' seemed to skip off the page into her head. 'It says "Lilac Fairy,"' she said.

'Go on,' said Miss Thrupp, 'go on,' and Elizabeth went on. 'Li-lac Fai-ry. Spin-ning Wheel. Prince Charm-ing.' 'Ting. Ting. Ting,' went the bell.

'Good girl, those are difficult words!' said Miss Thrupp.

In sewing they began tray-cloths in embroidery stitches; perhaps it was from making the small-sized fairy things that Elizabeth's fingers had learned to be neat; the needle went in and out, plock, plock, plock, and there was not a trace of blood. 'You're getting quite nimble,' said Miss Thrupp, and she told the class, 'Nimble means clever and quick.'

'Does she mean I'm clever?' Elizabeth asked the little boy next to her. She could not believe it.

Soon it was summer. Fairy Doll had a Canterbury bell for a hat; her bed had a peony-petal cover now. She ate daisy poached eggs, rose-petal ham, and lavender rissoles. Lady's slipper and pimpernels were planted in the moss.

'What's the matter with Elizabeth?' asked Godfrey. 'She not half such a little duffer as she was.'

That was true. She was allowed to take the Sunday

newspapers in for Father, and Mother trusted her to wash up by herself.

'You can use my paint box if you like,' said Christabel.

'You can take your own bus money,' said Josie.

'Run to the shop,' said Mother, 'and get me a mop and a packet of matches, a pot of strawberry jam, half a pound of butter, and a pound of ginger nuts.'

'What have you brought?' she asked when Elizabeth came back.

'A pound of ginger nuts, half a pound of butter, a pot of strawberry jam, a packet of matches, and a mop,' said Elizabeth, counting them out.

'But you still can't ride the bicycle,' said Josie.

It grew hot. Fairy Doll had a nasturtium leaf for a sunshade, and Elizabeth made her a poppy doll. To make a poppy doll you turn the petals back and tie them down with a grass blade for a sash; the middle of the poppy makes the head, with the fuzz for hair, and for arms you take a bit of poppy stalk and thread it through under the petals; then the poppy doll is complete, except that it has only one leg. Perhaps that was why Fairy Doll did not play with hers.

Something was the matter with Fairy Doll; her dress had become a little draggled and dirty after all these months, but it was more than that; her wings looked limp, the wand in her hand was still. Something was

The Fairy Doll

the matter in Elizabeth too; the bell did not say, 'Ting' any more in her head. 'Dull, dull, dull,' it said.

'Dull?' asked Elizabeth.

'Dull. Dull. Dull.' It was more like a drum than a bell.

'Does it mean Fairy Doll is dull with me?' asked Elizabeth.

She felt sad; then she felt ashamed.

A fairy likes flying. Naturally. If you had wings you would like flying too. Sometimes Elizabeth would hold Fairy Doll up in the air and run with her; then the wings would lift, the wand would wave, the gauze dress fly back, but Elizabeth was too plump to run for long.

'I'll put her on my bicycle and fly her,' Godfrey offered.

'You mustn't touch her,' cried Elizabeth.

'Well, fly her yourself,' said Godfrey, offended, and he rode off.

'Fly her yourself.' 'Ting' went the bell, and it was a bell, not a drum. 'Ting. Ting. Fly. Fly.' So that was what Fairy Doll was wishing! Elizabeth went slowly into the garage and looked at the pale blue, still brand-new bicycle.

'It doesn't hurt so much to fall off in summer as in winter,' said Elizabeth, but her voice trembled. Her fingers trembled too, as she tied Fairy Doll onto the handlebars.

Then Elizabeth put her foot on the pedal. 'Push. Pedal, pedal,' she said and shut her eyes, but you cannot ride even the smallest bicycle with your eyes shut.

She had to open them, but it was too late to stop. The drive from the garage led down a slope to the gate, and 'Ting,' away went the bicycle with Elizabeth on it. For a moment she wobbled; then she saw the silver wings filling and thrilling as they rushed through the air, and the wand blew round and round. 'Pedal. Pedal, pedal.' It might have been Christabel talking, but it was not. 'Pedal.' Elizabeth's hair was blown back, the wind rushed past her; she felt she was flying too; she came to the gate and fell off. 'Ow!' groaned Elizabeth, but she had flown. She knew what Fairy Doll wanted. Her leg was bleeding, but she turned the bicycle round to start off down the drive again.

Elizabeth was late for tea.

'What *have* you been doing?' asked Christabel. 'There's no jam left.' But Elizabeth did not care.

'You've torn your frock. All the buns are gone,' said Godfrey, but Elizabeth did not care.

'You're all over scratches and dust,' said Josie. 'We've eaten the cake.' But Elizabeth still did not care.

'Well, where have you been?' asked Mother.

Elizabeth answered, 'Riding my bicycle.'

*

The Fairy Doll

Christabel was pleased. Godfrey was very pleased, but Josie said, 'Pooh! It isn't Elizabeth who does things, it's Fairy Doll.'

'Is it?' asked Elizabeth.

'Try without her and you'll see,' said Josie.

Elizabeth looked at Fairy Doll, who was sitting by her on the table. 'But I'm not without her,' said Elizabeth.

Autumn came and brought the fruit; briony berries were fairy plums and greengages; a single blackberry pip was a grape. A hazel nut was pork with crackling. In every garden people were making bonfires, and Elizabeth made one in the fairy garden; it was of pine needles and twigs, and she watched it carefully; its smoke went up no bigger than a feather. It was altogether a fairy time. In the wood she found toadstools so close together that they looked like chairs put ready for a concert; she gave a fairy concert, but, 'It ought to be crickets and nightingales,' said Elizabeth. There were silver trails over the leaves and grass. 'Fairy paths,' she said.

'Snails,' snapped Josie. No doubt about it, Josie was jealous.

School began, and Elizabeth was moved up; she was learning the twelve-times table, reading to herself, and knitting a scarf. She was allowed to ride her bicycle on the main road, and to stay up till half-past seven every night.

Then, on a late October day when the first frost was on the grass, Fairy Doll was lost.

Chapter 3

'You must have dropped her on the road,' said Mother.

'But I didn't.'

'Perhaps you left her at school.'

'I didn't.'

'In your satchel.' 'In your pocket . . .' 'On the counter in the shop.' 'In the bathroom.' 'On the bookshelf.' 'Behind the clock.' 'Up in the apple tree.'

'I didn't. I didn't. I didn't,' sobbed Elizabeth.

Everyone was very kind. They all looked everywhere, high and low, up and down, in and out. Godfrey said he looked under every leaf in the whole garden that was big enough. It was no good. Fairy Doll was lost.

Elizabeth went and lay down on the floor behind the cedar chest; she only came out to have a cup of milk and go to bed.

Next morning she went behind the chest and lay down again.

'Make her come out,' said Josie, who seemed curiously worried.

'Leave her alone,' said Mother.

'She must come out. She has to go to school.' But Elizabeth would not go to school. How could she? She could not say her tables now, or spell or read or sew,

The Fairy Doll

and she had not brushed her teeth. The tears made a wet place in the dust on the floor. 'And I can't ride my bicycle,' she said.

It was Christabel's birthday. Christabel was twelve. Elizabeth had a present done up in yellow paper; it was a peppermint lollipop, but she did not give it to Christabel.

She stayed most of the day behind the cedar chest, and a day can feel like weeks when you are seven years old.

'Make her come out,' said Josie.

At four o'clock Mother came up. 'Great-Grandmother has come for the birthday tea,' she said.

'Great-Grandmother?' Elizabeth lay very still.

'I should come down if I were you,' said Mother.

Last time Great-Grandmother came she had sent for Elizabeth and Elizabeth had come with a tearstained face. It was tearstained now, but, 'I could wash it,' said Elizabeth and from somewhere she thought she heard a 'ting'. Her dress had been dirty; it was dirty now, but, 'I could change it,' said Elizabeth, and she heard another 'ting'. It was faint and faraway; it could not have been a 'ting' because the chest was empty, the fairy doll was gone, but it sounded like a 'ting'. Very slowly Elizabeth sat up.

'Good afternoon, Elizabeth,' said Great-Grandmother. No one else took any notice as Elizabeth, brushed and clean, in a clean dress, put the present by

Christabel and slid into her own place.

She was stiff from lying on the floor, her head ached and her throat was sore from crying, and she was hungry.

Mother gave her a cup of tea; the tea was sweet and hot, and there were minced chicken sandwiches with lettuce, shortcake biscuits, chocolate tarts, sponge fingers, and meringues, besides the birthday cake. Mother passed the sandwiches to Elizabeth and gave her another cup of tea. Elizabeth began to feel much better.

Christabel's cake was pink and white. It had CHRISTABEL, HAPPY BIRTHDAY written on it, and twelve candles.

'And I,' said Great-Grandmother, 'am eight times twelve.' A dewdrop slid down her nose and twinkled. 'Eight times twelve. Who can tell me what that is?' asked Great-Grandmother.

With her eyes on the dewdrop, before any of the others could answer – 'Ting.' 'Ninety-six,' said Elizabeth.

After tea they had races. One was The Button, the Thread, and the Needle. 'I can race that,' said Great-Grandmother. 'I'll have Elizabeth for my partner.'

Great-Grandmother threaded the needle as she sat in a chair. Elizabeth had to run with the button, sew it to a patch of cloth, and run back. 'I can't . . .' she began, but, 'Nimble fingers,' said Great-Grandmother; the stitches flew in and out, the button was on, Elizabeth ran back, and she and Great-Grandmother won the double prize, magic pencils that wrote in four colours.

'Dear me, how annoying!' said Great-Grandmother. 'I had meant to stop at the shop and get a few things – some silver polish, a packet of Lux, a one-and-sixpenny duster, and a nutmeg – and I forgot. Elizabeth, hop on your bicycle and get them for me.'

'But I can't . . .'

'Here's five shillings,' said Great-Grandmother. 'Bring me the change.'

'Ting.' Before Elizabeth knew where she was, she was out on the road, riding her bicycle and perfectly steady. Soon she was back with all the things and one-and-fourpence change for Great-Grandmother.

'Then were the "tings" me?' asked Elizabeth, puzzled. She could not believe it. 'I thought they were Fairy Doll.'

'I thought so too,' said Josie. She sounded disappointed.

'How could they be?' asked Godfrey.

'They couldn't,' said Christabel, who after all was twelve now and ought to know. 'Don't be silly,' said Christabel. 'She was just a doll.'

'*Fairy* Doll.' It was Great-Grandmother who corrected Christabel, but her voice sounded high up and far away – As if it came from somewhere else? asked Elizabeth.

Chapter 4

In the country, November and December are the best times for hedges, but now no one picked the old man's beard for a mattress, or winter berries to bake; no one went to the wood for fresh moss and new toadstools. The fairy house was broken up; the bicycle basket was on the bicycle.

For Christmas they each chose what they would get.

'A writing case,' said Christabel.

'A reversing engine, Number Fifty-one, for my Hornby trains,' said Godfrey.

'A kitchen set,' said Josie. Elizabeth did not know what she wanted. 'Another fairy doll?' suggested Christabel.

'Another! There isn't another,' said Elizabeth, shocked. 'She was Fairy Doll.'

On Christmas Eve the tree was set up in the drawing room. Mother opened the cedar chest and brought the decorations down, the tinsel and the icicles, the witch balls and trumpets and bells, the lights and candle clips. There were new candles, new boxes of sweets, new little bags of nuts, shining new coins, and new crackers. 'But what shall we put at the top?' asked Christabel.

Elizabeth ran out of the room, upstairs to the cedar chest.

The Fairy Doll

She was going to cast herself down – 'and stay there; I don't want Christmas,' said Elizabeth – but the lid of the chest was open, and, on top of a pile of blankets and folded summer vests, she saw the cotton-reel box that had held Fairy Doll.

'Empty,' said Elizabeth. 'Empty.'

She was just beginning to sob when, 'Look in the box,' went a loud, clear 'ting'. 'Look in the box.'

Elizabeth stopped in the middle of a sob, but she was cleverer now, and she argued. 'Why?' asked Elizabeth.

The 'ting' took no notice. 'Look in the box.'

'Why? It's *empty*.'

'Look in the box.'

'It's *empty*.'

'Look.'

It was more than a 'ting', it was a stir, as if the box were alive, as if – a wand were waving?

Slowly Elizabeth put out her hand. The lid of the box flew off – 'Did I open it?' asked Elizabeth. She heard the blue tissue paper rustle – 'Did I rustle it?' – and out, in her hand, came Fairy Doll.

'But how?' asked Christabel. 'How? And how did Elizabeth *know*? I said, "What shall we put on top?" and –'

'She ran straight upstairs,' said Godfrey, 'and came back with Fairy Doll –'

'Who was lost,' said Josie. 'Wasn't she lost?'

'We don't understand,' they said, all three together.

*

You may think that when Josie was jealous she stole Fairy Doll and put her back in the cedar chest. I thought so too, but then why was Josie so surprised? And how was it that Fairy Doll was not draggled at all, but clean, in a fresh new dress, with new silver wings and another pair of mice-sewn shoes?

Perhaps it was Mother who found her and put her away because it was time that Elizabeth had 'tings' of her own. Mother could have made the dress and wings, but, 'I couldn't have sewn those shoes,' said Mother.

Fairy Doll looked straight in front of her, and the wand stirred gently, very gently in her hand.

Chapter 5

Fairy Doll went back in her place on the top of the Christmas tree. After Christmas she was laid away in the cedar chest till next year. 'She has done her work,' said Mother.

Christabel had her writing case; Godfrey had his engine; Josie, who was cured of being jealous, had a kitchen set with pots and pans, a pastry board, a rolling pin, and a kettle. Elizabeth had a long-clothes baby doll, with eyes that opened and shut.

She loves the baby doll, but every time she goes up and down the stairs she stops on the landing and puts her hand on the cedar chest; every time she does it – it may be her imagination – from inside comes a faint glass 'ting' that is like a Christmas bell.

The Story of
Holly & Ivy

This is a story about wishing. It is also about a doll and a little girl. It begins with the doll.

Her name, of course, was Holly.

It could not have been anything else, for she was dressed for Christmas in a red dress, and red shoes, though her petticoat and socks were green.

She was ten inches high and carefully jointed; she had real gold hair, brown glass eyes, and teeth like tiny china pearls.

It was the morning of Christmas Eve, the last day before Christmas. The toys in Mr Blossom's toyshop in the little country town stirred and shook themselves after the long night. 'We must be sold today,' they said.

'Today?' asked Holly. She had been unpacked only the day before and was the newest toy in the shop.

Outside in the street it was snowing, but the toyshop window was lit and warm – it had been lit all night. The spinning tops showed their glinting colours, the balls their bands of red and yellow and blue; the trains were ready to run round and round. There were steamboats and electric boats; the sailing boats shook out their fresh white sails. The clockwork toys had each its private key; the tea sets gleamed in their boxes. There were aeroplanes, trumpets, and doll perambulators; the rocking horses looked as if they were prancing, and the teddy bears held up their furry arms. There was every kind of stuffed animal – rabbits and lions and tigers, dogs and cats, even turtles with real shells.

Tales from the Dolls' House

The dolls were on a long glass shelf decorated with tinsel – baby dolls and bride dolls, with bridesmaids in every colour, a boy doll in a kilt and another who was a sailor. One girl doll was holding her gloves, another had an umbrella. They were all beautiful, but none of them had been sold.

'We must be sold today,' said the dolls.

'Today,' said Holly.

Like the teddy bears, the dolls held out their arms. Toys, of course, think the opposite way to you. 'We shall have a little boy or girl for Christmas,' said the toys.

'Will I?' asked Holly.

'We shall have homes.'

'Will I?' asked Holly.

The toys knew what homes were like from the broken dolls who came to the shop to be mended.

'There are warm fires and lights,' said the dolls, 'rooms filled with lovely things. We feel children's hands.'

'Bah! Children's hands are rough,' said the big toy owl who sat on a pretend branch below the dolls. 'They are rough. They can squeeze.'

'I want to be squeezed,' said a little elephant.

'We have never felt a child's hands,' said two baby hippopotamuses. They were made of grey velvet, and their pink velvet mouths were open and as wide as the rest of them. Their names were Mallow and Wallow.

The Story of Holly & Ivy

'We have never felt a child's hands.'

Neither, of course, had Holly.

The owl's name was Abracadabra. He was so big and important that he thought the toyshop belonged to him.

'I thought it belonged to Mr Blossom,' said Holly.

'Hsst! T-whoo!' said Abracadabra, which was his way of being cross. 'Does a new little doll dare to speak?'

'Be careful. Be careful,' the dolls warned Holly.

Abracadabra had widespread wings marked with yellow and brown, a big hooked beak, and white felt feet like claws. Above his eyes were two fierce black tufts, and the eyes themselves were so big and green that they made green shadows on his round white cheeks. His eyes saw everything, even at night. Even the biggest toys were afraid of Abracadabra. Mallow and Wallow shook on their round stubby feet each time he spoke.

'He might think we're mice,' said Mallow and Wallow.

'My mice,' said Abracadabra.

'Mr Blossom's mice,' said Holly.

Holly's place on the glass shelf was quite close to Abracadabra. He gave her a look with his green eyes. 'This is the last day for shopping,' said Abracadabra. 'Tomorrow the shop will be shut.'

A shiver went round all the dolls, but Holly

383

knew Abracadabra was talking to her.

'But the fathers and mothers will come today,' said the little elephant. He was called Crumple because his skin did not fit but hung in comfortable folds round his neck and his knees. He had a scarlet flannel saddle hung with bells, and his trunk, his mouth, and his tail all turned up, which gave him a cheerful expression. It was easy for Crumple to be cheerful; on his saddle was a ticket marked 'Sold'. He had only to be made into a parcel.

'Will I be a parcel?' asked Holly.

'I am sure you will,' said Crumple, and he waved his trunk at her and told the dolls, 'You will be put into Christmas stockings.'

'Oooh!' said the dolls longingly.

'Or hung on Christmas trees.'

'Aaaah!' said the dolls.

'But you won't all be sold,' said Abracadabra, and Holly knew he was talking to her.

The sound of the key in the lock was heard. It was Mr Blossom come to open the shop. Peter the shop boy was close behind him. 'We shall be busy today,' said Mr Blossom.

'Yes-sir,' said Peter.

There could be no more talking, but, 'We can wish. We must wish,' whispered the dolls, and Holly whispered, 'I am wishing.'

'Hoo! Hoo!' went Abracadabra. It did not matter

if Peter and Mr Blossom heard him; it was his toy-owl sound. 'Hoo! Hoo!' They did not know but the toys all knew that it was Abracadabra's way of laughing.

The toys thought that all children have homes, but all children have not.

Far away in the city was a big house called St Agnes's, where thirty boys and girls had to live together, but now, for three days, they were saying 'Goodbye' to St Agnes's. 'A kind lady – or gentleman – has asked you for Christmas,' Miss Shepherd, who looked after them all, had told them, and one by one the children were called for or taken to the train. Soon there would be no one left in the big house but Miss Shepherd and Ivy.

Ivy was a little girl, six years old with straight hair cut in a fringe, blue-grey eyes, and a turned-up nose. She had a green coat the colour of her name, and red gloves, but no lady or gentleman had asked for her for Christmas. 'I don't care,' said Ivy.

Sometimes in Ivy there was an empty feeling, and the emptiness ached; it ached so much that she had to say something quickly in case she cried, and, 'I don't care at all,' said Ivy.

'You will care,' said the last boy, Barnabas, who was waiting for a taxi. 'Cook has gone, the maids have gone, and Miss Shepherd is going to her sister. You will care,' said Barnabas.

'I won't,' said Ivy, and she said more quickly, 'I'm going to my grandmother.'

'You haven't got a grandmother,' said Barnabas. 'We don't have them.' That was true. The boys and girls at St Agnes's had no fathers and mothers, let alone grandmothers.

'But I have,' said Ivy. 'At Appleton.'

I do not know how that name came into Ivy's head. Perhaps she had heard it somewhere. She said it again. 'In Appleton.'

'Bet you haven't,' said Barnabas, and he went on saying that until his taxi came.

When Barnabas had gone Miss Shepherd said, 'Ivy, I shall have to send you to the country, to our Infants' Home.'

'Infants are babies,' said Ivy. 'I'm not a baby.'

But Miss Shepherd only said, 'There is nowhere else for you to go.'

'I'll go to my grandmother,' said Ivy.

'You haven't got a grandmother,' said Miss Shepherd. 'I'm sorry to send you to the Infants' Home, for there won't be much for you to see there or anyone to talk to, but I don't know what else to do with you. My sister has influenza and I have to go and nurse her.'

'I'll help you,' said Ivy.

'You might catch it,' said Miss Shepherd. 'That wouldn't do.' And she took Ivy to the station and put her on the train.

She put Ivy's suitcase in the rack and gave her a packet of sandwiches, an apple, a ticket, two shillings, and a parcel that was her Christmas present; on to Ivy's coat she pinned a label with the address of the Infants' Home. 'Be a good girl,' said Miss Shepherd.

When Miss Shepherd had gone Ivy tore the label off and threw it out of the window. 'I'm going to my grandmother,' said Ivy.

All day long people came in and out of the toyshop. Mr Blossom and Peter were so busy they could hardly snatch a cup of tea.

Crumple was made into a parcel and taken away; teddy bears and sailing ships were brought out of the window; dolls were lifted down from the shelf. The boy doll in the kilt and the doll with gloves were sold, and baby dolls and brides.

Holly held out her arms and smiled her china smile. Each time a little girl came to the window and looked, pressing her face against the glass, Holly asked, 'Are you my Christmas girl?' Each time the shop door opened she was sure it was for her.

'I am here. I am Holly'; and she wished, 'Ask for me. Lift me down. Ask!' But nobody asked.

'Hoo! Hoo!' said Abracadabra.

Ivy was still in the train. She had eaten her sandwiches almost at once and opened her present. She had hoped and believed she would have a doll this Christmas, but the present was a pencil box. A doll would have filled up the emptiness – and now it ached so much that Ivy had to press her lips together tightly, and, 'My grandmother will give me a doll,' she said out loud.

'Will she, dear?' asked a lady sitting opposite, and the people in the carriage all looked at Ivy and smiled. 'And where does your grandmother live?' asked a gentleman.

'In Appleton,' said Ivy.

The lady nodded. 'That will be two or three stations,' she said.

Then . . . there is an Appleton, thought Ivy.

The lady got out, more people got in, and the train went on. Ivy grew sleepy watching the snowflakes fly past the window. The train seemed to be going very fast, and she leaned her head against the carriage cushions and shut her eyes. When she opened them the train had stopped at a small station and the people in her carriage were all getting out. The gentleman lifted her suitcase down from the rack. 'A . p . . t . n,' said the notice boards. Ivy could not read very well but she knew A was for 'Appleton'.

Forgetting all about her suitcase and the pencil box, she jumped down from the train, slammed the carriage door behind her, and followed the crowd of people as they went through the station gate. The ticket collector had so many tickets he did not look at hers; in a moment Ivy was out in the street, and the train chuffed out of the station. 'I don't care,' said Ivy. 'This is where my grandmother lives.'

The country town looked pleasant and clean after the city. There were cobbled streets going up and down, and houses with gables overhanging the pavements and roofs jumbled together. Some of the houses had windows with many small panes; some had doors with brass knockers. The paint was bright and the curtains clean. 'I like where my grandmother lives,' said Ivy.

Presently she came to the market square where the Christmas market was going on. There were stalls of turkeys and geese, fruit stalls with oranges, apples, nuts, and tangerines that are like small oranges wrapped in silver paper. Some stalls had holly, mistletoe, and Christmas trees, some had flowers; there were stalls of china and glass and one with wooden spoons and bowls. A woman was selling balloons and an old man was cooking hot chestnuts. Men were shouting, the women had shopping bags and baskets, the children were running, everyone was buying or selling and laughing. Ivy had spent all her life in St Agnes's; she had not seen a market before; and, 'I won't look for my grandmother yet,' said Ivy.

In the toyshop Mr Blossom had never made so much money, Peter had never worked so hard. Peter was fifteen; he had red cheeks and a smile as wide as Mallow's and Wallow's; he took good care of the toys and did everything he could to help Mr Blossom. Whish! went the brown paper as Peter pulled it off the roll, whirr! went the string ball, snip-snap, the scissors cut off the string. He did up dozens of parcels, ran up and down the stepladder, fetched and carried and took away. 'That abominable boy will sell every toy in the shop,' grumbled Abracadabra.

'What's abominable?' asked Holly.

'It means not good,' said dolls, 'but he is good. Dear, dear Peter!' whispered the dolls, but Abracadabra's green eyes had caught the light from a passing car. They gave a flash and, rattle-bang! Peter fell down the stepladder from top to bottom. He bumped his elbow, grazed his knee, and tore a big hole in his pocket. 'Hold on! Go slow!' said Mr Blossom.

'Yes-sir,' said poor Peter in a very little voice.

'Did you see that, did you see that?' whispered the dolls. Holly wished she were farther away from Abracadabra.

Soon all the baby dolls but one were sold and most of the teddy bears. Mallow and Wallow were taken for twin boys' stockings; they were done up in two little parcels and carried away. Hardly a ball was left, and not a single aeroplane. The sailor doll was sold, and the doll with the umbrella, but still no one had asked for Holly.

Dolls are not like us; we are alive as soon as we are

born, but dolls are not really alive until they are played with. 'I want to be played with,' said Holly, 'I want someone to move my arms and legs, to make me open and shut my eyes. I wish! I wish!' said Holly.

It began to be dark. The dusk made the lighted window shine so brightly that everyone stopped to look in. The children pressed their faces so closely against the glass that the tips of their noses looked like white cherries. Holly held out her arms and smiled her china smile, but the children walked away. 'Stop. Stop,' wished Holly, but they did not stop.

Abracadabra's eyes shone in the dusk. Holly began to be very much afraid.

One person stopped, but it was not a boy or a girl. It was Mrs Jones, the policeman's wife from down the street. She was passing the toyshop on her way home when Holly's red dress caught her eye. 'Pretty!' said Mrs Jones and stopped.

You and I would have felt Holly's wish at once, but Mrs Jones had no children and it was so long since she had known a doll that she did not understand; only a feeling stirred in her that she had not had for a long time, a feeling of Christmas, and when she got home she told Mr Jones, 'This year we shall have a tree.'

'Don't be daft,' said Mr Jones, but when Mrs Jones had put her shopping away, a chicken and a small plum-pudding for her and Mr Jones's Christmas dinner, a piece of fish for the cat, and a dozen fine handkerchiefs which were Mr Jones's present, she went back to the market and bought some holly, mistletoe, and a Christmas tree.

'A tree with tinsel,' said Mrs Jones. She bought some tinsel. 'And candles,' she said.

'Candles are prettier than electric light.' She brought twelve red candles. 'They need candle clips,' she said, and bought twelve of those. And a tree should have some balls, thought Mrs Jones, glass balls in jewel colours, ruby-red, emerald-green, and gold. She bought some balls and a box of tiny silver crackers and a tinsel star. When she got home she stood the tree in the window and dressed it, putting the star on the top.

'Who is to look at it?' asked Mr Jones.

Mrs Jones thought for a moment and said, 'Christmas needs children, Albert.' Albert was Mr Jones's name. 'I wonder,' said Mrs Jones. 'Couldn't we find a little girl?'

'What's the matter with you today, my dear?' said Mr Jones. 'How could we find a little girl? You're daft.' And it was a little sadly that Mrs Jones put holly along the chimney shelf, hung mistletoe in the hall, tied a bunch of holly on the doorknocker, and went back to her housework.

Ivy was happy in the market. She walked round and round the stalls, looking at all the things; sometimes a snowflake fell on her head but she shook it off;

sometimes one stuck to her cheek, but she put out her tongue and licked it away. She bought a bag of chestnuts from the chestnut man; they were hot in her hands and she ate them one by one. She had a cup of tea from a tea stall on wheels, and from a sweet stall she bought a toffee apple. When her legs grew tired she sat down on a step and wrapped the ends of her coat round her knees. When she was cold she started to walk again.

Soon lights were lit all along the stalls; they looked like stars. The crowd grew thicker. People laughed and stamped in the snow to keep their feet warm; Ivy stamped too. The stall-keepers shouted and called for people to come and buy. Ivy bought a blue balloon.

At St Agnes's a telegraph boy rang the bell. He had a telegram for Miss Shepherd from the Infants' Home. It said, IVY NOT ARRIVED. SUPPOSE SHE IS WITH YOU. MERRY CHRISTMAS.

The boy rang and rang, but there was no one at St Agnes's to answer the bell, and at last he put a notice in the letterbox, got on his bicycle, and rode away.

In her house down the street Mrs Jones kept looking at the Christmas tree. 'Oughtn't there to be presents?' she asked. It was so long since she had had a tree of her own that she could not be sure. She took Mr Jones's handkerchiefs, wrapped them in white paper and tied them with some red ribbon she had by her, and put the parcel at the foot of the tree. That looked better but still not quite right.

'There ought to be toys,' said Mrs Jones, and she called to Mr Jones, 'Albert!'

Mr Jones looked up from the newspaper he was reading.

'Would it be very silly, Albert?' asked Mrs Jones.

'Would what be silly?'

'Would it be silly to buy . . . a little doll?'

'What is the matter with you today?' asked Mr Jones, and he said again, 'You're daft.'

Soon it was time for him to go on duty.

'I shall be out all night,' he told Mrs Jones.

'Two of the men are away sick. I shall take a short sleep at the police station and go on duty again. See you in the morning,' said Mr Jones.

He kissed Mrs Jones goodbye and went out, but put his head round the door again. 'Have a good breakfast waiting for me,' said Mr Jones.

In the toyshop it was closing time.

'What does that mean?' asked Holly.

'That it's over,' said Abracadabra.

'Over?' Holly did not understand.

Mr Blossom pulled the blind down on the door and put up a notice: 'Closed'.

'Closed. Hoo! Hoo!' said Abracadabra.

Mr Blossom was so tired he told Peter to tidy the

shop. 'And you can lock up. Can I trust you?' asked Mr Blossom.

'Yes-sir,' said Peter.

'Be careful of the key,' said Mr Blossom.

'Yes-sir,' said Peter proudly. It was the first time Mr Blossom had trusted him with the key.

'You have been a good boy,' said Mr Blossom as he was going. 'You may choose any toy you like – except the expensive ones like air guns or electric trains. Yes, choose yourself a toy,' said Mr Blossom. 'Good night.'

When Mr Blossom had gone, 'A toy!' said Peter, and he asked, 'What does he think I am? A blooming kid?'

Peter swept up the bits of paper and string and straw and put them in the rubbish bin at the back of the shop. He was so tired he forgot to put the lid on the bin. Then he dusted the counter, but he was too tired to do any more, so he put on his overcoat to go home. He turned out the lights – it was no use lighting the window now that the shopping was over – stepped outside, and closed and locked the door. If he had waited a moment he would have heard a stirring, a noise, tiny whimperings. 'What about us? What about us?' It was the toys.

'Go home and good riddance!' said Abracadabra to Peter; but the toys cried, 'Don't go! Don't go!'

Peter heard nothing. He put the key in his jacket

pocket to keep it quite safe and turned to run home.

The key fell straight through the torn pocket into the snow. It did not make a sound.

'Hoo! Hoo!' said Abracadabra, and the snowflakes began to cover the key as Peter ran off.

The market was over as well. The crowd had gone, the stalls were packing up, the last Christmas trees were being sold. Ivy had spent all her money, the blue balloon had burst, her legs ached with tiredness, and she shivered.

Then the lights went out; there were only pools of yellow from the lamp posts, with patches of darkness between. A bit of paper blew against Ivy's legs, making her jump. Suddenly the market place seemed large and strange; she would have liked to see Miss Shepherd.

You might think that Ivy cried, but she was not that kind of little girl. Though the empty feeling ached inside her she pressed her lips tightly together, then said, 'It's time I looked for my grandmother,' and started off to look.

She walked up the cobbled streets between the houses.

How cosy they seemed, with their lighted windows; smoke was going up from every chimney. 'There are fires and beds and supper,' said Ivy. Some of the houses had wreaths of holly on their front doors, paper chains and garlands in their rooms; and in almost every window was a Christmas tree.

When Ivy looked in she could see children. In one house they were sitting round a table, eating; in another they were hanging stockings from the chimney shelf; in some they were doing up parcels, but, 'I must look for a house with a tree and no children,' said Ivy.

She knew there would be a tree, 'Because my grandmother is expecting me,' said Ivy.

The toyshop was still and dark. 'Thank goodness!' said Abracadabra.

'But people can't see us,' said Holly.

'Why should they see us?' asked Abracadabra. 'It's over. People have all gone home. The children are going to bed.' He sounded pleased. 'There will be no more shopping,' said Abracadabra, and the whisper rang round the toys, 'No shopping. No shopping.'

'Then . . . we are the ones not sold,' said a doll.

There was a long silence.

'I can be sold any time,' said a bride doll at last. 'Weddings are always.'

'I am in yellow, with primroses,' said a bridesmaid. 'I shall be sold in the spring.'

'I am in pink, with roses,' said another. 'They will buy me in the summer.'

But Holly had a red dress, for Christmas. What would be done with her?

'You will be put back into stock,' said Abracadabra.

'Please . . . what is stock?' whispered Holly.

'It is shut up and dark,' said Abracadabra, as if he liked that very much. 'No one sees you or disturbs you. You get covered with dust, and I shall be there,' said Abracadabra.

Holly wished she could crack.

'This is my grandmother's house,' said Ivy, but when she got to the house it was not. That happened several times. 'Then it's that one,' she said, but it was not that one either. She began to be very cold and tired.

Somebody came down the street. Even in the snow his tread was loud. It was a big policeman. (As a matter of fact, it was Mr Jones.)

Ivy knew as well as you or I know that policemen are kind people and do not like little girls to wander about alone after dark in a strange town. 'He might send me to the Infants' Home,' said Ivy and, quick as a mouse going into its hole, she whisked into a passage between two shops.

'Queer!' said Mr Jones. 'I thought I saw something green.'

At the end of the passage was a shed, and Ivy whisked into it and stood behind the door. There was something odd about that shed – it was warm. Ivy did not know how an empty shed could be warm on a cold night, but I shall tell you.

The Story of Holly & Ivy

The shed belonged to a baker and was built against the wall behind his oven. All day he had been baking bread and rolls for Christmas, and the oven was still hot. When Ivy put her hand on the wall she had to take it away quickly, for the wall was baking hot.

Soon she stopped shivering. In a corner was a pile of flour sacks, and she sat down on them.

A lamp in the passageway outside gave just enough light. Ivy's legs began to feel heavy and warm; her fingers and toes seem to uncurl and stretch in the warmth, while her eyelids seemed to curl up. She gave a great yawn.

Then she took off her coat, lay down on the sacks, and spread the coat over her.

In a moment she was fast asleep.

The toyshop was close by the passage. It was too dark to be noticed, though Abracadabra's eyes shone like green lamps.

'Shopping is over. Hoo! Hoo!' said Abracadabra.

'Over. Over,' mourned the toys.

They did not know and Abracadabra did not know that it is when shopping is over that Christmas begins.

Soon it was not dark, for the snow had stopped and the moon came up and lighted all the town. The roofs sparkled with frost as did the snow on the pavements and roads. In the toyshop window the toys showed, not as bright as day, but bright as moonlight, which is

399

far more beautiful. Holly's dress looked a pale red, and her hair was pale gold.

Dolls do not lie down to go to sleep; they only do that when you remember to put them to bed and, as you often forget, they would be tired if they had to wait; they can sleep where they stand or sit, and now the dolls in the toyshop window slept in their places, all but Holly. She could not go to sleep. She was a Christmas doll and it was beginning to be Christmas. She could not know why, but she was excited. Then all at once, softly, bells began to ring.

Long after most children are in bed, on Christmas Eve, the church bells in towns and villages begin to ring. Soon the clocks strike twelve and it is Christmas.

Holly heard the bells and – what was this? People were walking in the street – hurrying.

'Hsst! T-whoo!' said Abracadabra at them as they passed, but they took no notice.

'Then . . . it has started,' said Holly.

'What has started?' said Abracadabra.

'It,' said Holly. She could not explain better than that for she did not know yet what 'it' meant – this was, after all, her first Christmas – but the bells grew louder and more and more people passed. Then, it may have been the pin of Holly's price ticket, or a spine of tinsel come loose from the shelf, but Holly felt a tiny pricking as sharp as a prickle on a holly leaf. 'Wish,' said the prickle. 'Wish.'

'But – the shop is closed,' said Holly. 'The children are in bed. Abracadabra says I must go into sto –' The prickle interrupted. 'Wish. Wish!' said the prickle. 'Wish!' It went on till Holly wished.

Ivy thought the bells woke her or perhaps the passing feet, but then why did she feel something sharp like a thistle or a hard straw in one of the sacks? She sat up, but she was half-asleep and she thought the feet were the St Agnes's children marching down to breakfast and the bells were the breakfast bell. Then she saw she was still in the shed, though it was filled with a new light, a strange silver light. 'Moonlight?' asked Ivy and rubbed her eyes. She was warm and comfortable on the sacks under the green coat – though there were great white patches on it from the flour – too warm and comfortable to move, and she lay down, but again she felt that thistle or sharp straw. The light seemed to be calling her, the bells, the hurrying feet; the prickle seemed to tell her to get up.

Ivy put on her coat and went out.

Outside in the passage the footsteps sounded so loud that she guessed it was the policeman. She waited until they had passed before she dared come out.

In the street the moonlight was so bright that once again Ivy thought it was morning and she was in St Agnes's and the bells were the breakfast bell. 'Only . . . there are so many of them,' said sleepy Ivy.

She walked a few steps to the toyshop. She did not know how it came to be there and she thought she was in her St Agnes's bedroom and it was filled with toys. Then: 'Not toys,' said Ivy, 'a toy,' and she was wide-awake. She did not even see Abracadabra glaring at her with his green eyes; she looked straight at Holly.

She saw Holly's dress and socks and shoes. She is red and green too, thought Ivy. She saw Holly's hair, brown eyes, little teeth, and beautiful joints. They were just what Ivy liked and, 'My Christmas doll!' said Ivy.

Holly saw Ivy's face pressed against the window as she had seen so many children's faces that day, but, 'This one is different,' said Holly.

Ivy's hands in their woollen gloves held to the ledge where it said, BLOSSOM, HIGH-CLASS TOYS AND GAMES. Holly looked at Ivy's hands. Soon they will be holding me, thought Holly. Ivy's coat even in the moonlight was as beautiful a green as Holly's dress was a beautiful red, so that they seemed to match, and, 'My Christmas girl!' said Holly.

Ivy had to go to the shed again to get warm, but I cannot tell you how many times she came back to look at Holly.

'My Christmas doll!'

'My Christmas girl!'

'But the window is in between,' said Abracadabra.

The window was in between and the toyshop door was locked, but even if it had been open Ivy had no

402

money. 'Hoo! Hoo!' said Abracadabra, but, remember, not only Holly but Ivy was wishing now.

'I wish . . .'

'I wish . . .'

The toys woke up. 'A child,' they whispered, 'a child.' And they wished too.

Wishes are powerful things. Ivy stepped back from the window and Abracadabra's eyes grew pale as, cr-runch went something under Ivy's heel. It was something hidden just under the snow.

'Hisst!' said Abracadabra.

'T-whoo!' But Ivy bent down and picked up a key.

In the moonlight it was bright silver. 'Peter's key. Peter's key,' whispered the toys.

Footsteps sounded in the street, people were coming from church; Ivy put the key in her pocket and quickly ran back to the shed.

She had to wait a long time for the people to pass as they stopped to say 'Merry Christmas' to one another, to give each other parcels; and Ivy sat down on the sacks to rest. Presently she gave another great yawn. Presently she lay down and spread her coat over her. Presently she went to sleep.

The toys had gone to sleep too. 'But I can't,' said Holly. 'I must wait for my Christmas girl.'

She stayed awake for a long time, but she was only a little doll . . . and presently she fell asleep where she stood.

*

Ivy dreamed that the shed was hung with holly wreaths and lit with candles. The berries were the colour of the Christmas doll's dress and the candle flames were as bright as her hair. 'A-aaah!' said Ivy.

Holly dreamed that two arms were cradling her, that hands were holding her, that her dress was beginning to be rumpled and her eyes made to open and shut. 'A-aaah!' said Holly.

Abracadabra kept his green eyes wide open, but he could not stop the moon from going down, nor the coming of Christmas Day.

Very early on Christmas morning Mrs Jones got up and tidied her living room. She lit a fire, swept the hearth, and dusted the furniture. She laid a table for breakfast with a pink and white cloth, her best blue china, a loaf of crusty bread, a pat of new butter in a glass dish, honey in a blue pot, a bowl of sugar, and a jug of milk. She had some fresh brown eggs and, in the kitchen, she put sausages to sizzle in a pan. Then she set the teapot to warm on the hob, lighted the candles on the Christmas tree, and sat down by the fire to wait.

The baker's oven cooled in the night and Ivy woke with the cold. The shed was icy; Ivy's eyelashes were stuck together with rime, and the tip of her nose felt frozen. When she tried to stand up, her legs were so stiff that she almost fell over; when she put on her coat her fingers were so numb that they could not do up the buttons. Ivy was a sensible little girl; she knew she had to get warm and she did not cry, but, 'I m-must h-hop and sk-skip,' she said through her chattering teeth, and there in the shed she swung her arms, in-out, out-in, and clapped her hands. Outside she tried to run, but her legs felt heavy and her head seemed to swim. 'I m-must f-find m-my g-g-grandmother qu-qu-quickly,' said Ivy.

She went into the street, and how cold it was there! The wind blew under her coat; the snow on the pavements had turned to ice and was slippery. She tried to hop, but the snow was like glass. Ivy fingers and nose hurt in the cold. 'If-f I l-look at m-my d-d-doll, I m-might-t f-feel b-b-b-better,' said Ivy, but she turned the wrong way.

It was the wrong way for the toyshop, but perhaps it was the right way for Ivy, for a hundred yards down the street she came to the Joneses' house.

I must look for a house with a tree and no children. That is what she had said. Now she looked in at the window and there was no sign of any children but there was a Christmas tree lit. Ivy saw the fire – 'To w-warm m-me,' whispered Ivy, and, oh, she was cold! She saw the table with the pink and white cloth, blue china, bread and butter, honey and milk, the teapot warming – 'My b-breakfast,' whispered Ivy and, oh, she

405

was hungry! She saw Mrs Jones sitting by the fire, in her clean apron, waiting. Ivy stood quite still. Then: 'My g-g-grandmother,' whispered Ivy.

Holly woke with a start. 'Oh! I have been asleep,' said Holly in dismay. 'Oh! I must have missed my little Christmas girl.'

'She won't be back,' said Abracadabra. 'It's Christmas Day. She's playing with her new toys.'

'I am her new toy,' said Holly.

'Hoo! Hoo!' said Abracadabra.

'I am,' said Holly, and she wished. I think her wish was bigger than Abracadabra, for when Ivy lifted her hand to Mrs Jones's knocker, a prickle from the bunch of holly ran into her finger. 'Ow!' said Ivy. The prickle was so sharp that she took her hand down, and 'F-first I must g-get my d-d-doll,' said Ivy.

If Ivy had stopped to think she would have known she could not get her doll. How could she when the shop was locked and the window was in between? Besides, Holly was not Ivy's doll and had not even been sold. A wise person would have known this, but sometimes it is better to feel a prickle than to be wise.

'Hullo,' said Ivy to Holly through the toyshop window. 'G-g-good morning.'

Holly could not say 'Hullo' back, but she could wish Ivy good morning – with a doll's wish.

In the daylight Holly was even more beautiful than

she had been by moonlight, Ivy was even dearer.

'A little girl!' sneered Abracadabra. 'There are hundreds of little girls.'

'Not for me,' said Holly.

'A little doll!' sneered Abracadabra. 'There are hundreds of little dolls,' and if Ivy could have heard him through the window she would have said, 'Not for me.'

Ivy gazed at Holly through the window.

She gazed so hard she did not hear footsteps coming down the street, heavy steps and light ones and a queer snuffling sound. The heavy steps were Mr Jones's, the light ones were Peter's, and the snuffling sound was Peter trying not to cry.

'I put it in my pocket,' Peter was saying. 'I forgot my pocket was torn. Oh, what shall I do? What shall I do?' said Peter.

Mr Jones patted his shoulder and asked, 'What sort of key was it now?'

A key? Ivy turned round. She saw Mr Jones and jumped. Then she made herself as small as she could against the window.

'A big iron key, but it looked like silver,' said Peter. He and Mr Jones began to look along the pavement.

It looked like silver. Ivy could feel the edges of the key in her pocket, but – If I go away softly the policeman won't notice me, thought Ivy.

'Mr Blossom trusted me,' said Peter. His wide smile

was gone and his face looked quite pale. I don't like boys, thought Ivy, but Peter was saying, 'He trusted me. He'll never trust me again,' and though Peter was a big boy, when he said that he looked as if he really might burst into tears.

A boy cry? asked Ivy. She had never seen Barnabas cry. I didn't know boys could, thought Ivy.

The toys had all wakened again. 'Poor Peter. Poor Peter'; and the whisper ran around:

'Wish. Wish Peter may find the key. Wish.'

'For that careless boy?' said Abracadabra. 'Why, he might have had us all stolen.'

Peter was saying that himself. 'A thief might have picked it up,' he said.

'It w-wasn't a th-thief. It was m-m-me,' said Ivy and put her hand in her pocket and pulled out the key. 'S-so you n-needn't c-c-cry,' said Ivy to Peter.

Can you imagine how Peter's tears disappeared and his smile came back? 'Cry? Who'd cry?' said Peter scornfully, and Ivy thought it better not to say, 'You.'

Mr Jones put the key in the lock, and it fitted. 'I suppose I had better go in,' said Peter, 'and see if everything's all right.'

'Well, I'm going home,' said Mr Jones. 'You know where I live. If anything's wrong, pop in.' It was as he turned to go home that Mr Jones saw Ivy. 'So – there was something green,' said Mr Jones.

Ivy knew how she must look; her coat and her hair,

her socks and her shoes were dusted with flour from the sacks, she had not been able to comb her hair because she had no comb, her face had smears across it from the toffee apple; and, 'I think you are lost,' said Mr Jones.

His voice was so kind that the empty feeling ached in Ivy; it felt so empty that her mouth began to tremble. She could not shut her lips, but, 'I'm n-not l-lost,' said Ivy. 'I'm g-g-going to m-my g-g-g-grandmother.'

'I see,' said Mr Jones. He looked at Ivy again. 'Where does your grandmother live?' asked Mr Jones.

'H-here,' said Ivy.

'Show me,' said Mr Jones and held out his hand.

Ivy took his hand and led him down the street to the Joneses' house. 'This is m-my g-g-grandmother's,' said Ivy.

Mr Jones seemed rather surprised. 'Are you sure?' asked Mr Jones.

'Qu-quite sure,' said Ivy. 'She has m-my b-breakfast ready.'

'Did you say . . . your breakfast?' asked Mr Jones.

'Of course,' said Ivy, 'l-look in at the w-window. There,' she told him. 'Th-there's my Ch-Christmas t-tree.'

Mr Jones thought a moment. Then: 'Perhaps it is your Christmas tree,' he said.

'Sh-shall we kn-knock?' asked Ivy, but, 'You needn't knock,' said Mr Jones. 'You can come in.'

*

The toys were all in their places when Peter opened the door. 'No thanks to you,' said Abracadabra.

Perhaps Peter heard him, for Peter said, 'Thanks to that little girl.'

I do not know how it was, but Peter had the idea that Ivy was Mr Jones's little girl. 'He was kind to me,' said Peter, 'and so was she.' Peter was very grateful, and, 'What can I do for them?' he asked. Then: 'I know,' said Peter. Mr Blossom had told him to take any toy, and, 'I'll take her a doll,' said Peter. 'I can slip it into their house easy, without saying a word, but – what doll would she like?' asked Peter.

'A bride doll,' said Abracadabra with a gleam of his eyes.

A bride doll was standing in the corner, and Peter went to pick her up, but he must have put his hand on the pin of her price ticket or a wire in the orange-blossom flowers on her dress, for, 'Ow!' said Peter and drew back his hand.

Abracadabra looked at Holly. Holly smiled.

'All little girls like baby dolls,' said Abracadabra. 'Take her a baby doll.'

There was one baby doll left. She was in the window; Peter reached to take her out, but the safety-pin on the baby doll's bib must have been undone, for, 'Ow!' cried Peter and drew back his hand.

'Hsst! T-whoo!' said Abracadabra to Holly. Holly smiled.

It was the same with the primrose bridesmaid.

'Ow!' cried Peter. The same with the rose. 'Ow!' And, 'Here, I'm getting fed up,' said Peter. 'Who's trying this on?' I do not know what made him look at Abracadabra. Abracadabra's eyes gleamed, but in her place just above Abracadabra, Peter saw Holly.

'Why, of course! The little red Christmas doll,' said Peter. 'The very thing!' But as he stepped up to the glass shelf Abracadabra was there.

Peter said that Abracadabra must have toppled, for a toy owl cannot fly, but it seemed for a moment that Abracadabra was right in his face; the green eyes were close, the spread wings, the hooked beak, and the claws. Peter let out a cry and hit Abracadabra, who fell on the floor. 'Out of my way!' cried Peter, and he gave Abracadabra a kick. Then Abracadabra did fly. He went sailing across the shop and landed head down in the rubbish bin.

'Oooh! Aaah!' cried the toys in terror, but Peter sprang after him and shut the lid down tight.

Then he picked up Holly from the shelf in the window and ran pell-mell to the Joneses'.

When Mr Jones and Ivy came in Mrs Jones was in the kitchen with a fork in her hand, turning the sausages. Mr Jones told Ivy to wait in the hall.

'Merry Christmas,' said Mr Jones to Mrs Jones and kissed her.

'Merry Christmas,' said Mrs Jones, but she sounded a little sad.

Mr Jones had a present in his pocket for Mrs Jones, a little gold brooch. He took it out, unwrapped it, and pinned it to her dress. 'Oh, how pretty, Albert!' said Mrs Jones, but she still sounded sad.

'I have another Christmas present for you,' said Mr Jones and laughed. 'It has two legs,' said Mr Jones.

'Two legs?' asked Mrs Jones, and Mr Jones laughed again.

'It can walk and talk,' said Mr Jones and laughed still more, and then he brought Ivy in.

When Mrs Jones saw Ivy she did not laugh; for a moment she stood still, then she dropped the fork and knelt down on the floor and put her hands on Ivy's shoulders. 'Oh, Albert!' said Mrs Jones. 'Albert!' She looked at Ivy for a long time and tears came into her eyes and rolled down her cheeks. Ivy, with her glove, wiped the tears away and the emptiness went out of Ivy and never came back.

'Dearie me!' said Mrs Jones, getting to her feet, 'what am I thinking of? You must have a hot bath at once.'

'Breakfast first,' said Mr Jones, and Ivy asked, 'Couldn't I see my Christmas tree?'

Mrs Jones's living room was as bright and clean as it had looked through the window. The fire was warm

412

on Ivy's legs, the table was close to her now, and in the window was the tree – 'With a star on the top,' whispered Ivy.

'But why, oh why,' Mrs Jones was saying to Mr Jones outside the door, 'why didn't I buy that little doll?'

'And the shops are shut,' whispered Mr Jones. 'We shall have to explain.'

Ivy did not hear them. 'Red candles!' she was whispering. 'Silver crackers! Glass balls . . . !'

'Well, I'll be danged!' said Mr Jones, for, at the foot of the tree, by the parcel of handkerchiefs, stood Holly.

Though Mrs Jones was a little young to be a grandmother, she and Mr Jones adopted Ivy, which means they took her as their own and, of course, Holly as well. Miss Shepherd came to visit them and arrange this. 'Please tell Barnabas,' said Ivy.

Mrs Jones made Ivy a green dress like Holly's red one but with a red petticoat and red socks. She made Holly a red coat like Ivy's green one and knitted her a pair of tiny green woollen gloves so that they matched when they went out.

They pass the toyshop often, but there is no Abracadabra.

'Where is the owl?' Mr Blossom had asked when the shop opened again, and Peter had to say, 'I put him in the rubbish bin.'

'Good gracious me!' said Mr Blossom. 'Get him out

at once,' but when they lifted the lid Abracadabra was not there.

'Sir, the dustman must have taken him away,' said Peter, standing up stiff and straight. I do not know if that was true, but Abracadabra was never seen again.

'Never seen again,' said the toys. They sounded happy. 'Never seen again,' and long, long afterward in the toyshop they told tales of Abracadabra.

Sometimes Holly and Ivy meet Crumple, who waves his trunk at them. Once they saw Mallow and Wallow put out on a windowsill. They often see Peter and Mr Blossom; in spite of Abracadabra's disappearance, Mr Blossom trusts Peter.

'But if you had not found the key,' says Peter to Ivy.

'If I had not come to look at Holly,' says Ivy.

'If I had not gone to Mr Jones,' says Peter.

'If Mrs Jones had not bought the Christmas tree' – but it goes further back than that. If Ivy had not slept in the shed . . . If the baker had not lit his oven . . . If Ivy had not got out of the train . . . If Barnabas had not laughed at Ivy . . . If Holly . . .

'If I had not wished,' says Holly.

I told you it was a story about wishing.

Candy Floss

For Jane who thought of it

This is the tune Jack's music box played

Ah, my dear old Au-gus-tine, Au-gus-tine, Au-gus-tine,

Ah, my dear old Au-gus-tine, ev-ery-thing's gone –

Mon-ey's gone, sweet-heart's gone – all is gone, Au-gus-tine,

Ah, my dear old Au-gus-tine, ev-ery-thing's gone.

Once upon a time there was a doll who lived in a coconut shy.

You and I can say we live in London, or Chichester, or in Connecticut, France, Japan, Honolulu, or the country or town where we do live. She lived in a coconut shy.

A coconut shy is part of a fair. People come to it and pay their money to throw wooden balls at coconuts set up on posts. If anyone hits a coconut off the post he can keep it. It is quite difficult, but lots of nuts are won, and it is great fun.

This particular shy was kept by a young man called Jack.

There are many coconut shies in a fair, but Jack's was different. It had the same three-sided tent, the same red and white posts for the nuts, the same scarlet box stands for the balls; it had the same flags and notices and Jack called out the same call: 'Three balls f'r threepence! Seven f'r a tanner!' (A tanner is what Jack called a sixpence.) All these were the same, but still this shy was different, for beside it, on a stool, Jack's dog sat up and begged by a little mechanical organ that Jack had found and mended till it played (he called it his music box). On top of the box was a little wooden horse, and as the music played – though it could play only one tune – the horse turned round and round and frisked up and down. On the horse's back sat a beautiful little doll.

The dog's name was Cocoa, the horse's name was Nuts, and the doll was Candy Floss.

A fair is noisy with music and shouting, with whistles and bangs and laughing and squeals as people go on the big wheel, the merry-go-rounds, or the bumper cars. Jack's music box had to play very loudly to be heard at all, but Cocoa, Nuts, and Candy Floss did not mind its noise; indeed, they liked it; no other shy had a music box, let alone a dog that begged, a horse that frisked, or a doll that turned round and round. A great many people came to Jack's shy to look at them – and stayed to buy balls and shy them at the nuts.

'We help Jack,' said Candy Floss, Cocoa, and Nuts.

Jack was thin and dark and young. He wore jeans, an old coat full of holes, and an old felt hat; in his ears were golden rings.

Cocoa was brown and tufty like a poodle; he wore a collar for every day and a red, blue, and white bow for work. Cocoa's work was to guard the music box, Nuts, Candy Floss, and the old drawer where Jack kept the lolly (which was what he called money). Cocoa had also to sit on a stool and beg, but he could get down when he liked, and under the stool was a bowl marked 'Dog' and filled with clean water, so that he was quite comfortable.

Nuts was painted white with black spots; his neck was arched and he held his forelegs up. He had a black-painted mane and wore a red harness hung with bells.

Candy Floss

Cocoa and Nuts were pretty, but prettiest of all was Candy Floss; she was made of china, with china cheeks and ears and nose, and she had a little china smile. Her eyes were glass, blue as bluebells; her hair was fine and gold, like spun toffee. She was dressed in a pink gauze skirt with a strip of gauze for a bodice. When she needed a new dress Jack would soak the old one off with hot water, fluff up a new one and stick it on with glue. On her feet were painted dancing shoes as red as bright red cherries.

The music box played:

Cocoa begged, Nuts frisked, Candy Floss turned round and round. All the children made their fathers and mothers stop to look. When they stopped, the fathers would buy balls and if anybody made a nut fall down Jack handed out a beautiful new coconut. He was kept very busy, calling out his call, picking up the balls; and the heap of pennies and sixpences in the lolly drawer grew bigger.

went the music box; Cocoa begged, Nuts frisked, and

Candy Floss turned round and round.

When the coconuts were all gone Jack would empty the lolly drawer, put out the lights, and close the shy. He shut off the music box and let Cocoa get down. Nuts was covered over with an old red cloth so that he could sleep; Jack put Candy Floss into his pocket (there was a hole handy so that she could see out) and, with Cocoa at his heels, went round the fair.

They went on the big merry-go-rounds where the big steam organs played 'Yankee Doodle' and 'Colonel Bogey' and other tunes. Jack sat on a horse or a wooden swan, a camel or an elephant, with Cocoa on the saddle in front of him and Candy Floss safe in his pocket; round they went, helter-skelter, until Candy Floss was dizzy. The little merry-go-rounds had buses, engines, and motor-cars that were too small for Jack, but sometimes Candy Floss and Cocoa sat in a car by themselves. Here the music was nursery rhymes, and the children tooted the horns. Toot. Toot-toot-toot. Candy Floss wished she could toot a horn.

Sometimes they went to the Bingo booths and tried to win prizes. Once Jack had won a silk handkerchief, bright purple printed with shamrocks in emerald-green. Cocoa and Candy Floss thought it a most beautiful prize and Jack always wore it round his neck.

Sometimes they went on the bumper cars. When the cars bumped into one another the girls shut their eyes and squealed; Candy Floss's eyes would not shut, but she would have liked to squeal.

Best of all they went on the big wheel, with its seats that went up and up in the air high over the fair and the lights, so high that Candy Floss trembled, even though she was in Jack's pocket.

When they were hungry they would eat fair food. Sometimes they ate hot dogs from the hot-dog stall; Cocoa had one to himself but Candy Floss had the tip end of Jack's. Sometimes they had fish and chips at the fried-fish bar; Cocoa had whole fish and Candy Floss had a chip. Often they had toffee apples; Cocoa used to get his stuck on his jaw and had to stand on his head to get it off. Sometimes they had ice-cream and Jack made a tiny cone out of a cigarette paper for Candy Floss.

When they were tired they came back to an old van that Jack had bought dirt cheap (which was what he called buying for very little money). He had mended it and now it would go anywhere. Jack put the music box and Nuts in the van too, so that they would all be together. Then he closed the doors and they all lay down to sleep.

Jack slept on the floor of the van on some sacks and an old sleeping-bag. Cocoa slept at Jack's feet. Candy Floss slept in the empty lolly drawer which Jack put beside his pillow; the sixpences and pennies had been put in a stocking that Jack kept in a secret place. He folded up the shamrock handkerchief to make the drawer soft for Candy Floss and tucked one end round her for a blanket.

As she lay in the drawer Candy Floss could feel Jack big and warm beside her; she could hear Cocoa breathing, and knew Nuts was under the cloth. Outside, the music of the fair went on; through the van window the stars looked like sixpences. Soon Candy Floss was fast asleep.

Fairs do not stay in one place very long, only a day, two days, perhaps a week. Then Jack would pack up the coconut shy, the lights and the flags, the posts, the nuts, the stands, and the wooden balls. He would take down the three-sided tent, put everything on the van, start it up, and drive away. The music box with Nuts travelled on the floor in front, Cocoa sat on the seat, but Candy Floss had the best place of all: Jack made the shamrock handkerchief into a sling for her and hung it on the driving mirror. Candy Floss could watch the road and see everywhere they went.

Sometimes the new fair was at a seaside town. Jack would stop the van and they would have a picnic on the beach. Cocoa would chase crabs, Nuts had some seaweed hay, and Jack found Candy Floss a shell for a plate.

Sometimes the fair was in the country and they picnicked in a wood. Cocoa chased rabbits, not crabs, Nuts had moss for straw, and Jack found Candy

426

Candy Floss

Floss an acorn cup for a drinking bowl.

Sometimes they stopped in a field. Cocoa would have liked to chase sheep but he did not dare. Jack made daisy-chain reins for Nuts, Candy Floss had a wild rose for a hat; but no matter where they stopped to picnic, sooner or later the van would drive on to another fairground and Jack would put up the shy.

Cocoa would be brushed and his bow put on, and he would get up on his stool while Jack filled the bowl marked 'Dog'. The cloth came off the music box and Nuts would be polished with a rag until he shone. Then Jack would fluff up Candy Floss's dress and with his own comb spread out her hair. He washed her face (sometimes, I am sorry to say, with spit) and sat her carefully on the saddle and switched on the music and lights. 'Three f'r threepence! Seven f'r a tanner!' Jack would cry.

went the music box; Cocoa begged, Nuts frisked, and Candy Floss turned round and round.

Sometimes the other fair people laughed at Jack about what they called his toys; but, 'Shut up out of that,' he would say. 'Toys? They're partners.' (Only he said 'pardners.')

'A doll for a partner? Garn!' they would jeer.

'Doll! She's my luck,' said Jack.

That was true. Jack's shy had more people and took in more pennies and sixpences than any other shy.

Cocoa, Nuts, and Candy Floss were proud to be Jack's partners; Candy Floss was very proud to be his luck.

Then one Easter they came to the heath high up above London which was the biggest fair of all (a heath is a big open space, covered with grass). Only the very best shies and merry-go-rounds, the biggest wheels were there. The Bingos had expensive prizes, there were a mouse circus, three rifle ranges, and stalls where you could smash china. There were toy-sellers and balloon-sellers, paper flowers and paper umbrellas. There were rows and rows of hot-dog stalls, fish bars, and toffee-apple shops.

Cocoa had a new bow. Nuts had new silver bells. Candy Floss had a new pink dress like a cloud. Jack painted the posts and bought a pile of new coconuts.

'Goin' to make more lolly'n ever we done,' said Jack. 'More sixpences'n stars in the sky.'

went the music box; and how well Cocoa begged, how gaily Nuts frisked, and Candy Floss turned round and round as gracefully as a dancer. More and more people

Candy Floss

began to come – Hundreds of people, thought Candy Floss. The wooden balls flew; pennies and sixpences poured into the lolly drawer.

'That's my luck!' cried Jack, and Candy Floss felt very proud.

Now not far from the heath, in a big house on the hill leading down from the heath to the town, there lived a girl called Clementina Davenport.

She was seven years old, with brown hair cut in a fringe, brown eyes, a small straight nose, and a small red mouth. She would have been pretty if she had not looked so cross. She looked cross because she *was* cross. She said she had nothing to do.

'I don't know *what* to do with Clementina,' said her mother. 'What can I give her to make her happy?'

Clementina had a day nursery and a night nursery all to herself, and a garden to play in. She had a nurse who was not allowed to tell her to sit up or pay attention or eat her pudding or any of the other things you and I are told.

She had a dolls' house, a white piano, cupboards full of toys, and two bookcases filled with books. She had a toy kitten in a basket, a toy poodle in another, and a real kitten and a real poodle as well. She had a cage of budgerigars and a pony to ride. Last Christmas her father gave her a pale blue bicycle, and her mother a watch, a painting box, and a painting book. Still Clementina had nothing to do.

429

'What *am* I to do with Clementina?' asked her mother, and she gave her a new television set and a pair of roller skates.

You might think Clementina had everything she wanted, but no, she was still quite good at wants and, on Easter Monday afternoon when the garden was full of daffodils and blossom, the sound of the fair came from the heath, over the wall, into the garden; and, 'I want to go to the fair,' said Clementina.

Another way in which Clementina was not like you or me was that for her 'I want' was the same as 'I shall.'

'*Not* a nasty common fair!' said her mother.

'I *want* to go,' said Clementina and stamped her foot, and so her father put on his hat, fetched his walking-stick, and took her to the fair.

Of course she went on everything: on the little merry-go-rounds where she rode on a bus and wanted to change to an engine, then changed to a car and back to the bus; on the big merry-go-rounds where she rode on a swan and changed to a camel and changed to a horse. She went on the bumper cars where she did not squeal but was angry when her car was hit; on the swing boats where she did not want to stop; and on the big wheel where she wanted to stop at once and shrieked so that they had to slow it and take her down. She cried at Bingo when she did not win a prize and screamed when the mice ran into the ring in the mouse circus.

Candy Floss

Her father bought her a toffee apple which she licked once and threw away, a balloon which she burst, and a paper umbrella with which she hit at people's legs.

Having everything you want can make you very tired. When Clementina was tired she whined. 'I don't like fairs,' whined Clementina, 'I want to go home.' (Only she said, 'I wa-ant to go ho-o-o-ome.')

'Come along then,' said her father.

'Fetch the car,' said Clementina, but motor-cars cannot go into fairs; and, 'I'm afraid you will have to walk,' said her father.

Clementina was getting ready to cry when she heard a gay loud sound:

and a call, 'Three f'r threepence! Seven f'r a tanner!' and she turned round and saw Candy Floss.

She saw Candy Floss sitting on Nuts, turning round and round as Nuts frisked up and down. Clementina saw the red shoes, the pink gauze, the way the blue eyes shone, the gold-spun hair, and, 'I want that doll,' said Clementina.

People often asked to buy Candy Floss, or Cocoa or Nuts; then Jack would laugh and say, 'You'll have to buy me as well. We're pardners,' and the people would laugh too, for they knew they could not buy Jack.

'Candy Floss? Why, she's my luck, couldn't sell that,' Jack would say. 'Pretty as a pi'ture, ain't she?' said Jack.

Now Clementina's father came to Jack. 'My little girl would like to buy your doll.'

'Sorry, sir,' said Jack. 'Not f'r sale.'

'I want her,' said Clementina.

'I will give you a pound,' said Clementina's father to Jack.

A pound is forty silver sixpences; but, 'Not f'r five hundred pounds,' said Jack.

'You see, Clementina,' said her father.

'Give him five hundred pounds,' said Clementina.

Her father walked away and Jack smiled at Clementina. 'I said *not* f'r five hundred pounds, little missy.'

I cannot tell you how furious was Clementina. She scowled at Jack (scowl means to make an ugly face). Jack stepped closer to Candy Floss and Cocoa growled; and, 'You cut along to yer pa,' said Jack to Clementina. Jack, of course, treated her as if she were any little girl, and she did not like that.

She made herself as tall as she could and said, 'Do you know who I am? I am Clementina Davenport.'

'And I'm Jack and these are Cocoa, Nuts, and Candy Floss,' said Jack.

'I am Clementina Davenport,' said Clementina scornfully. 'I live in a big house. I have a room full of toys and a pony. I have a bicycle and twenty pairs of shoes.

Candy Floss

'That's nice f'r you,' said Jack, 'but you can't have Candy Floss.'

I believe that was the first time anyone had ever said 'can't' to Clementina.

Jack though he had settled it. In any case he was too busy picking up balls, taking in pennies and sixpences, handing out coconuts, and calling his call to pay much attention to Clementina. 'Cut off,' he told her, but Clementina did not cut off. She came nearer.

Cocoa, Nuts, and Candy Floss watched her out of the corners of their eyes.

Clementina was pretending not to be interested, but she came nearer still. If Candy Floss and Nuts had been breathing they would have held their breath.

Clementina came close and at that moment Cocoa got down to take a lap of water from his bowl. (It was not Cocoa's fault; he had never known a girl like Clementina.)

Nuts tried to turn faster, but he could only turn as fast as the music went. He wanted to kick, but he had to hold his forelegs up; he tried to shake his silver bells, but they did not make enough noise.

As Clementina's hand came out Candy Floss shrieked, 'Help! Help!' but a doll's shriek has no sound. She tried to cling like a burr to the saddle, but she was too small.

When Jack turned round Candy Floss had gone. There was no sign of Clementina.

When Clementina snatched Candy Floss, quick-as-a-cat-can-wink-its-eye she hid her in the paper umbrella and ran after her father.

Candy Floss was head-downward, which made her dizzy. The umbrella banged against Clementina's legs as she ran and that gave Candy Floss great bumps. She trembled with terror as she felt herself being carried far away; but she had not been brought up in a fair for nothing. She was used to being dizzy (on the merry-go-rounds), used to being bumped (on the bumper cars), used to trembling (on the big wheel), and when, in the big house on the hill, Clementina took her out of the umbrella Candy Floss looked almost as pretty and calm as she had on Nuts's saddle but china can be cold and hard; she made herself cold and hard in Clementina's hand and her eyes looked as if they were the brightest, clearest glass.

Dolls cannot talk aloud; they talk in wishes. You and I have often felt them wish and we know how clear that can be, but Clementina had never played long enough with any of her dolls to feel a wish. She had never felt anything at all.

'But you will,' said Candy Floss, 'you will.'

Clementina turned all her dolls'-house dolls out of the dolls' house, higgledy-piggledy on to the floor. 'You will live in the dolls' house,' she told Candy Floss.

'I live in a coconut shy,' said Candy Floss and her dress caught on the prim little chairs and tables and her hair caught on the shells that edged the scrap-pictures. Every time Clementina moved her she upset something. When she had knocked down a lamp, spilled a vase of flowers, and pulled the cloth off a table, Clementina took her out.

'Don't live in the dolls' house then,' said Clementina.

'You must wear another dress,' said Clementina and tried to take the pink one off, but she did not know, as Jack knew, how to soften the glue. All she did was to tear the gauze. Then she tried to put another dress over the top of the gauze skirt, but it stuck out and Candy Floss made her arms so stiff they would not go in the sleeves. Clementina lost patience and threw the dress on the floor.

She made a charming supper for Candy Floss: a daisy poached egg, some green grass spinach, and a blossom fruit salad with paint sauce. She had never taken such trouble over a supper before, but Candy Floss would not touch it.

'I eat hot dogs,' said Candy Floss, 'a chip, or a toffee apple.' Nor would she take any notice of the dolls' house's best blue and white china. 'I eat off a shell,' said Candy Floss. 'I drink from an acorn bowl.'

'Eat it up,' said Clementina, but Candy Floss tumbled slowly forward on to the supper and lay with her face in the blossom fruit salad.

'I shall put you to bed,' scolded Clementina and

435

she got out the dolls'-house bed.

'I don't sleep in a bed,' said Candy Floss, 'I sleep in a lolly drawer,' and she made herself stiff so that her feet stuck out. When Clementina tucked them in, Candy Floss's head stuck out. Clementina put the bedclothes round her but they sprang up again at once. 'Are you trying to fight me?' asked Clementina.

Candy Floss did not answer, but the bedclothes sprang up again.

'Well, you can sit on a chair all night,' said Clementina and she took out a dolls'-house chair.

'I don't sit on a chair,' said Candy Floss, 'I sit on Nuts,' and as soon as Clementina put her on the chair she fell off.

'Sit!' said Clementina in a terrible voice, but a doll brought up in the noise and shouts of a fair is not to be frightened by a little girl's voice and Candy Floss did not blink an eye. 'Sit!' said Clementina and she sat Candy Floss hard on the chair. *Snap*, the chair legs broke.

Clementina stood looking at the pieces in her hand; she looked as if she were thinking. And if Candy Floss's little china mouth had not been smiling already, I should have said she smiled.

But she did not smile in the night. Clementina left her on the table when she went to bed and all night long Candy Floss lay on the cold table in that strange room.

Candy Floss

There was no van; no music box with Nuts asleep under the old red cloth; no sound of Cocoa breathing; no Jack to feel big and warm; no lolly drawer to make a bed; no shamrock handkerchief. There was no music from the fair, no sixpence stars.

'And how can I get back?' asked Candy Floss. 'I *can't* get back. Oh, how will the shy go on? What will Jack do without his luck?' And all night the frightening words beat in her head: 'No luck. No luck. No Jack. No luck. No Nuts or Cocoa. No sixpences. No luck! No luck! No luck!'

Dolls cannot cry but they can feel. In the night Candy Floss felt so much she thought that she must crack.

Next morning it began again. Clementina took Candy Floss into the garden. 'You must go in my dolls'-house perambulator,' said Clementina.

'I go in a pocket,' said Candy Floss, and she would not fit in the perambulator. She held her head up so that it would not go under the hood and made her legs stiff so that they would not go in either. Clementina shook her until her eyes came loose in her head.

'You belong to me now,' said Clementina.

'I belong to Jack.'

Candy Floss, as we know, could not say these things aloud, but now Clementina was beginning to feel them. Clementina was not used to feeling; the more she felt, the angrier she grew, and she thought of something dreadful to say to Candy Floss. 'Pooh!' said Clementina. 'You're only a doll. The shops are full of dolls. Jack will have another doll by now. Do you think he wouldn't have bought another doll to take your place?'

Candy Floss seemed to sway in Clementina's hand. Another doll in her place! In all her places! On Nuts's back; in Jack's pocket; in the lolly drawer in the shamrock handkerchief. Another doll to be Jack's luck! What shall I do? thought Candy Floss. What can I do? And she cried out with such a big wish that she fell out of Clementina's hand on to the path and a crack ran down her back. 'Jack! Jack! Cocoa! Nuts! Help! Help! Help! cried Candy Floss.

At that moment, in the fair, the merry-go-rounds started up.

All the merry-go-rounds up and down the heath began to play. The big wheel started and the rifles cracked in the rifle ranges. People began to cry 'Bingo!' and the toy-sellers and balloon-sellers started to shout. All the music in the fair began to play, louder and louder until it sounded as if the whole fair were in the garden.

Clementina picked Candy Floss up off the path and what had happened? Candy Floss was cracked; her eyes were loose, the shine had gone out of her hair, her face was covered with paint where she had fallen into the salad, and her dress was torn. As for its pink, you know how brown and dull pink spun sugar can go. Candy Floss's dress looked just like that.

'You're horrid,' said Clementina and she threw Candy Floss back on to the path.

The merry-go-round and the fair music seem to say that too, 'You're horrid,' but they were saying it to Clementina.

'I think I shall go indoors and paint,' said Clementina. She went in but the fair music came into the house and now, as Clementina listened, she heard other things as well. 'She belongs to Jack.' 'You're horrid.' 'Cruel Clementina,' said the music.

'I won't sit still. I shall skip,' said Clementina, but though she skipped up to a hundred times she could not shut out that music. 'She belongs to Jack.' 'Cruel Clementina.' 'Poor Candy Floss;' and the big wheel turning – you could see the top of it from the garden – seemed to say, 'I can see. I see everything.'

When lunchtime came Clementina did not want any lunch. 'Are you ill?' asked her nurse and made Clementina lie down on her bed with a picture book. 'You look quite bad,' said the nurse.

'I don't!' shouted Clementina and hid under her blanket because that was what she did not want to feel, bad; but the bed and the picture book, even the blanket, could not shut out the fair, and the music never stopped: 'Bad Clementina.' 'Cruel Clementina.'

'She belongs to Jack.' 'Poor Candy Floss.'

Clementina put her head under the pillow.

Under the pillow she could not hear the music but she heard something else: thumpity-bump; thumpity-bump; it was her own heart beating. Clementina had not known she had a heart before; now it thumped just like the merry-go-round engine, and what was it saying? 'Poor Candy Floss. Poor Candy Floss,' inside Clementina.

She lay very still. She was listening. Then she began to cry.

By and by Clementina sat up. She got out of bed and put on her shoes; then, just as she was, rumpled and crumpled from lying on the bed and tear-stained from crying, she tiptoed out of the room and went down the stairs into the garden, where she picked up Candy Floss and she tiptoed to the gate.

No one was about. She opened the gate and ran.

She ran up the hill to the heath and into the fair, past the balloon-man and the toy-sellers, the fish-and-chips bar, the hot-dog stands and the toffee-apple stalls. She ran past the little merry-go-rounds with the buses and cars, and the big merry-go-rounds with the horses and swans, past the Bingos, the mouse circus, the rifle ranges, and the big wheel . . . and then she stopped.

The coconut shy was closed.

No lights shone; no coconuts were set up on the red and white posts. The balls were stacked in their scarlet stands. The music box was covered with the old red cloth. Nuts could not be seen. Cocoa lay on the ground with his head on his paws; now and again he whimpered.

Jack was sitting on a box, hunched and still. When people came to the shy he shook his head. 'My luck's gone,' he said, and Cocoa put up his nose and howled.

Clementina had meant to put Candy Floss back on Nuts and then run away as fast as she could, but she could not bear it when she saw how miserable she had made them all. She could not bear to see Nuts covered up, Cocoa whimpering, Jack's sad face; and, without thinking or waiting, she cried, 'Oh *please*, don't be so sorry! I have brought her back.'

Jack stood up. Cocoa stood up. The cloth slithered off the music box and there was Nuts, standing up. 'Brought her *back*? asked Jack, and Clementina forgot all about being Clementina Davenport in the big house on the hill; and, 'Yes, I'm Clementina. I took her,' she said and burst into tears.

When Jack saw what Clementina had done to Candy Floss he looked very, very grave and Cocoa growled; but Jack was used to mending things and in no time at all he had borrowed some china cement from the china-smashing stall and filled in the crack. He would not let Clementina hold Candy Floss but he let her watch, though Cocoa still growled softly under his breath. Very gently he touched the loosened eyes with glue and made them firm again. He washed the torn skirt off and glued a fresh one on and cleaned the paint off Candy Floss's face; then he spun out her hair again and she looked as good as new. Cocoa stopped growling and Clementina actually smiled.

Then in a jiffy (which was what Jack called a moment) he put fresh coconuts on the posts and opened the ball stands. He put Cocoa's bow on and told him to jump on the stool; he ran over Nuts's paint with a rag so that it shone; then he put Candy Floss in the saddle and switched on the music box.

went the music box.

'Three balls f'r threepence! Seven f'r a tanner!' called Jack. His shout sounded so joyful, Cocoa begged so cleverly, Nuts frisked so happily, and Candy Floss turned so gaily that the crowds flocked to the shy. 'Come'n help!' called Jack to Clementina and Clementina began to pick up the balls.

But who was this coming? It was Clementina's father and mother and with them the nurse and all the maids and a policeman, because there had been *such* a fuss when they had missed Clementina. They had searched all through the fair. Now they stopped at the coconut shy.

Candy Floss

'Is *that* Clementina?' asked her father and mother, the nurse and the maids.

The cross look had gone from Clementina's face; she was too busy to be cross. Her cheeks were as pink as Candy Floss's dress; her eyes were shining as if they were made of glass; her hair looked almost gold.

'*Can* it be Clementina?' asked her father and mother, the nurse and the maids.

'Clementina, Clementina!' they called amazed.

'Three f'r threepence! Seven f'r a tanner!' yelled Clementina.

'What *am* I to do with her? cried her mother.

It was the policeman who answered, the policeman who had been called out to look for Clementina. 'If I was you, mum,' said the policeman, 'I should leave her alone.'

Clementina was allowed to stay all afternoon at the shy. Her father and mother thought it was they who allowed her; Jack thought it was Jack. She worked so hard picking up balls that he gave her two sixpences for herself, and Clementina was prouder of those sixpences than of all the pound notes in her money box (she calls it a lolly box now). 'I *earned* them,' said Clementina.

When her nurse came to take her home she had to say good-bye to Jack, Cocoa, Nuts, and Candy Floss; but, 'Not good-bye; so long,' said Jack.

'So long?' asked Clementina.

443

'So long as there's fairs we'll be back,' said Jack. 'Come'n look f'r us.'

When Clementina was in bed and happily asleep the fair went on.

went the music box.

'Three f'r threepence! Seven f'r a tanner!' called Jack. Cocoa begged, Nuts frisked and Candy Floss went round and round.

Impunity Jane

The Story of a Pocket Doll

For Richard Leigh Foster

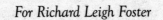

'I'm Imp-imp-impunity Jane'

Once there was a little doll who belonged in a pocket. That was what *she* thought. Everyone else thought she belonged in a dolls' house. They put her in one but, as you will see, she ended up in a pocket.

She was four inches high and made of thick china; her arms and legs were joined to her with loops of strong wire; she had painted blue eyes, a red mouth, rosy cheeks, and painted shoes and socks; the shoes were brown, the socks white with blue edges. Her wig of yellow hair was stuck on with strong firm glue. She had no clothes, but written in the middle of her back with a pencil was:

IMPUNITY JANE

This was in London, England, many years ago, when the streets were lit with gas and boys wore sailor suits and girls had many heavy petticoats. The little doll was in a toy shop. She sat on the counter near a skipping rope, a telescope, and a sailing ship; she was quite at home among these adventurous toys.

Into the toy shop came an old lady and a little girl.

'Grandma?' said the little girl.

'What is it, Effie?' asked the old lady.

'That little doll would just go in my dolls' house!' said Effie.

'But I don't want to go in a dolls' house,' said the little doll. 'I want to be a skipping rope and dance out into the world, or a sailing ship and go to sea, or a telescope and see the stars!' But she was only a little fivepence-halfpenny doll and in a moment she was sold.

The shop woman was about to wrap her up when the old lady said, 'Don't put her in paper. She can go in my pocket.'

'Won't she hurt?' said Effie.

'This little doll is very strongly made,' said the shop woman. 'Why, you could drop her with impunity.'

'I know "imp",' said Effie. 'That's a naughty little magic person. But what is impunity?'

'Impunity means escaping without hurt,' said the old lady.

'That is what I am going to do forever and ever,' said the little doll, and she decided that it should be her name. 'Imp-imp-impunity,' she sang.

Effie called her Jane; afterwards, other children called her Ann or Polly or Belinda, but that did not matter; her name was Impunity Jane.

She went in Grandma's pocket.

Impunity Jane's eyes were so small that she could see through the weave of the pocket. As Effie and Grandma walked home, she saw the bright daylight and sun; she saw trees and grass and the people on the pavements; she saw horses trotting (in those days there were horse buses and carriages, not cars). 'Oh, I wish I were a little horse!' cried Impunity Jane.

It was twelve o'clock and the bells were chiming from the church steeples. Impunity Jane heard them, and bicycle bells as well. 'Oh, I wish I were a bell!' cried Impunity Jane.

In the park girls and boys were sending shuttlecocks up into the air (in those days children played with shuttlecocks), and Impunity Jane wanted to be a shuttlecock flying up.

In the barracks a soldier was blowing a bugle; it sounded so brave and exciting that it seemed to ring right through her. 'A bugle, a horse, a bell, a shuttlecock – oh, I want to be everything!' cried Impunity Jane.

But she was only a doll; she was taken out of Grandma's pocket, put into Effie's dolls' house, and made to sit on a bead cushion. Have you ever sat on a bead cushion? They are hard and cold, and, to a little doll, the beads are as big as pebbles.

There she sat. 'I want to go in a pocket, a pocket, a pocket,' wished Impunity Jane, but nobody heard.

Dolls, of course, cannot talk. They can only make wishes that some people can feel.

A dolls' house by itself is just a thing, like a cupboard full of china or a silent musical box; it can live only if it is used and played with. Some children are not good at playing; Effie was one. She liked pressing flowers. She

453

did not feel Impunity Jane wishing in the dolls' house.

'I want to go out in a pocket,' wished Impunity Jane.

Effie did not feel a thing!

Presently Effie grew up, and another child, Elizabeth, had the dolls' house. There were changes in the nursery; the old oil lamp and the candles were taken away, and there was gas light, like that in the streets. Elizabeth's nurse did not wear a high cap, as Effie's nurse had, and Elizabeth's dresses were shorter than Effie's had been; nor did she wear quite so many petticoats.

Elizabeth liked sewing doll clothes; she made clothes for Impunity Jane, but the stitches, to a little doll, were like carving knives. Elizabeth made a dress and a tiny muff. The dress was white with blue sprigs, the muff was cotton wool. Impunity Jane would have liked to have worn it as a hat; it could have been like that soldier's cap – and far off she seemed to hear the bugle – but, no, it was a muff. After she was dressed Elizabeth put her carefully back on the bead cushion.

Through the dolls'-house window Impunity Jane could see Elizabeth's brother playing with his clockwork railway under the table; round and round whirred the shining fast train. 'Oh! I wish I were a train,' said Impunity Jane.

The years went by; Elizabeth grew up and Ethel had the dolls' house. Now the nursery (and the street outside) had electric lights, and there was an electric stove; the old high fender where Effie's and Elizabeth's socks and vests used to dry was taken away. Ethel did not have any petticoats at all, she wore a jersey and skirt and knickers to match.

Ethel liked lessons. She bought a school set with her pocket money, little doll books and a doll blackboard; she taught Impunity Jane reading and writing and arithmetic, and how to draw a thimble and a blackberry and how to sing a scale.

Through the open door Impunity Jane could see Ethel's brother run off down the stairs and take his hoop.

'Do re mi fa so la ti do,' sang Ethel.

'Fa! Fa!' said Impunity Jane.

After Ethel there was Ellen, who kept the dolls' house shut.

Ellen wore grey flannel shorts and her curls were tied up in a pony tail. She went to a day school and, if her mother went out in the evening, she had a 'sitter'.

Ellen was too busy to play; she listened to the radio or stayed for hours in the living-room, looking at television.

Impunity Jane had now sat on the bead cushion for more than fifty years. 'Take me out,' she would wish into Ellen as hard as she could. Impunity Jane nearly cracked with wishing.

Ellen felt nothing at all.

*

Then one day Ellen's mother said, 'Ellen, you had better get out all your toys Your cousin Gideon is coming to tea.'

Ellen pouted and was cross because she did not like boys, and she had to open the dolls' house and dust its furniture and carpets. Everything was thick with dust, even Impunity Jane. She had felt it settling on her, and it made her miserable. The clothes with the big stitches, the lessons, had been better than dust.

'Gideon! Gideon! What a silly name!' said Ellen.

To Impunity Jane it did not sound silly. 'G-G-G' – the sound was hard and gay, and she seemed to hear the bugle again, brave and exciting.

Gideon was a boy of seven with brown eyes and curly hair. When he laughed his nose had small wrinkles at the sides, and when he was very pleased – or frightened or ashamed – his cheeks grew red.

From the first moment he came into the nursery he was interested in the dolls' house. 'Let me play with it,' he said, and he bent down and looked into the rooms.

'You can move the furniture about and put out the cups and saucers, as long as you put them all back,' said Ellen.

'*That's* not playing!' said Gideon. 'Can't we put the dolls' house up a tree?'

'A tree? Why, the birds might nest in it!' said Ellen.

'Do you think they would?' asked Gideon, and he laughed with pleasure. 'Think of robins and wrens sitting on the tables and chairs!'

Impunity Jane laughed too.

'Let's put it on a raft and float it on the river,' said
Gideon.

'Don't be silly,' said Ellen. 'It might be swept away
and go right out to sea.'

'Then fishes could come into it,' said Gideon.

'Fishes!'

Impunity Jane became excited, but Ellen still said,
'No.'

Gideon looked at Impunity Jane on the bead
cushion. 'Does that little doll just sit there doing
nothing?' he asked.

'What could she do?' asked Ellen.

Gideon did not answer, but he looked at Impunity
Jane with his bright brown eyes; they twinkled, and
suddenly Impunity Jane knew she could make Gideon
feel. 'Rescue me,' wished Impunity Jane as hard as she
could. 'Gideon, rescue me. Don't leave me here, here
where Effie and Elizabeth and Ethel and Ellen have
kept me so long. Gideon! *Gideon!*'

But Gideon was tired of Ellen and the nursery. 'I
think I'll take a ball out into the garden,' he said.

'Gideon! Gideon, I shall crack!' cried Impunity
Jane. 'G-I-D-E-O-N! G-I-D-E-O-N!'

Gideon stopped and looked at Impunity Jane; then
he looked round at Ellen. Ellen was eating cherries
from a plate her mother and brought in; she ought

really to have shared them with Gideon, but she gobbled most of them up; now she was counting the stones. 'Tinker, tailor, soldier, sailor,' counted Ellen.

'Gideon, Gideon,' wished Impunity Jane.

'Rich man, poor man, beggar man' – and just as Ellen said, 'Thief,' Gideon, his cheeks red, slid his hand into the dolls' house, picked up Impunity Jane, and put her into his pocket.

Ages and ages ago Impunity Jane had been in Grandma's pocket, but Grandma's pocket was nothing to Gideon's. To begin with, Gideon's pockets often had real holes in them, and Impunity Jane could put her head right through them into the world. Sometimes she had to hold on to the edges to avoid falling out altogether, but she was not afraid.

'I'm Imp-imp-impunity,' she sang.

Grandma had not run, and oh! the feeling of running, spinning through the air! Grandma had not skated nor ridden on a scooter. 'I can skate and I can scoot,' said Impunity Jane.

Grandma had not swung; Gideon went on the swings in the park, and Impunity Jane went too, high and higher, high in the air.

Grandma had not climbed trees; Gideon climbed to the very top, and there he took Impunity Jane out of his pocket and sat her on one of the boughs; she could see far over houses and steeples and trees, and feel the bough moving in the wind.

Impunity Jane

'I feel the wind. I feel the wind!' cried Impunity Jane.

In Grandma's pocket there had been only Impunity Jane and a folded white handkerchief that smelled of lavender water. In Gideon's pockets were all kinds of things. Impunity Jane never knew what she would find there – string and corks, sweets and sweet-papers, nuts, cigarette cards with beautiful pictures, an important message, a knife with a broken handle, some useful screws and tacks, a bit of pencil, and, for a long time, a little brown snail.

The snail had a polished brown shell with smoke-curl markings. Gideon used to take her out and put her down to eat on the grass; then a head with two horns like a little cow came out at one side of the shell and a small curved tail at the other; the tail left a smeary silvery trail like glue; it made the inside of Gideon's pocket beautifully sticky. Gideon called the snail Ann Rushout because of the slow way she put out her horns.

'I once had a chestnut as a pretend snail,' said Gideon, 'but a real snail's much better.'

Impunity Jane thought so too.

But in all this happiness there was a worry. It worried Gideon, and so, of course, it worried Impunity Jane. (If dolls can make you feel, you make them feel as well.)

The worry was this. Gideon was a boy, and boys do not have dolls, not even in their pockets.

'They would call me "sissy",' said Gideon, and his cheeks grew red.

On the corner of the street a gang of boys used to meet; they met in the park as well. The leader of the gang was Joe McCallaghan. Joe McCallaghan had brown hair that was stiff as a brush, a turned-up nose, freckles, and grey eyes. He wore a green wolf cub jersey and a belt bristling with knives; he had every kind of knife, and he had bows and arrows, an air gun, a space helmet, and a bicycle with a dual brake control, a lamp, and a bell. He was nine years old and Gideon was only seven but, 'He quite likes me,' said Gideon.

Once Joe McCallaghan pulled a face at Gideon. 'Of course, I couldn't *think* of pulling one at him,' said Gideon. 'He knows me but I can't know him – yet.'

Once Gideon had a new catapult, and Joe McCallaghan took it into his hand to look at it. Gideon trembled while Joe McCallaghan stretched the catapult, twanged it, and handed it back. 'Decent weapon,' said Joe McCallaghan. Gideon would have said 'Jolly wizard!' But how ordinary that sounded now! 'Decent weapon, decent weapon,' said Gideon over and over again.

Impunity Jane heard him and her china seemed to grow cold. Suppose Joe McCallaghan, or one of the gang, should find out what Gideon had in his pocket?

'I should die,' said Gideon.

'But I don't look like a proper doll,' Impunity Jane tried to say.

That was true. The white dress with the sprigs had been so smeared by Ann Rushout that Gideon had taken if off and thrown it away. Impunity Jane no longer had dresses with stitches like knives; her dresses had no stitches at all. Gideon dressed her in a leaf, or some feathers, or a piece of rag; sometimes he buttoned the rag with a berry. If you can imagine a dirty little gypsy doll, that is how Impunity Jane looked now.

'I'm not a proper doll,' she pleaded, but Gideon did not hear.

'Gideon, will you mail this letter for me?' his mother asked one afternoon.

Gideon took the letter and ran downstairs and out into the street. Ann Rushout lay curled in her shell, but Impunity Jane put her head out through a brand-new hole. Gideon scuffed up the dust with the toes of his new shoes, and Impunity Jane admired the puffs and the rainbow specks of it in the sun (you look at dust in the sun), and so they came to the postbox.

Gideon stood on tiptoe, and had just posted the letter when – 'Hands up! said Joe McCallaghan. He stepped out from behind the postbox, and the gang came from round the corner where they had been hiding.

Gideon was surrounded.

Impunity Jane could feel his heart beating in big

jerks. She felt cold and stiff. Even Ann Rushout woke up and put out her two little horns.

'Search him,' said Joe McCallaghan to a boy called Puggy.

Impunity Jane slid quickly to the bottom of Gideon's pocket and lay there under Ann Rushout, the cork, the sweets, the pencil, and the string.

Puggy ran his hands over Gideon like a policeman and then searched his pockets. The first thing he found was Ann Rushout. 'A snail. Ugh!' said Puggy and nearly dropped her.

'It's a beautiful snail,' said Joe McCallaghan, and the gang looked at Gideon with more respect.

Puggy brought out the cork, the sweets – Joe McCallaghan tried one through the paper with his teeth and handed it back – the pencil, a lucky sixpence, the knife – 'Broken,' said Puggy scornfully, and Gideon grew red. Puggy brought out the string. Then Impunity Jane felt his fingers round close her, and out she came into the light of day.

Gideon's cheeks had been red; now they went dark, dark crimson. Impunity Jane lay stiffly as Puggy handed her to Joe McCallaghan; the berry she had been wearing broke off and rolled in the gutter.

'A doll!' said Joe McCallaghan in disgust.

'Sissy!' said Puggy. 'Sissy!'

'Sissy got a dolly,' the gang jeered and waited to see what Joe McCallaghan would do.

Impunity Jane

'You're a sissy,' said Joe McCallaghan to Gideon as if he were disappointed.

Impunity Jane lay stiffly in his hand. 'I'm Imp-imp-impunity,' she tried to sing, but no words came.

Then Gideon said something he did not know he could say. He did not know how he thought of it; it might have come out of the air, the sky, the pavement, but amazingly it came out of Gideon himself. 'I'm not a sissy,' said Gideon. 'She isn't a doll, she's a model. I use her in my model train.'

'A model?' said Joe McCallaghan and looked at Impunity Jane again.

'Will he throw me in the gutter like the berry?' thought Impunity Jane. 'Will he put me down and tread on me? Break me with his heel?'

'A model,' said Gideon firmly.

'She can be a fireman or a porter or a driver or a sailor,' he added.

'A sailor?' said Joe McCallaghan, and he looked at Impunity Jane again. 'I wonder if she would go in my model yacht,' he said. 'I had a lead sailor, but he fell overboard.'

'She wouldn't fall overboard,' said Gideon.

Joe McCallaghan looked at her again. 'Mind if I take her to the pond?' he said over his shoulder to Gideon.

Now began such a life for Impunity Jane. She, a little pocket doll, was one of a gang of boys! Because of her, Gideon, her Gideon, was allowed to be in the gang too. 'It's only fair,' said Joe McCallaghan, whom we can now call Joe, 'it's only fair, if we use her, to let him in.'

Can you imagine how it feels, if you are a little doll, to sit on the deck of a yacht and go splashing across a pond? You are sent off with a hard push among ducks as big as icebergs, over ripples as big as waves. Most people would have been afraid and fallen overboard, like the lead sailor, but, 'Imp-imp-impunity,' sang Impunity Jane and reached the far side wet but perfectly safe.

She went up in aeroplanes. Once she was nearly lost when she was tied to a balloon; she might have floated over to France, but Gideon and Joe ran and ran, and at last they caught her in a garden square, where they had to climb the railings and were caught themselves by an old lady, who said she would complain to the police. When they explained that Impunity Jane was being carried off to France the old lady understood and let them off.

The gang used Impunity Jane for many things: she lived in igloos and wigwams, ranch-houses, forts and rocket ships. Once she was put on a Catherine Wheel until Joe thought her hair might catch fire and took her off, but she saw the lovely bright fireworks go blazing round in a shower of bangs and sparks.

She was with Joe and Gideon when they ran away to sea, and with them when they came back again because it was time for dinner. 'Better wait till after Christmas,' said Joe. Gideon agreed – he was getting a bicycle for Christmas – but Impunity Jane was sorry; she wanted to see the sea.

Next day she was happy again because they started digging a hole through to Australia, and she wanted to see Australia. When they pretended the hole was a gold mine, she was happy to see the gold, and when the gold mine was a cave and they wanted a fossilized mouse, she was ready to be a fossilized mouse.

'I say, will you sell her?' Joe asked Gideon.

Gideon shook his head, though it made him red to do it. 'You can borrow her when you want to,' he said: 'But she's mine.'

But Impunity Jane was not Gideon's, she was Ellen's.

The gang was a very honourable gang. 'One finger wet, one finger dry,' they said, and drew them across their throats; that meant they would not tell a lie. Gideon knew that even without fingers they would never steal, and he, Gideon, had stolen Impunity Jane.

She and Gideon remembered what Ellen had said as she counted cherrystones (do you remember?). 'Rich man, poor man, beggar man, thief,' said Ellen.

'Thief! Thief!'

Sometimes, to Gideon, Impunity Jane felt as heavy as lead in his pocket; sometimes Impunity Jane felt as heavy and cold as lead herself. 'I'm a thief!' said Gideon and grew red.

Impunity Jane could not bear Gideon to be unhappy. All night she lay awake in his pyjama pocket. 'What shall I do?' asked Impunity Jane. She asked Ann Rushout. Ann Rushout said nothing, but in the end the answer came. Perhaps it came out of the night, or Ann's shell, or out of Gideon's pocket, or even out of Impunity Jane herself. The answer was very cruel. It said, 'You must wish Gideon to put you back.'

'Back? In the dolls' house?' said Impunity Jane. 'Back, with Ellen, Ellen who kept it shut?' And she said slowly, 'Ellen was worse than Ethel or Elizabeth or Effie. I can't go back,' said Impunity Jane, 'I can't!' But, from far off, she seemed to hear the bugle telling her to be brave, and she knew she must wish, 'Gideon, put me back.'

She wanted to say, 'Gideon, hold me tightly,' but she said, 'Gideon, put me back.'

So Gideon went back to Ellen's house with Impunity Jane in his pocket. He meant to edge round the nursery door while his mother talked to Ellen's mother, then open the dolls' house and slip Impunity Jane inside and on to the bead cushion. He went upstairs, opened the nursery door, and took Impunity Jane in his hand.

It was the last minute. 'No more pockets,' said Impunity Jane. 'No more running and skating and swinging in the air. No more igloos and ripples. No rags and berries for frocks. No more Ann Rushout. No more warm dirty fingers. No more feeling the wind.

No more Joe, no gang, not even Puggy. No more . . . Gideon!' cried Impunity Jane – and she cracked.

But what was happening in Ellen's nursery? The dolls' house was not in its place – it was on the table with a great many other toys, and there was Ellen sorting them and doing them up in parcels.

'I'm going to give all my toys away,' said Ellen with a toss of her head. 'I'm too old to play with them any more. 'I'm going to boarding-school. Wouldn't you like to go to boarding-school?' she said to Gideon.

'No,' said Gideon.

'Of course, you're still a *little* boy,' said Ellen. 'You still like toys.'

'Yes,' said Gideon, and his fingers tightened on Impunity Jane.

'Would you like a toy?' asked Ellen who was polishing a musical box.

'Yes,' said Gideon.

'What would you like?' asked Ellen.

'Please,' said Gideon. His cheeks were bright red. 'Please' – and he gulped – 'could I have' – gulp – 'the pocket doll' – gulp – 'from the dolls' house?'

'Take her,' said Ellen without looking up.

Gideon has a bicycle now. Impunity Jane rides on it with him. Sometimes she is tied to the handle-bars, but sometimes Gideon keeps her where she likes to be best of all, in his pocket. Now Impunity Jane is not only his model, she is his mascot, which means she brings him luck.

The crack was mended with china cement by Gideon's mother.

Ellen went to boarding-school.

As for the dolls' house, it was given away.

As for the bead cushion, it was lost.